# TAX RETURN

Jim Pollard

Copyright © 2017 Jim Pollard
All rights reserved.
KDP Edition ISBN: 978-1-5210022-0-9

Published by Tartaruga Books
www.notonlywords.co.uk/tartaruga
tartaruga.books@icloud.com

'Things as certain as death and taxes,
can be more firmly believ'd.'
Daniel Defoe,
*The Political History of the Devil*, 1726


'Trickle-down theory:
the less than elegant metaphor that if one
feeds the horse enough oats,
some will pass through to the road for the sparrows.'
Economist John Kenneth Galbraith,
*The Culture of Contentment*, 1992

# Contents

**Part One**   7
'Arguably the worst pub on the South Coast.'

**Part Two**   75
'You do know that I've never arrested anybody before.'

**Part Three**   147
'You remember that story about George Best and Miss World...?'

**Part Four**   225
'I can't enjoy a cake. I just taste self-loathing and guilt.'

**Part Five**   295
'It's Jaws all over again.'

**Part Six**   357
'Returning to the scene of the crime?'

**Who's Who in Biscuit Town and beyond**   387

**Acknowledgements**   392

# 1:
# 'Arguably The Worst Pub On The South Coast.'

# 1.1.

Once the dust had settled, thick, black and burnt, the small seaside town was left wondering, scratching its collective head. The students' house had burned with such efficiency. Could it have been arson? The Chief Fire Officer himself had attended and poked around in the building's charred skeleton. A crime of this nature would have been rare indeed in Biscuit Town, as the sleepy South Coast resort was still affectionately known. It wasn't arson but the truth was strange enough. Pip Henley knew how lucky she was to be alive and was determined that the experience would change her.

She had started out with such good intentions.

A childhood gilded with privilege had left Pip not the rounded and curious person she longed to be, but insecure and guilty. Was the First Class Honours degree she was expected to achieve down not to her but to all those private tutors, ponies, pools and untold toys? She was smart enough to know that being in line for a First did not mean she was a genius. (Tommy Lockhart was also in line for a First and, anyway, a B.Ed wasn't really an academic degree, was it?) The dialogue inside her head ran a repetitive refrain: if she was so smart, why couldn't she figure out exactly why her housemates didn't like her? She knew it was something to do with her pampered background but she couldn't understand why nobody could see beyond that. She was a good person. She was good.

She prized goodness for its own sake but, in truth, she also wanted the dividend of goodness: popularity and a sense of self-worth. Was that so wrong? Perhaps she was too concerned with the one to truly experience the other? She worried that not understanding other people, yet yearning for their approval, was a combustible combination, particularly in her chosen profession. Teachers needed an understanding of human nature and a strong moral core, a clear sense of right and wrong. Not to still be children themselves. She'd have swapped her bucket of privilege for a soupçon of self-confidence in a flash. Instead, was she trying to buy it?

The house was hers and the rent she charged was peanuts.

Being Pip, she felt bad charging rent to people who were already borrowing to pay their tuition fees. She didn't really need the money but – and she'd rehearsed these arguments a million times – the alternatives were to live with spoilt brats like herself who wouldn't notice the rent (but that would keep her locked in the loop of entitlement from which she so yearned to escape) or not to charge rent at all, which would have left her feeling like Lady Muck and never knowing if her tenants were friends or parasites. It was a burden. Except, of course, it was only a burden in rich kid land. Most of her fellow students would never own their own home. Did all the children of the rich feel like this or was it just her? Born under a sad sign. Why couldn't she just enjoy her good fortune?

True, the house was quite a long way from campus – her father's condition when buying it for her had been that she should remain nearby. But there were buses and trains. Tommy had his bike and she was always ready with a lift in the Mini Cooper. She knew that money couldn't buy you love but when you had it, it was tempting to try. She'd buy rounds, buy meals, stock up at Waitrose. She'd bought Melissa a dress at American Apparel and told her how good she looked in it – and she hadn't been lying. Inspired by the loose peasant top with billowing sleeves that Melissa had 'sourced', as she put it, in a charity shop and by Tommy's protracted Led Zeppelin phase, she'd organised a 70s retro night for them all.

Pip invited some people from her course but even as she was doing it, she didn't expect them to come. Was it the apologetic tone in her tiny voice that made her so easy to turn down? The way she always seemed to be fiddling with her long lank hair, wrapping it round a stubby finger. She kidded herself it was the distance and the myriad attractions of Brighton on a Saturday night.

It was likely to be just the five of them, the housemates. Maybe six if Melissa had a new boyfriend in tow. Tommy was coming and, if Tommy was coming, then Josh, his cheerleader in chief, would be there too. The pair were round the corner in the local. 'Arguably the worst pub on the South Coast,' Tommy always called it.

'Do you need the "arguably" in that sentence?' Josh had asked.

'Arguably not.'

Pip envied their easy manner.

Tanisha would come. She was Nigerian and had more important things to worry about than whether people liked her or not. She was the only one who took Pip as she came and paid the rent promptly and with pleasure that it wasn't, as it might so easily have been, more. Tanisha thought she was blessed to be living in a semi by the sea. Why couldn't the others? Why couldn't Melissa?

Melissa was in her room, ostensibly working on an assignment. As Pip arranged the floor cushions she'd bought, she wondered whether Melissa would come down and help. Probably not. Melissa Brink had perfected the art of arriving just as all the work had been done. Melissa was directly above, so she could certainly hear what was going on. She had the master bedroom – Pip's guilt again. Pip had the second bedroom, Tanisha the box room which she kept neat as a show-home, and Tommy the converted loft.

Pip arranged the fondue set, another charity shop find: a shining stainless steel star in the middle of the table. In B&Q to buy some fuel for the fondue's little burner, she had been interrogated about her age. Wasn't it supposed to be a blessing in Western society to look young? But it just made her feel like a child and her concerns and preoccupations seem childish. She'd even, thinking ahead since she'd never held a fondue party before, purchased a small hand-held fire extinguisher. Would an irresponsible kid have done that? She stationed it under the table and hoped she'd never have to think of it again.

It was a generally happy household. (She was trying to reassure herself now.) They enjoyed the garden which between them they kept just the civilised side of wild. They each had a chair. Tommy had reclaimed them from a skip. They would often – well, occasionally – sit outside shooting the breeze as the sun went down. Depending on the prevailing wind, you could hear either the sea or the gentle civilised hum and chatter from the bowling green, the occasional click-clack of the bowls colliding. Hell, she'd once even seen Melissa dead-heading in pink mittens. Decent houses at knockdown rents were as rare as an unmolested traffic cone on campus and that had no doubt been the attraction for Tommy, who Pip knew to nod to from her course, and Melissa. When the pair had moved in, they'd been an item – a kind of golden couple with her eyes and his charm – but their union hadn't lasted the closer proximity of a shared house for more than a week or two. Their liaison had given Tommy and Melissa each just enough of the drug that was the other to appreciate its attractions, yet provide immunity to its full effects. Clearly – to Pip anyway – they remained mutually fascinated. Big beasts stalking warily around each other.

Pip had been cooking with Melissa once – an unaccustomed girlie moment – and Tommy had walked in.

'Make us a cup of tea, will you, doll?' he had said to Melissa, patting her backside proprietorially as he passed. Next thing Pip knew Melissa was putting the kettle on.

When Melissa had contracted food poisoning (not the same occasion), Tommy had taken her to hospital in a taxi, plied her with water, quizzed the triage nurse and waited the three hours.

Yes, there might not have been enough room for two centres of attention in the house but there was still something. Perhaps not big beasts so much as beautiful butterflies unwilling or unable to settle.

The 70s effect was completed with some candles (scented ones to disguise the smell of the cannabis Tommy would surely bring), some paper lanterns, a couple of loosely-knitted hippy blankets, canned lager and several bottles of Piat d'Or. She'd covered the sofa with a silk sheet for the full boudoir effect.

It wasn't just altruism. Pip needed her party. It had been a tough week. On the Thursday, one of the girls in her teaching practice class had been hit by a falling rock. They'd been on the beach, a 'field trip', and Pip had been talking about the local fossils – so much more interesting than just seeing them in the museum, she had thought – when nature provided its own lesson in erosion.

'But where do fossils come from, Miss?' That was the question that had started it.

If Biscuit Town was known for anything other than biscuits, it was for fossils. When the Stern & Feltman factory had been built in the nineteenth century, an impressive Cretaceous collection had been unearthed. The best ones – the unbroken ammonites – were in

London but the remnants adorned the town museum. In an attempt to excite her charges with the delights of physical geography, Pip had organised a little outing. The headteacher, Ms Greene, had been quite keen: 'provided there's no bad behaviour' which was not a guarantee Pip could really make. The class's usual Geography teacher was off sick so a surly supply teacher accompanied the party unenthusiastically.

'I mean, Miss, if these fossils are old dead animals, how were they made?'

The beach during school time was quite a challenge to an apprentice pedagogue. To any child, the beach was for playing.

'Can we go in the sea?'

'Can we play beach cricket?'

'Can we build a castle?'

'Can we play musical towels?'

'Will there be Wi Fi?'

The answer to all these questions was no. Pip felt like a real kill-joy.

'Musical towels?' she asked.

'It's like musical chairs,' little Kirsty Carlisle explained, 'except you have towels and you take towels away.' That sounded like great fun to Pip and she realised that she hadn't really thought this through. Standing there on the beach in the shadow of the cliff talking about finding fossils, well it was still 'chalk and talk', wasn't it. But with a lot more chalk.

Then suddenly Kirsty was bowled over as if she were a skittle. Pip had been talking to her one minute, a big-eyed child with bouncy full-bodied brown hair Pip would have killed for. The next moment Kirsty was on the ground, eyes wider still, time standing still as the grass-topped lump of white rock bounced, spun, rolled and finally came to rest in the middle of the sand. Pip remembered her initial thought: that rock was too big to have been thrown by one of the other pupils.

You couldn't control what flew through your mind in the heat of the moment and these automatic, instinctive reactions were, Pip felt, very revealing. She felt ashamed that her first response effectively boiled down to something as selfish as 'phew, at least it wasn't my fault'.

The thought – itself as bold, random and unstoppable as a falling boulder – had been eating at her ever since. It ate at her now as she waited, nibbling on crisps and Doritos.

The silence had been broken by Sunil yelling that he'd seen the rock fall down the side of the cliff. Pip had coped well from then on. She applied a temporary bandage fashioned from a packet of tissues and a summer scarf and got the bleeding girl to hospital, instructing the rest of the class to walk back to school in the custody of the surly supply teacher. While Kirsty was getting stitches, Pip had contacted the child's parents, reported the incident to Ms Greene and even called the Council – all within twenty minutes of it happening. Why did she choose to focus on that 100% human initial reaction rather than on her subsequent efficiency and calm? Perhaps because it played in perfect harmony with Pip's impression of herself as an accident waiting to happen.

Still alone an hour after the appointed start time, Pip brushed her hair again. She had been trying to recreate the look of 70s icon Farrah Fawcett, the blonde in Charlie's Angels. She'd found a picture on the internet. Of course, Pip wasn't blonde but that wasn't the issue. Her hair was long, which ought to have been lovely, but instead it was always so dry. She was forever washing it or thinking that she ought. Styling it was like trying to style split-ended straw. Still, it was too late to condition it again now. Took ages to dry and she was too self-conscious to walk around the house with a towel as a turban. Not right at a 70s party, anyway. Pip opened the first of the bottles of wine and spilled it down her rainbow kaftan. Perhaps if she started washing her hair, they'd all turn up. Opening a bottle by yourself was pathetic with the result that she was angry and hence clumsy and being clumsy made her feel fat.

She wasn't going to cry. Tanisha had found her crying once and instead of the comforting arm and soothing words, her flatmate had merely shaken her head and said: 'too absorbed by self'. The words had made her tears freeze because we all know the truth when we meet it.

She found the Led Zeppelin she'd specially downloaded on iTunes. Then she laid down on the carpet and opened her atlas, a big one. A3-size pages. Perhaps larger. Thick vellum paper. As so often in her life, looking longingly at maps of places where she might be instead took her out of herself and reduced her discomfort. Communication breakdown, Robert Plant screamed. It's always the same.

# 1.2.

Gary Shad's thumb bobbed like a leaping salmon as he scrolled through his tweets. One eye on the screen, one eye on his pint, one eye on the door, one eye on the main chance, you needed to get up early to put one past old Gaz.

He was vaping. Tried to be subtle about it. Landlord didn't like it much, though he hadn't outright banned it. Couldn't afford to lose the punters, could he? And he, Gary, had no need to provoke unnecessary fights, so he stood by the open window. The Smugglers' was a 70s cavern that looked more like a working men's club than a traditional pub. Too big now for the dwindling number of customers, furnished with neglect, out-of-date posters and peeling paint, its neon sign long since spent. Pitiful. Stuck in a past that was never too glorious anyway. Biscuit Town all over.

Gaz looked out through a grimy, seagull-shat-upon pane of glass at the boozer's four wooden tables dropped seemingly randomly on the balding grass. Slightly more popular after the smoking ban, then slightly less since the world and his wife started vaping, they were like a picnic area in a no-longer-used lay-by, a beauty spot that wasn't any longer. Fucking hole really. To call this cesspit a beer garden, as the fading wooden notice by the front double doors claimed, was to play faster and looser with the English fucking language than an army of Spanish school kids trying to order a 99. The benches were built into the tables and at least two were rotten, eaten away by the sea air and seagull shit. There were a couple of inverted flowerpots serving as ashtrays but the furthest table, hidden from the bar and so popular with underage loiterers, was paddling in a sea of dog-ends.

Jess obviously hadn't been in yet. She'd clear up that sort of mess.

Gaz tugged deep on his e-ciggie. A mix of berries – raspberry – and grape and then a soft menthol kick. Like sweets at school really. Used to smoke to look big and grown up back in the day and now it was the opposite: vaping as an excuse to gorge on sweet, addictive kiddie flavours. Always found a way to play tricks on you, life. Gotta roll with it.

Fags were part of what had kept him beanpole thin and he didn't want to start running to fat now. He liked being, well, he called it lean. Jacky, his first girl, had said that naked, with his red tightly-cropped hair, he looked like a Swan Vesta safety match. Cracked them both up. Nice girl Jacky – but not the one.

They said there was no smoke without fire – and they'd been saying that about Gary's dodgy doings since he was a kid – but it wasn't true anymore, was it? Not with the sweetie juice. Plenty of smoke without fire. He took another big toke and walked back to his seat at the bar.

A couple of students were giving it some. Politics. That cunt of a Prime Minister was due in town, wasn't he? One of the students had seen a TV programme or something. Big Ron, the ex-copper, was installed at the next seat but one at the bar. Like Gaz, he was trying to ignore it all. The mouthiest student was another two seats along. It was a bit like in a public lavatory: bloke, space, bloke, space, bloke. Not that any punters were actually pissing up against the bar. (Although Gaz had seen that in one of the tastier dives in Brighton back in the day. Bloke who was too lazy or pissed to walk to the bog, peeing in his own pint glass and then standing it on the counter like a cocktail.) The mouthy student's mate disturbed the pattern a little. He was at the next seat to motor mouth but round the corner. 'S'right, Tommy,' the mate kept saying. 'S'right, Tommy.'

Ron was trying to lose himself in the crossword. Gaz had respect for Ron even though he'd nicked him once. They were cut from the same stuff really and both knew that politics as spouted by politicians and students was about as far away from life on the street as left was from right.

Gaz perched on his bar stool. Seated but poised. Ready to move in a flash.

He scrolled. Could he really be the only dickhead who had figured Twitter out? Felt like it but he couldn't share what he knew, so he'd never know. Ironic really, given that Twitter was supposedly all about sharing. Like Quality Street. Ha. Bloke in Brighton that he'd been following. Tweets a couple of times a day of the 'my dick's so big, it seats six' variety – bars he's in, cocktails he's drinking. Odd bit of bollocks about Apple, their arty-farty computers as well as boasting about his phone. (Pal, we've all got bloody iPhones. This is the 21st century.) Anyway, it was obvious from this twat's tweets that he had a fair few computers, internet dealer maybe. It was also obvious from his Twitter location, the bars he tweeted about and from a cursory knowledge of said location that he lived in the arse-bandit district of Kemptown. Didn't even have to follow him home. No, there was an app for that. (And a thing called the phone book. Ha.) Gaz knew where he lived now. Just a matter of waiting for him to tweet he was going on holiday or more likely tell us all he was enjoying Sex On A Beach. Ha. Well, the joke's on you, Brighton boy. Candy from a baby.

It had started with this kid into Formula 1. Well, Gary liked that. Fancied himself as a bit of a driver. Had no idea how Shitter worked back then, couldn't see the fucking point but the girlfriend was wetting herself about it. Anyway, it was Lewis Hamilton and Jensen Button, refuelling rules, diffusers, tyre width and what have you. Kid knew his stuff so Gaz kept an eye. Then the kid mentioned Angmering. Mentioned a pub that he called his local. Mentioned he got the train to work. Gary felt like he was getting warm but he didn't know why. Penny dropped when the kid mentioned his own car. Some hi-tech sporty thing. Gary didn't really know but Spicer knew all about it. Not many of them sort of motors in Angmering. Very warm. And easy to serve yourself during office hours. Stole it and sold it abroad within the hour. Sweet as. Ha. That's how the Twitter twatter patter started.

And now he'd got two on the go. The Brighton queen was good but @Gav_3 was potentially better. Only been tweeting like a twot for a few days but already Gary knew that he, Gav, was a banker and that he lived in Estuary Sands, that new estate for the loaded not a stone's throw from this very shithole. Ripe for the plucking. A bit of a reccy needed – Gary hadn't seen the place yet, but everybody this side of Brighton knew how bling-ketty-bling it was – and a few more details of a personal nature but it was well on the way. He was another big dick tweeter was Gav, a boaster, and they were so careless, it was criminal. This Gav had a Russian wife and Gary was pretty sure Jess, his favourite barmaid, had told him she au-paired for a couple in Estuary Sands with a Russian wife. Could be a coincidence but there couldn't be that many mail-order brideskis up there, could there? Unless Biscuit Town had got a job lot.

Gary put his phone down on the bar. His dog was rolling over on her back – wanted her tummy tickled. What a slapper she was. But they all loved her, the pub punters, the dumb mutt walkers of the rec. Jess liked her too. (Where was she?) And who could be scared of a bloke with a poodle? French, he called her. French the poodle. Well, they have a lot of them in France, don't they? It was a passport, a pooch, a passport to civilised society. And a lot easier than having the tatts taken off. When they saw the dog, they didn't see the tatts. It helped you to get to know people and in Gaz's business getting to know people helped big style. Twitter had taken it to a new level, the getting-to-know-people biz: 65 million tweets a day they said – that was about 750 tweets a second. That was a lot of little chats in the park or the pub. Search on locations, words and hashtags and it was as easy as falling off a bar stool to find a local yokel with more front than sense. Hashtags. Hark at him. Gaz the geek. He should start #wanttobeburgled. Ha. Wouldn't do it, of course. It was that sort of cocky crap that got you caught.

'Don't let that bloody mutt get dog hairs all over my carpet.' It was the dulcet tones of Vic Hooper, the permanently pissed-off landlord.

'It's not her,' said Gaz. 'The carpet's so sticky it's giving her a bloody Brazilian. What do you clean it with? Coca Cola?'

'Clean it,' snorted Ron. 'It hasn't been cleaned since the Royal Wedding.'

'Whose Royal Wedding?' quipped Gaz. 'Victoria's.'

Ron laughed.

'Fuck off,' said Vic.

Suddenly, a volley of fresh air disturbed the deathly fug as the double doors wheezed open. A new punter. Everybody looked up. But it was only Darren and Hovis. If Jess was the reason Gaz popped into The Smugglers' more often than any sane man should, then Darren and Hovis were the reason he ought to avoid it. Thick as pigshit but, since they'd all been at school together, Gaz was obliged to pass the time of day with them. Pretending they were mates because they had been once. Small town stuff. Biscuit Town all over. Gaz had broken into his first house with Hovis. Bunking off. One sunny afternoon. Hovis had been fatter than Gaz – still was – so they'd decided that Hovis should climb through the open window first. Theory being that if Hovis could get in then so could Gaz. Stupid git Hovis had squeezed his blubber through but then put his foot in the goldfish tank. Water and squirming fish all over the shag. Gaz figured that next time if he, as the skinniest, went in first, he could let his accomplice in through the door afterwards. On-the-job learning they call that. Thanks Hovis. Darren and Hovis were showing Vic some posters, laying them out on the bar like a couple of salesmen. Posters for what? Could be anything – there was all sorts of stuff happening in Biscuit Town if you knew where to look. Gaz knew but didn't care. He'd be leaving soon. Very soon.

'United Kingdom Independence Party,' read Vic, slowly as a primary school kid with undiagnosed dyslexia and a glass eye.

'It's the kippers!' squawked the student kid.

'Kippers for breakfast, Tommy,' said his mate.

'Kipper ties,' said Tommy even louder, tugging at his mate's tie which was a big fat purple thing. Were they back in fashion?

The mate started fiddling with his tie, flapping it. 'It's a purple kipper, a purple kipper.'

Like a couple of kids.

Hovis wasn't happy. Moved his bulk towards them but he was about as threatening as a beach ball.

Vic was shaking his slow heavy head. He had a fleck of spittle on his pock-marked cheek. Or was it beer? 'I'd like to help you, lads, but...'

'Come on Vic,' said Hovis. 'If it wasn't for Nigel Farage, half the pubs in Britain would have closed.'

'Half the pubs in Britain have closed,' said Ron without lifting his head from his paper. He was filling in the crossword like a man plucking a chicken.

'No,' said Vic. 'I'd like to help you lads but I serve whoever comes through that door.'

'Same cheery smile for everyone eh, Vic? No matter their provenance,' smirked Tommy.

Vic cast a stony stare at the student kid, Tommy, but didn't say anything. 'No politics, no religion, no Southampton and no Bournemouth. Them's the house rules.' Vic was a Portsmouth supporter. They were largely self-enforcing, the house rules. Rare indeed was the punter who wanted to discuss Bournemouth's football team and only a man who had lost his religion or, like Gaz, had never had one to begin with would choose to spend any time in The Smugglers'.

'It's not politics, it's common sense,' said Hovis. 'Taking our jobs...'

'Pushing down wages,' said Darren.

'Yes, well, I can't afford to pay.' Vic stopped himself with an unconvincing cough. 'Anyway, it's still politics,' he said. 'People come down the pub to enjoy themselves.'

Gaz surveyed the assembly and it brought a smile to his thin lips. The Smugglers' merry crew were disguising their enjoyment admirably.

'Go on, lads,' said Ron. 'You heard what Victor said.'

Sling your hook was implied, not said. No need to be confrontational. Another way in which Gaz could see that he and Ron were alike. He'd have learned that on the beat. Gaz watched as Ron returned to his crossword. He was making like it was all nothing but Gaz could tell that it made him feel good that these lads who were less than half his age and, presumably, had push come to shove, physically stronger, heeded what he said and shuffled off, posters rolled up under their flabby arms. Ron Newton may have been retired but he still cut a figure in the town, had a certain respect.

'It's global capitalism that's pushing down wages,' said Tommy. 'You are attacking the symptom, not the cause.'

Hovis and Darren were at the door. They didn't look back. It was possible that they didn't realise that Tommy was talking to them. Perhaps they just didn't understand what he'd said. Gaz wasn't sure that he did.

'Global capitalism, eh,' said Ron, still not looking up.

'Ron,' hissed Vic.

'More and more wealth is concentrated in the hands of fewer and fewer,' said Tommy.

'Politics,' said Vic.

'It's not politics,' Tommy said. 'It's economics.' And then louder: 'Trickle-down economics, lads.'

But Hovis and Darren were gone.

'Trickle-down,' Ron repeated.

'The idea that if the rich get richer then more crumbs will fall from their tables.'

'The only thing trickling down here is the beer,' muttered Vic bitterly. 'Trickling very slowly.'

French was on her feet, rubbing against Gaz's leg. Tired of lounging on a gluey carpet, no doubt. Probably keen for a trickle herself. That fucking dirty carpet was economics, the faded sign was economics, the whole bloody heap of crap that was Biscuit Town was economics. To call something economics was like calling it nothing at all. But Gaz didn't say anything. What did students know? Gaz didn't have anything against books. Quite liked them in fact. But they were pleasure. No substitute for the real thing. He looked at the time on his phone.

'Jess not working till later?' he asked. Conversational. Ran his hand over his hair – a little bit long.

'No,' said Vic.

'It's economics,' said Ron, again without looking up.

Gaz bounced off his bar stool and gave French's lead a little tug. 'Come on, girl.'

# 1.3.

Pip had tidied the lounge and was using candlelight, a second silk sheet (was it Melissa's?) and a number of throws to – quite cleverly, she thought – remove the room's stern Victorian edges. Alongside the large patchwork scatter cushions, she had installed a rattan wicker bucket chair that looked like one she'd once seen Twiggy photographed in. Sipping wine as she went, she rearranged the cooked meats and stirred a little more cider into the fondue. Back in the kitchen, she put the potatoes back on a low heat to keep them warm. Then she chopped up more crispy bread. (She had enough baguette to open a boulangerie.) She found two more candles and lit those too. Eventually, there was the sound of a key in the front door. Pip froze. With excitement, with fear, she wasn't quite sure. She necked the glass anyway to douse her tingling anxiety.

Tanisha, back from the library, appeared in the door frame.

'Hello, Pip. It is your 1970s night,' she said, unhitching a multi-coloured woven headscarf.

'Our 70s night,' said Pip. 'And your scarf is just perfect.' Pip had a full glass of wine in Tanisha's hand before Tanisha had even put her bag down.

'This is 1970s music?'

'This is Led Zeppelin.'

'That is a funny name.' Tanisha sipped her wine. She looked around the room. Pip could see she was impressed. 'Your hair looks nice,' said Tanisha.

'It's a Farrah Fawcett. From Charlie's Angels. The original ones.'

'I see. Are they a 1970s pop group too?'

Pip smiled. It was too complicated to explain.

Tanisha was rearranging the coffee table which was already piled with books, trying to find some space for her own. Pip's enormous atlas was open in the middle of the carpet. For some reason, she didn't go over and close it.

Melissa, who had presumably heard Tanisha return and figured that it was now safe to descend, did just that. She had the pale blue peasant top on. Pip was pleased to see that. She also had a matching floral-print wraparound skirt and no bra. As the top's split sleeves settled like sails, Pip and Tanisha were treated to a profile of a pert, bouncing tit. Another art that Melissa had perfected was that of being just tarty enough. Her new boyfriend would be coming, Melissa announced. Pip didn't bother to register his name. He would, no doubt, be suitably drooling, attentive and – ultimately – disappointed.

'She got cancer,' said Melissa, nodding in Pip's general direction.
'What?' said Pip.
'Farrah Fawcett.' Pip felt inspected. Melissa had put her own natural curls up in a bandana. 'That is a Farrah Fawcett, isn't it?'

Pip instinctively clutched at her hair and felt like a child.

'Cancer of the arse,' said Melissa helping herself to a glass and filling it.

'We all die of something,' said Tanisha. She had pulled her laptop from her bag.

The other two girls looked at their African housemate. Tanisha was wearing scruffy jeans and a plain top, probably from Primark, but there was something other worldly about her. There always had been. Her bone structure so delicate, her mahogany skin like a perfectly-fired clay. She was the tallest of the three. Statuesque was the word and right now she was both as present and as absent as a statue in the middle of a town square. A different astral plane. We all die of something. It was easy for her to say. It took rich Pip and pretty Melissa with their different rings of protection a moment to realise that she was indeed simply stating a biological fact.

'I'll put my laptop away,' said Tanisha.

Tommy arrived. He and Josh had been to the pub. Melissa's boyfriend arrived. He hadn't been to the pub. He didn't want to spoil his chances, so his only concession to 70s attire was a kipper tie – even broader than Josh's. ('My grandad's,' he claimed.) He had a bottle of wine and, for Melissa, a bunch of flowers. Melissa accepted them as if they were the very least she expected. It was left to Pip to find a vase for them, Tanisha to snip the stems to make them fit.

'No phones,' said Tommy. 'This is real life.'

That was why everybody liked Tommy. That sort of remark. Everybody turned off the sound on their phones, even Melissa whose beeping, buzzing smartphone was a house party in its own right. Tommy had charisma in his veins.

'You all right?' he asked Pip, touching her on the forearm for just a beat longer than it took to touch someone. 'I heard about what happened on the beach.'

'Yes, she's fine, Kirsty, the little girl. Needed ten stitches though.'

'No, I mean you. How are you?'

'Me? I'm cool. I'm...' Pip really didn't know how to answer those sorts of questions.

They drank wine and had fun with the fondue, topping the burner up regularly from the bottle of meths, opening and shutting the air holes like kids in the chemistry lab. Josh rolled a joint and gave it, along with a simpering smile, to Tanisha. He had no chance, Pip thought. Tanisha was head and shoulders taller than Josh for a start.

'Tanisha is a pretty name,' he said.

'It means born on a Monday,' said Tanisha, taking a toke and laughing.

'What's the booze?' asked Tommy. He wore a T-shirt that said 'Here Comes The Sun', a pair of beige Oxford bags broad enough to serve as a tent and a glue-on porn moustache, yet somehow he still managed to look cool, in control and like a man with just the right dash of vulnerability beneath his confidence to get pretty much anything he wanted. 'In the fondue, I mean. Is it meths?'

'It's cider and white wine,' smiled Pip.

Tommy's bread, not for the first time, fell into the bubbling cheese. He and Josh insisting on sword-fighting with the fondue forks.

'Awesome,' said Josh.

And it was. For the first time, Pip felt that all the effort had been worthwhile. Tanisha nibbled on a gherkin – the girl ate next to nothing – while the boyfriend fed Melissa cheese-sodden baguette like a slave feeding a deity or a keeper feeding a seal depending on your take on the reclining Melissa.

Pip was talking about a lesson idea she'd had. 'It's a geography lesson but for older children than the ones I have now.'

'Go on,' said Tommy. And, for a few minutes, Pip became the focus of the conversation. She was, as she might have put it, 'holding court' – and that was perhaps the most awesome thing of all.

'I'd take a T-shirt – like your T-shirt, Tommy – and show its journey: all the countries it passed through, all the different workers in the chain who played a part.'

'Cool. It would make a great wall chart.'

'The statistics are all well and good,' she said. 'But, by telling the stories of half a dozen people, you make it real.'

'That's sick, Pip.'

'I want to show how trade is making the world smaller, how technology is driving down commodity and labour prices and how marketing and politics are making both these things seem both desirable and inevitable.' Pip stopped to breathe. That had been quite a mouthful, the words lining up like lemmings. Everyone was looking at her. Had she over-egged the pudding?

'Not sure that's on the national curriculum,' said Tommy. 'But you're welcome to the T-shirt.' He removed it to a chorus of whistles and cheers. Tommy wasn't ripped in any way but his chest had both shape and softness, a few delicate yet masculine tufts of chest hair. Pip leaned back in her chair, a little breathless and not quite sure why. Melissa rolled big eyes.

'So is this a real 70s party or what?' asked Josh, breaking the silence. He was rolling another joint while still capable.

'What do you mean? A real 70s party?'

'Do we throw our car keys in the hat and take our pick?' He was trying to look meaningfully at Tanisha as he said this but his nerve didn't quite hold.

There was a lull in the music, a reverberating bass note or two before Jimmy Page cranked it up, and it coincided not with laughter but a pregnant pause in the conversation as the residents of 27 Hampshire Drive looked at Pip. Pip coughed and rose from her seat.

'I'll open another bottle,' she said.

'Except Pip's the only one with a car,' said Tommy, fork-fishing his bread with one hand, toking on the joint with the other. Crash went

Jimmy's guitar. Crash.

'And who'd want to pick out her keys?' said someone.

The music was loud again and Pip had her back to the table. She had been looking for a corkscrew before realising that she didn't need one. Screw-top. Screw it. Screw-top. She took the bottle into the kitchen with her all the same and steadied herself on the working surface. Deep breath. Had someone really said that? Pip wasn't sure. She couldn't say whether the voice had been male or female. She couldn't really be certain if she'd heard it through her ears or just inside her paranoid head. She was drunk. She had to put it down to being drunk.

Back in the lounge, Tommy had produced a red balloon which he appeared to be deflating into his mouth.

'£60 a bottle on ebay,' he squeaked and reacted as if this remark was the punch-line to the funniest joke in the world. He laughed for a minute before suddenly going silent. The faraway look in his eyes was every bit as other worldly as anything in Tanisha's African queen demeanour. Pip topped up everybody's glasses with a brisk efficiency. She had no idea what was going on. Had Tommy been laughing at her? Now pretending he hadn't been? She picked the quarter joint out of the ashtray – Harp stays sharp, the charity shop ashtray read – and took a tiny tug. It burned her lungs.

'Is he alright?' she asked, squinting through watering eyes.

Josh, she could see by his reaction, wasn't entirely sure.

'Dude?' he asked, giving Tommy a tentative poke.

He didn't get poked back. Tommy was somewhere the other side of Alpha Centauri. For a long moment the room watched, so quiet you could almost hear the candles flickering. Tommy's pupils dilated and contracted twice slowly.

'Dude', Josh said, again.

'Is he breathing?' Melissa asked. She was getting bored. Her boyfriend, out of his chair now, pulling down his cuffs, was preparing to perform heart massage or something else suitably heroic. And then Tommy opened his eyes. He nodded slowly – as if he had just understood something complicated.

'Be calm, my people,' he said, stretching his eyes. 'Be zen. Be beautiful. It's nitrous oxide – the one-minute harmless high. Delivery method: the humble balloon.'

'We use nitrous oxide as an anaesthetic in dentistry,' said Tanisha. 'It is not harmless.'

Tommy took the canister, pumped the balloon up and handed it to Josh. 'It is legal, though,' he said.

'So it can't be that bad,' said Josh.

Tommy pumped. He handed another balloon to Melissa and then a third to her boyfriend. 'Bitches?' he said to Tanisha and Pip, raising an eyebrow. 'This would cost you laaaaaarge on the street.' He put on an American twang.

'A balloon,' said Melissa's boyfriend. 'That's why it's called a party drug.' He laughed at his own joke.

Tanisha got up. 'I'm going for a walk,' she said.

'No,' said Pip.

'No,' said Josh.

'You can come too, Josh,' said Tanisha, with a short laugh. Pip knew he wouldn't. Tanisha too. Cruelly, she offered him his jacket, a threadbare not at all retro military-style thing.

'No,' said Josh. 'I think I'll just...'

With all the falsely gay abandon of a man backed against the edge of a cliff and forced to jump, Josh inhaled deeply on his balloon. It farted; he wheezed and then his head fell off his shoulders.

'What's it like?' asked Pip. She was watching Josh's lolling features with no little consternation but she was fascinated all the same. There could be a PhD in this stuff.

'Everything just goes in slow motion,' said Tommy. 'It's fine. It's fun.' Pip heard the front door slam. Tanisha, the voice of sanity, had departed, leaving Pip's painfully desperate need to be liked as the loudest voice in her head. 'I heard every word you were saying,' said Tommy. 'All of you. Don't worry.'

Melissa and her boyfriend looked at each other conspiratorially, then he emptied the gas from his balloon into her mouth while she emptied hers into his.

'Gross,' said Josh.

Pip was the only possible focus for Tommy's attention now and he gave it as good as he always gave it. Pip knew what it was all about, the Lockhart charm. She'd seen it all before in its gushing insincerity. But it was such a lovely way to be suckered. 'Absolutely fantastic idea, Pip, my friend,' he said. He raised a glass to her, a little unsteadily. 'A fondue. A fun do.'

He handed her the canister and watched her intently as she began to fill a balloon for him. He took the full balloon from her and placed it between his lips. Then, taking the canister from her, he began to inflate a balloon for her. Pump, pump. It was a yellow balloon, expanding like her ego. As he pumped, he kept his eyes fixed on hers and she, foolish, foolish, frustrated girl that she was, kept her eyes fixed on his. Oh, Philippa Henley, have you no shame? His smile got bigger and bigger. The balloon did the same. Eventually he stopped and handed the swollen object to her.

'I think that's enough, don't you, young lady?'

'There's enough to take off in here,' she said. 'You know, like the old man in Up.'

Tommy laughed. 'That was a funny film,' he said and then he looked at her again. 'You've had a tough week, Pip,' he said. 'The crumbling cliff...'

She smiled – touched he remembered. 'I wanted to show them where the fossils come from,' she said.

'You should have taken them to the shopping centre,' said Tommy, with a wink. Then he opened wide and sucked in a bagful of nitrous oxide. 'Go on Pip. Have a laugh. It's laughing gas. You deserve it.' He was still laughing and he was still looking at her, yet he was already a million miles away. Pip needed to be back by his side, basking in the warm skin-tingling sunshine of his attention. Laughing gas. That's exactly what you need, sad girl. Some laughing gas. She opened her mouth and squeezed.

For a beat, there was nothing but, as she went to comment to that effect, not a syllable emerged. Tommy's T-shirt, she saw. Purple. He was using it to wipe the damp table. The angry scimitar flicker of a phalanx of candles. A sudden table cloth.

# 1.4.

Ron could feel an itch, a nagging tug, in his trigger finger. As he became aware of it, the finger began to jerk like a knee kicking under the doctor's hammer. He had never used it in anger, the trigger finger, the odd time at the funfair, the charity fundraiser but not on the job, not as a beat copper in Biscuit Town. He focused on the feeling. The tug. That's what you were supposed to do.

He turned the sound up on the side of his phone and tried to bury the earbuds deeper in his ears. Not easy with all that bloody hair. More hair in his ears these days than on his fucking bollocks. He had Martha's Mindfulness practice on his mobile. One of the younger lads on the course had shown him how to put it on a phone. He had the shorter 'practice'. He had begun listening to it when he felt himself losing it.

'What are you feeling in your right hand, in this moment?' said Martha in her infuriatingly calm monotone.

Ron tried to refocus on his twitching fingers. Tried to imagine that it was the anger leaving his body, like electricity from a broken cable bucking and kicking into nothing. Fucking do-gooders. He was very angry. And given that they'd identified hypertension, first mild and then moderate, at every single one of his police medicals, that could not be a good thing.

Martha, the Mindfulness teacher, had frizzy lilac hair and eyes that looked as if they might dissolve into tears at any moment. Ron quite liked her. The social worker type who saw the good in everyone. Ron had met more than his fair share of them in his years on the Force. Little Johnny may have burgled 97 houses to feed his drug habit but he's nice to his mother. Martha, though, looked like she might also have actually lived a bit. She wasn't one of those politically correct regurgitators of claptrap. Not like those bloody charity muggers in the pub. University of Life, Martha. Like Ron himself.

'The mind will wander. That's what minds do,' intoned Martha. 'Just gently – and with kindness – take the mind back to this body scan and to the sensations in your right arm.'

Bloody hell, he was crap at this. She was right, Martha – the way the mind wanders. He used to think he was good at concentrating. Perhaps he was. Once. But the right hand. When he thought of it, it shook. And, when his hand shook, it made him think of Eileen. Started in the hand with her but now she was shaking all over. Like a rag doll – a rag doll in the hands of an angry child.

Martha was coming towards the end. Ron had listened to her 'body scan practice (shorter)' often enough to know that. Only the left arm left now. And he wanted to swing with that one like he used to when he boxed. Right-handed but swung harder and heavier with the left. It was Charlie Frasier, his first boxing trainer in the Met, who'd spotted that and turned him into a southpaw.

Ron looked at the half-gone pint of beer he'd set on the beer garden table. He could make a pint last 90 minutes now. That was retirement for you. He put his hands into the small of his back and eased the shoulders back, stretching the spine and taking a deep breath of tobacco-stained air. How could you be this angry with a bunch of bloody women in pink T-shirts? Mindfulness wasn't easy at the best of times and, after a pint and a half of fizz and a gutful of patronising bullshit, it was next to impossible.

'And, if you have closed your eyes, allow them to open,' said Martha. 'Fine just as you are. In this moment.' Then the bells. Those two little silver discs that Martha used to signal the end of the 'practice'. Tinkle, tinkle. He was supposed to be relaxed now but he was about as relaxed as a man with a late night appointment with the Kray twins.

Ron had been enjoying a quiet drink. Well, the nearest thing you could get to a quiet drink in The Smugglers'. For all that it attracted fewer and fewer customers, there still always seemed to be something bubbling in there, something about to kick off. Nothing serious but it was never exactly relaxing either. The owner, Vic Hooper, was a nervy, unsettled and unsettling man at the best of times. Vic needed a few pints of Mindfulness himself. Of course, it couldn't be easy: the customers fewer and poorer, the bills bigger and more frequent. But Vic just didn't seem to get that, when the chips were down, you had to try harder to get the customers. Half-hearted attempts at karaoke and the odd meat raffle weren't going to cut it in the social media age. Even Ron knew that much and he didn't really know what social media was. But Vic had always been a glass half-empty sort of bloke, even back in the days when The Smugglers' was rammed. Perhaps all publicans were. The eye for the empty glass.

Some half a dozen drinkers, none of them exactly caning the stuff. Tommy, the student, the only person saying anything much. He'd started it – Ron's feeling of unease. The bloody cancer girls had just made it worse.

Ron knew that Tommy was a student, thought that he looked like an arse with his 70s sideburns and strides and knew that he talked bollocks but he couldn't help liking the kid all the same. How did you explain that? Ron had always fancied himself a shrewd judge of character when he was on the Force – able to sort the wheat from the chaff even as the lines between the cons and the law were blurring and bending. The kid Tommy just didn't take anything too seriously, including himself, and that was infectious. Ron admired it. He had probably taken – took – life way too seriously. The best laid plans. He and Eileen had been planning a cruise for the summer.

Ron found himself asking Tommy about the little girl who'd got hit by a stone. 'Student teacher from your place, wasn't it?'

'You sure it wasn't one of the other sprogs?' Vic had snorted. 'Throwing a stone, I mean. The cliff hasn't moved for years.'

Ron wasn't so sure about that but he didn't say anything. He'd only come in for a quiet drink.

'Well, Vic,' said Tommy, reasonably, 'they've closed a bit of the beach. And the Council wouldn't do that for nothing, would they?'

This spun off in the usual direction. Older punters on the kids of today, the minor misdemeanours, the kicked fences, the litter, the lack of respect...

Eventually Tommy and his sidekick had downed their pints and taken off. Somewhere better to go. Ron was grimly aware that he had no particular place to go and was condemned to Vic's piss-inducing keg fizz or a night at home alone with the television. He laboured over his pint, drinking it as slowly as he could, leafing disinterestedly through the Daily Mirror. He was looking for a crossword or a sudoku or codeword or any sort of puzzle really (as Eileen got weaker, his need for number and letter distractions got stronger) but he couldn't stop thinking about Tommy's parting shot. 'This is the thing, Vic,' Tommy had said as he slid off the bar stool. 'And it's not me saying it, it's Oxfam, but one per cent of the world's population owns as much as the remaining 99% put together. One percent.' He and his pal walked across the sticky floorboards and, at the door, he stopped and turned theatrically: 'You see what happens when people don't want to talk about politics?' The doors creaked and swung arthritically as Tommy and his oversized trousers disappeared.

While he still had a clear head, Ron had started manipulating the figures. He'd always liked Maths problems. If two men take an hour to dig a hole, how many holes can three men dig in four hours? He picked up a half-sized bookie's biro that was lying on the bar. (Had Vic been gambling away whatever slim profits he was making?) Those rich guys. The top one per cent. If he had his sums right, they could afford to give away half of what they had and still own a quarter of the world's wealth. Was that right? It sounded absurd. It sounded medieval. Tommy had said that 80 people owned as much wealth as more than 3.5 billion of the poorest people. He said it had been on the telly so he surely wasn't making it up. How many fucking noughts was a billion? Eighty people! You could fit twice that number in The Smugglers' and still have room for a barn dance. It took him out of himself for half an hour or so and that was a good thing. But it disconcerted him all the same.

There had been about half of dozen of them – the women – and they'd have stood out without the pink T-shirts and collecting boxes. Groups of unchaperoned women were not seen in The Smugglers' as a rule. Groups of unchaperoned cockroaches would have been wary. Not that this group needed chaperoning. They were well capable of looking after themselves. That Deborah Gann had always used her boobs like weapons and nobody argued with Ruby Tuesday, certainly none of her husbands had ever dared. Ruby shook a collecting tin. She was an out-of-the-bottle blonde with soot-heavy mascara and bright pink lipstick to match the T-shirt. 'I Beat Cancer', said the

T-shirt. Certainly explained why she'd lost a few pounds.

Cancer was just the topic he didn't want to talk about, but he couldn't help putting his pen down. He watched the tin rattling for a moment, Ruby half-bullying, half-flattering the punters out of their pennies. 'Come on, darling – is that a wallet in your pocket or are you just pleased to see me?'

'So you beat cancer, did you, Ruby?' Ron had heard himself asking.

Ruby twirled and nearly lost her footing. Perhaps this wasn't their first pub. That and/or the pencil-thin heels begging for mercy beneath those still substantial calves. There was a date printed on the back of the T-shirt.

'That's the day you beat cancer, is it?'

'That's right, Ron Newton – the day I sent it running for its mummy. Like Charlie Reed,' she cackled.

Charlie Reed was one of Ruby's exes. Ron could already feel the hackles rising. And not out of sympathy for Charlie, whom he'd once nicked for receiving stolen fish fingers. But he had noticed that the girls all had similar slogans printed on their T-shirts or written on cardboard and attached to their T-shirts with safety pins. My dad beat cancer. My friend Sally beat cancer. Jenny beat cancer.

'So how do you beat cancer, then?' he asked.

The others looked at Ruby. It must have seemed, to them, like a daft question. 'You fight it,' she said. 'You refuse to accept it. You live your life.' She looked around for support.

'You just say no,' said someone.

'What a load of crap,' said Ron.

He was aware of Vic Hooper hissing 'Ron' under his breath. Vic was serving the girls and didn't want to miss slaking Ruby's substantial thirst. Ron didn't have anything against Ruby. Liked a brassy blonde as much as the next man. But this was just fucking crap. 'You don't fight cancer.'

Someone gave him a leaflet which said that you did. Fight cancer, it read.

'My wife has cancer and she is going to die,' said Ron. He shocked himself saying this. Hearing himself admit, for the first time, that Eileen was going to die. He looked down and then he forced himself to look up, to eyeball everyone around him. 'Are you saying that she wants to? Are you saying she just isn't trying hard enough, even as every bone in her fucking body is being eaten away from the inside? She's not fighting hard enough.'

'I'm sorry to hear that,' said someone.

'You don't beat cancer. You just get lucky,' said Ron.

'We just want to do something,' said Deborah Gann. 'For charity.'

'You're doing it for yourself. You're buying into some Children in Need Pudsey fucking Bear bollocks that you can beat death with a sponsored bloody swim. Didn't get your mum this time, the cancer, Debbie? Maybe next time around.'

Deborah Gann looked like she'd been shot. The pub was silent now. Silent, bar Vic's unheeded hissing. 'And my Eileen, is she some weak, pathetic person because she's losing and she's losing fast? And I'm not talking about her fucking hair-loss. You're all fucking children unable to accept reality. In your little pink T-shirts like you're eight years old. Fucking grow up.' Ron got up, picked up his pint and walked out.

Twenty minutes later, his heart was still beating thirteen to the dozen.

'This your phone, Ron?'

What?

'Are you all right, Ron?'

A soft voice. Ron looked round. It was Jessica, the barmaid. He hadn't noticed her arrive. She was another Gann. She was related to Debbie, Ron knew that, so therefore related to the cancer-licking mother too. Jess wore jogging bottoms and a baggy T-shirt. It wasn't pink. Ron's legs suddenly felt wobbly and Jess's hand, as it touched his forearm, was gentle enough to push him over, the proverbial feather. He allowed himself to sit at the table. 'Thanks, I...'

She showed him the phone. A modern one with a transparent plastic protector around its bevelled edges. He looked up at her and, despite himself, had to smile. 'Does that really look like my phone?' said Ron. 'Do I look like a rapper?'

Jess smiled. 'Since you put it like that...'

'It's Gary Shad's – saw him glued to it earlier.'

'He lives in my block, so that's easy, anyway.'

'I'm sorry about what I said,' said Ron.

'About Auntie Lou?' said Jess. 'It's fine. I agree with you. She was just very, very lucky.'

Jess put the phone down and began emptying the ashtrays. Ron sipped.

Jess picked up dead cigarette butts and piled them in the ashtray on Ron's table. 'Luck. I mean, it's all anything comes down to, isn't it?"

'It is,' said Ron. 'And they told us it was hard work was rewarded.' He couldn't stop thinking about the bloody one per cent and wondering how many of them had ever done a proper day's work in their lives. For Pete's sake, Ron, why have you never asked yourself that before? Why does it take some student ...

'Sorry to hear about your wife, Ron,' said Jess. 'She used to teach me.'

Ron had a picture of his wife sitting at the kitchen table marking. Two neat piles of exercise books: marked and unmarked. 'Another five minutes,' she'd say as Ron went up to bed.

'I didn't know that, love,' Ron said.

Suddenly, Gary Shad's phone flashed into life – a spit of light in the gathering gloom, a wedge of text appearing. Jess picked it up.

'Looks like Gary's expecting a parcel,' she said. 'A book...'

'A book ...'

Jess and Ron's astonished eyes met. 'Did she use to teach Gary too?'

'She did.' The smirk on Jessica's lips matched that on Ron's own. Shad the bookworm was an incongruity to rank with Ron the rapper.

'She must have been a bloody amazing teacher if she got him interested in books.'

'She was pretty amazing,' said Jess. 'You know, for a teacher.'

Ron felt a pain in his chest. He had an urge to know everything about his wife's career as he realised that, beyond knowing what she did and where she did it, he knew very little indeed. But before he could ask Jess what she remembered, his attention was caught by a young pasty-faced man approaching, ignoring them both and helping himself to a couple of the more substantial dog-ends.

'Hey,' said Jess but her heart wasn't in it. Ron watched as she eyed the lad up and down. He was stick-thin with acne and a black plastic leather jacket. He didn't look English – something about the hair or the eyes. Both were lifeless. Jessica produced a packet of fags and offered him one. He took it without a word and lit it himself with a stick-thin plastic lighter.

'You working on the estate?' said Jess. 'I've seen you...'

'Thank you for the cigarette,' said the kid as if reciting from a phrase book.

Ron gestured at the bench opposite him and the kid sat down. His greasy jeans had holes in them and not the trendy kind.

'Do you want a drink, son?' he made the appropriate drink-downing gesture and noticed his hand had finally stopped twitching.

'I have no money.'

'It's OK,' said Ron. 'I had no money when I was your age. What do you want?'

The kid looked confused and turned to Jess. 'Lager?' she ventured. 'Like Tyskie? Lager?'

The kid nodded.

'When you're ready, Jess. No rush,' said Ron.

'Where are you from?' Ron asked the kid. His first guess had been that he was aged about 22, 23 but now he reckoned he was younger.

The kid told him. Ron had never heard of it. 'Poland,' the kid added. 'I leave home to earn money.'

'That's why we all leave home. Is it much better money here?'

'No. They say yes. But is no.'

'How much do you make?'

Kid looked blank.

'How much do you earn?'

Blanker. Ron put his hand in his pocket and pulled out a pile of change and a couple of rogue notes. He pushed the money across the table. 'In one hour.' He held up a finger and made a swivelling gesture with it around his watch face. 'How much money in one hour?'

The kid shied away from the money. As if Ron was testing him to nick it. Ron did the thing with his finger again. 'One hour. Work. How much money? You.' He pointed.

The kid looked at Ron and then at the money. He picked up the tenner and gave it back to Ron. Shook his head. He did the same with the fiver. Then he started counting the coins, stacking them quickly like a croupier. He pushed a little pile back to Ron.

'£2.75,' said Ron. 'In an hour you earn £2.75?'

The kid nodded. 'Two pound seventy five hour.'

What was the phrase the students had used? Trickle-down economy? The tiniest of trickles in this case. Ron, who considered himself worldly-wise, was surprised by how little it was.

Jess came back with the drinks. Ron gave her the tenner he was holding.

'This lad says he earns £2.75 an hour,' said Ron. 'That can't be right, can it? What's the minimum wage?'

'That's an easy one,' said Jess. 'It's what Vic pays me.'

'And always with a cheery smile, I'd wager,' said Ron. It was a joke. He looked at Jess and knew he should smile himself but he couldn't quite eke one out. Jess stretched her lips a little, widened her eyes but she wasn't really smiling either. Instead, she told him how much the minimum wage was. It wasn't a lot but it was a lot more than £2.75 an hour.

'Prentice,' said the kid. He'd necked half his pint already. 'Ape Prentice.'

'Apprentice,' said Jess. 'He's an apprentice. Paid as an apprentice. You work at the warehouse?'

Glimmer of recognition. The kid's pint was three-quarters gone now. Like Ron at his age.

'There's a warehouse on the estate for, well, you won't have heard of them, Ron.' This time Jess did smile. 'Internet fashion company. Cheap stuff. Wear it twice and bin it. You know.' Ron didn't know. He was still wearing shirts he'd bought in the 1980s. 'They say they're training them so that makes them apprentices.'

'But doesn't the Job Centre...?' Ron trailed off. The Job Centre was just something he'd heard about, heard someone mention somewhere at some time. An answer for a crossword perhaps. He had no idea how it worked. Last time he looked, the Job Centre was called the Labour Exchange.

'They bring them straight from Poland,' said Jess. 'Talk to Darren about it.'

'He was in earlier.'

'UKIP posters?'

Ron nodded. He could see Darren's point of view all of a sudden. Born and bred round the corner and couldn't even get a slave-wage job in the local warehouse. As a young man, Ron had boarded the coach to London, worked a week on a building site, a fortnight as a tea boy in an office off the Strand and then joined the Met. It had been a lot easier back then. But he could see the Polish kid's point of view too. Looking for something better? You couldn't condemn a man for that, could you? Might as well condemn him for breathing. When did Sergeant Ronald Newton (retired) become so fucking reasonable? Martha would be proud of him.

'So you get training, do you?' he asked the kid. It was hard to believe that a lad who could barely string a sentence together in English was getting any training at all.

The kid drained the rest of his beer. Ron repeated himself. 'You get training?'

'No,' said the kid. 'I walk.'

Ron became aware of Jess snatching up Gary Shad's mobile and dialling with panicked punches of the finger at about the same moment as he became aware of the black smoke – a cloud of which was now zeppelined over The Smugglers'.

'Fire,' said Jess. 'Hampshire Drive, I think.'

A brace of flames punched the sky and Ron, as he sprung from his seat, upset his pint of beer.

# 1.5.

Tommy Lockhart's purple T-shirt had been pre-faded, dyed to look old as its 70s slogan. 'Here Comes The Sun', it read in retro lettering that had also been deliberately aged.

The cotton in Tommy's T-shirt had been harvested by a man named Baxter Thomas. However, for the purposes of Pip's wall chart, its long journey had begun not in a Mississippi cotton field but in a Wisconsin lab where its genes had been designed for maximum yield. (Pip avoided genetically-modified foods in her diet; she had no idea there were genetically-modified T-shirts. Who knew? As Melissa might have said.) So by the time Baxter harvested it, it had already travelled the best part of 1,000 miles.

When Baxter looked out of the window of the cab of his picker, he could feel its power beneath him, 600-horse power, swallowing up the cotton three metres at a time. Genetically-modified cotton plants were rich. The picker gorged itself on T-shirts.

It wasn't the worst job in the world. On these early mornings, the flecks of white cotton twinkling in the thin sun, it was like harvesting a sea of stars.

Of course, Baxter didn't need to look out of the picker window if he didn't want to. The picker – a strong, smart and very expensive green beast – drove itself. Auto-pilot. If he wanted to see what was going on, he need only consult the iPad-style screen at his right hand, the very same screen his boss could see from the comfort of his office back at the ranch. In that sense, Baxter could feel the power above him too. He was a minder rather than a driver, a big man but he felt like a tiny and fragile cog inside that picker which grew around him like a robot.

His family had been picking cotton for years. So had his boss's. Since Baxter was black and his boss was white, the relationship had changed a little down the generations but not as much as it ought, not as much as the evidence of a black man in the White House might suggest. As the picker, like a dog that knows the route of its favourite walk, turned its tight, precise U-turn at the end of the plantation field, Baxter's boss was watching. As Baxter relieved himself into a bottle, the picker trundling on, his boss was watching.

Tommy's T-shirt, still not purple and not even yet fabric, had then been shipped to Indonesia where the cotton picked and baled in the USA was, using monstrous machines built in Japan and Germany, spun, stretched and twisted, first into enough rope to tie up a nation of prisoners and then into yarn. The yarn was turned into fabric and dyed by workers with multicoloured hands.

Then it went to Bangladesh where it landed in the palms of Puja Alam, the machinist.

Puja was not like Baxter. Cotton was not in her family. She was the first generation of her family to live and work in a city. She had left her village with the express and sole purpose of taking one of the lowest paid jobs in the world, an economic migrant for 80 dollars a month. She lived in a shared single room without running water in a poorer corner of Dhaka.

At dawn, she joined the great march of workers to the factory. For as many hours a day as she could manage, she was a magician. With just her sewing machine and her bare hands, she would conjure up a T-shirt from a piece of fabric in a few moments. She had no contract as such and the hours (and which of them counted as 'overtime') were at the whim of the supervisor. She was one of the lucky ones though. She had a face mask and didn't cough as much as some of the other girls. Sometimes you couldn't see the girl at the next machine because the air was so thick with cotton fluff.

Puja was 21 years old.

She worked her wizardry on Tommy's pumped-up purple T-shirt, finally sewing in the all-important Peter Robb label. She understood the individual words of the slogan 'Here Comes The Sun', although not exactly why anyone would want to have them printed on a T-shirt. Was it a joke? T-shirts were often in-jokes. She didn't understand why anyone would want a T-shirt that had been deliberately made to look so old either. She checked the most important seams, the one at the V of the neck and the ones where the arms join the shoulder. But should she bother if the point of this T-shirt was that it should look like it had already been worn for a lifetime? She was a lightening fast worker but there was never enough time to check them all, anyway.

Puja knew several people who had been killed when the Rana Plaza building collapsed: the worst garment factory accident ever, people said. Over 1,000 had died, twice as many injured. She had heard of others being killed in fires, the doors to the workplace locked and chained shut to prevent the workers leaving. But the truth was that Puja was better off than many in her country and sent most of her salary back to her family in her village. She pushed the T-shirt to one side and a colleague folded it and placed it in a pile.

After folding and bagging and batching and boxing, the T-shirt finally came to rest in a 20-foot standard shipping container where nobody came near it for the best part of a month although, at one point, as the vessel heaved through the Red Sea, a sailor called Jesús leaned against the container and checked he had enough Marlboro to get through the Suez Canal. The container hit port in England and was attached to a container lorry. It was driven by Dave, an overweight man with angina counting down the days to his retirement. He had no idea what he'd do with all the free time but he was looking forward to it all the same. His wife Glennis was making a list of jobs for him so he wouldn't be under her feet.

Five and a half hour trip. A14 and A1. Not the worst job in the world but not what it used to be.

At the Stufff factory in Northumbria, the T-shirt had been tracked and packed in regulation time by a Geordie lad whose father had been a National Union of Mineworkers branch secretary for a decade and whose name had been painted by a sign-writer on the Board of Honour that used to hang in the miners' club. Lee missed his father but he was glad he was dead. His father was so proud of his work and the lads he did it with. He'd have hated him to have seen what work had come down to.

Tommy hadn't paid for special delivery so the parcel took a couple of days to arrive but it still made it in good time for the party where it ended its short life doused in a highly-flammable material after Tommy had used it to mop up spilled meths.

Pip was right. It would have made a great wall chart, a great lesson.

Pip opened her eyes. Or perhaps she didn't open them. Perhaps they just slid back into focus – clunk, whirr, like a self-focusing SLR camera. She saw the embroidered throw on fire. The coffee table, the books, were going like an oven. Then she smelt the smoke. As she moved, the curtains went up and the fire danced across the carpet, island-hopping the cushions. She appeared to be on the floor in the middle of the room. There seemed to be candles in various states of blaze all over the place. Where was everyone? Half-pulling herself up, she opened her mouth but choked before she could yell. She hit the deck again and saw the now-empty meths bottle on the opposite side of the lounge. She remembered the meths being spilled. No sooner had she seen the carpet with its purple highway, the T-shirt or meths or both, than the flames engulfed it. Cushions, throws, the bookcases, the rattan chair with a snap and a crackle.

Fire extinguisher.

She rolled under the table. (Under the table would be safer, wouldn't it?) And groped around. There were flames mounting one of the table legs. A solid metal canister materialised cold against her palm. She picked it up and squeezed. The fire hesitated. But wasn't this gas supposed to be foam? And then the fire embraced its new playmate and laughed, roared and smoked up to new and greater heights. An inferno now, out of the door and up the stairs. The canister fell from her hands. N2O, Pip read.

# 1.6.

Colin Graham tapped his foot, straightened his collar and looked at his watch. He straightened the creases in his trousers and looked up at the station clock. His mind was wandering away from his shift, which was ticking to an end, and towards the twins' birthday. He needed to leave promptly to maximise the time that he was at their party. Tap, tap went his hand on his thigh. Susie had made that very clear. And she was right. Absolutely. He straightened the collar and the seams once again. He buttoned a rogue button. Sharp working rig. Sharp thinking. He downed a cup of water. Cool head. Clear thinking. Tap, tap, tap went his foot on the floor. It was your thinking that kept you alive in a fire. Knowing instinctively what to do and doing it automatically. Keep your mind on the bloody job, Colin.

Actually, in truth, it wasn't the twins' birthday that was distracting him, was it? They'd be delighted if he turned up for just five minutes. Piggyback each round the lounge. Sorted. It was the letter. Not sorted.

He took the letter out of his pocket. Was about to read it again but then thought better of it. He knew every bloody word already. Didn't know what to think about it though – that was the thing. Didn't know how to react. Colin was used to knowing how to react. He was used to knowing what he thought about something. He was a man who knew his own mind. But lately, that had been getting harder. Suddenly, life seemed to be full of pros and cons. Was that what getting old was all about? Indecision. He wasn't sure. Was cancer still the death sentence it used to be? His paternal grandfather and uncle had both died of it. Diagnosis to death had taken about five minutes in the case of Uncle Ian. That's how Colin remembered it anyway, although he was a teenager back then, so had other things on his mind. On the other hand, he knew that Sedge's wife had had it for years and was still going strong, so...

Maybe that was then and this is now.

Colin wasn't sure. The doctors weren't sure either. They couldn't tell him whether he'd got the big C yet anyway, so perhaps he shouldn't be worrying at all. The blood test was 'frequently inconclusive' which made you wonder why they bothered with it. Another grey area. Colin was not fond of grey areas. He liked clarity. Black and white. Right and wrong. That was probably why he hated smoke so much: too grey.

'There are false positives and false negatives, Mr Graham,' the consultant had said. Colin had given him a false smile.

So he refolded the letter, got up and walked across to his locker. It was at this point that he realised that he was still wearing his bloody boots. Not good on the carpet. So much for the cool head and clear thinking. He was surprised nobody had said anything but perhaps his colleagues sensed his mood better than he did and were steering well clear. He'd been downstairs for an hour or so checking out the new hydraulic cutting equipment – any distraction – and had forgotten to take the things off. Idiot.

He opened the door of his locker. The pictures of Susie and the twins sellotaped to the back of it, the manuals and handbooks, towels (two), spare rig, waterproofs, the knee brace he sometimes wore when playing volleyball – a place for everything and everything in its place. He put the letter on top of the folded towels. Then he changed his mind and put it in the pocket of his waterproofs. He tidied his documents, clipping the pages on the new hydraulics into his binder. Then he straightened the picture of Susie. It was comforting to him that, if he did catch one on a call, then his locker at least was immaculate. No mess, no dirty clothes, no pin-ups. It reflected him as he'd want to be reflected. It was bad enough that a bereaved widow should have to clear her husband's locker. You wouldn't want her to find it plastered with half-naked models, would you? The lads told him he was a doom merchant. Of course, the rules said you weren't supposed to have pin-ups or similar in your locker, anyway – sexist, unprofessional, 'not the image you'd want to associate with a modern fire service' and so on and so forth – but half the lads did. Even Sedge had a fading photo of Gabby Garnier in that shampoo advert.

There was a bit of an argument going on as to what channel to watch on the telly. (Colin wasn't the only person who was going off shift and was therefore itchy as a schoolboy at three thirty.) Dave Sedgeley was a fan of some gameshow. Someone else wanted the news channel but mainly because he fancied the presenter. Butch, the union rep, was clutching the remote, twirling it like a baton as one of the kids tried to grab it. Butch was babbling about a documentary he'd seen, in which they'd said that 80 people were as rich as the 3.5 billion poorest put together. Never missed a chance, did Butch.

'What, in this country?'

'There aren't 3.5 billion people in this country, you muppet.'

Colin had seen the documentary too but he didn't say anything. The union was all well and good but Butch was a troublemaker, really – bad for morale.

'Well, in Africa, what do you expect? Turn the fucking channel over.'

A couple of the younger bucks came in from the gym. They were arguing about the static bikes and who'd been fastest over the Tour de France stage simulator. Colin watched it all, head surveying the entire room like a slowly panning camera. It was as if he were seeing the station and his colleagues for the first time.

Or the last.

God, he was a doom merchant.

He needed to get out of these boots. He used the stairs. The noise from the TV, noise from the gym, noise from the chatter, they were all receding behind him when, suddenly, there was silence. Funny how there always was just before the shout went up. The trumpet sounded and Lena, the disembodied robotic voice, announced it. Colin was one of the first at the appliance even though he'd had to go via the Watchroom for the print-out: house in Biscuit Town. Well, at least it wasn't the old factory again.

'BA,' shouted Colin, as he counted them onto the appliance. 'Make sure you've got your BA.' He grabbed the BA board and hopped on as Sedge put on the beacon.

As they hurtled through the streets, Colin operated the blue and twos and then, as the two-tone siren began to cry, flicked on the radio.

Sedge rattled through the gears. 'Well?'

'Student house, it seems,' said Colin.

'Marijuana factory?'

'Maybe.' Colin looked up as an unexpected flicker of orange caught his eye. 'Fuck,' he said.

'What?'

'We're still half a mile away and I can already see the flames.'

'Shoot,' said Sedge.

The engine revved. Colin was concerned about the blaze spreading. There were garages at the back of the houses on Hampshire Drive and a wooden clubhouse on the bowling green. He checked with the radio operator that a second appliance was following and was told the WM had just returned from his visit and was right behind. Colin detected in himself some relief that he would no longer be the senior officer. This was not a feeling he had ever felt before. He usually liked being in charge. He'd been flying on autopilot and the sensation brought him back down to earth with a bump. He realised he could hardly breathe. He felt as if he needed BA just to breathe normally.

'I was born round here,' Colin heard himself saying. Why had he said that? 'I...' He paused. 'How's your wife, Dave?'

Sedge tossed him a stern sideways glance. Narrow road. Big fire engine. Irritating parked cars.

'Sorry, not the time,' said Colin.

Sedge concentrated on the road. 'They think it might have come back,' he said eventually. 'Needs some tests, you know.'

'Sorry, mate.'

'There's a lot of it about,' said Sedge. 'She's quite bright about it really. I don't know. Debbie Gann's asked her to do some sort of fundraiser. Don't know if she will or not.'

'Debbie Gann's got cancer?' said Colin. Mortality striking one of your schoolyard squeezes was a face-slapping reminder of your own. Colin remembered spinning her round the dancefloor to 'The Night' by Frankie Valli. All night. She could dance, could Debbie.

'No, her mother. Think she's in remission, though. But Ron Newton's wife...'

Sedge hit the brakes. There were people on the streets now and, as they swung round into Hampshire Drive, a cat skipped out of the way, his eyes lighting up in the headlights. Colin was gathering up equipment. Cancer could wait. One of the new kids was still fiddling with his boots as the appliance came to a halt and the crew swung into action.

'We need at least one more pump, Sedge,' said Colin as he jumped from the cab. Fuck, that hurt his knee. He went into automatic: gather, evaluate, formulate, implement, re-evaluate. Done it dozens of times.

Colin looked at the house. The ground floor was alive with fire, the windows cracking. No sign of any residents. He looked back over his shoulder, the crew were moving ladders and hoses into position. He could hear the second appliance in the distance. The cat was now sitting on a gate post, not a care in the world. A fox disappeared up an alley with considerably more urgency.

'Is there anybody in there?' asked Richards.

Richards was the sharpest of the younger lads – shame he couldn't lose that bloody earring.

'Student house. Multi-occupancy.'

Colin looked at Richards and made a decision. 'Take this, son. The Watch Manager's about to arrive.'

He gave Richards the BA board and the identification tag from his own Breathing Apparatus. Quite what he was doing he wasn't quite sure since he was, at that moment, the senior officer. But he suddenly felt far more expendable than these young, fit lads in his charge. Each had his whole life ahead of him.

'We'll want someone round the back,' he said to Richards. 'When McCormack gets here.' He gestured towards the arriving appliance which was less than 50 yards away now.

As good as here.

As he eased the face mask into position with his right hand, his left automatically reached over his shoulder to check his air cylinder was secure and in place. These were movements he'd made a thousand times before and they made him feel settled. He had two men with BA at the door already. One of them – was it Gupta? – had the hose reel. But the lads were hesitating. He knew it was unprofessional but he couldn't help himself. It was as if part of him thought he may never have the chance again. As if this could be the last time. He pushed past Gupta and delivered a size eleven boot to the front door's sweet spot. It swung open.

Colin knew these houses. Probably been in one in this very street. Certainly one like it. The narrow hallway. Bulked up in his rig, he felt as if he had to breathe in to squeeze between its hugging walls.

The smoke was thick, possibly thicker than usual. Door on the left? Yes. Wide open.

Shuffles in. He can see the orange glow. The lounge is ablaze. The fire growls. His colleague is beside him. A shorter man. Must be Gupta. Has the high-pressure hose reel. The white flash of steam as Gupta unloads a jet. The fire gasps like an exploding geyser. Lounge empty. He moves towards where he expects the kitchen to be. Walks into a laid table. (Knocked-through lounge-diner. They all had that.) The place settings suddenly very clear before his eyes – is that a fondue? – and then smoke swirling again. Another jet. Dining room empty. Feels his way round the table. Another door. Open. Kitchen full of smoke. Sees a fridge. Kitchen empty. As well as the lounge, there is fire in the dining area and the hallway. The frame of the door he entered through just seconds before is beginning to bite. He gestures to Gupta. Colin's getting hot. It happens like that. One moment you're OK and, the next, frying inside your rig. Back in the hallway, the fire, by the sounds of it anyway, is everywhere. Crackling and barking. Something pops. Perhaps a lightbulb, perhaps something larger. Colin refocuses on his breathing, the steady scuba sound inside his mask. He's calm. When you're young, you take great gulps of air which obviously reduces the time you can spend inside. The BA beeps at you when you have five minutes of air left. Colin is a light breather. He's lucky. He's never heard that beep in 25 years. Colin smells his own sweat as he climbs the stairs. The smoke is rising but the doors are all closed. The students all have their own rooms he presumes and that desire for a little privacy affords them protection. Opens each door in quick succession. Bathroom empty. Bog empty. Bedroom empty. Bedroom empty. There are more stairs. Loft conversion. Up the stairs. Door shut again. Door open. Loft room empty. Backwards down the narrow stairs. Then forwards down the second flight towards the fire that is at the foot of the stairs. His colleague is dousing it down. Good lad, Gupta. Colin is past it and out.

Back out in the front garden he could see again. The paramedics had arrived as well as McCormack's crew. He took his mask off – the fresh air, the assault of smells (wood, plastic, carpet, clothes, paint, gas) – and turned to Richards for an update.

'They're over there, Guv.'

Sitting on the garden wall were three young lads and standing up, a black girl was comforting a crying white girl. Nothing seriously wrong with any of them. The paramedics were hovering.

'The students,' said Richards, nodding in their general direction. 'The occupants. They were out the back garden. Pissed mostly. Lucky bastards.'

Colin counted them again. 'But there are only five of them,' he said. 'There were six places laid at that fucking table.'

Colin turned and ran back into the house. He was coughing before he could even get on his hands and knees. His eyes were burning and his knee, as he crawled along on all fours as fast as he could, was killing him – burning more than any flame. No piggybacks tonight. She was under the table. Just a touch was enough to tell him she was still alive. To pick her up and carry her out, he was going to have to stand in this. So he did, adrenalin lightening her dead weight. Coughing up whole lungs, he manoeuvred her through two doors without ever seeing either – the instinct of having felt his way in and out already. He deposited her on the lawn and the paramedics pounced. Colin bent double, hands on knees and coughed and coughed and coughed. In the distance he thought he could hear a train.

The crew from the second appliance had manoeuvred a hose reel around the side, presumably to come in through the kitchen. McCormack appeared at the corner of the house and clocked Colin. Excellent officer, McCormack. If they could contain it in the lounge. Colin's eyes were stinging like they were being pulled from their sockets with acid pliers. As he went to shout to McCormack, he felt a hand on his back and saw the high-vis shininess of a paramedic uniform. They were talking to him. He heard his own name a couple of times. But he couldn't hear them above the noise of the train, the noise of first, the train, and then, the music.

'You know you're gonna to lose more than you've found,' sings Frankie Valli.

Colin sees himself slumped on the familiar moquette, black-grey with red, yellow and sky-blue stripes. The musty smell of the railway carriage. Feet up on the seat opposite. Folds up his music mag. He is primed for the first sight of the sea: the ice blue moment between the railway cutting and the Railway Bell where the grey grit ribbon of Prince's Street races down to the front – the bowling green, the tennis court, the outermost limb of the Crystal Flyer jutting out like a great steel elbow: where the train brakes and screeches and slowly slows past empty signal boxes and sidings, wild chamomile and black grass and that abandoned carriage in peeling Southern Rail green that is older than he is. A schoolboy's camp. A teenage hideaway. A treasure trove of stolen kisses and faint-sketch memories.

The big old clock on the station that always says twenty to six. The clock's Roman numerals (with the missing V on the six), the cast iron frame and the stone, for which the region was once famous, from which it hangs, to Colin they go together like fish and chips. Or fish and biscuits. This is Biscuit Town thanks to its famous factory. And if he remembers nothing else, he will always remember that smell: the strange bitter-sweet half fishmonger's, half bakery smell. Something like herring-flavoured Garibaldis or cod in butterscotch. On those summer days when the Channel was as calm as the duck pond in the park, it settled like smog.

# 1.7.

Jessica Gann bounced along the street in her favourite trainers, head full of song, happy in her headphones. Jess wasn't the whistling type and had a strong aversion to folk with terrible voices singing along with their music but occasionally the joy in the beat was just too much for her and she'd blurt out a line or two and then laugh. Sha-la-la-la-laaaargh. 'Why don't you come on over, Valerie?' she sang. 'Doo-doo-doo.'

She really wasn't built for tunes. Loved dancing though.

She was running late. Vic had had 'a couple of little things that need doing' and she had been too soft to say no – 11.30pm or not (and he stopped paying her at ten). She felt sorry for him, was how it was. The pub was too big for him and its sad Dad's Army of punters. End of. Now she was cold. Spring was supposed to be just around the corner but Jess had seen no evidence. She did up her retro, charity shop tracksuit top and pulled up the collar. Nearly home. The house fire two streets away, which had accompanied her all the way home, was finally beginning to die down. The cloud of smoke was thick and dark but, thanks to the sea breeze, dispersing. Too far away to afford any warmth but still too close to home. The wiring in her flat had already claimed two toasters.

'Evening.'

It was Gary Shad sitting on the wall outside their block, boots tap, tap tapping against the brick. For a moment he was lost in a cloud of a smoke too. Vaping, not burning. Gary's dog, the poodle French, sat obediently at his feet. Jess let her headphones slide down onto her shoulders and told her phone to stop playing. (She loved talking to her phone.)

'Hey, Gary,' said Jess. 'You left your phone in the pub.' She half-patted, half-stroked French on the head.

'Thanks, sweetheart,' said Gary. He didn't seem surprised, didn't reach for his pocket like you might expect. She fished it out of her tracksuit and placed it in his palm. As far as Jess knew, Gary Shad had never done a proper day's work in his life, so why did his hands look rougher than an old tree?

'You all right, Jess?' asked Gary, slightly over-friendly.

'Yeah.' Hesitant. 'Did the fire scare French?' It didn't look like it. The dog looked like she was watching telly.

Gary exhaled through tightly-pursed lips. 'Always someone worse off than yourself, isn't there?'

'Any news?'

'Seen a couple of ambulances.'

'That's...' Jess wasn't sure what it was, in fact. 'Well, see you later.'

'Jess,' said Gary, before she could move, a higher note in his voice. 'You still au-pairing?'

'You could call it that,' she replied, tentatively. 'Why? You looking to get into the domestic servitude line yourself?'

He ignored that. 'Russian, in't she? The lady of the house.'

There was a crack of a branch underfoot and then the rapid rubbery slip-slapping of training shoe on pavement. Jogger. On the other side on the street, head-to-toe in designer gear and seemingly oblivious to the smoke, was Gavin Henley. Jogging while Rome burned. For a moment his face was caught in the moonlight or a street lamp or perhaps the last flame from the fire and she had a clear view of him: inhaling, exhaling, that vein above his right eye pumping with purple rage. His tight black top said 'Run. Become' in day-glo lemon. Jess didn't realise that he ran down her street. Did he know she lived here? He was certainly a long way from home. Jess watched as he ran past, lost in his sweaty, teeth-grinding reverie.

'Ask him yourself,' she said when he was out of earshot.

'Is that him?' whistled Gary. 'Your boss?'

'Hasn't he seen the fire?' Gavin Henley hadn't looked up at the smoke once. 'Always in his bubble.'

'Amazed he comes down here in the cheap seats. Gav...'

'He runs miles. Mostly on the cliff-top at the back of Estuary Sands. I see him standing there just looking over the edge sometimes... Always in a bubble.' She trailed off. The Henleys' house, for all the money it represented, was not a happy home.

'Seriously loaded.' Gary left the remark hanging. It wasn't quite a question. And it too tottered on the edge of a cliff before tumbling into the night.

They watched the black-clad figure disappear up the street, behind the trees and then turn right to head towards the beach, the prom and, Jess assumed, the cliff path up over Moonshine Point and back home again. Three, maybe four miles.

A fire engine trundled by. Going away from the fire. No siren. No hurry. You could still smell the fire but you couldn't see it anymore.

'They must have it under control,' said Gary.

'Makes you think,' said Jess.

'That can't be good for his health – running through all the smoke,' said Gary.

Jess had known Gary since school and saw right through this old flannel. She didn't want to know why he was so interested in the Henleys, why he had called his Lordship 'Gav' when he clearly didn't know him. Instead, she leaned against the wall and manoeuvred a ciggie from the packet in her pocket.

'You trying to tempt me back on the weed?'

'Nope,' said Jess. 'You will have noticed, Gary, that I didn't actually offer you one.' She lit her fag and, for a moment, she smoked tobacco and he smoked what smelled like bubble gum.

'You remember Mrs Newton from primary school?' she said

through the smoke.

'Of course. The copper's wife.'

'She's got cancer.'

Gary didn't say anything at first but Jess knew that for all his front, Gary liked Mrs Newton well enough – they all did. 'You can't talk about cancer when you're smoking,' he muttered.

Jess had been thinking about Mrs Newton on the way home. Was that a sign that she was getting old? Nostalgia for her schooldays? More like it was because she felt stuck, like her life was going nowhere, and she was looking back into the past for some pointers. Singing like a schoolgirl wasn't going to make that nasty germ of a feeling go away, was it? Only a new life would do that.

Come on, Jessica, man up.

'You remember when we used to have a Maths test and she'd leave the answers on her desk, face down,' Jess went on.

'I do.' Gary's face lit up, remembering. 'Then she'd go out of the classroom, wouldn't she?'

'Daring us to look. She'd told us the answers were there "but you're only cheating yourself if you look". Remember?'

'Yes,' said Gary. 'You ever look?'

'No. That's the point. Nobody looked. And it wasn't that we were scared of her. It was just that we knew it was wrong and that was her point. She was a good teacher.'

'She was,' said Gary.

He looked at Jess. She was staring into the distance. The darkening night was eating up the smoke: the swirls from the fire and from their own smaller contributions, his sweetie juice, her fag, all disappearing into the blackening grey. She had steered Gary away from Gavin Henley nicely. And Gary knew that he'd been steered.

'I'm going to organise a tenants' meeting,' he said.

It took Jess a moment to absorb this. Gary Shad organising a tenants' meeting was like Auntie Debbie joining the Women's Institute – and winning a jam-making competition. She couldn't help smiling.

'I've got mould,' he said, eventually.

'That some new legal high you kids are taking?'

'Well, if it is, I should be loaded. Wiring's fucked too.'

Jess took a long drag. She knew what he meant but didn't say anything. When toaster #1 had gone up in black flames that smelled of burning tyres, she'd contacted the landlord. Absentee landlord as it turned out. There had been an agent. He'd been like 'yeah, yeah, yeah' for a week and a half before admitting he couldn't contact the landlord directly and that there was nothing more than a mailing address... It made Jess angry to think about it, so she didn't.

'What book you ordered?' she asked. It was an odd question to be asking anyone she realised, especially Gary Shad. When did books get so exotic? She'd quite enjoyed reading at school.

He looked at her as if she'd caught him out.

'I saw the notification on your phone,' she explained.

Gary didn't say anything, so Jess patted French. Lovely dog. Poodle but a proper pooch; full size, not some toy model.

'I'm doing dog-walking,' she said.

'Dog-walking?'

'Yeah. Take them over the rec.' She patted Gary's dog again.

'Haven't you got like 57 jobs, Jess?'

'Three, Gary.'

'I can't think of anyone I'd rather walk French,' said Gary. 'But it's the only exercise I get.'

Jess smiled at his attempt at gallantry and then at his admission of idleness.

'You split up with... what's er face, then?'

'Had to let her go,' he said like a boss after a redundancy.

Jess didn't buy it but she also let it go. 'Enjoy your book,' she said, stubbing her fag out on the top of the wall. 'When you're curled up in bed on your own.'

Jess walked up the drive. She could still walk. Knew Gary was watching. Just knew. That took her back to school in a different way. Some of the kids had called her 'the Prom Queen' then and sometimes she could still feel that power, even if she was wearing trackie bottoms. The conversation with Gary with its overtones of ageing and of mortality and of lack of control had made her feel uncomfortable. Mrs Newton was teaching her yet another lesson, wasn't she? That was the truth of it. Knowing a bloke was watching her arse was restorative. It was like her karma. They were both 'cards close to the chest' types, her and Gary Shad. Both turning into the sort of tight-lipped adults they'd despised as in-your-face teenagers, both kidding the world, if not themselves, that they were hard. The picture that flickered into her mind's eye was of Gary at the age of about 12 or 13, fighting in the playground at Plane Grove. He got so angry back then, the red face matching his hair. Funny how he was the one from school she still knew. Yet, in that very English way, didn't know at all.

The musty smell in the hall hung heavier than any smoke cloud. Slowly she turned the key in the lock.

She turned on the lights. There was a half-hearted flash like a broken ciggie lighter and then the leaden click that told her the fuses had blown. Shit.

Of course, she had fucking mould. You could smell it, almost taste it and, when she opened the curtains to get a little hit of the fading light, you could certainly see it, half-hidden by the sofa and the telly but there it was. No light, no shower, no hot food, no heat, she counted her problems on chilly fingers. Jess didn't do crying but, as she sat down in the semi-dark and contemplated an electricity-free night, she felt like it. Nobody knows what goes on behind closed doors. That was one of her mother's favourite sayings. But Jess could see how it applied to her, Jessica Jane Gann, metaphorically. Her true feelings were behind a closed door, a closed door that was brightly painted with happy faces and funny slogans. Her front, her happy, joking face to the world, was a child's bedroom door.

Dorset Avenue must have been a decent road once. It was broad, with trees down both sides and big houses set back. They dated from when they'd built the Stern & Feltman biscuit factory and before. She had this idea that Charles Feltman himself had once lived on the road. Where had she got that from? School again? But now it was a shit-hole. Most of the houses had been turned into flats, some of them the tiniest bedsits. Her place wasn't the worst – number 31 had been turned into 17 separate rat-holes – but it was pretty bad. Nothing had been done to number 27 in the two years she'd lived there. Tell a lie, maybe they'd cut the grass once. Her one-bedroom tip with en-suite asthma triggers had mould on half the walls. You could smell it even from outside the cheap chipboard front door. Half of her was terrified the place was going to go up in flames. The other half of her wished it would.

It seemed to Jess as if she had lived her whole life waiting for something that was just around the corner. It wasn't that she wasn't busy. Far from it. Hardly had time to fart. But she was always busy doing the same thing – working in the pub (three to four nights a week), doing the au-pairing style of thing at the Henleys' (three to four days a week) or walking the dogs (the rest of the time). The odd night out. Oh yeah, and she'd had a date some time back in the Middle Ages. She was 'three jobs Jess' and she still couldn't afford the rent on somewhere decent. Where had all the time gone since she'd left Plane Grove and why had nearly all of it been downhill?

She had considered moving back to her mum's but that would be real tail-between-the-legs stuff – and would certainly mean sleeping on the sofa. Auntie Debbie's? She had room. Great Auntie Lou's? Well, the humiliation would be much the same. But, family the size of hers, there was a limit to how long you could put off inviting one of them round. Please don't come over, Valerie. Doo-doo-doo. Or anyone else, thanks. Her mum had been once or twice early doors – before the mould started seeping through the cheap wallpaper and before the first toaster exploded. Perhaps she should just leave. Cost of living was cheaper up North, wasn't it? Trouble was there were no bankers looking for home helps up North or cash-rich, time-poor tarts prepared to pay you to walk their fat dogs. The one good thing was that at least she had no kids to inflict this crap on but, at the same time, she often felt the crappiest thing about her life was that she had no kids. Was that what they called a paradox?

Ron knew the footpath like the back of his hand. They were both rough, gnarled old things. He'd walked from town over Moonshine Point to the cottage at Carter's Green thousands of times, literally thousands. It nearly always helped. After a tough shift it had been his comedown. Some used alcohol, exercise or sex but Ron used a nice clifftop walk – safer and more effective. It cleared the head. It was the space between work and home, the space that had allowed him, unlike so many coppers, to remain sober, remain married and remain the right side of sane. But would it still work without Eileen?

Late as it was, he still had no desire to go home. The house smelled of her and that got him where it hurt. He had no idea what the smell was, part her, part him, part dust and clean sheets, but he'd recognise it until the day he died. He could burn toast and boil beans in that kitchen for a year and it would still reek of Eileen. He'd been sitting on the prom watching the beach disappear: sand, sea and sky, three different shades of grey, blurring and blending with each other. It was a bit like modern art, a study in grey. Ron didn't much like modern art but had found this oddly beautiful. Now that those greys were turning into a single black, he was trying to dawdle home but he wasn't very good at it, dawdling – found it difficult to walk more slowly than the regimented rhythm of a copper on the beat.

The one thing Ron couldn't bring himself to say to anyone, even to himself, were those three and a half words: it's not fair. He'd heard so many cons recite that particular mantra – this injustice or that unlucky break. For Ron, you knuckled down and worked and you got what you deserved. Except you clearly didn't. For a while it seemed to work. The police exams, the promotions. But he'd given his life to the British state, taken a fucking bullet for the British state. Eileen was just the same. The number of 50-hour-plus weeks they'd put in – him at the station, her at the school. How many kids – citizens of the British state – had Eileen nursed, nurtured, cared for and cajoled? Teacher, head of year, senior teacher, deputy head teacher. He didn't know what half of them were. They were just job titles. But her rise through the ranks had been much the same as his. Both of them servants to the state and how did the British state react when the going got tough? By saying, sorry your life is just too expensive. You've done your bit. Thanks very much. Now do us a favour and drop dead. Naive, that was the word. He'd just been so fucking naive.

Of course, life was unfair – you were a fool if you didn't know it and a bigger one if you forgot it.

Lost in his thoughts, Ron didn't see the bloke at first. What's more, the bloke was dressed in black and standing where, by rights, nobody should have been standing, way too close to the edge. The heavy breathing was perturbing and Ron felt himself tense. But it wasn't anything to worry about, not a fugitive but a jogger – one of the newbies from the new estate probably.

'I wouldn't go too close to the edge,' Ron said. 'Did you not hear about the little girl?'

The bloke had his hands on his hips trying to catch his breath. He didn't say anything and in the dark Ron couldn't make out his features, but something in the body language said that he was listening.

'Falling debris.' Ron took a step closer as the bloke stepped away from the edge. The waves crashed around down below like a drunken giant. The wind whistled. Ron looked up at the white moon. 'But it is awe-inspiring,' he said.

Again, there was no reply. Ron was not unfamiliar with this scenario. Talking was, by definition, humanising which made it a great leveller – and not just in police work. No wonder so many men were so taciturn, doggedly trying to avoid conversation in order to cling onto the sense of difference or of superiority that gave their existence meaning. It wasn't just cons, it was men in general really. Including rich joggers in tight black lycra with banal hi-vis slogans who thought they'd bought a slice of the South Coast.

'Take care,' said Ron. 'The footpath I'm standing on used to be, well, on the other side of where you're standing. Disappeared in about 1975.'

# 1.8.

The slow rise and fall of his solid chest was the only sign that Colin Graham was still alive. Gill watched, lost like a child in a maze, as she followed the various tubes that led from her son's arms and face. They terminated in machines and drips and endless questions. A square, cream plastic-cased LCD device, as old-fashioned as yesterday's science fiction, had reduced Colin's life to numbers – heart rate, blood pressure, others that Gill didn't recognise. A green light pulsed on and off with each heavy breath.

'Wake up, you big fat bastard,' said Gill in a voice so quiet only she could hear. No matter. She had still used the b-word in public for the first time ever. It made her feel a teeny bit better. She was alone anyway, apart from her son, of course, and you didn't need to be a doctor to tell that he wouldn't be going anywhere anytime soon, wouldn't be erecting any extendable ladders or rescuing any damsels in distress. Of course, she'd always known that this was a possibility even when her heart had been pounding with pride at Colin in uniform, Colin receiving a commendation or Colin presenting her with two perfectly-matching grandchildren at the first time of asking. Pride before the fall. Hubris punished.

Hospitals, she was learning, ran on adrenalin surges and waiting: peaks and troughs like a heart monitor.

The last nurse had left half an hour earlier with a short 'better run'. Better, indeed. Running was a good idea, Gill thought but she didn't move. She hadn't run for years. She stayed seated where she'd been seated for a good hour, her bottom welded into the doughy brown cushion of a rusty metal-framed seat. Why were hospitals so hot?

She creaked to her feet, the seat eventually permitting her skirt to pull stickily away. She looked away from Colin and out of the window instead. Was this intensive care? She couldn't remember what they'd said. You certainly wouldn't call it hospital clean. The windows were shabby and smeared. Gill paused, inclined her head to get a different angle. It wasn't Graham and Graham Sunview Plus double-glazing, that's for sure.

Her own windows were immaculate.

Would Colin be better off at home? If he was going to die, she'd prefer...

She looked back at Colin and then, with two firm hands, she took the sheet that he was lying under and folded it, just as if she were making the bed, upwards to cover his face.

She wasn't sure what had compelled her to this, her hands had just done it in that automatic way, like wiping a surface or removing a boiling pan. A mother's hands. She looked at her handiwork. Colin's breathing caused the sheet to balloon and contract around his mouth. He had a distinctive nose, big like his father's and Colin had been very aware of it as a child. Without it, he'd have been as prettily handsome as his little brother, Gill realised. She'd never consciously thought that before. As it was, even shrouded in sheet, her eldest was very recognisable. It was Colin and this is what Colin would look like if he died. They'd cover his face and she'd walk in to see this. Would she be able to take it? Perhaps that's why she had done it. Just to see. The sensation made her nauseous but she wasn't going to faint and she didn't need to sit down.

Instead, she breathed deeply a couple of times and tried to be mindful. Mindfulness was a technique her GP had suggested when Gill had complained about the drugs not working anymore.

'You mean just be aware?' Gill had asked. Surely, if just being aware could help, they never would have invented Prozac.

'Yes. Be mindful of what's going on in the moment you're living and how you're responding to it.'

'Live in the moment?"

Her GP, an overweight man called Conway with a salt and pepper beard, nodded.

'But isn't living in the moment the crime for which we blame our feckless youth?'

'I think that might be living for the moment. We're not talking about worship of the present here, just simple acceptance of its inevitability and appreciation thereof.'

'What?'

'I think it means that if the sun's shining, enjoy it, Gill,' Dr Conway had said with a shrug. 'It's a Buddhist thing.'

She could see Dr Conway as a little Buddha, in the lotus position, pot belly boiling over his loin cloth. This image made her smile to herself which, for some reason, made her think of Colin and of husband Cliff and of number two son Andrew and then want to cry.

Gill wondered whether Cliff knew about Colin, his fireman son (or firefighter as they called them now). And, if he did know, whether he cared. Cared enough to leave London, get in the car and drive down to the coast. She had her own ideas about this but they were as changeable as the wind. She didn't really know for sure any more now than she had ever known anything for sure during their fifteen-year marriage or down the muddle of years since. Maybe he would appear. More likely he'd turn up at the old house and wonder where she'd gone. Maybe Andrew the youngest would do the same. Andrew would probably wait until she'd gone to bed and then try but fail to not wake her as he sneaked in. She was used to it. The sneaking-in. But when he was living at home, a wild oats-sowing youth, and she said 'where the hell do you think you've been?', she meant 'where the hell do you think you've been for the last four hours since you said you'd be back by 10.30 and it's a school night', not 'where the hell do you think you've been for the last 10 years? I thought you were dead.' She knew she wouldn't say that anyway. Not to either of them. She'd be only too pleased to see them whatever the horror of the circumstances. Probably ask one of them to change the battery in the carriage clock instead. Gill was piqued with herself. This was not being mindful.

She folded the sheet back down again and made the bed neatly around Colin, tucking him in tight just as he used to beg her to as a child. One last look. Her son was in exactly the same position, making exactly the same rasping breathing noise as he had been when she'd arrived. The same applied to the instruments. Unchanged. The sun may have been going down outside but, inside this bedroom, time was standing still.

Gill walked more slowly than usual and waited for the lift rather than taking the stairs. She shared it with an empty bed trolley and two porters, one black and tall, one white and short. They were exchanging tips for Plumpton and observations on that 'posh fucker'. It took her a moment or two to realise that they were talking about the Prime Minister.

'Did a ward round, did he?'

That's right, the Prime Minister had visited the hospital.

'Yeah.'

'You see him?'

'No. Ray did. Shook his hand.'

'Not a firm handshake, I would wager.' The black man – coloured was the word Gill instinctively reached for but she knew that wasn't right any more – was clutching a styrofoam beaker of steaming coffee-scented liquid which swirled and threatened to spill as the lift came to a clunking halt on the ground floor. The pair took off in opposite directions as the doors opened, the one with the coffee ambling with the bed trolley, the other, with a far more purposeful stride, unbuttoning his green three-quarter length coat. Home time.

'There's No Panic,' he shouted back over his shoulder. 'The 4.40.'

Here, in the main entrance lobby, a brick-built pagoda-like affair, the hospital was a little busier. The desk at which volunteers – Friends of the Hospital – usually sat pointing folk in the right direction was now unmanned, leaving visitors to pore over maps and colour-coded lists of departments and floors. A family sprinted in, gangling pre-teen girl sliding to a halt as she found herself in an enclosed public space. Dad arrived, car keys jangling, open-neck checked shirt, then mum a little overweight, overdressed and over-encumbered with bags and a cool-box. There wasn't a nurse or doctor to be seen. The porter, who now had his coat over his arm, exchanged a word or two with the girl in the little Nissen hut that rented out televisions to long-stay patients. Gill intended to get one for Colin tomorrow. Pointless probably but what could you do? Through the revolving doors she could see a cacophony of lights – street lamps, the cars in the car park and those still out on the road.

She stopped and started to read the noticeboard. There was something about outside that didn't look very appealing. But the noticeboard was another gloomy affair: all support groups, hospices and funerals. A big poster for the Friends of the Hospital drawn by a child. She counted seven different religious offerings: six brands of Christianity and an Islam. It was like trying to choose cornflakes in the supermarket. Or perhaps get Special K instead. Didn't they all believe in the same God? What was the point of it? Weren't you supposed to get more religious as you got older? But Gill just got more and more annoyed with it all. Don't we all know what's right and wrong without having to get so hysterical about it?

Something lurking in the corner caught her eye. A coffee machine. The home to the styrofoam cups. She didn't much want a cup of coffee but she didn't much want to go outside either.

The machine was out of order but there was a restaurant apparently, two sets of doors and a cold corridor or two away. It was the porter who told her – 'just follow the pink, love, you can't miss it' – a last helping hand before he disappeared into the night with thoughts of sure things and a politician's promises. The PM hadn't been to see Colin, had he? Gill followed the pink: arrows on the wall, peeling footprint-shaped stickers on the black, grey, black, grey floor tiles.

The restaurant was home to a distressed-looking beige couple with several cups on their table. Most of the other tables were empty but their shiny surfaces were cluttered with trays and wrappers, cans and half-eaten sandwiches. The couple's conversation, quiet already, dropped a notch as Gill entered. They huddled a little closer, the woman pulling a thick brown overcoat tighter than tight.

At the counter, the only other customer was a big man now going to fat. He stood solid as a boxer but his face looked like it had gone down in the second round and was still absorbing the blow. He didn't watch the change being counted into his fleshy palm, allowing his head to turn vacantly from side to side without actually seeing.

'Sugar's on the side,' said the assistant.

She was probably West Indian. About the same age as the man Gill would estimate and about his weight too. She'd seen it all before, this catering assistant. People like this lost soul, who longed to go home; people like Gill who didn't want to. The assistant slid the till shut with a big, ring-encrusted hand and a hoop of plastic yellow bangle bounced up her forearm and descended again as she turned to Gill.

'Coffee,' said Gill. 'No, tea.'

Something Cliff had once said to her about only ever trusting the tea in a transport café made her change her mind. This wasn't a transport café and her husband's advice had only ever proven sporadically useful in the past but, for some reason, she thought of it and chose to follow it.

'To drink here?'

'Yes, please.'

A teabag on the end of a string, a steaming surge of hot water.

But, at least, she got a proper china cup. That was the advantage of drinking it in.

Gill looked up from swirling her teabag to notice that the man in front of her still hadn't sat down. What was he looking for now? The flavour? Wouldn't find that in a paper sachet. Then Gill realised that the man was looking at her – indeed, he actually appeared to be waiting for her. He had a frown-etched face and rheumy eyes, a too-tight suit which he clearly didn't wear very often. He had loosened an incongruously-loud tie that went with neither the shirt, the suit nor the location, but he had not unbuttoned his collar. 'I never forget a face,' he said.

'I'm sorry?' said Gill, surprising herself with this casual Americanism.

'The Mindfulness course at the Friends' Meeting House.'

Gill was struggling.

'Ron Newton,' the man insisted. He had the slightest of limps. 'I always wear a red tracksuit. Have a big red blanket.'

Gill remembered. It wasn't a nutter, thank the Lord. 'Hello,' she said. 'Fancy meeting you ...'

Ron smiled. 'I met the Prime Minister.'

'Really. How long was he here?'

'About ten minutes, I should think. Kissed a few babies, shook a few hands – one of them was mine.'

'Have you washed it?' asked Gill.

'Twice.' Ron Newton looked at his hand and laughed.

They'd shuffled to a table which was slightly less shell-shocked than the others. 'Shall we?' said Ron, easing out a chair for Gill. She couldn't help but smile at this old school gesture. Nor could she help herself beginning to tidy the table, stacking cups and plates into a single tower. 'Why can't people...'

'I know,' said Ron. 'Always expect someone else to clean up after them. Sorry, I didn't mean to finish your sentence.'

'Don't apologise. It's curiously reassuring after the day...' She took her first sip of steaming hot tea.

'Fireman, isn't he? Your son.'

Gill coughed, feeling hot and not just with the excess of tea. 'How did you know?'

'It's a small town, Mrs Graham. Policemen. Firemen. We're as good as colleagues really. I'm a retired police sergeant. I actually knew your other son. Many years...'

Gill was relieved that Sergeant Newton had not finished this particular sentence. She could do without any unbidden reminders of Andrew's misdemeanours, thank you very much.

'Injured. In a fire.' She cleared her throat. Her eyes were watering. 'Colin.'

'That business with the students?'

'Yes. I don't really know what happened. One of his colleagues is supposed to be... He's in a coma.' She cleared her throat again and said it again, more loudly. 'He's in a coma.'

'I'm sorry to hear that.' Ron deliberately spilled some of his tea into the saucer and then slurped it up from that – a gesture Gill hadn't seen for years and which was every bit as reassuring as the policeman's habit of finishing her sentences. She remembered him from the Mindfulness course now. His wife was ill but she didn't think he'd ever said with what. The only thing he really ever said about Mindfulness was that he couldn't 'get it' and Martha would tell him that, when it came to Mindfulness, there was nothing to 'get'.

'But there must be,' Ron would say, looking for support from among his fellow students for this most obvious of propositions.

'Do you enjoy the Mindfulness?' Ron asked, as if reading her mind.

'Not really. I hope I might find it useful though. I really do need to keep my mind from wandering now.'

'My doctor suggested I start when Eileen was ill,' said Ron.

'Do you find it useful?'

Ron laughed. 'I'm not sure it's designed for ex-coppers,' he said. 'Although Martha's very patient.'

'She is.' Gill took a sip of tea for courage. 'What's wrong with your wife, Sergeant Newton?'

'Cancer. She's going to...'

They both took drafts of tea.

'There is a drug but, well, I don't know. There is but there isn't. Too expensive or something. I don't quite understand. I mean a pill's a pill, isn't it? It's not silver-plated as far as I know.'

'I'm sorry.' She'd heard of this. Postcode lottery they called it. 'Is it very ...'

'Costs more than a thousand pounds a week, apparently. Must be plated with bloody gold at that price – excuse my French.'

'I'm sorry.'

'Might give her one more Christmas. I've asked if I can pay for it myself but they keep talking about protocols and precedents. I'm going to put the house on the market anyway but, unless I give it away, I can't see it selling.' He paused. 'In time.'

'That's... How is she right now? In herself I mean.'

'Weak. Quiet.' Gill could tell Ron was struggling for words. Unable to describe his dying wife and who could blame him? She put her hand on his and they both finished their tea.

'Did you talk to him?' he asked after a moment or two.

'Pardon?'

'Did you talk to him? Your son.'

'Well, not really.' Gill honestly hadn't thought about it. But no, she hadn't. Apart from telling him to 'wake up'. Why hadn't she? She coughed. 'Do you? Talk to your wife, I mean?'

'I do now, Mrs Graham. Or I try, anyway. She sleeps a lot. She never used to sleep. Up at the crack...'

Ron paused and returned to the point. 'But when she was under, after the surgery: not a word. Just silent prayer.' He fiddled with his cup, ostensibly trying to reattach the flimsy white lid to the empty cup but really just fiddling like a man with Rosary. 'And I've never been a religious man. Eileen, yes. But not me. And all the time I'm thinking: say something. What if she doesn't come round? Tell her how you feel. Tell her you love...' He stumbled on the word. 'I knew she could hear, the nurses had told me. But I had nothing.'

Gill gazed deep into her china cup. 'They told me the same thing. They want you to talk, the nurses, but.'

'We're English,' said Ron. 'We don't do talking, do we? Not proper talking. We do tea.'

The pair looked at each other and, without blinking, communicated. Gill felt an urge to tell Sergeant Newton absolutely everything, heart and soul. Her sick mother, her absent husband, her contrasting children. She cleared her throat instead. The policeman got up.

'Perhaps I'll see you again, Mrs Graham,' said Ron. He was still holding his beaker in his hand and, before setting it back on the table, he pulled a fragment of it off, flakes of polystyrene tumbling to the floor. 'Looks like we're both going to be here for a while, doesn't it?'

Gill nodded. The cup stood there as if someone had taken a bite out of it. Ron stood there in much the same way.

'Are we mindful?' Gill asked.

'Are we even awake?' Ron replied, completing between them the phrase with which Martha began every Mindfulness class. As a catchphrase it was hardly Tommy Cooper but they both smiled all the same.

'We should volunteer for the Friends of the Hospital,' Gill said. She wasn't quite sure why – perhaps it was the recruitment poster or the thought of the unmanned desk.

'That's an idea.'

'Would you like another tea?' asked Gill. She smiled. 'Since that's what we do.'

A volley of raindrops splattered onto the windowpane and slid down slowly. Then a few more. Heavier. The cafeteria's handful of customers all looked up as one.

'And it's raining now,' Gill heard herself saying.

Someone tutted, presumably at a precipitation that the BBC had failed to forecast rather than at Gill's statement of the obvious.

Ron nodded, put his hand in his pocket and extracted his wallet. 'Trickle-down economics,' he said.

# 1.9.

Gill was constantly aware of Colin from the corner of her eye but she couldn't look at him directly. This was strange since his eyes were closed anyway but she was reading him the newspapers and felt very self-conscious.

How he would have laughed as she stumbled over the sports section. Were all the footballers South American these days? And what was a transfer window? Her father had run a double-glazing business all his life but she'd never once heard of a transfer window. The front pages weren't a lot better. She couldn't figure it out. One of the papers was saying that, to bail out the banks, the amount of cash currently borrowed by the government had risen by £7 billion to a total of £124 billion. The other paper seemed to be saying that the country was bankrupt because of social security scroungers. Now Gill knew that job seekers thingy – whatever they called National Insurance now – was not much more than £60. She knew that for a fact since that was what Colin's Susie had been offered when she lost her job at the out-of-town. It took a lot of £60s to make whatever-it-was billion. Some said that it would be all right if all the immigrants went home. Well, that didn't sound very Christian. Gill also wasn't keen because of that nice Chinese lad – well, Chinese-looking lad – who did her nails. Well, they were all foreigners working there, weren't they? Behind those face masks. The place would shut down without them and then where would we be? Well, she'd be doing her own cuticles presumably. Could that really be good for the economy? None of it added up.

'Is the bitch coming?' asked Pip. She was eating Doritos like a ravenous piranha. Stressed on a number of levels. Not least by the presence of her father. She'd never been in the hospital and now she felt like she lived there. First, little Kirsty. Then, the fireman. Well… never two but three. She didn't believe that. Wasn't superstitious, at all. But she could imagine her mother saying it. Her real mother. 'Never two but three, Philippa.'

'How am I supposed to answer that?' said her father. He shook his head. Was that a smile she saw? She honestly couldn't tell with him these days. Didn't understand him at all. 'If you mean your mother…' Yes, it was a smile. Well, an evil grin really.

'My step mother, as you know full well. The one with the fake tits.'

'Let's just get this over with, shall we?'

Gavin Henley straightened his tie and pushed the hospital door. A big stride in to get some momentum and then marching, marching purposefully. He hated hospitals like the plague. He hated what they did. Care. He hated what they represented. Death. He hated the antiseptic cleanliness and the smell of bleached sanctimony. He hated the neediness, the simpering, the self-sacrifice, the dignity (God, he hated that word the most). They stood for everything that he loathed and the knowledge that with every passing day the likelihood of his needing the services of one had come another 24 hours closer was doing his head in. Private medicine took care of a lot of the shit but even an army of private nurses couldn't mop up the inevitable. Was this what they called a mid-life crisis? This wasn't his place and this wasn't his thing.

'You know what you're going to say?' said Pip, catching up with him.

'Yes.'

Her kaftan was a safety hazard really, always threatening to trip her up. It was new. The rainbow one stank of smoke and she'd thrown it away. Part of the retail therapy Melissa and Tommy had taken her on in Brighton after the fire. Tommy didn't really do guilt – and it wasn't really his fault anyway, one of those things – but he'd been kind to her.

Gavin didn't do gratitude but the truth is that this fireman had saved his daughter's life and he needed to thank him. Man to man. He didn't know if he loved his daughter so he didn't know whether this was really about her or not. (He wasn't sure what love was about at the best of times. It had to be about more than what gave you an erection. But, if it was about more than that, well... perhaps he'd never felt it.) More like it was about him and the indignity of having to be grateful. On a certain level, he hated the bloody fireman who had put him in this position. He was in a coma, apparently, this fireman. Gavin believed that he, Gavin J Henley, was rich because of the risks he was man enough to take in business. It was because of his risks that he deserved his wealth. But he wouldn't risk a coma for anyone. So was this fireman fucker a better man than him? It took some mental gymnastics to persuade himself otherwise. How bloody dare he? Just a man in a uniform.

Fit nurse at 11 o'clock, clocking him, clocking her. Clocking the Brioni suit. Italian. When the economy went down the toilet in the late noughties – not my fault, guv – Brioni introduced their most expensive line of suits ever. Gavin loved that. It excited him more than the fit nurse, truth be told. No time for getting into that. Loved even more the fact that he already wore the gorgeous brand when that particular line came on tap. Wore it before everybody else did. Just like James Bond. (He and Daniel Craig were both 5'10" which was well above average height if anyone was counting, which Gavin wasn't.) He felt the testosterone course through him and it made his dick twinge.

God, she'd rather he didn't smile. That slimy thing he'd squeezed out for the nurse made her feel sick. Did he think he was sexy? Really, did this grease-ball of a man think he was sexy? Pip hated him and hated her dependence upon him. She binned her Doritos bag and its cheese-infused flakes of burning orange.

'It's in here,' she said.

Gill looked up from her newspaper. The sound of the door interrupted her reverie. Had she been talking aloud? Two people. Click went one of the monitors. A man and a younger – well, you should say a woman but she looked like a girl to Gill. Click went the monitor.

Was this man a new consultant? Rather flash for a doctor. More like a second-hand car salesman. And this girl? No, they must have come to the wrong room.

'Hello,' said the girl. 'I'm Philippa Henley.'

'Hello,' said Gill.

'Pip. I'm the student...'

Gill looked at her as she took in what she was being told.

Not an unattractive girl. A little overweight. Dressed like a hippy. Hair like parcel twine. So this was the girl Colin had risked his life for? She knew she ought not to think of it like that. It was a job, wasn't it? A vocation. The job of a brave son. But she couldn't pretend that this wasn't her first thought: was this girl worth it? Was she worth making your children orphans for, Colin? Was she worth making your wife a widow? Was she worth abandoning me for? She managed a very insincere smile. After Cliff and Andrew, was she worth abandoning me for? Gill felt wretched.

'Is he...?' said Pip.

'The same as ever,' said Gill. 'The same as when they wheeled him in, I'm told.'

'I'm sorry to hear that. He was...'

'A very brave man,' Gill snapped. 'Yes, I know that.'

Gill felt doubly wretched. She looked again at the pair. Father and daughter perhaps. She folded the paper and put it next to the others on Colin's bed. She gestured towards two chairs.

'Sorry,' she said. 'I'm rather frazzled.'

Pip sat down. Gavin put his coat on the chair but remained upright. 'I'd rather stand,' he said.

'They've said all sorts of things,' said Gill. 'Most of it I don't really understand. They mentioned cyanide though.' She coughed. 'I understood that. In the smoke, I'm told. There are all sorts of chemicals in the smoke. Including cyanide.'

Pip felt the burning at the back of her own throat. She desperately didn't want to cough. 'Yes,' she said.

'How are you, dear?' asked Gill. She smiled again, much more sincerely this time. This child was alive because her son was a hero.

'I'm fine,' said Pip. 'Thank you for... I'm very grateful...'

Gill was aware of the man standing at her shoulder. Why wouldn't he sit down? Scared of hospitals probably. Most men were. She looked up at him and indicated the seat again. 'Please...'

Gavin cleared his throat as he did when he wanted to speak at team meetings. It was a subtle gesture, one you had to be listening to hear. It echoed around the white cell of a room and ricocheted off the heart monitor. 'Are you his mother?' he asked.

'Yes,' said the woman. She kept turning her head awkwardly and expecting him to sit. He would sit when he wanted to sit.

'I'm Gavin Henley,' he said. 'Philippa's father. I've taken some time out of my schedule because I wanted to say...' He stopped. Refocused. 'I wanted to let you know how... My wife and I are both...'

Gill, fed up with straining her neck to see this man, rose slightly from her chair – not enough to come unstuck – and swivelled the legs around through 45 degrees – away from Colin and towards the man who was not prepared to sit with him. 'Yes,' she said without having or giving any indication that she had the remotest idea what he was talking about. 'Yes?'

'It was a... a gesture of the highest...'

'What?' said Gill, getting up. 'A gesture of the highest what?' Futility she was thinking. Thoughtlessness. Idiotic stupidity. She was facing the man now.

'He's trying to say "thank you",' said Pip. 'My father is trying to say "thank you".' She had no idea why she was bailing him out. To save Mrs Graham perhaps, who looked as unsure of how to proceed as her father did. 'He's not used to it,' she said. 'He wants to say thank you for saving his daughter's life.'

'I know full well what he's saying. What I don't understand is why he's not saying it.'

Gavin had never been speechless in his life and he was buggered if he would be now. 'If there is anything I can do, anything at all. I am not without means.' Why wouldn't the words come out right? He was not an emotional man. Why wouldn't the words come out right? 'I imagine this must be a difficult, an expensive... a difficult time for you, Mrs...'

'Dad.'

'Graham.'

'Mrs Graham, I can write you a cheque now...' He produced a pen from inside his jacket.

'I'm sorry?'

'Dad.'

'Or arrange a transfer, whatever is most convenient...'

'Dad!'

'Fifty thousand?'

Gill went down like a feather, the strength had gone from her legs just as if the carpet had been pulled from underneath her, and she found herself seated once again. She pulled her skirt down, automatically. Her shoes suddenly felt tight and her calves tired and sore. The tears that she didn't think she had in her began to roll gently down her cheeks. They came not in a dramatic flood but in a lethargic slow weep. She put her heavy head into her gently-shaking hands. It steadied them.

'I'm sorry, Mrs Graham,' began Pip. She didn't know whether to get up or remain in the chair. She was hot but didn't want to take her jacket off now. How could that be the right thing to do? Her father was standing erect looking out of the window, pretending that he was no longer there. She wanted to kill him. Mrs Graham sobbed almost silently. The heart monitor blinked. A moment passed. Pip's throat was screaming sore. Another moment. Another sob. Then she was aware of her father removing his cheque book from his coat pocket. She was mortified.

'Dad, you can't put a price...' Pip could avoid coughing no longer. Her throat rattled like a collecting tin.

Mrs Graham looked at her. 'You can,' she said sharply.

She put her hands down and turned to Pip's father. 'Please make it payable to Mr Ronald Newton. Fifty thousand, you say.'

Her father had his pen poised. 'I thought your name was Graham. Is that your maiden...'

'Mr whatever your wretched name is, all the money in the world won't help my son right now.'

'Well then, I...'

'But Mr Newton is a police officer, a local police officer, a man who has walked the beat of this town for years. You do live in this town, I take it, Mr ...? His wife is dying of cancer and the treatment she needs is too expensive for the NHS...'

'You want me to give my money to someone else?'

'I want you to put your money where it can be of most use.' Mrs Graham had regained her composure. 'It's a gesture of the highest generosity, Sir, and I would like to put it where it can be of most use.' Pip watched open-mouthed and unblinking as Mrs Graham moved in for the kill. 'I'm sure that's what Colin would want,' she said.

Pip's father stepped back as if he'd taken a small bullet. Did he look down? Blink to avoid eye contact? Pip had never seen her father look wounded before.

'My offer was for you and your family, Mrs Graham,' he said, reasserting himself. 'It is. Not.' Eyes down. 'Transferable.'

'Dad.'

'Fine, write the cheque to me then. Gillian Graham. No "e" on Graham.'

'But... how do I know that you'll ... I'm afraid I can't do that. I no longer have confidence that the money will be used as I intend.'

'That's rather the point of a gift. That it be used as the recipient intends. Not the giver.'

'What about other people who have this...'

'Liver cancer. Mrs Newton has liver cancer.'

'Liver cancer. What will they do?'

'I'm told it's rare. The county is hardly crawling with them, if that's what you mean. You won't be setting a precedent.'

'If I give this policeman the money, it will... it will distort the market.'

'I don't know what you mean,' said Mrs Graham. 'But that is the most ridiculous thing I've ever heard.'

Pip's father snorted. Anyone who didn't understand the market was worthy only of contempt. Would he have the last word? Of course he would. 'I hope your son wakes up,' he said before turning on his perfectly-shined black heel and walking out of the door. Pip looked at Mrs Graham.

'I wish I could speak to him like that,' said Pip.

'Despicable man,' said Mrs Graham to nobody in particular.

'I wish I could speak to him like that too,' said Pip.

'Absolutely despicable.'

Pip took a last look at her saviour, at the tubes that were keeping him alive. 'I'm so grateful for what your son did for me, Mrs Graham.'

'I know you are, dear,' said Mrs Graham and patted her on the arm.

## 2:
# 'You Do Know That I've Never Arrested Anybody Before.'

# 2.1.

DS Christophe Caton was not a keen reader of the local Police Federation newsletter. But at the moment he got the call, that is exactly what he was doing. That and studiously avoiding answering a text message from his mother.

When you were as close to suspended as it was possible to be without actually leaving the office, there wasn't a lot else to do. The magazine was called 'The Job', but that was really a description of the process of reading the thing. That was a job and a half. The pay freeze, the messing-about with retirement ages, the abolition of special priority allowances – all the usual suspects filled the newsletter's shrill pages. Chris was supposed to be filing, but filing irritated him even more than the Police Federation's persecution complex. The papers in the wrong files, the files in the wrong place, the items filed upside down, the items filed back to front, the paperclips that had fallen off, the staples that hadn't been put in properly and stabbed your fingers, the items that should have been stapled but which had only been clipped, the stuff pertaining to a case long closed that was still sitting on someone's desk when it should have been locked in a cabinet. And top of the list – the oscar of idiocies: why, oh, why, could nobody in the Met use a fucking computer? They'd only been around 40 years. It made him so angry. The paperless office? As likely as the perfect crime.

He'd decked a suspect. That was why he was on 'non-operational duties' – gardening leave without the garden, basically. Chris had hit the guy, not because the suspect wouldn't tell him something he knew, but because he couldn't tell him something he didn't know. As that penny dropped, Chris had lost control of his fist. He realised that the pair of them had been sitting there chewing the fat for over an hour while some bastard was getting the distance on him. He hated people getting a distance on him.

Crime made him angry, which ought to be a good quality in a copper – not a bad one, anyway. But, in Christophe Caton, it was just too random. Serious crime made him angry. Petty crime made him angry. White collar crime, blue collar crime, polka-dot yellow collar crime, they all made his blood boil. His temper was a permanently taut bungee cord, always on the edge of snapping. This made him largely unsuitable for police work, except in comparison with all the other forms of work for which it made him even less suitable.

Particularly annoying was the appalling mismanagement at pretty much every level of the Metropolitan Police. The Federation newsletter had a point that this was probably not the best time to be shafting the average copper's pension and benefits. It wasn't about the money. It was about the effect of these decisions on morale. The Met was a complete mess, that much was clear, even to the spiders in the basement and the dogs in the street. It was congenitally incapable of reacting appropriately. Chris knew why. He reckoned quite a few others within the Met knew why too, but nobody spoke about it. The truth was that insofar as it affected them, the British police lived by the spirit of the law (and sometimes barely by that); insofar as it affected everyone else, they lived by the letter. It was a recipe for acting too precipitously on one hand, too late on the other. A recipe for disaster.

As he rose from his threadbare swivel chair and elevated himself to his full height, he allowed the newsletter to fall from his hand into the waste bin below. No point complaining about zero pay or zero hours. Nothing was going to change if the politicians didn't take the ordinary officers with them. And taking his pension wasn't about to achieve that. But the politicians didn't really know or care about the ordinary officer anyway. Ordinary officers were for council estates, rough Saturday nights and fences' lock-ups: the shabby, dirty, twilight places that were a world away from celebrity shoulder-rubbing and portentous red boxes. The days of a copper on the door at Number 10 were long gone. The elite had always had their own schools, their own hospitals and their own jobs. Now they had their own coppers too. And he wasn't just thinking of the elite's own special unit of the Met: Protection Command. He was thinking private security, the grown-up version of those clowns who'd clamped his car in Clapham that time. Missed a decent collar thanks to those muppets.

It was one law for the rich and one law for the rest. That much he'd learned. And that's why, within the Force, there was one law for the police and one law for the rest. Perhaps that wasn't an appropriate response but it was, at least, a logical one.

The clock on the wall was approaching seven. Chris had been coming in as early as possible in the morning. This enabled him both to avoid colleagues and to minimise the risk of road rage. Something must have been happening if the DCI was already in. He took a deep breath and swallowed the latest wave of anger that was rising inside him. The job had once been an effective outlet for anger. Slamming a drunk up against the wall or hurling some small-time brainless arsehole over a bonnet, all that TV stuff used to make him feel like a just avenger. Now, it just disgusted him. Once the exercise of his self-righteous rage had doused down his burning self-loathing, now it was just more fuel to the fire. What was he doing to make the world a better place? He straightened his tie – instinct – and cleared his throat. Then he took the four paces across the pock-marked lino floor to the DCI's office and knocked firmly.

'Chrissie,' said Detective Chief Inspector Corrigan, opening the door. He was up and fiddling around with his computer.

'Guv,' said Chris with a tone of surprise. Corrigan had been giving him a wide berth since the latest incident. Now he sounded pleased to see him.

Generally, the guv's arse was welded to his chair, his lard-laden girth wedged between the armrests like the doughnut between his fingers. Chris could count on one hand the number of times he'd seen DCI Corrigan out of his chair so it must be serious. Corrigan was breathing like a blast furnace. With one hand, he was poking ham-fistedly at his computer keyboard: a gloved boxer trying to defuse a bomb. With the other, he was rattling a reluctant key in a seemingly long-forgotten filing cabinet.

'What's the matter with this fucking thing?'

Chris wasn't sure to which thing he was referring. Generally, Corrigan was a red-faced man with a fiery nose and a fiery world-weary temper to (almost) match Caton's own. Today only the latter was in evidence. He looked bed-sheet pale.

'Movie premiere. Party. Toilets. Head wound.' He was speaking between gulps of breath, a full sentence out of the question. 'Middle of Soho.'

The inspector's computer screen stuttered into life – the home page of a well-known online mail order website appearing. Chris thought it an odd moment to be internet shopping but he didn't say anything.

'It's him,' said Corrigan pointing at the screen as if he'd just spotted Jack the Ripper.

Chris peered at the screen. The site seemed to be going large on some Tolkien movie tie-in. 'You mean the Hobbit?'

'I mean the bloke who set up this fucking site. He's dead.'

Chris didn't know Jack Sender but, like everybody else in the country, he knew his website. For online shopping, Stufff was the first port of call. First it had been music, then books and then pretty much everything else. 'Stufff it' had become shorthand for 'buy it online'. The apparent murder of a bigwig dot-com geek-turned-businessman like Sender at a party in central London was about as high-profile as it got. The Guv was Senior Investigating Officer. It was all hands on deck, all shoulders to the grindstone, all men to the pump – the Guv was running all the clichés up the flagpole to see who would salute them. It boiled down to this: because of the hour and because everybody else was busy, he needed Chris, gardening leave or not. He needed someone to go tell the dead man's wife.

'She's French apparently, according to the Wikipedia,' said Corrigan. 'And, well, you're a frog, aren't you, Caton?'

'Half a frog, guv, yes. My mother is French.'

'Half frog and half stout British lion, eh, Caton?' Corrigan wittered on a bit more but Caton was only half listening. At least he'd be getting out of the office.

The media had stolen a march on them. Already there were crowds of hacks and telly crews around the hotel where the reception had been taking place, with feeds flying to all four corners of the planet. An Oscar-winning actress, who'd been at the party, had already tweeted about it. That had been retweeted a hundred times or more and already the speculation had started.

Chris opened up Twitter on his phone and put it on the passenger seat. Beep, beep, beep. Suicide was a popular theory but Corrigan had shown him SOCO's initial photographs and Chris doubted that very much. The size, shape and angle of the blow on the head would have required Sender to be double-jointed and endowed with an arm five feet long. A business rival. A jealous lover. Mistaken identity (Jack Sender looked a lot like former Manchester United central defender Nemanja Vidić). A dissatisfied customer. All of these hypotheses and more were swirling around cyberspace but the Met were tight-lipped.

'Let's keep cool,' Corrigan had said. 'What we're saying, if we have to say anything, is that it was probably a mugging gone wrong.'

It was possible. That wouldn't have been Chris's take though. Nor Corrigan's either probably, but it was the DCI's job to play down the snowballing conjecture, if only to keep the politicians on the leash for as long as poss. Back in the 90s, there'd been a guy who used to hide in the toilets before big West End events and then mugged some unsuspecting celeb or corporate big shot while they were taking a leak. The MO wasn't dissimilar.

Internally there was a little of what Corrigan liked to call 'robust humour' about a publisher who had tweeted 'good riddance' on hearing of the death. The publisher had been picked up at one of Soho's cheaper restaurants. Denied the killing, of course, but said he'd happily confess if the arresting officers would allow him to piss over the corpse.

Chris pulled up at the gatehouse to the gated community in south-east London in which Sender had lived and furnished his ID. The security guard looked him up and down, didn't touch the ID and reached instead for the wall-mounted telephone. This post was one or two up from nightclub bouncer. This was a respectable joint.

'If you don't know why I'm here, put the telly on,' said Chris.

'I know why you're here.'

'Does she?' asked Chris. 'Mrs Sender.'

'Ms Garnier-Sender,' said the doorman with a twinkle.

'Garnier?' said Chris. 'Not Gabrielle Garnier, as was?'

'The very same.'

# 2.2.

Twitter had told her before the police did.

Surely, the news of your husband's death ought to be delivered with a sombre voice, an arm round the shoulder and, this being England, a nice cup of tea. But Gabby Garnier-Sender got the message in less than 140 characters from a variety of sources, most of whom were not anywhere near the scene, her vibrating phone bouncing on the coffee table and spinning with text as post after post scrolled into view. #Senderdead was trending alongside a TV talent show, upcycled furniture and a paddle-boarding cat.

It was Jacqui Elliot who had introduced her to Twitter. ('It's like text-messaging the world,' Jacqui had said.) So Gabby would have still been sitting there, happily reading her novel in blissful ignorance, had Jacqui not one day used a brief 'it's awesome' introduction to the latest, greatest thing on the internet as a pretext to show off her brand new silver-and-diamond-encrusted iPhone. Tacky.

But then Jack had gone out and bought an even blingier one. V tacky.

Gabby turned off her own tastefully bling-free phone and put it on the other side of the room. Then she let herself be eaten up by the Italian sofa, kicked off her slippers and curled up. She fancied that cup of tea but it was a long way to the kitchen.

It ought to be possible, she imagined, for most wives, on learning of the murder of their husband, to quantify their feelings in fewer that 140 characters. Four letters would surely be enough for most wives. But Gabby could not. The complexity of what she was feeling defied all reduction. I'm shocked that it could happen but if it can happen I'm not surprised it's happened to him. I feel exposed, scared yet it's as if a weight. And that's it: 140 characters all gone before she had even scraped the surface of her emotions. Somehow she knew Jack was dead even when the reports were just of a vague 'incident', the sort of fifty shades of absolutely nothing that the internet thrived on. She knew what had happened, had for some time, but still didn't know how she felt about it or how she wanted to feel about it.

So she picked up her book again, read three words again and put it down again.

She picked it up, read two words and put it down again. She had no idea why she was doing this. Perhaps, in some way, it made her think that Jack wasn't dead. And that therefore her life was the same old boring romp in paradise that it had been yesterday.

She'd started the book the previous week-end on the beach. Yes, it may have been mid-winter but she'd passed the week-end, as she frequently did, on the beach. Shell Beach on Saint Barths. Their holiday retreat. Their bolthole. Their 'love nest' (according to the celebrity mags). This last produced a tear of sorts, squeezed out from between her battling lashes. She wanted to cry properly but couldn't. Perhaps it would come.

'You been walking on eggshell beach?' Jack would ask when she pattered into the villa in her flip-flops and walked into the acre of shower. It was sweet. It wasn't without warmth, yet it contained, like all his jokes, a stone in its heart. Did he believe he walked on eggshells with her?

She ate up these detective novels. Life and death, like so much in the world, was something that happened to other people. It was entertainment. Whodunnit this time? It wasn't real life like, well, a week-end on the other side of the world. Now suddenly it was. And perhaps the reason there were no tears was that she felt that she deserved it in some way, this rude awakening to the real world. She wasn't stupid and she hadn't always been rolling in it. She hadn't been born rich, so she knew how enormously privileged with a capital everything she'd become. Il y a un temps pour tout.

When she did her philanthropic work, she was always described as Gabby Garnier-Sender, entrepreneur and former model. It was the former model that everyone saw. It was not just because she wasn't, by even the most gymnastic stretch of the imagination, a true entrepreneur (unless you wanted to call a cupcake shop in New England that she'd visited twice an enterprise). It was not just that in the UK media meta-narrative – Jack's term, not hers – you were always labelled with the first thing for which you were famous, regardless of what you did later. No, her luck had changed the day she hit puberty and, twenty plus years later, she wasn't so pickled in privilege that she'd forgotten it.

There was a sound which, at first, she couldn't place as it tinkle-tinkled into her consciousness. It was like coming around from sleep and waiting for your head to clear. But, when it rang again, she recognised it as the doorbell. She hadn't heard the doorbell for years. Was the entryphone not working?

Even as he was pumping the bell, DS Caton realised he should be using the entryphone and buzzed that too. Wouldn't one or the other suffice? Then he spotted the CCTV camera above the door and waved his ID at it for good measure. How many entry systems did you need? He was wondering whether there was anyone in – he'd been told that Sender and his wife had recently returned from the Antilles but perhaps she had stayed out there – when the door wobbled open hesitantly. It was indeed Gabby Garnier, the former model, in carpet slippers.

'Hello, I wasn't sure if you were...' he tailed off. 'Security tried to call you from the gate.'

'Sorry, I was miles away,' she said. 'I'd asked for the buzzer to be turned off.'

'Still on holiday?'

She flicked him a look that said 'how did you know?' Big eyes under bigger lashes.

'They told me you'd been away, someone somewhere must have said something,' he said, spluttering. She didn't have a hair out of place. It looked like chocolate silk.

She smiled. 'Holiday? My whole life has been a holiday. Certainly, my whole marriage. Time to pay for it, isn't it?'

'I'm sorry,' said Chris. 'You've obviously heard. We usually try to keep it out of the media until the next of kin have been...'

'DMed on Twitter. Yes, well, you'd better come in. Sorry it took me so long to get to the door. I don't think I've answered a door for ten years.'

'You have staff?'

She tried another smile. 'Well, it's not exactly Downton Abbey. The cleaning staff wouldn't normally be here when we are. Usually only Louisa, my PA. But she doesn't come in until 9.30. So here I am, husbandless, PA-less and forced to answer my own door.' She half-laughed and bowed her head. She seemed more nervous than he was – not unusual in the circumstances. Nobody knew how to behave when a murder was announced.

'I may need to talk to them all,' Chris said, producing a notebook from inside his pocket.

She followed the gesture and then began laughing as if he'd told the funniest of jokes.

'You still use a notebook?' she giggled. 'Don't you have something more hi-tech? Everybody else does.' She gestured for him to sit down but, even with her hand over her mouth, she couldn't stop laughing. 'Please excuse me. Police cutbacks, is it?'

'Well, it is but that's not the reason why I use a notebook,' Chris's voice sounded stiff and prim to him. He perched on the edge of the deep, velour sofa, wary of losing himself in its lushness if he sat on it properly.

'No, of course not. Sorry.'

Gabby watched as the policeman jabbed the pen into action with his thumb and wrote her name in his book. She didn't say anything. She was used to people knowing her name. The policeman had shocking dress sense. She was used to that too. Policemen and security men. Was it a job requirement? It wasn't a Columbo mac or anything quite as bad as that. The offence against good taste was in the colours. The policeman was wearing half a dozen. Some pastel, some vibrant, topping a big-shouldered 70s-style brown leather jacket off with a thin 80s-style navy tie. A car crash, really. Concentrate Gabby, snapped the voice in her head. It sounded like her mother's. She tried to refocus on the point in question: the murder of her husband. There was a pause as she and the policeman both looked at the packet of cigarettes on the coffee table. She'd been trying to give up. Had given up really. But as soon as she'd heard, she'd found herself lighting up. It was as if something inside her had told her that it was the thing to do. This was what was expected when your husband was killed. She extended an index fingernail and gently drew the packet across the walnut table-top towards her.

'Cigarette?'

Chris didn't smoke. Not a single cigarette had passed his lips for one year, six months, two weeks and, what, a day or two. Just the odd half tonne of nicotine chewing gum. But he had this idea, something he'd got from a social worker once, that you could bond with someone better by sharing something with them. So, if he was interviewing someone who wanted tea, he had tea. If he was in a pub with a lager drinker, he'd drink lager. If a supermodel wanted to offer him a fag, he'd have a fag.

'Thanks,' he said.

She lit their cigarettes and there was another pause. Gabby was trying to find the right 140 characters for the policeman. I know I should be crying but I'm not sure I cared very much so I've been sitting here weighing up what's good and bad about being single again. That was 145. She didn't say anything. Next to the fag packet, Chris noticed, was a novel. Some sort of detective crap.

'My wife likes him,' Chris said, nodding at the cover. He wasn't married and had never heard of the author.

'Really? I should think your wife gets quite enough murder and brutality in reality. Being married to a policeman.'

He didn't quite know how to respond. 'You don't get enough murder and brutality?' he began.

'I don't get enough reality,' she said.

She picked up the book. 'I was reading this the last time I saw him,' she said. 'When we were in the Antilles. Before the car took him back to the airport. I was angry because he wanted to go home early. Back to England, home, I mean.'

'Did he want to go home to go to that party?' asked Chris.

'I don't know.'

'What was the last thing he said to you?'

The ex-model took the book in both hands and held it up. He'd seen people do something similar with the Bible when swearing on it in court. She spoke very slowly and deliberately, as if trying to remember the exact words. 'He said: "You're not reading another one of those stupid things, are you? They're all the same. They all begin with a dead body with its head stoved in."'

Chris was unsure again. He took a long drag. 'Did your husband have any enemies?'

'About 3,300.'

Chris coughed. 'That's a very precise number.'

'That's the number of people who worked for the shit.'

Gabby felt a tear sprint from the corner of her eye, slide down a lash and leap for freedom. It landed with a dead splat on the jacket of the book which she was still clutching. Finally, she had started crying.

Chris hesitated before putting his hand on hers. 'They all begin with a body,' he said, 'but they all end with an arrest.'

This did not sound as comforting as he had hoped and she slumped under another bigger wave of tears and onto his shoulder. Nobody had put their head on his shoulder for three years, two months and about a week and a half. It relaxed him a little – like they'd turned the temperature down slightly on his hot tin roof. He allowed himself to settle back a little into the sofa.

There were several moments of warm comforting silence before Chris's phone buzzed with a text message, vibrating in his jacket pocket between her chin and his chest. They ignored it. Another zap followed less than a minute later.

'I'm sorry,' said Chris, sitting up and pulling the phone from his pocket. 'The station probably want me to...'

'I think I'm going mad,' said Gabby, straightening first her spine and then her hair. 'I want to tweet something.'

Chris read the message but his mind was elsewhere. 'Was your husband on Twitter, Mrs Sender?'

'Yes.'

'I presume you follow him.'

"Nominally, yes.' Gabby sat up. This is what she should have been doing. Acting, not tweeting. The policeman offered her a tatty-looking packet of service-station tissues which she reacted to as the kind gesture it was intended to be, rather than as the health and safety risk it was.

'Shall we look at his feed?'

Gabby nodded. She stubbed out her cigarette with a punch and a grind.

Chris watched her. He'd just had Gabrielle Garnier's perfect head on his shoulder and it was fazing him in a number of ways, not all of them unpleasant. He shook his own imperfect head. The only thing he knew for certain was that now was not the time and that the time, like a winning lottery ticket caught on the breeze, might never come again. Perhaps that was two things he knew. And perhaps that was wisdom. Anyway, that was beside the point. Time to get down to business. That was the point. He had his phone in the palm of his hand before either of them could blink.

'What's your husband's Twitter name, Mrs Sender?'

'@JackStufff or @Stufffchief, something like that. Hold on.' She got up. 'I've got it on my phone around here somewhere.' She walked around the vast room. 'The trouble with big houses is it's so easy to lose...' Chris watched her. They'd both spotted her phone on an occasional table by the French windows. He watched as she picked the phone up and bayoneted it back into life with a nail. He watched as she swiped through apps and scrolled down the screen.

'@StufffCEO', she said. Then he watched as all the colour drained from her face and she put a hand out onto the window to steady herself. Her mouth was as wide as her eyes. She was rocking on her feet and Chris noticed for the first time that the slippers she was wearing were a man's pair and too large for her.

'Mrs Sender?' Chris was up from the couch.

'He's still tweeting,' said Gabby. 'Jack's still tweeting.'

# 2.3.

Gill picked up the pot from the window sill, a stunted, lop-sided, hastily-glazed affair that Colin had made at school. It was ugly: the ugliest item in the room by far and, of course, the one she loved the most – certainly at this moment. In fact, it was pretty much the only item that was hers rather than her mother's. She looked around. Yes, in this room, it was the only thing of hers. She still considered the house her mother's home, not hers. Mother's and father's. Trying to kid herself she was just staying the week-end. Or at least, until Colin was up and about again, and Susie and the kids were able to go home. She dusted the stump of a pot for the 467th time and put it back on the window sill. This was not being mindful at all.

She took another lungful of lemon-and-vinegar-flavoured air.

Concentrate on the moment. Look out of window and across road to recreation ground – what is the difference between a recreation ground and a park? – mindfully. The twins were playing. Outside at last. They were so easily bored compared to Colin and Andrew as children. A game of one-onto-one football so far as Gill could see. Wouldn't it make more sense to pass the ball to each other rather shooting all the time? There was more shouting and running to collect the ball than there was actual football. But they seemed to know the rules, each appealing occasionally to an invisible referee. Was that not a sign of intelligence, inventing your own games? Well, they used to say it was when hers were young, but it was probably considered a sign of terminal delinquency now. Everything changes. Milk and sunshine are bad for you now and coffee and crosswords are good for you.

The kids knew their father was in hospital. But what did it mean to them? Did they understand? Gill suspected that children understood things better than adults, better than adults dared imagine they did. And while she and Susie might have pussyfooted around the terminology – coma, hypoxic, prognosis – the twins understood. But there was a debate, all the same. Whether or not they should visit their father. Not handled brilliantly by her or Susie. Susie had said that Jake and Ryan wouldn't be able to handle seeing their father in a coma. Gill had said that seeing him like that would help them to accept the worst if the worst happened. Susie had burst into tears.

'I wasn't saying he's going to ....'

Gill hadn't been able to say the word for all that she couldn't stop thinking about it. 'I was just saying.'

Susie had stepped outside and smoked a cigarette in the front garden, much to the chagrin of Mrs Hennessey. Gill had seen that through the living room window too. It made her smile, Mrs Hennessey's outraged expression as Susie stood among the roses puffing. Mrs Hennessey looked like she'd discovered a particularly large, particularly chewy sweet stuck to her false teeth. Then Gill hoped Susie hadn't seen her smiling and felt guilty. But when Susie came back inside, she'd called the kids, dry-eyed, and taken them to the hospital. It was the first time Gill had seen her daughter-in-law smoke. First time she'd seen her cry too.

They hadn't been gone long – little more than the time it took to walk there and back – and Gill had hardly begun to get the lunch on. The boys were silent afterwards. Ryan even read a book, something that would have been the cause for some celebration under other circumstances. They ate salad – salad! – with barely a murmur.

'Was Dad a hero?' Jake asked eventually. He was picking and poking his way through his favourite corner pot yoghurt, a dessert that usually didn't touch the sides.

'He is a hero, yes,' said Susie. 'He saved a girl's life.'

Jake put his spoon down. He wanted more.

'He went back into the fire to rescue her,' said Susie.

Ryan carried on eating slow, measured spoonfuls.

'Why?' asked Jake.

'Because otherwise she'd be dead.'

'And now he's dead.'

'He's not dead,' said Susie, a little squeak in her voice. 'I told you he's in a coma and I explained to you what it means to be in a coma, didn't I?'

'It looks the same as being dead,' said Jake.

You couldn't argue with that, not really, so Gill had started stacking the plates.

They were out in force, the dog walkers. Also the handful of mums who ran round the park pushing their pushchairs and then did their various big-bottomed stretches and bends, using the handles of their pushchairs as a barre. They started at about 11, the exercise girls. The exhausting girls. You knew it was time because a Council van pulled up and the Council workers in their high-visibility jackets took their 'tea break'. Gill started to count the dogs, name their owners. Perhaps even a full complement today. It had only just brightened up so this was their first chance to get out. She watched them. Mindfully, checked them off an imaginary list.

There was Peter Penney who used to run the newsagent's. His lad was a policeman. The dog's name was Lenny. Lenny Penney. It was a mongrel with wild grey frizzy hair. Like a cartoon dog that had got its paw stuck in the power socket. Actually it did look like a cartoon dog, that cartoon dog that Colin used to like. Drawn with a big fat felt pen, it used to shimmer on the screen. Memory like a sieve. Had a video. First time round it had been on before the evening news, the programme – the Magic Roundabout slot. What was the wretched dog's name?

Funny music too.

There was old Mrs Browne, sitting on the bench. Well, Gill said old but actually Mrs Browne was younger than she was. Had a tougher old life though. Cliff and Colin and Andrew may have given her a whole head of white hairs. Each. But at least they were all still alive. Mrs Browne had buried her two sons. The oldest – Martin, wasn't it? – a friend of Andrew's, had been hit by a car. The youngest was even worse. Nobody really knew what had happened to him. Mark. Pulled out of the estuary, already dead. The bench Mrs Browne was sitting on had their names on it. A plaque. That was why she walked half-way across town to walk her dog here. After Mark had drowned, the town had had a collection for her – raised enough to buy a hundred benches.

Gill watched as Mrs Browne – Camila, her name was (Spanish, Gill thought) – raised a heavy hand to toss an arthritic ball for Bouncer. Bouncer was a bounding canine lump of hippy happiness. A big dog. Gill thought the breed was Newfoundland. Whereas Mr Penney's dog was long-haired and frizzy, Camila's was equally long-haired but in a shaggy way. Bouncer was a walking shaggy dog story, into everything and never finished with anything. He had all the lust for life that his owner now so understandably lacked; Bouncer had enough energy for Camila and everyone else in Biscuit Town.

When he tired of the ball – Camila couldn't really throw it far enough – Bouncer scampered and darted with the two retired greyhounds and gave the pair a run for their money. The greyhounds were owned by a small, quiet woman who wore a gaberdine mac regardless of the weather. Gill had never known her name. The dogs' names were something obvious, a double act like Laurel and Hardy. The woman sat, if she ever sat, on the other side of the rec with Mr Sweetman, the English teacher who used to work with Andrew at Plane Grove.

'Mr Sweetman isn't' had been her son's assessment of his then colleague and Gill had had no grounds to disagree, having never exchanged more than a handful of words with the man. He certainly had a surly, down-turned expression that didn't invite conversation. His dog was a slightly overweight Corgi that was as much a loner as its owner appeared to be. While most of the dogs ran around randomly in the middle of the park, Sweetman's Corgi skulked in the trees around the edge: the same three trunks, always sniffing, never seemingly peeing. She wasn't quite sure whether Sweetman had retired or not. She couldn't see him at Plane Grove Academy, somehow. Sometimes he was in the park during working hours, other times not for weeks. It revealed a grim truth: since she'd been at her mother's, she'd become more au fait with the dogs and their owners than she'd care to admit. They'd become her daytime television.

Mr Hafiz came waddling across the park, Oscar, his white terrier, yapping at his tottering heels. Like the ogling Council workers, Mr Hafiz too wore a bright yellow hi-vis jacket. Dangerous job, dog-walking. Did everyone have hi-vis jackets these days? Should she have one for pruning the roses? Hafiz shouted something at the mac lady. She waved. And then there was that younger man with his poodle. Strange combination that. The man had muscles, dark blue tattoos and the shortest of short hair. He looked like a football hooligan as far as Gill could see, yet he'd got a poodle like a French maid. The poodle liked Bouncer and Bouncer liked everybody so there was a lot of nosing going on. Gill was not sure which was which sex.

'Count it down,' shouted the gym instructor – short, slim and androgynous. 'Three!'

'Two,' screamed the girls. 'One!'

'Shake it out. Shake it out.'

So now it was her turn. For dog walking. Make the full set. She could hear Demetrius, her mother's dog, pacing the kitchen. As night follows day, the thought of her mother made her feel guilty although, as ever, she wasn't quite sure about what. Because she worried about Colin dying but not her mother? Maybe. But Gill had long since made peace with the idea of her mother dying before she, Gill, did so there was no shock at its imminence. The idea of her first born – big, smiling bundle of boy – not being there any more was wholly different. Any cool, rational, detached analysis told her that she had nothing to feel guilty about. But that wasn't how it worked. Her mother had booked herself into a convalescent home before even discussing it with Gill – 'convalescing from what?' Colin had asked – and had left her daughter running between two oversized houses. Rightly or wrongly, Gill had moved herself plus Susie and the boys into the larger of the two properties – her mother's – when Colin had the accident and it became obvious that Susie was falling apart. She was accepting that she was the rock and was trying to make it a little easier for herself so to be. Should she feel bad about that? The evidence was that her mother was now falling apart too. She was saying she wanted to 'come home to die'. What exactly that meant, Gill didn't know. Yes, her mother's mobility wasn't great, that was a fact. She'd either need to sleep downstairs or get a stairlift. (Although the latter had previously been vetoed on the grounds that it would ruin the Laura Ashley wallpaper.) And that would complicate things. If mother was sleeping downstairs, the twins couldn't really stay. Therefore neither could Susie. Yet Susie, as she constantly said, found it 'calming' to have Gill 'under the same roof'. And, if truth be told, Gill liked having her daughter-in-law and grandchildren around – they provided normality as well as company. There was nothing terminally wrong with her mother – simply a whole medicine cabinet full of little things. Inevitable at her age. Gill knew herself how the mildest thing could feel like the final straw when you were depressed and, let's face it, who wouldn't be depressed all alone at her mother's age? The home opined that she was 'quite poorly in herself' and that another move would kill her. She could see Cliff raising his eyes at that one and quoting first Mandy Rice Davies and then the home's 'outrageous' fees. 'Is that for a month or a year?' Would bringing her home be giving her implicit permission to die? And did Gill have the right to refuse such permission anyway if that's what her mother wanted, even if there was no absolute medical reason for it? Gill had been over every inch of this before, like a prisoner in the tiniest of exercise yards, and, as for the prisoner, there was no obvious way out.

Demetrius, Dimmy for short, was an enormous Golden Retriever who no longer got enough exercise of any type and was taking over the back of the house. She walked back down the hall and opened the kitchen door. Dimmy was out like a bullet. She opened the front door and he was over the road before she could even think of the traffic. Fortunately the road was empty. Not so much as a bicycle. During the Silver Jubilee celebrations, Gill's mother had joked that the road was so dead you could have had a street party everyday. The road was busier now but still quiet. It could, theoretically, be used as a rat-run to the new houses, Estuary Sands, though – and that was a worry. (That was the main reason she had signed the petition against the development if the truth be told.) But the new residents, not being locals, didn't know that. Not yet, anyway. Gill pocketed the door keys, realised that she hadn't made-up and was still in her slippers but decided that, with Colin in a coma, she really didn't care.

'Dimmy,' she shouted. 'Wait for …' The word 'mummy' was caught and smothered before it was really born.

# 2.4.

Gabby could feel the colour coming back to her cheeks. She had gulped two cups of tea (fancied something stronger but not with a policeman in the house). She was at the sink. It was not a part of the house she was familiar with and it had taken her ages to locate any washing-up liquid. She didn't want to use the dishwasher (just as well really, since she didn't know how to use it). She wanted the distraction of housekeeping. She washed her cup and the policeman's. She washed the pot. She dried. She put away. She unpeeled the rubber gloves. She washed her hands.

Gabby realised that she had on her feet the only part of Jack that she really loved: his slippers. My heart has been in cold storage for years in an empty marriage. Now I can breathe. My life is no longer a reading list. I'm glad he's dead. That was 140 characters exactly. Was she heartless or had she been given another chance?

Either way, she had to psyche herself up for the forthcoming ordeal. Against change of fortune set a brave heart. This policeman, Caton, would be taking her in. Scotland Yard, presumably. There was nothing to worry about as such, no problem with her alibi. She'd arrived back at about eight which the airline could confirm, had taken a taxi which the driver could confirm and then there was CCTV all over the estate and at home. It would all be routine but not pleasant all the same. She could do without her picture in the paper but couldn't see how, under the circumstances, that could be avoided.

As she gazed out of the window onto the vast garden, she heard the door. That was not unexpected – DS Caton had been on the telephone and she was expecting a report – but what was unexpected was that he appeared to be speaking French and addressing it to her.

'Il faut que vous dites quelque chose, Madame Sender. En français, bien sûr.'

His accent wasn't at all bad for an Englishman (although there were the usual errors with the subjunctive). But why was he speaking French?

'Say something?' she said. 'I mean, mais pourquoi?'

'Mon chef m'a envoyé parce que nous sommes tous les deux Français. C'est-à-dire moitié Français en mon cas.'

Half French, that explained half the accent and all the grammar. 'Moi, je suis Française de souche,' said Gabby with a smirk. 'Mais pourquoi parle-t-on français?' Caton was waving the phone in her general direction – presumably so that whoever was at the other end could hear her speak French. The policeman's boss?

'Ma mère est une vraie Parisienne,' announced Caton proudly.

Mum from Paris. That explained the other half of the accent. 'Ah bon? Je viens de Marseille.'

'Je comprends maintenant pourquoi tu es partie de la France.'

She laughed at that – most Parisians saw Marseille as the sort of town you wouldn't be sad to leave.

'Yes, that's the point, guv. Barely a word. Well, they're hardly ever here, are they?'

Gabby couldn't hear the other side of the conversation – just a gruff rumble. What was going on?

'Well, would you live in England if you could afford not to?' Caton said.

Rumble.

'OK, guv, thanks. Will do.' He hung up and then turned to Gabby with a smile.

'I'm your Family Liaison Officer,' he said.

Corrigan had wanted Chris back at the station which was the last thing that Chris wanted. It was partly the excitement of the case, the excitement of Gabby, possibly, but frankly he would have tried to stay on the case if it had been a cat up a tree. Corrigan also wanted to interview 'the wife' and wanted Chris to bring her in with him. Chris had told Corrigan that Gabby couldn't speak English well enough for an interrogation, so he'd need to translate if they wanted to question her. That being so, it would make sense for him (Chris) to stay with her and for him (Corrigan) to make him (Chris) Family Liaison Officer. Quite possibly Corrigan knew he was being fed a line, but Chris had rightly guessed that his boss needed all hands on deck and wasn't about to argue. Corrigan had even agreed to let Chris get Gabby's initial statement. All the same, it wouldn't look good for Chris if someone did interview Gabby later and she began spouting the Queen's like a Roedean girl. He'd have to deal with that one sooner or later.

'Did you tell him I couldn't speak English?' asked Gabby.

Sooner, then. Brains as well as beauty. Well, it was only to be expected. 'To be precise, I didn't tell him that you could,' said Chris hesitantly.

'O-kay,' said Gabby, slowly. 'Are you going to tell me why?'

'Well... qu'est-ce que tu veux que j'te dise?'

'If you're going to tutoie me, then clearly we know each other well enough for you to tell me the truth.'

'Did I tutoie you? Sorry, I always do that. It's difficult when you don't actually live in a country to keep up with cultural changes like...' Chris was babbling. 'You know, it's not easy to know which contexts are considered formal and which informal.'

'I think telling someone his or her spouse is dead is generally pretty formal.'

'Good point. Yes, you're right. Sorry about that.' Chris cleared his throat despite having no desire to do so and waved his mobile extravagantly in Gabby's direction. 'Anyway, we've had some feedback from your husband's social media agency.'

He began scrolling through his texts even though the communication had not been in that form. But, despite the distraction of a hundred rolling messages, Chris was aware of Gabby Sender's eyes fixed on him, holding him as securely as any handcuffs.

'Why,' she asked, 'did you tell your commanding officer that I couldn't speak English?'

'I'm on gardening leave,' said Chris.

'I see. And you want to stay and do my garden?'

'Is there another tea?' asked Chris.

'No', said Gabby. She had very big eyes at the best of times and when in hard-stare mode they were laser-like, eating into his soggy soul. He was aware of her moving across the room and extracting his phone from his hand.

'It's not on the phone,' he said, suddenly aware she was reading his messages. 'It's...'

'When are you coming to see me, you loathsome reptile, question mark,' read Gabby, aloud. He couldn't hear the smirk or see the smirk but smirk he knew there was. 'This from your hashtag wife?'

'I don't actually have a hashtag... It's from my mother,' said Chris, wretchedly.

Gabby was still looking at him, whether still with irritation or now with pity, he didn't care to know. Each was as bad as the other really. And then he was saved by the bell as Gabby's own phone buzzed into action.

In her grief, if that was the right word, Gabby had forgotten all about the social media agency which handled Jack's Twitter account, along with much other social media nonsense as part of their corporate contract with Stufff. The agency had been aware of his death but unaware that there had been some tweets scheduled in advance. They'd realised something was wrong when one of the tweets was widely retweeted tagged as Sender's 'delivery from the #grave' and similar. Not that they'd bothered to warn her until she contacted them. The necessary action had been taken, they had told her – which Gabby took to mean that some poor intern had been fired. Chris had read them the Riot Act so intimidatingly that Gabby hadn't been sure whether he was faking the anger or not. He'd demanded their help to find the killer and they, in their guilt, had agreed.

The thing was that Jack, or his social media agency, it wasn't yet clear, had been dangerously reckless about tweeting his location. He had tweeted that he'd be attending the party several days before and had referred to it on at least two further occasions. He'd announced his arrival. Could it be that he'd signed his own death warrant?

Gabby put the call on the speaker phone.

'Mrs Sender?' said a tentative little voice. 'It's Neil from the agency.' He didn't sound much more than an intern himself.

'Hello Neil.'

'Is the officer still with you?'

'DS Caton here too,' said Chris stuffily.

'We're putting together a list of all Mr Sender's followers,' said Neil, 'with as much personal detail as we can find so you can interview them.'

'Good.'

'But there are a lot of them.'

Gabby had a thought. 'But if you were stalking someone for...' she hesitated over the word, 'malicious reasons, would you follow them? I mean, formally follow? Wouldn't you just read their tweets anonymously?'

Chris shot her a glance – already it was clear that she was smarter than any partner he'd had in the Met.

'Does anyone particularly stand out? On the list, I mean?' said Chris.

'There's one guy who is chasing an order.'

'That can't be unusual.'

'Let me read some of the tweets. Where's my effing order Sender you B? Er, you big effing C I want my B, effing, different B-ing order. I'm editing some of the language.'

'Yes, I think we get that. But is that so strange? I've sent a few messages like that myself. Minus the language.'

'He goes on to threaten Mr Sender and he says, I'm sorry Mrs Sender, that he knows where he lives. And then there's the postcode. Your postcode.'

'Right.' Gabby and Chris exchanged glances. It wasn't a massive amount to go on but it did represent their first lead.

'Do we know anything about this guy?'

'Everything,' said Neil. 'Right down to his address and phone number. The order number checked out. He did have an order and it was six weeks late. Is six weeks late.'

'What is it? The order?'

'A book about getting the best out of social networks, would you believe?'

Chris was getting more interested.

'There's one more unusual thing. We've checked his Twitter profile and he's been a member of Twitter for ages but he doesn't follow anyone and, apart from these tweets to Mr Sender, has never tweeted.'

That was fishy. 'What was it you said, Gabby? "If you were stalking someone for malicious reasons, would you follow them"?'

Gabby nodded.

'Where does he live?' asked Chris.

Neil told him.

'Is that in Shropshire?' said Gabby.

'No, South Coast,' said Chris. 'They call it "Biscuit Town". Neil, send us all his details.'

'I'll text them right now, Officer.'

Gabby hung up. 'There must be thousands of people who have

joined Twitter and never used it,' she said. 'It doesn't prove anything.'

'No, but he is using it, isn't he?' Chris had a plan hatching. 'And why order a book on social networking if you're not interested?' He knew from Corrigan that SOCO had next to nothing. As a crime scene, the toilet where Sender had been found was as compromised as a vicar in a brothel. Traces of pretty much everything and everyone everywhere. It would take a bit of trawling through. He'd also fed back to Corrigan Gabby's remark about Sender's 3,300 employees so he knew his boss had some seriously time-consuming work to do there too. Stufff had at least half-a-dozen delivery centres in the UK and dozens worldwide.

'Would Sender's employees be any more discontent than those in any other large corporation?' Corrigan had asked.

'They tag them,' said Chris.

'What, like our electronic tagging?'

'The very same. The Peckham Rolex. They know exactly where they are, even when they're in the crapper.'

'Bloody hell, they didn't use to do that in Woolworth's.' Chris could imagine Corrigan's head shaking from side to side like the wise old sage he fancied himself to be. '3,300 staff?'

'In the UK. Loads more at Christmas. Lot of agency. Only takes one.' Chris egged the pudding. 'Send me the SOCO pix, guv. I can have a look at them. Try to ease the load. Nothing else much to do.'

'This is dangerously close to active duty, Caton,' Corrigan had said but he'd sent the pictures anyway.

Gabby's phone pinged, returning Chris to the matter at hand.

'Neil?' he asked.

She nodded and showed him the message. Address. Phone. Order number. Book title.

'Do you want to go for a drive?' asked Chris.

'OK,' said Gabby. 'Let me just change out of these slippers.'

# 2.5.

Bouncer and French were going nose to nose. 'These two need to get a room,' Gary said and got a half-laugh from a couple of faces.

Gaz wouldn't have minded getting a room himself with one or two of the girls from the exercise class. Perhaps at the same time. The yummy mummies, they called them. He couldn't help looking at them. Blokes didn't have a choice. It was in the jeans, ha. Pushing their buggies and stretching their lithe lycras. Just a room, mind. He wasn't doing sprogs – and they all seemed to have them, those little, screaming, shitting designer accessories. It was an odd ambition, really – the continuation of the species. Was it rational on a planet of seven billion people? Did all these honeys really need to make 'mini-mes' when there were so many people in the world who didn't have the benefit of contraception. To Gaz, it was further evidence that the human species had not moved far from the cave.

Then the skirt who'd just moved in over the road appeared. He'd noticed her before – something in her sadness. She was the polar opposite of the yummies with all their squealing and counting and high-fiving. She looked like she had all the shit of the world and then some weighing her down, to say nothing of the bags of shopping. She moved slowly, walking across the grass like she was wearing concrete shoes. Thin as a stick. All in black, like somebody had died. And not black lycra. Maybe somebody had. Gaz, who could be gallant, felt for her. He moved towards her, letting the shoulders loose.

'You want a hand with those, sweetheart?'

The girl was a bit taken. Didn't seem like she had even clocked him. (Losing your touch, Gaz.) Lost in her own little world of pain. You saw it all the time. There were so many miserable women.

'Oi, Mum, you got my Haribo.'

Shit, those two kids playing football were hers. Must be older than she looked. Must be more attached. Too late now. She was offering him the bags with the saddest smile he'd ever seen. Still Gary could be gallant – even if those shopping bags did appear to be full of fucking bricks.

'You all right, darling?' he asked. So miserable, you got to feel sorry for them.

Gill watched as Susie approached. Dimmy was walk-running in the middle of the park, trying to get Bouncer's attention. Demetrius was probably five times the age of Bouncer, had a gammy leg and was overweight but the sight of the younger dog reinvigorated the older. It was the same with humans, Gill supposed – the way she used to be able to find the energy to play with the twins when they were still of an age of wanting to play with their granny.

The woman in the gaberdine mac appeared to be clearing up after the fat Corgi. Must be very good friends, her and Mr Sweetman, if she cleared up his doggie's doings. Gill tried to disengage her mind from gossip and pointless speculation about people she didn't know and didn't truly care about.

She was half talking to Camila, sitting on her sons' bench, but it was like getting blood out of a stone.

'Least it's stopped raining,' she said.

Camila said something in reply. It was not that Camila didn't speak, it was that you couldn't hear what she was saying. Perhaps the dogs could hear her. Perhaps that's why Bouncer was such a mad thing. He could hear her in his ear all day long – speaking dog. Camila had said something about the rain or Spain or something happening again.

Gill guessed. 'Not the best spring.' The sun was trying its best though – spitting out some rays from a suffocating sky.

Camila said something else. Now she was either talking about erections or the election. Gill guessed the latter.

'I imagine they'll sort themselves out,' she said.

'Doesn't matter who you vote for, the government always gets in,' said Camila audibly.

Gill found her head turning, as if a statue had spoken. Camila raised her head at Bouncer's imminent arrival and her eyes locked with Gill's. Gill could not remember ever really making eye contact with Camila before. She had beautiful brown eyes that were all the more beautiful for the sadness locked up inside them. The eyes smiled and the lips, slowly, as if they were out of practice, eventually, followed. Gill smiled too and they both even giggled a little – Gill, in her concern for Colin, understanding in a visceral way for once rather than a sympathetic one how Camila must have felt all these years. Of course, Gill was way too English to say anything to this effect but for a moment all was right. This is what being human is, isn't it? The reason we talk to people. Then Bouncer was on Camila, great bear-like paws muddying her faded print skirt. She extracted the ball, dripping saliva, from the dog's mouth. Gill knew what the neighbourly thing to do was and she'd been so well brought up that she couldn't help but do it. Handful of dog spit or not, she took the ball from Camila and hurled it as far as she could – two, three times as far as Camila managed. Bouncer was in dog heaven. They watched as he canter-capered after it, the ball bouncing once and dying in the damp-top turf.

'Well, you can't throw from a seated position, can you?' Gill said. She was surreptitiously trying to shake canine expectorate from her unvarnished finger nails.

Camila said something as she rummaged in her handbag. Gill wiggled her thumb. There was a globule of dog drool the size and tenacity of a limpet clinging to it. Camila produced a crumpled but clean Kleenex from a thick wad of same and handed it to Gill.

Gill had just enough time to say 'thank you' before the returning Bouncer dropped the well-drooled ball at her feet. The limpet finally gave in. It wriggled free from Gill's thumb enjoying an airborne moment before landing on the tip of Bouncer's nose from where it disappeared in the flick of a sinewy pink tongue.

Gill dearly wished she hadn't noticed this. She fixed her expression in a different direction. Not that the football hooligan talking to Susie was much more pleasing on the eye. Not, as she'd heard Jake and Ryan say, eye candy. The way children spoke, it was like the doctors. You knew what the words meant, near enough, even though you'd never heard them before. All those tattoos. And did he have a red tattoo on his head or was that dye? No man henna-ed his hair in her day. What could you say? Not eye candy at all, but you saw young girls covered head-to-foot with them. Tattoos. Awful. And red hair.

Green hair. Purple hair. (Are you going to list all the colours, Gill?) The hooligan appeared to be trying to take the bags from Susie as the kids appeared to be trying to rummage through them for sweets or some such. Those bags are going to split if they're not careful, Gill stopped herself from saying.

'Wait. Can you wait?' said Susie but there was no force in her voice, no sense that she meant it. Gill was lip-reading rather than hearing. Well, she had been too soft with them long before all this business with Colin came along and knocked the stuffing out of her. Not much stuffing to knock if truth be told. The twins gave no indication of having heard her.

'Didn't you get any Haribo? whined Ryan.

'Oi.' It was the football hooligan speaking this time – loud and clear – and this time there was no doubt that the twins had heard as they sprung to a sloppy attention like a pair of green squaddies. 'Your mother says wait.'

The hooligan scowled first at Jake and then at Ryan and then he marched towards Gill, holding the bags out in front of him, one gripped in each fist as if the contents might wriggle free, like kittens for the drowning. She could see now that he didn't have dyed hair or a red tattoo. He was a redhead. Susie followed in his wake, a coil more spring in her step. The boys exchanged glances and tagged along behind, Jake gathering up the ball with a dispirited flick of the toe. Gill became aware of a smile hovering on the corner of her lips as she watched the procession.

'Thank you,' Susie said with Gill, almost in unison, as the bags were deposited in front of the bench, in reach of both Gill and Camila – the football hooligan perhaps unsure in whose direction Susie was heading.

'Sorry,' said the hooligan. 'But they'd have split those bags, the way they were carrying on.'

'Quite' was all Gill could manage.

Susie gave Gill a shy smile. Gill was embarrassed by the Lidl bags and wanted them out of public sight before Mrs Hennessey appeared for her morning constitutional. Gill knew full well that this was snobbery of the worst kind, wondered whether there was a good kind, and congratulated herself on at least recognising her snobbishness rather than denying it. Dr Conway had, after all, said something about acceptance being a good thing. Now that was the most preposterous and absurd notion she'd ever heard. Flew in the face of everything she had been taught for 60 odd years and sounded, to paraphrase her ex-husband, like the biggest pile of horse manure ever but right now, she'd settle for it. It was a lot less stressful. Acceptance. Perhaps there was a progress after all. Mindfully, she picked up a bag while mindfully avoiding looking at what she was carrying. Full of sweets and crisps probably.

## 2.6.

'You remember the fire at the biscuit factory, Colin? It can't have been long after you joined the brigade. They had three big wooden sheds that they used for storage and they all went up. All three. Like matchwood. Do you remember the smell? The whole town smelled like burnt biscuit. After the fire there was just ash all over the yard, a black sooty sea. The wind picking it up and sprinkling it across the town like black rain.' Ron looked at the prone Colin Graham and became aware that he was still holding Eileen's urn in his hands. 'You remember?'

He had some time to kill before he started his shift with the Friends of the Hospital. He was scheduled for the 'where to go' desk which is what he'd been angling for. It was more him than, say, working in the shop. Giving directions... well, it was a bit like directing the traffic. Perhaps he should erect a little platform for himself in the vestibule.

He couldn't really say why he had chosen to spend those spare moments visiting Colin. He'd not known the younger man particularly well: a mutual respect that didn't go beyond the curtest of nods of the head. A very English thing. He couldn't have told you the names of Colin's kids – though he knew he had them – and he certainly couldn't have told you what he drank in the pub. He knew that Colin had had a trial for Brighton as a kid – blokes tended to know that sort of stuff about each other – so assumed he must be a Seagulls fan. But he didn't actually know. All he did know was that he was solid, one of the best. How, while knowing so little about the man, could he be so sure that he knew that? Something so, what was the word, intangible? It was part of the unspoken compact of the emergency services. Did he know Colin was solid or simply, for the sake of his own survival, have to believe it?

Perhaps it was something to do with him being Gill's lad. 'Me and your mother have volunteered from the Friends of the Hospital,' he'd told Colin as soon as he'd sat down.

Perhaps he just needed to sit beside a hospital bed one last time and had manufactured a reason.

Colin's machine bleeped and winked with a metronomic perfection. Not like Eileen's at the end. They couldn't even get a cannula into her towards the end. Skin drier than parchment.

'We just beat Victoria Park,' he said. 'Carter's Green that is. Close match but my four won comfortably.' Too comfortably really. He hadn't needed to concentrate and that had allowed the mind to wander. His bowling bag was on the floor beside the chair. He hadn't yet resorted to wheels on his bowling bag. He carried his bag and even carried it to and from the house to the green and back. Rarely used the car. He'd always made the game as physical as possible – size 5 bowl, extra heavy. Well, it wasn't boxing, was it? Bowling. A little dull he'd always found it, to tell the truth. One end much like another, but what were you to do? Age caught up on us all. Eileen had always encouraged him. Got him out of the house and the action of bending to bowl was good for his mobility, kept the limp to a minimum.

Ron looked at the urn. He'd just picked it up from the crematorium. He'd expected it to take longer – the process of picking it up – but it was all over. Eileen. She no longer even required paperwork. Should he have had the urn engraved? No point if he was only going to scatter the contents. He thought about the photos he'd found when he'd been going through Eileen's things, the ones he didn't know she had kept, like the first time at their campsite. Him with his shirt off, washing in the communal sinks. The French blokes drowning themselves in cologne, him with a bar of Lifebuoy. He didn't even know she'd taken that one. 'Le Camping', Eileen had called it (although she had pronounced it properly even then: le compeen). Driving down, Ron had assumed she'd been joking and that its real name would be something more, well, French but there it was plastered over the entrance, all over the local map: Le Camping. It became a bit of a standing joke during the holiday. They'd go out for Le Dinner and order Le Bottle Of Wine. They'd go for Le Walk in Le Afternoon. Each uttering was delivered in the most excruciating French accent: ze valk in zer aff-tair-noon. They had had a fair bit of Le Sex too. Ron examined the urn. Not much for a life's work.

There was a noise behind him and the door opened.

This wasn't the first time that Pip had looked in on Colin. As the weather improved, she'd taken to working in the hospital's small but neatly-tended Italian-style sunken garden, piggybacking on the NHS's wi-fi. It was quiet, the bowling green next door provided a gentle soundtrack (not unlike in the house), but apart from the odd smoker, it was often quite deserted: a lot more pleasant place to work than at home (which wasn't her home, by the way) with the wicked stepmother. True, there was one chap who seemed to be there all the time, blue surgical smock and wheeling his IV line but he was harmless. He wore a heavy neck chain, more like a mayoral trapping of office than a rapper's bling, and never sat down. He just stood there watching the carp in the pool, an expression very much like a hooked fish himself, fingering his neckwear as if it were a magic lamp.

Usually, she'd just peep in through the window pane to see if Colin was still there and to watch the machines for a moment. He always was there and, for Pip, the predominant emotion in a torment of them was relief. Still there. Still alive. Were she to find his bed empty, what would she conclude? That he'd died or that he was up and about and looking for his fire helmet? The former. Did that make her a pessimist? A Cassandra? Or just a realist? She'd read up, of course. Most comas lasted two to four weeks. Colin Graham was pushing at the outer limits of that. And your chances of coming out of one depended on your Glasgow Coma Score. Colin's score wasn't the lowest you could get – the nurse had told her he had some 'appropriate, even encouraging motor responses' – but it wasn't good. Let's put it this way, if you got the sort of score, proportionately, that Colin Graham was getting in his Glasgows in your finals, you'd be lucky to get a pass, even in Sociology.

Today, however, Pip pushed the door and walked in. The nurse had told her that he already had someone in with him and Pip had hoped it might be his mother. Another chance to apologise – although a million apologies couldn't make amends for her arsehole of a father. She wasn't expecting a man.

Ron looked up. He had assumed a nurse, but this was a very strange uniform. A girl wearing a big baggy hippy thing with purples and reds. Highly inappropriate for nursing duties. She was too young to be the wife. A sister, perhaps?

'Oh,' said Pip. 'Sorry. Are you Mr Graham's father?'

Ron smiled. 'No, love. I'm, well, sort of a work colleague.'

'Is there any change?'

'I don't know, love. I've not been in…'

Pip nodded slowly in a way that she knew was ham – a gesture learned from the telly? 'Are you a firefighter, then?' He looked a bit old to be a fireman but then it was a very stressful job.

'No, I'm retired now. I used to be a policeman. The emergency services, you know, we all, well, work together.' Cough. 'The attestation to public service.' Ron was wondering why he was trying to justify his presence. 'Are you…?'

'I'm nothing,' said Pip. 'Well, I'm the one he…' Pip wasn't able to complete the sentence. 'You know.'

Pip didn't wait to be invited, she sat down anyway, her legs suddenly jelly beneath her.

They both looked at Colin for a moment or two, at the rising and falling of his chest.

'He,' said Ron, taking a breath and finding the right word, 'is a brave man'.

'Yes,' said Pip. 'He is.'

She looked across the bed and saw what the policeman was cradling in his hands. Ron became aware of the girl's gaze and suddenly, with neither wishing it, both his eyes and hers were trained not on the breathing Colin but on the unbreathing polished metal receptacle on Ron's lap.

'Were you a local police officer?' asked Pip, hesitantly.

Ron nodded.

'Has your wife got cancer?' This question even more hesitant than the first.

Ron nodded. 'She had cancer,' he said.

There was a long silence, eyes on the urn.

'You must know Mrs Graham well,' said Pip, immediately aware of how ambiguous this clumsy formation was.

'Not really. We both volunteer for the Friends of the Hospital.'

There was another silence. Pip knew but she had to be sure she knew. Something inside her, something insensitive and insecure made her plough on.

'A sort of liver cancer?'

'Yes. How do you...?' He looked up. 'Do you work here?'

'No, sorry, Mrs Graham told me and my father...'

'What? That is none of her...' The man was looking not at the urn now but directly at her. Pip squirmed. His eyes weren't piercing. They somehow managed to be watery and hollow at the same time.

'My father. He's. Rich. He offered Mrs Graham money. To help with her son.' Squirm. Pip had made this excruciating for both of them. 'And she said he should give it to you instead.'

Ron took a moment to take this in. The sequence of events. 'That was...'

He was about to say 'that was very generous of her' but that wasn't actually what, in his heart, he wanted to say.

'How much was it?' he blurted. His head felt heavy and the urn was glued to his fingers and palms with sweat.

'Fifty, I think.'

'What?'

'Fifty thousand pounds.'

Ron couldn't even nod his head. He felt that, if he tried, it would fall off and roll across the hospital floor, wibble-wobble like a badly-biased bowl.

'Might have given her till Christmas,' he said. The urn and his hands were welded together, a single item of lead.

When he had said those exact same words to Gill Graham in the hospital canteen – well, something similar, anyway – 'till Christmas' hadn't seemed like anything at all. A couple of months. Well, when you'd lived for sixty odd years, what was a couple of months? But now, as he looked at the girl and then at Colin Graham and then at the urn containing all that was materially left of Eileen, it felt like all the time in the world. One more Christmas. His head throbbed. He couldn't really focus. Right now, what wouldn't he give for one more Christmas?

A couple of hours later, Pip was sitting in the Italian garden as Sergeant Newton left the building. She realised that she'd been keeping an eye on the door for just this moment. She wished she'd handled her conversation with him better but what could she possibly say now? Stupid girl. The former policeman was a big man but slouched over now in a heavy black anorak and running to fat. The man with the neck chain in the blue smock appeared to be looking at him too.

'Where's he gone?' said the man.

'To see his friend,' said Pip. Mr Neck Chain had never said a word before and it seemed an odd question, but she wasn't going to be rude.

The man looked at Pip as if she were mad. 'He's broken,' he said.

He certainly was but Pip didn't say anything. Then, as she turned her attention back to her iPad, she realised that Mr Neck Chain hadn't been talking about Sergeant Newton at all.

Presiding over the pool, keeping a watchful eye on the koi carp, there had been a statue of a little cherub. He rather resembled – or had rather resembled – the one in Brussels although he wasn't peeing and he was made of stone. Now all that was left on the plinth were two little mossy green feet, cut off at the ankle. The hospital had obviously cleared up as the body was nowhere to be seen.

'Bloody hoodlum kids,' said Mr Neck Chain.

'Or the wind,' said Pip. The corrosive effect of the sea wind and rain could well have taken its toll. (Had she not sworn off field trips, there may have been a geography lesson in this.) It struck her as symbolic though. Like Sergeant Newton, the statue had been swept off its feet. And like all the bodies in the hospital...

In her mind's eye she saw the stone cherub being carried away on a stretcher by ambulance men.

Well, she hoped that wouldn't happen to the fireman.

# 2.7.

'We need the phone,' said Chris, taking a serious bite of his apple. 'Wait until he uses the phone.'

Gabby wondered exactly what, given that she had a dead husband back home in London, she was doing sitting with a deranged fruit-devouring policeman in some obscure English seaside town, watching a lot of fat women and dogs run round a shabby park. The policeman – Chris – had his binoculars (actually Jack's binoculars) trained on the dog walkers. 'I'll take him. You get the phone,' he said through flecks of apple.

'OK,' said Gabby. 'But you do know that I've never arrested anybody before.'

This was the first time she'd been out 'on her own' in ages. She had stood down the security guard people shortly after news of Jack's death had broken.

'I'd need Mr Sender's authority for something like that, Miss,' the voice on the phone had said, instantly regretting it.

'I want to keep a low profile,' Gabby had said.

Actually perhaps life wasn't so different. She had substituted a plain-clothed security guard with souped-up muscle, rapid eyes and a sense of menacing suspicion for a plain-clothed policeman with same. And at least it was brightening up, the grey lace veil of sea mist that had been sitting over the town dissolving.

'How do you know it's him?' asked Gabby.

Chris kept the binoculars trained. 'Woman in his block told me he was walking his dog. Young, male, red-haired. Nobody else remotely matches that description.'

That was true. The man Chris had taken to calling 'the suspect' was the only male under 60.

'Sure you don't want one?' Crunch went the apple. 'Those bloody jogging women keep getting in the way.'

Chris had been getting more and more hyped up on the journey down, psyching himself up for the job in hand. It was worse than the catwalk. Gabby just couldn't bring herself to believe that this man, 'the suspect', was the man who had murdered Jack. It all seemed so surreal. A game almost. Although she could see that it was anything but a game to Chris. If this person was the killer... well, the fact that Chris had presumably broken pretty much every police rule in bringing her down here wouldn't matter, would it? If he wasn't...

The exercise instructor was barking out orders like a blonde-haired sergeant major, her pony-tail doing burpees of its own. 'Just think of all the fat you're burning. Think of all those nasty calories. Come on, come on, last lap.' It was like Gabby's locked-up catwalk conscience had risen from its slumber, got up and put on a tracksuit.

'They'll stop in a minute and start doing some static exercises. No, thanks.'

'How do you know?'

'I just know about exercise classes. Believe me.'

Chris looked at her. 'Don't you eat apples?'

'I don't eat anything. Once a model...'

Chris made a grunting sound. The brown paper bag sat between their seats. Gabby knew that it contained three apples. Counting food. That she was good at. Eating it was the challenge.

Chris scanned the park with his binoculars.

'OK, this is it.'

'The suspect' was walking across the grass away from the other dog walkers. His red head – was that dye? – was bowed down, his hands out in front of him, so he was either praying or texting. His dog was not, yet, following. The man stopped. 'French,' he yelled. 'French!'

'French?' repeated Gabby.

Chris took the final bite of his apple and set the slim core on the dashboard.

'I think it's the name of his dog,' Chris said. He leaned over onto the back seat and produced a grimy-looking black baseball cap which he dropped in Gabby's lap.

'Must be the poodle then,' said Gabby. There was a big, soppy poodle rolling on its back looking for some attention. 'What am I supposed to do with the cap – clean the windows?'

'French! Come here.'

'Put it on. Hide the hair. If that dog comes, he'll be away in two minutes. OK, Gabby, we'll walk across the park together towards the suspect. I'll take him. You make sure you get the phone. He might try to lose it. Or break it.'

Chris was out of the car before Gabby could object. She inspected the interior of the cap and decided it was better not to look too closely. She settled for making it as large as possible and pulling it down over her head, stuffing as much hair as possible up inside it. She opened the door and swung herself out. Chris was circling the back of the vehicle. Then, for reasons she would have been unable to explain but which had something to do with a new beginning, she leaned back in, took an apple from the bag and began to shine it on her jacket. In for a centime.

'Ma chérie,' said Chris offering her his arm as Gabby joined him on the pavement. Click went the doors of the car. 'Quick,' said Chris, in French. 'Before the dog obeys.'

'Why are you speaking French this time?' asked Gabby.

'Because we are French tourists enjoying a day out at the beach, of course,' said Chris in French. He pocketed the car keys.

'You really don't dress French,' said Gabby. She wanted to straighten – or better still, remove – that ridiculous tie. He was without doubt the worst dressed man she'd been seen in public with. A fact she felt a lot better about than she ought to under the circumstances. She took a bite of the apple. It was crisp. It was sweet. It was like liquid sherbet dancing around the inside of her mouth.

'They've stopped,' said Chris, still in French. He was referring to the jogging mothers who were now assembled around their buggies and prams, stretching and straining. Gabby found it odd that they would do that in public. It was showing off. As a former professional show-off, she knew it when she saw it.

She and Chris walked on. Gabby took another bite – smaller this time, a nibble.

'As-tu une pomme?' asked Chris. It sounded like a first-year French lesson.

'Oui, mon poulet. J'ai une pomme.'

'Remember you need to grab the phone. You're going to struggle to do that with an apple in your hand.'

The suspect had stopped in the middle of the park now. 'French, you tart!' he bellowed. Gabby and Chris were about thirty seconds away when the dog finally got up and started walking reluctantly towards her master.

'If there's any trouble, we chase him in their direction. The exercisers. They will slow him down.'

'Trouble doesn't really translate directly in this context,' said Gabby. She hurled her unfinished apple across the grass – a baseball pitcher in her cap. Progress. She'd had two bites. 'You need to say souci or difficulté.'

Then Gabby realised what he actually had said but, before she could add 'what do you mean? Trouble?', Chris was running towards the suspect from one direction and half a dozen dogs were doing the same from the opposite – chasing after her attractively ball-shaped flying apple.

There was an unfortunate set of angles. Or lack of them. Enormous hairy dog like the one in Peter Pan. Policeman. Tempting apple. They were in a straight line. The dog took Chris out just as he was extending his hand to feel the T-shirted suspect's metaphorical collar. Chris was on his back under three or four dogs before you could say 'chien'. The suspect looked round at the barking kerfuffle. A flash of silver. The suspect and Gabby both saw it at about the same time. In Chris's hands, a rattling pair of handcuffs. The suspect looked at Chris who was being licked to death, looked at Gabby, looked at the cuffs once again and started sprinting, his poodle following.

Chris was up on his knees and then down again as an overweight Retriever that had finally built up enough momentum to join in the fun was unable to stop and ploughed into him. She couldn't tell whether Chris or the dog yelped loudest. Gabby had no choice. She started to chase the suspect. He was running towards the exercising women. They had now switched to yoga and were saluting the sun in a chubby unison. The instructor who looked like a boy on steroids but had hair down to her backside continued to bark instructions. Not very Yin. Gabby ran but she was losing the race. She wasn't in heels as such, no Louboutin stilettos, just an inch or so, but her purple pixie boots weren't designed for jogging.

'Stop that man,' she yelled. She didn't know where that came from. It was what they shouted in films. 'Stop him.'

Her baseball cap fell off and now her hair was in her eyes. 'Stop him', she yelled through a mouthful of mane.

At this moment another track-suited woman came into the park from the entrance towards which the suspect was heading. She had another half a dozen dogs on a variety of leads. Dog walker. The beasts fanned out as they entered the park like dogs doing Reservoir Dogs. The suspect had to apply the brakes and divert towards the exercising girls. Gabby was suddenly much closer – about ten yards behind. As she reached out to grab, a gust of wind or her electrifying speed or perhaps both whipped the hair away from her eyes, causing it to twist and wriggle behind her, just as it had in the 'Body and Bounce' shampoo commercial that had made her a household name.

'That's Gabby Garnier,' shouted one of the women.

'Yes – and I'm Buffy the Vampire Slayer.'

'It is. It is. Look.' The sun saluting ceased and they all looked at her.

'Not me, him' shouted Gabby, pointing as the suspect scooted past the sea of gawping faces. Off the grass now and onto the asphalt path, he had circumnavigated the dogs and was just a handful of strides from the exit gate.

The instructor grabbed the nearest pram. Bright pink canopy, it was one of those high-tech efforts, all super-light, super-strength metals, more like a four-by-four than a push-chair. A run-up, then she pushed it. This woman was fit. It moved like a day-glo torpedo hitting the suspect, scooping him up like a JCB and, as the pram fell over, depositing him in the flowerbed. Gabby had time for two thoughts – what about the baby the now prone suspect had just sat on in the pram and what the hell was she going to do when she caught the man – before she landed on top of him like a whale on a trampoline.

Gabby was aware of his hands flailing. One caught her in the stomach. But she concentrated on his head, focusing all her attention on pushing it as deep into the dirt as she could. It wasn't a tattoo or a dye, he was a red-head with a number one on the clippers. Keep his face in the dirt. Now he was kicking. Ow. Gabby took a heel in the back. Where was his phone?

'You're right, it's Gabby fucking Garnier,' said a middle-aged woman in pastel blue jogging bottoms as she grabbed one of the suspect's legs.

A younger woman, with chubby red cheeks, screamed with delight as she pinned down the other leg. 'The phone,' yelled Gabby.

Could she hold him? She couldn't. But they could. There were four or five exercisers now, each with an arm or a leg of the suspect. 'Girl power,' someone shouted. And then Chris was there and the cuffs were sliding on and the rights were being read. '...if you do not mention when questioned something you later rely on in court...' incanted Chris – and Gabby realised just what she was involved in as suddenly she was surrounded by lycra-laden females, in the eye of a high-vis oestrogen tornado.

'Have you joined the police force, Gabby?' She was pulled to her feet.

'Do you really use that shampoo, Gabby?' Someone was dusting dirt off her jacket.

'Can you sign my sports bra, Gabby?' Another product she'd once advertised. Gabby looked around for the phone and saw the still-upturned buggy.

'The baby!,' she said.

'It's all right,' said the woman in the blue joggings. Gabby noticed the colour matched her hair. She was a lot older than she looked. 'There's no baby. It's my daughter's old one. But the class is called "Pushchairs and Press-Ups" so to join you need...'

Gabby finished the sentence for her. 'A pushchair. Right.'

The women all looked round as Chris pulled the suspect to his feet.

'Gary Shad,' said the woman in blue in a sing-song voice. 'And what have you been up to now?'

The red-cheeked woman squealed again. She hadn't really stopped in fact. But now she was holding a ringing phone. 'I found it on the ...'

'It's mine,' said the suspect. Cuffed behind his back, he couldn't actually take hold of it. The ringtone jingled on.

'Gabby,' said Chris. He nodded at the phone. 'Can you...'

Gabby knew her way around a smartphone at least and tapped it into action. She held it up by the suspect's ear.

He coughed. 'Hello?'

Pause.

'Not right now, mate, no. I'm a bit busy. I've just been arrested by Gabby Garnier.'

Pause.

'Yes, the supermodel.'

The suspect looked at Gabby for the first time. 'He hung up,' he said. 'Didn't believe...'

Gabby shrugged as the big hairy dog arrived, dropping the half-eaten apple in a marinade of doggy drool at her aching feet.

'Why did you buy apples?' she asked Chris.

'I like them' he said, pleased as Punch as he attached himself to the suspect with a second pair of cuffs. 'And I thought you'd prefer something healthy.'

Jess was standing there looking at him and Gary, for once, was speechless. Looked like he was going to get a room, after all. A fucking cell. He had dirt all over his face. He allowed his head to incline towards the ground and felt the cuffs cut into his wrists. French appeared, initiating a bit of arse-smelling with one of Jess's dogs.

Jess instinctively pulled her pooch away. A subtle up-yours. As if her dog nuzzling French might contaminate hers with Gaz's fuck-witted stupidity by association. What a twat you've been, Gaz. Too cocky.

He remembered their last conversation, he and Jess, the night of the fire. Mrs Newton and the Maths tests. Gary had, on one occasion, sneaked up to Mrs Newton's desk and turned over the page on which the teacher had said she had written the Maths answers. But she hadn't been telling the truth. The sheet had been blank except for four words spelling out the question 'How do you feel?' Even as a little primary school kid, Gary Shad knew the answer to that one. He felt terrible and had never told anyone about it. He felt much the same inside now, a toxic, snaking knot of shame in the stomach.

'Jess, can you look after French for me?' he said.

# 2.8.

Tommy was stuck on Josh Finkelstein's floor and it was more than a mere mortal could endure.

Teacher training already represented a million and one compromises with his teenage dreams, but he wasn't an idiot and understood that he needed to work until he figured out something better. It certainly wasn't a vocation to him as it seemed to be to, say, Pip. Studying something you were interested in for its own sake was all very well for the rich kids – and was to be applauded intellectually – but it wasn't practical in his case. His mother had been desperate for kids but, after years of failing to find Mr Right, was deep into her forties and clutching at straws when Tommy's dad found himself in the wrong place at the wrong time, a younger man completely unprepared for fatherhood. He had disappeared before Tommy was born and his mum had raised him on her own on a pittance and without a relative within fifty miles. Now it was Tommy's turn to bring home some bacon. In hindsight, those teenage dreams had been vague, nebulous things, anyway – morphing into each other like images in the very low-tech kaleidoscope that he'd so loved when the other kids were getting their first consuls. Tommy wasn't bitter or bothered about any of this, not even angry with his father whom he suspected he resembled in temperament. Something would turn up.

He had an A in looks and a B in brains, so perhaps he'd just marry above himself like the pretty poor girls in the great novels. Josh's floor, however, was another matter – enough to make even the most committed scholar consider dropping out.

After the fire, the fabulous free lunch that was Pip Henley's house had ceased to be served. According to Tanisha, they'd been 'blessed' with 27 Hampshire Drive – and she should know. Hallelujah. A real counter of blessings, the girl knew every verse of the Bible by number and spoke of Elijah and Daniel and the rest of the cast of many colours as others spoke of characters in Eastenders. She was full-on in that way.

'If we were so blessed, why was the place smitten with fire and brimstone?' Tommy demanded over a coffee in the refectory. The four former housemates plus the inevitable Josh were all there reflecting on their various solutions to post-fire homelessness.

'That was nothing to do with God, Tommy. That was to do with you buying stupid drugs from some stupid boy in some stupid nightclub.'

Tanisha smiled broadly and exposed a pristine set of sparkling teeth – impressed with her command of colloquialism, presumably.

'Well, you can't argue with that, Tom,' chimed Josh. He was a little bit smitten himself – in his case with Tanisha's slender perfection rather than fire and brimstone. Tommy had to admit that he was wearying of his sidekick.

'It was outside the club, actually. Anyway, why is the one a human act and the other an act of God?'

'You surely not suggesting you burning down lovely house was an act of God?'

Tommy noted the grammar was less tight when Tanisha was less uptight but he wasn't the sort to make a cheap point like that.

'That's exactly what it was,' said Tommy. 'That's exactly what they call it in insurance land, isn't it? An act of God.'

'Insurance land is not to turn to for spiritual guidance.'

Even Tommy had to admit that that was a fact. 'It just seems to me that us finding the house, us losing the house, they're equally random acts.'

'Only to man who can't see difference,' said Tanisha.

Tommy knew he was beaten. 'We're in "moves in mysterious ways" territory now, aren't we?'

'We are.'

Tommy also knew why he was a little peeved with Tanisha. It wasn't just that she was one of the few females who seemed impervious to his admittedly decidedly non-spiritual charms but also that Tanisha really did appear to have been 'blessed' once again. Tommy preferred to call it 'landing on your feet' but, however you put it, some crusty old geezer she'd met at church had offered Tanisha his spare room.

'And you think that's down to a shared interest in bible studies, do you?' Josh had muttered with some irritation.

She had a bloody en-suite bathroom, for Christ's sake. Very blessed. And he was sleeping on a cold floor in a smelly room.

Pip couldn't stop apologising, as if the fire had been her fault and nobody thought that. They'd been a bunch of selfish idiots to leave someone alone when she was gassed up and a bunch of drunken idiots to do it in a room full of candles. And Tommy's meths-soaked T-shirt, well, he felt especially bad about that. Probably what Pip was really apologising for was that she was living at her old man's luxury new pad up at Estuary Sands. En-suite bathroom was probably the very least of it. En-suite everything. En-suite free.

'I wish you could all stay at mine,' said Pip, as if reading his mind.

Nobody really fancied that but they were grateful for the sentiment.

'Where are you living, Mel?'

Melissa shuffled in her seat. She took a quick sip of frothy strength. 'Moved in with Piers,' she muttered under her breath. The stage whisper was very un-Melissa like, but Tommy heard well enough. He wasn't surprised and, in truth, wasn't too disappointed. Piers did have the twin advantages of living just round the corner from campus and having a car. And these were advantages to Melissa's friends like Tommy, almost as much as they were to Melissa herself. The fact that she was a little sheepish about admitting her living arrangements to the group he took as a good sign.

'Is he the boy who came to the party?' asked Pip. 'I never did get his name.'

'That's right,' said Melissa, formally. 'He's been very supportive.'

Tommy saw it clearly at that moment. Support was what Melissa needed and, while Piers may have been a bit of a prat (and frankly about three divisions below Melissa in the looks league), he was around to provide it – presumably without demanding too much in return. You couldn't blame the girl. She needed to look after herself. They all did. Everyone did. Of all those involved in the fire, Melissa had, on the face of it, been the most affected. She had found it hardest to come to terms with the sometimes thin line between life and death. Tommy knew she'd been with Pip to see the fireman in hospital. She had also suggested to Tommy that he and she take Pip out to 'cheer her up'. Tommy saw it as a kind gesture and had been happy to do it but, as it turned out, it had been Melissa who had most needed to talk about it, most needed to go over the events and most needed to share observations on how lucky they'd all been. Tommy knew from when he and Melissa had been going out that she was yet to lose anyone close to her. Her grandparents on both sides were still going strong. He'd met the Brinks, her father's parents, and the couple, well into their 70s, were out on the town (albeit Tunbridge Wells) more often than he and Melissa. Impressive energy. In that respect, Melissa still had some of that sense of a 'bubble of protection' that children have. Of course, intellectually she knew how the world worked but, until it actually happened, there was a gap between what she had known in her head and what she'd felt in her heart. He didn't reproach Melissa for it. Long may it continue.

'That's great, Mel,' he said. 'Piers is one of the good guys.'

Melissa smiled. She had a dress on and her hair up. A little more formal. A little more like the girlfriend of a public school boy than an oik like Tommy. But Tommy wasn't bothered. He knew he held the cards when it came down to it.

'Anyway, what about this?' said Melissa, waving a computer printout. 'They're looking for staff for the Beautiful Homes Show in London – hosts (welcomers they call them), waiting staff, front and back of house. Real money.'

Tommy felt like he had won a trick without even playing. Melissa had done this for him. She knew that he was sleeping on Josh's floor for almost entirely financial reasons. True, Josh and he were mates but styles were being cramped in a big way. It wasn't Josh's socks, it wasn't even his farts, it was his permanent presence. Yes, the smell was ripe but Josh hung around like a bad smell himself. Tommy hadn't realised how little a life Josh Finkelstein had without him. Tommy had been forced to scuttle off to the library for some me-time which, while it hadn't done his grades any harm, wasn't really what life was all about.

'Shall we apply then?' said Tommy.

Melissa was a practical girl with a great arse, so why couldn't he just sort it out with her? Was it simply that he wanted to play the field a bit first? Was he really that shallow? (Given that this speculation was essentially about whether Melissa was a possible life-partner and that he'd already conceded that the second most admirable quality in said putative partner was the exquisite roundness of her backside, he had to admit that he probably was.)

'Pretty much done,' said Melissa. 'All I need are the national insurance numbers of those interested. Piers's uncle – well, some relative anyway – is event manager. I provide the names and unless you turn up in your sweaty socks or your onesie – mentioning no names, Joshua and Philippa – we're in.'

She looked round the table, leaning forward to give each of her friends a high five. Tommy clapped her raised palm warmly. The phrase 'well, some relative anyway' said everything to Tommy about just how important Piers was to Melissa. Not so much.

'Happy as a pig in shit, Mel,' he said. Yes, he was about as shallow as an upturned paddling pool.

'I think you mean blessed,' said Tanisha. But she was beaming too. True they had a combined student debt in six figures, but it was a start.

# 2.9.

Chris stepped out of the police station and began to head for the hotel. Then he changed his mind and walked towards the front. Shit, merde and shit and merde in every other language under the sun. He walked briskly because he knew that Gary Shad would, odds on, be striding out of the very same door within the next five minutes and there was nothing worse than a smug con. A local uniform-carrier had been mooting a Section 18 authorisation but Chris couldn't see it. He wasn't much fussed anyway. Point was that, whatever Mr Shad may or may not have done in Biscuit Town, he had not – Chris kicked a stone that had somehow wandered off the beach and up the high street – been anywhere near the smoke on the night that Jack Sender died. Cast-iron alibi. Tenants meeting in his block of flats, half a dozen witnesses. It really was a fucker. The collar might not have put everything right but it would have gone a long way.

The stone Chris had kicked ricocheted off the wall beneath a shop window and bounced in front of a little kid on a tricycle. His dad, or perhaps some child molester, was walking behind him, steering the blue and yellow contraption with a handle attached to the seat.

'Careful,' said the bloke.

Chris considered clocking him, considered booking him on some spurious pretext, considered a whole host of pointless and petty responses in a nanosecond of pure and puerile brain energy. Neurones lashing out. The red mist. Instead, he took a deep intake of breath and raised his hand in an apologetic gesture.

He coughed and tried to look like a human being, rather than a deranged lunatic. It was early. Actually, it was a bit too early for, in the normal course of things, a dad to be taking a kid out on his bike. He spun round just as mum, or an accomplice armed with a picnic basket, emerged from the coffee shop and handed the kid a pink confection in a clear plastic cup. Big bent straw. Chris coughed again and walked normally. Of course, they're up early, Caton. They're on bloody holiday. You might have figured that out if you ever took one. Coffee was quite a good idea. He could see a place down by the prom with seats outside. It was funny how all seaside towns felt the same, perhaps that was part of their attraction. All designed with reference to the sea so you instinctively knew where the pier would be, or the amusement park with the big dipper. But, if he wanted this little South Coast sojourn to continue, he needed to move fast.

He had to figure out what to do before Corrigan summoned him back to London. He needed to get Gabby away too. She'd chatted to the pushchair exercise class, signed all sorts of crap for them and appealed to them to keep quiet but it could only be a matter of time before someone squealed. 'You'll never guess who I saw in the park yesterday...'

Corrigan had been happy to delay Gabby coming into the station. He didn't want a scrum of fashion photographers around Scotland Yard. But that couldn't last. Chris wondered if he could get hold of a laptop or something and type up Gabby's statement. That might satisfy the DCI for a little longer.

Perhaps they could go to Chris's mum's. She lived in a tiny village on the South Downs, not that far away really. Chris owed her a visit and she had an iPad (which Chris had bought for her and on which a report could be typed) and she and Gabby could speak French...

Chris wasn't really a coffee man. He was hyper enough already. A steady stream of thick muddy tea was his drug of choice. But occasionally, in the early morning, he liked the hit of a good strong coffee: three sips, three darts through the roof of the mouth and straight into the brain, no messing. One hundred and eighty. He kept his calm while negotiating the ridiculously intricate menu – three sizes of cup, four sizes of cardboard beaker, ten sorts of syrup, twenty sorts of milk, umpteen million sorts of coffee.

'Double expresso,' he hissed between gritted teeth. The place smelt not of coffee but of disinfectant and the sweetest sugary cake. The machine snorted steam. The staff, all young girls, all stick insects or beach balls, wore tight black T-shirts with a company logo on one tit and a name badge on the other. Tiffany – behind the counter. Melody – half-heartedly wiping a table-top. Boomers, the Happy Cuppa Coffee Company. A blackboard behind Tiffany's incomprehensibly complicated hairstyle listed a hundred and one varieties of muffin and concluded with some platitudinous bollocks about having 'a booming luvverly day'. Everything was styled in that almost-black-but-not-quite colour they called 'taupe'. Mole. Everything was mole-coloured – the colour of half-blind, worm-eating vermin that had destroyed his mum's garden.

'Size up to a Big Boomer, Sir?' asked Tiffany.

'What?'

She had to repeat it three times before he got it.

'What's a Big,' deep breath, 'Boomer?'

The girl pointed a nibbled nail at a cardboard cup the size of a bucket.

'That's a litre, isn't it?'

'Thirty-one ounces, Sir.'

'What are you talking about, you dozy tart, we have the fucking metric system in Europe,' said the voice in his head.

'No, thanks,' said the voice in his rictus-grinning mouth.

The head voice continued: 'which part of "a double expresso" don't you understand? A double. Not a triple. Not a quadruple. Not a fucking duodecadruple. Thirty-one ounces of expresso? I'd be on the fucking ceiling for a week and a half...'

'Shut up,' said a second head voice.

Chris emerged from the coffee shop with his coffee and three mini-muffins in a bag. (Because of some special promotional offer related to the time of day or the alignment of the planets or some such crap, three small muffins were cheaper than one big one.) He had taken the last two blueberry ones – weren't blueberries supposed to be a superfood? – and a third featuring some sickly, gooey white-chocolate shite. Nearly walked through a plate glass window. Not super at all. Only a day-glo sticker reading 'Booming Brilliant' saved his skin. By the time he sat down, his hand was shaking. The external seating area was a slice of street fenced off with fabric panels. Again the corporate colours. Again the corporate slogan. Booming bollocks. Deep breath. A bit of swearing under the breath. A big mouthful of cake-like mush. Yes, he kept his calm.

The Kremlin had sent him some photos from the crime scene but he hadn't really looked at them, so impatient had he been to get after

Shad. That was Chris all over: running like Usain Bolt up the first alley the investigation presented and not stopping even when it turned out to be a dead end.

He fired up his phone. Another missed call and a text message from the guv. The plan was to tell Corrigan he'd left his phone somewhere. Quite where, he wasn't sure. Wouldn't matter if he had the collar. But he didn't. He needed something to offer the guv, something the blokes in London hadn't got.

He scrolled through the pix from SOCO. Jack Sender had been bludgeoned to death in the nightclub toilet. Not pretty. There were photos of the body from different angles. A couple of snaps probably taken standing on a bog seat. A pile of bloodied hand towels with which perhaps someone had tried to save him. But the back of his head looked like someone had taken a bite out of it. A whole series of these. Chris's thumb did the screen jig as he scrolled through. Then there were several of the, what? The wall? No, the bathroom mirror. You could see the photographer in different positions, trying to keep himself out of the picture but a picture of what? Blood trickling down. At least that's what it looked like.

Chris stopped and zoomed with his fingers. He wasn't skilled at this. Too fiddly. It wasn't blood. It was a close-up of a word. Was it? No, it was a number. Scrawled on the bathroom mirror, in what looked like lipstick. Why hadn't he taken the time to look at this before? Corrigan hadn't said anything about it, but perhaps he hadn't seen it himself or, well, Chris wasn't actually on the investigation, was he, so why would Corrigan say anything? Chris's fingers were sticky with cake but he managed to zoom in on the number.

It appeared to be 3.4 B 1.8 M.

Although those two full-stops could just have been marks on the mirror, his hunch was that they were deliberate: they were both in the same place vis-a-vis the adjacent numbers. You might find a phone number scrawled on a mirror, or graffiti even, but not something like this. It was hard to believe that it wasn't in some way connected with the death. Some sort of code? A type of IP address? A password maybe? Websites always forced you to have such complicated passwords these days. A capital, a number, a punctuation mark... He sipped some coffee. He ate some cake.

Melody had come out and was ineffectually wiping tables and collecting cups. Why didn't she bring a tray?

He looked up and down the increasingly busy street. Was he looking for Gabby? Was that why he had bought three muffins? Somehow he couldn't see Gabby eating the greasy full English served at the hotel. A tiny queue had formed at the cashpoint opposite and Chris realised that he was short of money himself.

Gabby stepped out of the shower. It had offered two temperatures, hot and very hot, and now the phone box size en-suite was full of steam. She'd been in less steamy steam rooms. She wrote her name in the condensation on the bathroom mirror a couple of times before finding a switch for the extractor fan.

She was absolutely determined to make it down to breakfast. She was going to eat something. OK, not a full English. Not even a little Continental probably. But definitely something. Sure and certain. The shower wasn't big but it was warm and the towel, while it wasn't the thick, voluminous offering favoured by the fancier chains, was soft. Gabby was deciding that she quite liked provincial English hotels. The TV wasn't big – or even flat-screen – but it was working and what caught her eye, as she towelled herself down, was a map of France on the screen. She picked up the remote control from the bed and turned the volume up.

They were zooming in on the map. Then the face of someone she knew. She stopped in her tracks, wet footprints on the carpet. Well, Jack had known him and, as a result, she sold his coffee in her cake shop in New England. Or at least she thought she did. Perhaps she used to. Zak Thomas Brown, founder of one of the big coffee chains. He had been summer-skiing on a glacier in France, a spot Gabby knew well. There was a funicular train to the slopes. He had been found dead on the piste. Real name, according to the newsreader, not Zak or Zachary but Brian. The newsreader looked like she was struggling to keep a straight face. Gabby laughed, concluded that death was undignified and then went and vomited in the bathroom.

Her eyes watered and her head screamed. She had nothing really to vomit. She was chucking herself up. Suddenly, she was reliving the moment when she'd heard about Jack and finally, this time, reacting. She was hot and then she was very, very cold. Chicken flesh.

This hotel was a hole. She was a widow. This town was a hole. She was alone. What was she doing? What the fuck was going on? She spat a mouthful of sticky phlegm into the bowl and pulled on the first clothes she could find. Had to get out. Had to. She hesitated at the door of her room. This wasn't her. She stepped back inside to fire a toothbrush around her mouth but still she didn't bother with make-up and didn't look in the mirror. Handbag. She ran down the stairs (the lift was hopeless anyway and smelled of butterscotch) and was out of the door and catching her breath on the pavement before she realised she was looking for Chris.

She looked back up at the front of the hotel. Perhaps he was still in his room. She hauled her phone from her bag, like a mother pulling a child from quicksand. A couple of texts including one from Chris:
@ the police station

'Police station,' she mumbled to a bewildered passer-by who shook her off like a crumb.

Back into the hotel she went. The teenager on reception directed her.

Down to the front, turn left. A few half-steps, the street dance of someone who doesn't know where they're going.

Then she saw him queuing for money. Chris. She'd recognise that wretched jacket anywhere. She almost ran up to him.

'You OK?' he asked, 'you look...' He said 'flustered' but he meant fantastic. The lack of make-up. Not the time, Chris. Enter your pin.

As Chris tapped away at the cashpoint, Gabby showed him her phone. A picture of Zak Thomas Brown.

'He's dead,' she said.

Chris didn't recognise him. 'A friend of yours? I'm sorry.'

She grabbed inexpertly at Chris's hand, her palm greasy with stress. 'He was, he was, he just...'

Gabby looked away, looked up, swallowed a lungful of salty seaside air and, as she did, she caught sight of the coffee shop opposite. Her legs buckled beneath her as she collapsed backwards as if shot.

Boom. Right into Chris's arms, his hands splaying automatically to catch her and, in so doing, a hundred pounds in crisp, clean notes hopped and skipped off down the street on the breeze.

'Hey,' shouted Chris but Gabby was out. 'It's OK,' he said to passers-by. 'It's OK.' A mum despatched herself and a child on note-retrieving duties.

'Ooh, I say,' said the mother, suspecting drink.

Chris eased Gabby into a seated position against the wall. Light as a feather. He picked up her phone. It wasn't broken. Who was that guy? Did he recognise him? Was he another celebrity?

He scrolled down and Gabby had been reading a news story on a French gossip site. Chris read and, as he read, he too had the urge to take the weight off his feet before the shock of what he was taking in did it for him. He slid down the wall into a seated position beside Gabby. Zak Thomas Brown, the king of coffee, the inventor of the Big Boomer, was dead. The official line on the cause was that it was too early to say but a local blogger was reporting blood on the snow. Snow? Apparently there was writing in blood on the snow and then, Chris clicked, the Instagram: a series of numbers and letters in dripping, jagged scarlet. It was a photograph taken at distance. Was it really blood? The crime scene had been cordoned off. It certainly looked like some form of writing and in the same format as that on the mirror near Sender. He could see the M clearly. The photographer had noted the sequence anyway and the blog post included them: 3.1 B 8.6 M.

How irresponsible was that?

But it could give him the lead he needed for the guv.

'It might mean a million things,' Chris said to himself as he finally exhaled.

'Give the man the money, darling,' said the mum from behind the parapet of a bright red cagoule, and a timid child with a missing front tooth presented Chris with his set of tenners.

'Thank you,' said Chris, automatically looking at the notes. Instinctively counting. A prile of queens.

'Of course,' he said. 'Millions, billions. It's fucking money.'

There was a sharp intake of breath as the mother pulled her son away.

'Sorry,' said Chris.

'Some people...never...' Mum was away in big walking-boot strides, the little kid trailing behind, feet scurrying as if on a moving carpet.

'Gabby?' Chris realised, looking down at her, just how skinny she was. 'Have you eaten anything?'

Gabby wrested open her eyes. How the hell did he know? Bloody policemen. She wiped her eyes, remembered she wasn't made up and the feeling of nausea returned. Chris was pecking away at her telephone with his index finger.

'What are you doing?'

'I'm googling some figures,' he said. 'Pounds. Maybe euros.' He paused. 'Shit.'

'What's the matter,' she pulled herself up the wall so their heads were at the same height.

'Did you faint, Gabby?'

Chris handed her a muffin and she was eating it before she realised what she was doing. 'You need some sugar,' he said.

'What are you doing?'

'I'm googling these sequences, the figures, the ones found near the bodies, as billions and millions. Obviously numbers are all over the internet but I thought if I googled both pairs together... doesn't seem to work...'

'Hold on,' said Gabby. The sugar rush was heavenly. 'So there was writing by Jack's body too?'

'On the bathroom mirror, apparently.'

'Why didn't you tell me?'

'I didn't know until about five minutes ago.'

'Show me.' The blueberry on her tongue was like an injection.

Chris showed her the numbers he had been typing in. 'These two. 3.4 B 1.8 M – I'm trying 3.4 billion and 1.8 million.'

Gabby sat up and finished the muffin. 'They're familiar. Weren't Stufff's total sales £3.4 billion?' she said. 'What if you put all four numbers in?'

'Nothing.'

'And 3.1 B 8.6 M is the sequence from the French blogger?' she asked pointing at the screen with an elegant but unpainted nail.

Chris nodded. 'Come on, let's get you back to the hotel.'

Gabby allowed herself to be manoeuvred to her feet. She was feeling a little better. Having something to think about had helped. Actually, no – having something to eat had helped. Chris's hand was supporting her arm beneath her elbow, propelling her up the hill much as, in days of yore, the dedicated butler might have helped the aged maiden aunt into her bath chair. 'I think I need to get out of this town,' Gabby said.

Chris too was aware of the absurdity of the way he was handling Gabby – as if she were precious porcelain. He wanted to put his arm round her waist or her arm through his but, given that neither of those were going to happen, he instead gently let her go and allowed her to walk at her own pace.

'I've got just the place,' he said. No point thinking about it any more. It was going to happen. He was going to visit his mother.

Tiffany turned on the TV and for a moment she thought it was totally broken again. The shop logo was supersize on the screen. Boomers, the Happy Cuppa Coffee Company. Then they said that Zak Thomas Brown had been literally murdered. WTF. And she screamed a little.

'Melody!' she shouted. 'Melody!'

# 2.10.

Gabby wondered why she trusted Chris. Was the balance of her mind disturbed? That was the phrase, wasn't it? What had happened to Jack and now Zak certainly ought to have unbalanced her mind. But she felt quite the opposite of unbalanced. She felt centred.

She'd been panicking when she'd seen the Zak Thomas Brown news. She'd seen Chris and now she was relaxed again. How did you explain it? Was it the way he really owned that neglected scarecrow look? She tossed her few possessions into her bag, enjoying having so few. Feeling light.

Was it that they had something in common? Gabby stopped in mid-toss. That was a police tactic, wasn't it? She'd read enough thrillers, enough romans policiers to know that. Had he just played her with all that stuff in the car? She sat on the edge of the bed. After all, didn't he invent a wife in order to get closer to her? And she'd thought that she had been playing him. She'd been using – or thought she'd been using – a ploy she'd learned as a teenager: if you want a straight answer from a man, ask him while he's driving. But thinking back, it was him who had started the 'cards on the table' conversation.

They'd been in the car, on the way down to Biscuit Town. He'd got her talking – he called it an initial statement or something like that – and it was the usual line of questioning that she was familiar with from her diet of detective novels: alibi, last known movements, state of mind and marriage, 'tell me more about Jack', that sort of thing. He'd said he'd write it up and she'd need to sign it, but it had been very informal. He hadn't taken notes as he'd been driving. Very unorthodox, she could see in hindsight. Then he had ventured tentatively: 'I may know a little bit of how you're feeling.'

Gabby had doubted that. Since she didn't know how she was feeling, she had found it hard to believe that anyone else could have the faintest. She didn't say anything. She'd answered his questions but didn't fancy a chat or sympathy. They were on the M25. She continued simply to sit as she'd sat in so many taxis and cabs so often before. She was going with the flow.

'My father was murdered when I was a kid.' Chris put his foot down and accelerated past a couple of lorries.

She had not been expecting that.

'I'm sorry,' said Gabby eventually.

There was a pause as they turned off the motorway. The sky overhead, which had been three shades of grey, began to clear as they headed south. What was that about the road not taken or the road less travelled? A rusty old roadside sign that looked like something out of black and white television loomed up. The pole on which it was mounted was bent and the sign looked like it was bowing, welcoming you to the A294, a road Gabby had never even noticed before, for all those journeys around the M25. 'What happened?' she asked.

His father had been gunned down on the family's doorstep when Chris was four or five. He said he had a few fragments of memory of his father although how many were real and how many were the result of conversations with others, it was hard for him to say. The strongest memory was one of a sweetshop. His father buying him a bar of chocolate, a real treat. His mother probably not there. He couldn't remember anyway. It was the tiniest thing. The bar of chocolate looking enormous sitting in his hand and the smell, an indescribable smell that he would just occasionally get a hint of somewhere else – sweet, chocolatey, a little pinch of ready-rubbed tobacco and yet fishy. Perhaps, Chris had said, there'd been a fishmonger's or a chip shop next door. He'd never quite smelt the whole smell again – bits of it: the sweetness, the tobacco or the salty, seasidey fishiness – but never all together. There'd been another pause.

Surely, you couldn't make that up, Gabby thought. (Again, Gabrielle, are those novels you read not evidence that human beings can make anything up?)

'And your dad?' Gabby had prompted.

'Mistaken identity,' Chris had said. 'We lived in Brighton, in North Road. There was a drug dealer who'd upset someone at the same number North Gardens. Gardens-road. Road-gardens. Thought they were killing him, they killed my dad.'

'I'm so sorry, Chris.' Two pairs of eyes trained on the middle white line. 'What did he do, your dad?'

'Train driver. London to Brighton.'

'Were you there? When he was, you know.'

'No, round a friend's.'

'How do you tell a kid his dad has been shot?'

'You don't. For years, I thought he'd upped and left and never got in touch. Mum didn't tell me the truth until I was a teenager and by then the damage had been done.'

'What do you mean?'

'As a kid, Mum kept telling me that my father loved me but if so, where was he? That's what I kept asking myself. Made no sense. I became a nutter. I was a nutter. Expelled from a couple of schools. Always fighting.'

'You think she should have told you at the time?'

'I don't know. As you say, how do you tell a kid at nursery school his dad has been shot on the front doorstep?'

Chris punched through the gears. 'I don't know what he was thinking when he answered the door, but I always imagine that he thought he was letting me in.' Chris had slowed down for a roundabout, hands gripped white on the wheel. 'And I don't know if that makes me feel better or worse. I've never been able to think about it rationally. That place in my head. It's still like a burning room.'

There was nobody else on the road and Chris put his foot down. A bird of prey exploded from a gate post and overtook them as if they were going backwards. Gabby watched as it pulled away effortlessly. She wondered what it was.

'After he was killed, we moved to London. That's where I went to school. We had enough money. Mum earned OK money. She was a bookkeeper. I suppose she chose the job because it meant she could work from home. But it isn't really about money, is it? She was always there when I came back from school but it wasn't her I was hoping to find. Caught the train down to Brighton by myself when I was about eight or nine to look for him. It was me threatening to do something similar when I was a teenager... well, that's when she told me.'

'How was your mum when you were a kid?'

'Looking back, totally depressed. I can see that now. She never went out. I don't know why she didn't move back to France.'

'Why didn't she?'

'She says she didn't want to disrupt things for me...' He left it hanging.

'But...?'

'Well, at five, you can forget. I sometimes wonder, if we'd moved to France and I'd had a whole new country, whole new culture, new mother tongue...'

'You'd be running the CRS by now, they're all nutters.' Gabby stopped herself. 'Sorry.'

'No, it's fine. I feel better for having told you. I haven't told many...' Chris stared straight ahead at the road, hands still tight round the steering wheel. In truth, he didn't look a lot better.

'It was a genuine love story, my parents ... and that's something I suppose.'

Gabby had the sense that this final remark was as much for his own benefit as for hers and that he'd been trying to convince himself of it, the smallest of consolations, for some time. Apart from his hands which were holding onto the steering wheel for dear life, he looked fine – fierce but fine. A stiff upper lip that ran all the way down his arms to his tight, rigid fingers.

'Driving down this road somehow, it feels like yesterday.'

Gabby knew what he meant by that. She felt like they were driving back in time. That Jack was far away and long ago – a different dimension, even.

'Here we are,' Chris had said in a steady voice. 'Biscuit Town.'

And here they were. Gabby was checking through her purse. She owed Chris for the room. She had a wedge of euros from the Antilles but not a lot of sterling.

She rooted through a few old receipts. Was it really less than a week since she and Jack had been in that restaurant in Gustavia and Jack had dropped lobster spaghetti in his lap and she'd said it would teach him to go out in his swimming trunks? She remembered the waiter: in such a flap, so apologetic, as if he'd chucked the plate of spaghetti over Jack himself. She remembered too how Jack used to tease her for her habit of saving receipts. 'You're not a student, you know,' he'd say. She saw now, reading the receipt, that the restaurant hadn't charged for the spaghetti either. Gabby had always found that odd. The way the richer you got, the less you were expected to pay. She'd never liked it.

She took the euro notes out, straightened them, put them all the same way round and folded them back into her purse. And then the centime dropped.

# 2.11.

Chris was looking at himself in the mirror, trying to remember the last time he had wet-shaved. He assumed that he was doing it for his mother's benefit although it could conceivably have been for Gabby's. She'd certainly got under his skin. She was like a tranquilizer, murders or no murders.

Coming back from the cashpoint, Gabby had, much to his surprise, taken his arm as they went to cross the road. She had accepted his physical support as if they'd known each other for years, childhood friends (not that he had any of those). He'd helped her across the road and back up the hotel steps. They had passed an older couple descending in the opposite direction. The old man had been holding the old woman's arm in much the same way as Chris had been holding Gabby's. They looked happy enough on it, the woman whispering into the man's big old ears and he smiling with eyes that hadn't aged.

When Chris returned from reception where he'd been organising their checking-out, Gabby had been beaming like a child with a birthday cake.

'Thanks for the muffin,' she'd said.

'I've got another one if you like,' Chris had said.

'Save it for later,' she'd said.

He didn't want to eat the muffin, he wanted to eat her. The exchange, brief as it had been, managed to remind him both that he didn't have a relationship and that he didn't have any kids at the same time. And yet somehow it didn't make him feel particularly sad either. It was bitter-sweet and he couldn't help but smile. Perhaps they would be friends.

The face in the mirror was always about two or three incarnations ahead of the picture inside your head. There was a little more grey at the temple and, around the eyes, if not exactly crow's feet, then certainly crow's toes. Was his nose getting bigger? It was certainly getting hairier. And he needed some new clothes. Desperately. Looking in the mirror really was a mug's game. He pulled the razor across his cheek. The stubble seemed to be working its way up the face. And were his cheeks getting hollower? Short strokes around the bony bit of chin, a tricky area. He wondered what the old couple thought of them, him and Gabby, as their paths crossed.

The remaining mini-muffin complete with mini-napkin in its branded mini-bag was sitting there now, on the ledge shelf beneath his mirror over the sink.

Suddenly, his bedroom door flew open and Gabby was there, waving money at him.

Chris, face half-covered in shaving foam, felt oddly vulnerable. When was the last time anyone had seen him shave?

'I told you. It's official police business,' Chris said. 'I've paid for the rooms.'

'It's not that,' said Gabby. She took a deep breath.

'Is everything OK?' Chris asked. 'Don't worry, I haven't eaten the last muffin.'

'But what if those numbers were written by a Brit?' she said.

'What numbers?'

'By Zak Thomas Brown's body. On the ski slope.'

'What difference would that make?'

'A Brit wouldn't cross the seven and a Frog would read an uncrossed seven as a one.'

'Meaning?'

'Meaning instead of 3.1, try 3.7.'

Chris felt his hand threatening to shake and so concentrated on smooth strokes across the skin. 'Hmm,' he said, eventually.

'Well?' Gabby looked around for his phone to google on but she couldn't see it. Chris was dragging his feet. Why was he dragging his feet? He knew she was wrong? Feared she was right?

As Chris worked the razor, she spotted the muffin on the shelf and did something she hadn't done since she was a child. She unwrapped it and, after neatly folding and setting down the napkin, began working not on the cake but on the wrapper in which it had come: slurp-sucking it, licking the crumbs from the corrugations and then chewing on the paper until all the sweetness was gone and there remained nothing but a soggy blob.

'All done,' said Chris, rinsing his razor under a reluctant tap.

They exchanged glances. 'Well?' Gabby repeated. Chris was towelling himself.

The policeman's jacket was hanging up on the back of the door. He reached inside and slowly pulled out his phone.

Gabby watched. Chris was slow and precise. 'Well?' she said, for a third time. 'Any luck?'

'One site,' said Chris.

Gabby nodded – she really was feeling light and unencumbered – and they exchanged glances again. Gabby raised her hand, moving the as-yet-unbitten muffin in the direction of Chris's mouth. He opened wide and she popped it in. It had all happened in a second.

'Bingo,' she said.

## 2.12.

Cherrianne Dixon looked out of the office window at the crowd opposite. Ever since the death of coffee king Zak had started trending a couple of hours earlier, business at the Brighton Boomer's over the road had been, well, booming. What exactly they were trying to prove, these hipsters and hangers-on, she didn't know. Obviously there was a certain human sympathy but he had died on a ski slope and skiing in the summer sounded just about as decadent as it could get to Cherrianne. A man in his 50s on his own, on a glacier, in the early morning, with no helmet. Probably hit his head on a rock. Needless risk-taking. Wasn't that the alpha male all over?

The traffic crawled by, slowed by the crowds and their own curiosity. One vehicle was billowing smoke from its exhaust. Had it broken down? Cherri didn't like that at all. She sat back down in front of her screen and pulled her Beats by Dr Dre cans down over her ears, careful so as not to rough up her Marley twists. (Man come and man go but hair matter, as her big Jamaican Auntie Rita used to say.) She wondered, not for the first time, where Dan was. Probably out on his scooter. Or fishing. Not with them damn fools opposite, that's for sure. But she needed Dan because they were so busy it was sick. The website they'd set up together, corporatesponger.co.uk, was beginning to generate traffic. First the Stufff page after Jack Sender and now the Boomer's page after Zak Thomas Brown. It wasn't the way she hoped to change the world but, as Dan had put it, whatever works.

She wanted him back. If he wasn't on his scooter, he was probably in Gap. Boy lived in that damn shop. She wasn't dissing Gap. Not their clothes anyway. She'd bought this very T-shirt from the Boys' department there, thank you very much. She just preferred Peter Robb's. But it was all still consumerism, wasn't it? Shouldn't turn it into a fetish. But Dan did sometimes. Fetishise consumption. She worried about him. Way he cared for that scooter. Polishing the chrome. It was old school tool. Like a Mod scooter from the 1960s. Cool. Very cool. But just a bit of branded crap was all.

She had been fleshing out various sections of the company profiles on the website: tax affairs, labour relations, environmental record. Cherri thought it important to stress the environmental impact and not just the money. There was plenty of money but there was only one planet. And anyway, if you needed money, you could always print more of it. Quantitative easing, they called it. It sounded like a euphemism for taking a dump. She giggled. Get serious, girl.

There'd been a call she needed to discuss with Dan. He knew the journalist and she didn't. Posh boy called Blair Henry which was jokes because it sounded like his name was the wrong way round. She had googled him. Quite fit for a public schoolboy type. He was a financial journalist on one of the big old papers. Bare dry most of it but he'd quoted Dan in one of his pieces once. Dan had told Cherri a bit about Blair, called him an egomani-hack, which apparently meant that he was a journalist more interested in himself than in the story. Always looking for something that would make his name.

'Like what?' Cherri had asked.

'Well, Robert Peston, a financial journalist everyone has heard of.'

'How's he going to do that writing about interest rates?'

'Well, he wants to be like that dude from Goldman Sachs who coined the acronym Bric for the developing countries – Brazil,

Russia, India and China – in the noughties. He wants to do something like that,' Dan said. 'Trouble is everybody thinks he's a Chad, Ukraine, Nigeria, Turkey.'

Cherri had giggled at that too. She had given Dan a dressing down for blates sexism but she found it funny. She liked her cunt and didn't see why she shouldn't like the various words for it. Gays had reclaimed queer, why couldn't women reclaim cunt? Anyway, Blair Henry aka Henry Blair wanted Dan to call him back. As she pondered what to do, Cherri took a sip of skinny, tall Chai latte, purchased from Brewed Awakening, the independent coffee shop on the corner, three down from Boomer's. She took her cans off to concentrate. (Adele was old school too really but, man, that girl could sing. And Cherri respected her low profile. She weren't no slave to social media, Adele.) Then she took a sip of mango, pineapple and acai berry smoothie from Juice Willis and pondered some more. Finally, she took a big handful of Haribos from the bowl on her desk, picked out the egg-shaped ones and ate three of them. She could have eaten a thousand and not put on an ounce. She looked like a little boy. No boobs. No butt. The metabolism of an army of ants. Whatever works, muttered Cherri to herself, as she dived into Google.

Blair's newspaper's offices were in east London.

She went into the back-end of corporatesponger and found some on-site searches from that part of the city in the three-hour window before Blair had called. She whittled them down. Discounting the pornographic ones, a couple on Dan's name, one looking for a London Underground map, another hoping to buy sponges...

Was this it?

Someone in Blair's location had been looking at the company income and tax paid by Boomer's and then – this was very interesting – by Stufff – clicking back and forth between the one and the other. (On corporatesponger, they used a standard layout for tax stuff showing three figures: a company's income, estimated or reported, over whatever period; what they'd paid in tax; and what they should have paid if they'd paid corporation tax on the full amount.) These figures were, in Dan's words, 'set out in full so people could see how truly astronomical they were'. This meant the data sets often said, for example, 3,700,000,000 rather than 3.7 billion.

The figures did, as Dan intended, look astronomical but that did not mean they were easy to understand. In Cherri's opinion, these figures had the opposite effect from that intended, and had told Dan so. When billions looked much like millions, just strings of noughts, it was difficult to get a perspective on them. Six noughts? Nine noughts? These were numbers outside of people's perceptions, sums of money they'd never have in a hundred lifetimes. That's why it was easier for folk to get worked up about £50 of benefit fraud than about £50 million of tax fraud.

For Blair to be looking at the two companies which had lost their CEOs in unusual circumstances was too tidy to be a coincidence. But what did it mean? That the deaths were linked? Or at least that Blair thought they were.

What's more, and this was even more intriguing really, Blair wasn't the only person who had been searching on those two companies. Someone else had got there first. And this other user had entered the site via a search purely on the numbers – the amount of income and the amount of tax. In fact, it was his search on all four numbers (the income and tax paid by Stufff plus the income and tax paid by Boomer's) that had brought this other user to corporatesponger. Very precise. Straight to the site's 'Top 50 Spongers' page. Since 2000, Boomer's had made sales of, what, £3.7 billion pounds and paid just 8.6 million in corporation tax. For Stufff, corporatesponger had more detail. In the most recent year for which figures were available, Stufff had had a total income of £3.4 billion and paid just £1.8 million in tax on it. Very, very precise, given that these numbers did not cover the same financial period. How could anyone have happened upon them? No way was it an accident. Cherri became aware of her own heartbeat. This was like an exciting box-set. She felt like a detective.

Odd, and less precise, was that the same user had been searching for 3,100,000,000 as well as 3,700,000,000. Now Cherri was confused. This searcher had been on a mobile device so she had no idea where he, she or it was based. Seven? One? What did it mean?

She sat back and had another handful of Haribos. And, as she did, her blood ran cold. Did the extra number mean a third company involved somewhere? And did that mean a third death? Her blood ran colder still as she clicked back to the corporatesponger home page and saw that the figures in question for the periods in question for the companies in question were the very ones that corporatesponger used themselves to highlight the tax evasion problem. They were what Dan called their 'headline numbers'. OMG. Her hand, she noticed, was shaking a little over the keyboard. She had to tell Dan before he called Blair back and, just as she was thinking of him, the door opened behind her.

'Talk of the devil.'

The door slammed with a clunk. It was the heaviest door in the world anyway. Their trendy offices were refurbished like a factory with exposed brick and concrete and doors seemingly designed to stop a small explosion. Or one of Dan's farts. Dan would know what was going on.

'Put your hands on the table-top and don't move,' said a voice.

## 2.13.

Gabby let her eyes follow a wisp of cirrus cloud as it wafted, one of half a dozen zig-zags of chalky scribble, across an otherwise near cloudless sky. She wriggled a little, getting comfortable in an old-fashioned wooden deck chair. For all that had happened, quite how Chris had persuaded her to come to his mother's, she wasn't sure.

'Are we at the "meeting the parents" stage?' she had teased him and his cheeks had reddened.

'It'll be all over the internet that you're in Biscuit Town. One of those girls will squeal.'

She doubted that. In fact Jack seemed to have been forgotten, let alone her. The internet was now raging with outrage that Zak Thomas Brown's real name was Brian.

'I feel so cheated', whined one punter, #neverdrinkingboomersagain

Gabby welcomed the respite from it all, closed her eyes and enjoyed the feel of the sun on her cheeks. She listened to the birdsong and wondered which species they were. Her nose picked up the smell of La France Profonde by her right elbow. The mother seemed fine, so English in her cottage and country garden, and yet so French at the same time, serving Ricoré from an ancient tin drum but in a large bone china floral-patterned cup. Gabby found it amusing the way she spoke to her son and how the big tough, grumpy policeman suddenly seemed about five and a half years old.

'So here you are, n'est-ce pas? Nine months, one week and three days since Cri-Cri last visited his Maman.'

'Sorry, Mum, work, you know.'

'And it is only ze work that brings you 'ere now.'

Chris had explained about the suspect in Biscuit Town. Mrs Caton had expressed her enormous reservations about the place. 'C'est le bordel,' was perhaps her nicest remark.

'Well, it didn't work out,' said Chris. 'A mistake. Une fausse piste, Maman.'

Mrs Caton had seemed satisfied with that. 'And zis is your young lady, n'est-ce pas?'

Gabby had taken that one and played it straight back down the line, reassuring the diminutive but domineering figure in French. 'No, we're just friends, Madame Caton. But Christopher thought you'd like to speak French. I'm from Marseille.'

Even in low heels, Gabby towered over Mrs Caton, an odd and rare experience for her. She'd always been the shortest on the catwalk.

'Oh la la,' Mrs Caton had squealed. 'That is very good of you, Mademoiselle, since speaking French with my son is like a trip to a very bad dentist.'

She paused. 'And I have met a few ov zose, I must say. In zis country.'

Gabby was quite able to read the sub-text 'but not in France' without the aid of Chris's raised eyebrows.

'My mother believes all Englishmen have cold hands,' said Chris.

'It is twue, n'est-ce pas?'

Gabby smiled. 'I don't know. I haven't met all Englishmen.'

'Bof,' said Mrs Caton but there was a twinkle in her eye and Gabby thought she'd passed 'l'examen Maman'.

Gabby had been installed on the lush lawn before you could say 'jardin'. Ten minutes later, Chris had emerged from the cottage – a cute brick-built affair with two gable windows, plants climbing up the pipes and fading green volets. On the little lattice metal-topped outdoor table beside her, a French magazine and a magnifying glass.

'Oui, later, Maman,' was the passing shot over his shoulders as he juggled his car keys.

'It ees ze least you can do, non mais?' chimed Mrs Caton.

'If I don't get away, she'll have a lawnmower in my hand,' he had said to Gabby.

Gabby showed him the magnifying glass. 'This from your Sherlock Holmes period?'

'Mum's too vain to wear her glasses.'

'Where are you going?'

'If we've figured this out, then chances are others have too.'

'But nobody else knows there were numbers by Jack's body,' said Gabby. 'And all anyone seems interested in right now is Zak Thomas Brown's real name.'

'That may give us a head start but ...' And those were his last words as he got back in the car again.

Mrs Caton's coffee tasted like her own mother's. She too favoured the chicory and coffee blend – l'ami du petit-déjeuner, breakfast's friend, as the old TV ad had put it. Gabby had wisely allowed Mrs Caton to add a little sugar and a half a teaspoon of fortitude in the form of Nescafé. For medicinal purposes, Gabby had told herself, the restoration of her blood-sugar and energy levels. She had also accepted two Petit Beurre biscuits.

'You will have a big git?' Mrs Caton had said. 'Deux.'

Gabby had not understood and assumed it was the older woman's accent. 'A big git?'

Chris had no doubt noticed her furrowed brow. 'A big git is what I used to call a biscuit as a child,' he said. 'Allegedly. But I think it was more like bigit, wasn't it, Mother?'

'I don't remember any more,' Mrs Caton had sighed (in Parisian French, of course – always the best language for sighing in). Then she had turned to Gabby. 'Had he said it in ze French way, bis-kwi, I would have understood. I would 'ave been 'appy. But he had ze hardest "j" imaginable.'

'Hardest "g",' said Chris, adopting a cod French accent to add: 'I 'ad ze 'ardest "g" imaginable.'

'It was zo anti-French,' Mrs Caton had lamented which had made Gabby smile and now merited a nibble of big git.

Gabby had never accepted the A word in relation to herself. Anorexia was something for little girls and airhead teenagers trying to get into the fashion industry, not for a wise old bird with it all well behind her. But it was, and this she would admit, interesting how her first reaction on hearing of her husband's sudden and brutal death had been to eat even less. That was the mechanism she had turned to to regain control. Of course, it wasn't anorexia. Perhaps the same ball park? The stab of sugar, chicory and caffeine at the back of her throat fenced with her tonsils and tasted like home (although Gabby's mum served Chicorée Leroux rather than Ricoré, she too would often beef it up with a little instant coffee).

Madame Caton was so much smaller than the mental picture Gabby had painted from the information provided by her son but Gabby could see how what she lacked in stature she made up for in spirit. Five minutes inside the house had shown her what a warren it was. Not with rooms so much as books. They seemed to be everywhere. On shelves. On tables. In piles. One particularly tall tower appeared to be holding the ceiling up. 'Turn right at the double-entry ledgers and straight on past the cooked books,' Chris had said when directing her to a dusty spare room locked in La Belle Epoque.

'Cookery books?' Gabby had asked.

'No, cooked,' said Chris. 'I told you my mother used to be an accountant.'

Chris's mum had the almost orange, brushed leather skin of the ancient ladies of Cannes or Antibes. In their cases, their lined complexions were all about too much sun and too little to do. Perhaps it was in Mrs Caton's too, but surely also, to some extent, the result of what had happened to her: widowed young, husband murdered. Was this where Gabby was going? Was she a house guest at her own future?

Gabby looked up as the dressing-gowned mother advanced across the lawn, taking swift tight steps in a pair of flip-flops. She carried a walking stick that she didn't really need and used it instead to poke down actual or imagined inconsistencies or protrusions in the lawn. 'Moles,' she said in French.

When Cherrianne spun round in her office chair, there was a police warrant card in her face and a scruffily-dressed man towering over her.

'Interesting website,' said the policeman. Was he really a policeman? 'You alone?'

'Yes,' said Cherri hesitantly. 'To both.' He was preventing her from getting up. She smiled a little but she wasn't sure what to do, especially when he produced the handcuffs. Was he going to arrest her? She decided not to offer him a Haribo.

'You're the editor, are you?'

'Assistant editor.'

The policeman, alleged policeman, said nothing. Cherrianne could see he was reading her screen. That jacket was clapping. He had to be a genuine plain-clothes policeman in a jacket like that.

'What's this?'

'Search data.' The mobile phone search on the four different numbers was centre screen in big type. The policeman turned towards the screen, less interested in her all of a sudden, and as he moved she could have run out, but why should she? She hadn't done anything wrong and she wasn't the running type. He began fiddling inexpertly with her mouse.

'What exactly is it?' he asked.

'It's the internal search history on our site,' said Cherri. 'This. These four numbers. This is you, isn't it? You searched these numbers from your mobile phone.'

He didn't look round but she heard his voice harden. 'It shows where the searches were made from?'

'You think that Jack Sender and Zak Thomas Brown were both murdered and both by the same man, don't you?'

The policeman looked round sharply. Well vexed.

'Anybody else search on these numbers?'

She scrolled to Blair Henry's search.

'So, is this number in the other column the IP address?'

'Yes,' she said. He wasn't such a drongo then. 'But we can't tell exactly where the computer using that IP is, just the rough area.' There could be a big story here and Blair Henry might be onto it.

'You can't tell,' said the policeman. He had produced a notebook. 'But we can.'

Outside several cars were tooting. Cherri and the policeman looked out of the window to where the Boomer's crowd were beginning to spill into the road. The car Cherri had seen earlier did appear to have broken down and the owner was arguing with other road users. The smell of petrol and exhaust was wafting in through the open vent window.

'Name, son?'

'My name's Cherrianne.'

'Unusual name for a...'

'I'm a girl.'

'I'm a complete idiot, sorry – DS Caton, Metropolitan Police.' He looked up. 'I think the petrol fumes must have gone to my head.'

'Can you shut the window?' said Cherri. 'I can't reach.'

'Either that or my mother's undrinkable coffee.'

# 3:
# 'You Remember That Story About George Best And Miss World…?'

# 3.1.

**Sinister link between corporate killings**
**By Blair Henry**

New evidence suggests that the deaths of corporate bosses Jack Sender and Zak Thomas Brown may be linked to their tax affairs.

To a business world already struggling to come to terms with the loss of two of its biggest players, the news that their deaths may be related to their companies' tax policies and even to each other will come as a seismic aftershock.

Mr Sender, the founder of online store Stufff, was killed in an apparent nightclub mugging gone wrong in London. Mr Thomas Brown, the head of Boomers Coffee, was found on a summer glacier ski slope in south-east France where local police are still saying the most likely cause of death was an accident. Neither the Metropolitan nor the French police are linking the two deaths.

However, according to a local source, a sequence of figures was found painted in the snow not far from Thomas Brown's body. While local police have contested whether they were actually figures at all or just marks in the snow unconnected with the death, our research has found a link between these markings and the dead man. The sequence of figures, according to the local source, was 3.1 B 8.6 M.

We have discovered that 3.1 billion corresponds approximately to the estimated UK sales made by Boomers in the last five years (the official sales figure was actually even higher – £3.7 billion) while 8.6 million corresponds to the amount of corporation tax paid by the company in that period. The £8.6 million paid in tax is less than a quarter of one per cent of the sales figure, yet UK corporation tax, which is paid on profits, stood at 30% for much of the period. Boomers and Thomas Brown have long been criticised for tax avoidance although the company has always denied any wrongdoing.

Local blogger François Lecroix, who took the photo, said: 'the police took care of the body and, by the time they looked at the surrounding area, the snow had begun to melt. It was less obvious that they were letters and numbers, but I am sure they were.'

The question is: any paint on the piste must have been placed there deliberately and for what purpose if not to communicate something? Could these mystery figures explain why Zak Thomas Brown was killed?

There is similar data publicly available for Jack Sender's Stufff group, another global corporation that has been criticised for its tax avoidance strategies. This data, based on figures in the public domain and estimates, is collated by voluntary organisations and websites who monitor corporations' income, expenditure and tax behaviour.

# 3.2.

From behind his desk, Dan watched Cherri as she tapped away at her keyboard. He used to be a heads-down sort of guy, no-nonsense hard work, no short cuts. But, increasingly, he found himself just sitting there. Sometimes he just wanted to get out of the office and go fishing. Was he losing his mojo? Or only in comparison to Cherri?

She punctuated her coding with the occasional barely-audible mumble, followed by a sigh and a handful of Haribos. 'Needs PHP.' 'Where's that link?' 'Have to restyle.' He wondered if she knew just how much she talked to herself while working or whether she was too absorbed to notice.

He admired how good she was at what she did. Better than him. Perhaps not as fast, but she did it with cleaner code, hers were always stylish solutions rather than quick hacks. And to be a girl geek in a man's world and a black geek in a white world couldn't be easy on either count. But mostly he admired her contentment. She was so happy doing what she did. She loved coding, got such a kick out of refreshing the page and seeing the text shift six points to the left or seeing an image with a sexy new caption style. It was infectious. 'Yes!,' she'd say under her breath, the odd fist-pump if it was something really cool. It had kept Dan going in the early days when they had no hits and no money, Cherri's enthusiasm – better than coffee, Modafinil or cocaine. Cheaper too, since Cherri had never really bothered about money. She did corporatesponger.co.uk because she wanted to do it. She believed in it. Sometimes, increasingly, Dan wondered whether he really believed in anything.

When they'd started, he'd been pulling the all-nighters, sleeping in the office most of the time. He still had half of his stuff in the office cupboard and Cherri was still always complaining about the smell. 'It's either the fishing stuff or your socks, I don't know which.' But he never slept in the office any more. And if anyone worked late it was Cherri.

Visitor numbers were significantly up now. Blair Henry had name-checked the site in print and online in the wake of the so-called 'tax man' killings and traffic had gone through the roof. There was increased interest in their subject obviously, increased interest in the idea of corporates paying their fair share. That was good. Increased intellectual interest was not to be sneezed at. But there were also shedloads of rubber-neckers. You could tell that by the comments and emails they left. People who seemed to think that visiting the website that had surely been used by the killer was some sort of dark tourism, a smoking gun, the virtual equivalent of snapping a selfie at Ground Zero. In many ways, this emotional response interested Dan more. If corporatesponger's campaign was to advance, it needed people to get behind it with their hearts, not just their heads. And that applied to Dan Mann as much as to anyone else.

'We need a team meeting,' he announced, sliding his headphones off his shampoo shiny bonce and closing his laptop.

Conrad, the pasty-faced new kid Dan had hired to respond to the site's increased traffic and develop its social media profile, looked up. Conrad had darting eyes that were seldom still other than when focused on his screen. He eased one well-padded headphone can away from his ear. 'What?' Dan was ten yards away but he could still hear the banshee wail of Conrad's thrash metal.

Cherri wasn't listening to anything but the sound of her own fingers on the keys. She had her headphones on her desk. 'He means let's go down the pub,' she said – but she didn't look up or stop typing.

'I can't go down the pub,' said Conrad. 'I work until 5.30pm.'

Asking Conrad to take on social media had been a bit of a mistake really. At the interview, Dan had grilled him only on the technical side and Conrad had given answers that were, while perhaps overlong, always precise, detailed and accurate. Dan had added the social media brief as a bit of an afterthought because he was getting bored doing it himself. But there was a world of difference between code which was black and white and conversation which was anything but. 'You can't ask a geek to be a hack,' Blair Henry had said when Dan had complained to him. The point was that Conrad was probably the most literal man Dan had ever met. If Dan said 'tweet about the shocking new results of X, Y or Z', then Conrad would tweet 'tweet about the shocking new results of X, Y or Z'. Word for word, line for line just as if Dan had told him how to format a new bit of code.

'He's on the spectrum,' Cherri had announced at the end of Conrad's first day. 'And, if you didn't have the social skills of a gnat, you'd have noticed.'

Cherri was, he hoped, half joking. But she was half right too. Dan found it enormously difficult to see the world from someone else's point of view. He found writing a couple of lines of bollocks for the web or Facebook as easy as falling off a log and it never crossed his mind that someone else might not be able to do it.

Dan carried their three drinks in his two hands in a tight triangle.

'Craft beers all round,' he said settling them on the sanded wooden table. The pub looked more like a coffee shop to Cherri and it was quiet since it was still mid-afternoon. A bit brass monkeys too, so Cherri was glad she had her new black and silver T-shirt on. She'd bought it that lunchtime and just put it straight on over everything else. Result, she had about four layers on. But, in this cavernous bank-turned-pub, even that was barely enough. Cold beer wouldn't help any.

She didn't mind going to the pub, far from it, since Dan always said they were 'working, not drinking' and insisted on paying, but Dan seemed to be suggesting it increasingly frequently. It was as if he was getting bored of corporatesponger. It made no sense to her. He should be excited. They were doing what they'd set out to do: putting corporate greed in the shop window. They were beginning to get ads. They had even had a big US not-for-profit ask about sponsorship and a couple of enquiries from larger dot coms about a merger. Dan had given those enquiries more attention than she'd expected.

'What do you think?' he had said, sharing an email with her. 'Look at all those noughts.'

For some reason, Cherri hadn't told Dan about the police coming by and perhaps that was the reason. They'd always been on the same page. Now she wasn't so sure.

'Merger means takeover,' she'd said – repeating back to Dan something he himself had said in the early days when some pub acolyte had asked him what he'd do if Google or Comm-N wanted to buy corporatesponger.

'What it actually means is guaranteed work and income and someone else worrying about the bottom line.'

'Yes, but we'd still be working for the man,' Cherri had said. 'What would we do when the new owners started cutting corners on tax?'

Dan had pulled a face and given her a hard stare. 'Comm-N are getting into hardware, anyway,' was all he'd said.

Now he was all breezy. 'There's an American pale ale there. That's yours, Con. And a porter-style for Cherri. I've got a single hop summer ale.'

'Thanks,' they both said.

The late afternoon sun was making one last dying effort, spluttering through the colonial-style arched window. Dan raised his straw yellow pint to admire its colour.

When Cherri and Dan went to the pub, they usually shared the craft beers, each sampling the various options, but it was evident from the way Conrad was clutching his pint proprietorially that that wouldn't be happening today. Conrad was clearly a little surprised to find himself down the pub. With his choir-boy haircut and pristine checked shirt, he looked very young – and smelt of fabric softener

– so perhaps he got fed up with questions about his age. Cherri certainly knew all about that. However, she doubted that his youthful appearance was the main reason for his anxiety. It was the change in routine.

Cherri had tried to reassure the new recruit that, if Dan had said he could be out of the office, then it was OK to be out of the office since Dan was the boss, but still Conrad kept looking at his watch. 'My contract says my place of work is the corporatesponger office,' he insisted. He had a deep voice totally out of kilter with his slight appearance.

'It's OK,' said Cherri. 'Look, have you scheduled some tweets for this afternoon?'

'I've scheduled tweets for three-thirty, four and four-thirty,' he said.

'Good work,' said Cherri. What had he scheduled? Tweet about going to the pub. Tweet about going to the toilet.

'Nice T,' said Dan.

'Peter Robb,' said Cherri with a smile – their old Gap v Peter Robb argument. 'They're for kids really. I had to battle my way through a gaggle of screaming schoolgirls on their lunch break to buy one.' She sipped her beer. 'It was worse than Black Friday.'

'Did you get your hair pulled?' smirked Dan.

'They're just cheaper,' said Cherri. This was the truth but it wasn't the whole truth.

'You remember that crowd outside Boomer's the day Zak Brown got killed, Cherri?' Dan said. 'They were blocking the traffic in the street,' he added for Conrad's benefit. 'They were mostly kids too.'

Cherri nodded.

'Hundreds of people all desperate to buy a coffee. Biggest crowd ever. And the only thing that's changed between the morning where there's a little trickle of customers and the afternoon where there's a mob is that old Zak – or should we call him Brian? – has shaken off this mortal coil. What's that about?'

'It was freakish,' said Cherri. 'The sheep mentality. The need to be part of something bigger, maybe?'

'If we could harness that for sponger, we'd be in business.'

'You want a bunch of kids standing up for fair taxation?'

'Why not? You said yourself there's no mob like a mob of school-girls.'

Cherri had indeed said something like that, so she had a drink instead.

'Anyway, it's not about kids or not kids,' said Dan, getting animated. 'It's about the passion. Economics is so dry. Do you remember when we were talking about Blair Henry, Cherri, and you asked "how is he ever going to make a name for himself writing about interest rates?" Well, you were right – but suddenly all this dry economics is all over the papers. We've got to find a way to get a slice of it.'

'It's mostly froth in the newspapers,' said Cherri.

'And the sudoku,' said Conrad.

'Obviously this is not the way we'd have chosen for our issue to become the big issue,' Dan said. 'Of course not. But it has and we need to seize the day.'

'So what do you want to do?'

'I don't know. But I do know we don't do this just to provide information. I'm not a librarian. I do it to create change. I'm an activist. And this is our chance.'

'Well, we could be a bit more campaigny,' said Cherri. 'You know, make the links between low taxation and poor public services. Con can do that on social media.'

'We could – but even that could feel exploitative if it wasn't done right,' said Dan.

Cherri turned hastily to Conrad. 'He doesn't mean you wouldn't do it right, Con, he just means it's very, very difficult to get the balance.'

Conrad nodded. 'We could make T-shirts,' he said.

'I think Cherri's got enough T-shirts,' said Dan. He laughed and downed his beer.

'Badges then,' said Conrad.

Later that day, Dan was fishing. Hadn't even gone back to the office. Left Cherri and Con to get on with it.

They'd long since banned fishing off Brighton Pier so he'd either go to the Marina or cut along the coast somewhere, usually Biscuit Town where the catch was good and company quiet.

He was an odd guy. He'd always known that. He was a mod who fished, a geek who fished. Both were exponentially odd. But the Lambretta, with its broad platform, was actually perfect for resting your rod and fishing gear on. And fishing was, like coding, very binary. You caught something or you didn't. So perhaps it wasn't so odd. Whatever it was, it helped him think.

The team meeting had been an absolute disaster. Dan had always loved coding but Conrad, the geek's geek's geek, made him realise that he also wanted something more. Something more human. Code wasn't life, code was the pleasure in life, like a puzzle solved. It felt like something was happening, something that affected corporatesponger. Or was it the other way round: something was happening that corporatesponger had effected? Either way he needed to understand what it was. Solve a puzzle with a lot more variables. It was a windy day and the kite-surfers, the wind-surfers, the long-boarders, the short-boarders, the body-boarders, the paddle-boarders, Uncle Tom Wetsuit and all were out in force, a riot of candy colours. If you weren't surfing the zeitgeist, you were drowning. Dan knew that and he needed something to ride the wave that had been unleashed – corporatesponger might be the board but to really dance in the waves, he needed a sail too. Dan laughed. He was twirling his rubber-handled fish knife in his palm, like a majorette with her baton. Perhaps he should stick to code – metaphors weren't really his thing.

He eyed the rod. Still as a line of dead ASCII.

He used the knife's gut hook, a comma on the tip of the blade, to clean under his fingernails as he watched the surfers loop and leap, glide and slide. He didn't particularly enjoy gutting a fish, it was messy, but he enjoyed the fact that he could do it and do it well. Bystanders would watch. The seagulls would watch. It made him feel like Bear Grylls or someone, a human animal, and not just a geek who thought in binary. But today his rod sat there stoically. The eyes through which the line was threaded were a silent string of zeroes. He just had that feeling that he wouldn't be getting a bite.

# 3.3.

Smooth will take you a long way in the civil service. That's not smooth as in smarmy or even in slick, but smooth as in the simple absence of friction. Dominic Mason was such a public servant, a rolling stone gathering no moss, a fast streamer slipperier than a salmon. Whichever minister of whichever party had the fortune to find young Mason in his retinue soon came to regard him as the safest of safe pairs of hands. It was a mystery to Dominic at times. He was just doing his job as he perceived it. They frequently asked him to move with them when the inevitable reshuffle came. He never did. Why hitch yourself to another man's coat-tails? Especially when the average politician's trajectory was about as smooth as fell running.

Perhaps a black cat had crossed his path as a toddler or a flock of pigeons had deposited their multiple droppings on his pram. Whatever it was, he seemed to have picked life's four-leafed clover. That wasn't money. It wasn't looks or brains or any outstanding talent in any field at all. It was the ability to be baggage-less. This came, and he'd often thought about it, down to having been blessed with the appropriate amount of emotion for the situation. The past truly was another country to him. He was engaged enough to be engaging but would never, regardless of the provocation, be it at work or at home, lose his head. The injustices of childhood, his past failings, they were all water off this salmon's back. He was the iceman who was never cold. Sometimes it scared him – the certain knowledge that he could kill a man and then do a crossword on the train home – but even those feelings were appropriately short-lived and of low intensity.

When he read Blair Henry's article, he knew immediately that this was something to be alert to. Naturally, it was buried in the corner of the paper's website for now, but that meant nothing. That the paper wasn't splashing on it was down to one word: the 'approximately' in the first sentence of paragraph five. Henry had the rich smell of a good slow-cooking story in his nostrils; the editor remained to be convinced. This was how Watergate had started – very low key.

Dominic couldn't put his finger on it but there was something in the tone of the writing. Usually, and increasingly in the digital age, journalists overreached themselves, over-egged the story but, in this case, you could almost hear Henry holding back as if fearing himself the implications of what he was saying. The point of the final paragraph was hidden in plain sight, just like the information itself: all these figures were in the public domain. The killer could be anyone who found them. A serial killer who wanted to draw attention to corporate tax evasion? The potential impact was colossal in so many ways. The PM really ought to be informed of the possibility.

It had clearly been a monumental cock-up by the French police. Letting evidence melt was Jacques Tati really. But let's assume the numbers were seen near the body. (How could anyone make something like that up?) Had similar numbers been found near Sender's body? The Met had not said anything and the article was cleverly phrased, the author not actually claiming that such numbers did exist.

Online, Mason found footage of the French media conference at which they had played down the possibility of numbers in the snow. Very unconvincing. How did you say 'covering your arse' in French? There was only one way to put this story to bed for sure.

He picked up the phone.

Detective Chief Inspector Corrigan was, he would be the first to concede, confused. He was pacing his office, a big man in a small room, his still-warm mobile phone clutched in his chunky palm. DS Caton had gone AWOL. DS Caton was therefore due a gold-plated bollocking. Yet, DS Caton had given him more in one phone call than a whole team of so-called investigators on the ground in London had provided in the entire investigation. Corrigan set the phone down on the wobbly filing cabinet and picked up a cup of lukewarm tea instead. If DS Caton had been half as useful, half as cooperative, half as amenable when on active duty as he was when on gardening leave, he wouldn't have been on gardening leave in the first place.

On his computer screen Corrigan had the journalist's story. Caton had helped him to navigate to it. That alone was worth a Queen's

Police Medal as far as Corrigan was concerned. He struggled with the internet, he had to admit, found it difficult to send a text message if truth be told. Once, when his daughter had texted him to ask for a lift, he'd tried to reply 'right' and texted 'riot'. As if that girl needed any encouragement. (He'd imagined the headline: Met chief urges daughter to nightclub anarchy.) Every time you went to a page on the internet or opened something up on your phone, it looked different. And it was so fiddly: tiny buttons, weeny windows opening everywhere, kid-sized keys on the keyboard, a mouse. A bloody mouse. Even the names made it all sound lightweight and little. Still, that was the modern world for you, so that was modern policing too. He sipped at his tea. Barely hot enough, barely strong enough. He licked his lips. He was pleased to see that he still liked a juicy case. He worried about himself sometimes, wondered whether he was beginning to prefer the quiet life. It rejuvenated him to discover that it wasn't yet so.

Caton had confirmed the implication of the story. He had been to the office of some website in Brighton or something. Corrigan had already entertained the possibility of a link – both victims had had their heads smashed in, after all – but the numbers confirmed it and hinted strongly at the killer's motivation. The politicians would need to be informed now and that always complicated things. The involvement of the politicos was more convoluted than a hundred internets and a thousand mobile phones.

The desk phone rang.

'It's the Cabinet Office,' Corrigan was told. 'A Dominic Mason?'

Ten minutes earlier and he'd have been caught with his pants down. Thank you, Christopher Caton.

'Just wondering how you were getting on with those numbers by Sender's body?', said a casual voice at the other end of the phone. That information had not, officially anyway, left the police service and Corrigan, sensing a set-up, was able to reply quick as a flash:

'You've read Mr Henry's article, Mr Mason?'

The voice at the other end of the line hesitated.

Corrigan asked some questions to ascertain the caller's security clearance level and received the necessary replies.

He was alone in his office, his interlocutor ten minutes away, but he was still aware of leaning forward conspiratorially. 'We haven't officially released the sequence of figures by Sender's body but that may change,' Corrigan continued. 'It's a situation in a high state of flux. However, I can report we're linking the two deaths and that I'm grateful for your call as Downing Street probably needs to know.'

'Do we have confirmation from France of the Zak Thomas Brown numbers?'

Corrigan was impressed with the speed and fluidity with which Mason rebalanced himself after the initial wrong-footing.

'No, we haven't had the report from our French colleagues yet. There's a translators' strike, I believe.'

'I checked the numbers myself and they don't quite correspond with the tax figures of the two companies concerned. Do you think the killer had a different source or are we jumping to conclusions?'

'Ah,' said Corrigan in what he couldn't help but recognise as an 'I'm glad you asked me that' tone. 'It's all about how the French write sevens.' He then explained how a French man would read an uncrossed seven as a one, just as Caton had explained it to him.

'That is excellent police work, Officer.'

'A number of years at Interpol,' said Corrigan, not untruthfully.

'So it means the killer is British, not French?'

'It means he's probably an English speaker, yes.'

'Thank you, Officer, I'll talk to Downing Street and we'll be back in touch.'

'Good bye,' said Corrigan formally. He sat back in his office chair, exhaling with a certain relief. The chair had wheels as sensitive as a skateboard and his XXL momentum caused him to roll back across the lino and into the wall. The tea leapt in the cup but didn't spill over the top. He smiled to himself. There was much to do. Resources, for one. Already, Caton was saving him a lot of money by keeping the Sender spouse out of the way. Did he say she was staying at his mother's?! Corrigan shook his head in that world-weary way he'd noticed himself adopting. Caton and protocol were not words you'd find in the same sentence. First he'd earned another cup of tea and a doughnut.

For a moment the chief inspector's office was silent and that was long enough for him to realise that the office outside – the shop floor as he called it – was anything but. He looked out of his internal window onto open-plan excitement and arse-moving energy: officers dashing, chairs sliding, phones ringing, documents printing. Two detectives were running – but trying to do it discreetly – towards his office. The effect was comic, as if they were running from the knees down. Corrigan opened the door.

'It's Peter Robb, Sir.'

'The budget clothing...'

'I know who Peter Robb is,' said Corrigan. 'My teenage daughter lives in his shop on Oxford Street. Is he?'

'Yes, Sir.'

'Any numbers or letters?'

'No, Sir, just a cardboard sign hanging round his neck.'

'What does it say?'

'Tax Evading Super Scum.'

'Right, there seems to be a pattern emerging here.'

# 3.4.

Peter Robb was slumped against a wall. It looked like a changing room suite. The clothes on the hanging rail beside him were nearly as dishevelled as his own, a cheap-looking blue suit. His jacket sleeve was torn, his tie hung at half mast in the tight, tight knot of a rebellious schoolboy. His knees were tucked up against his chest – as if he had been trying to protect himself – and one shoe was missing. His lank blonde hair was even more wayward than usual and the right side was matted red with blood. There was also a little blood around the right eye – both eyes were closed – and he was sitting in a pool of the stuff. Hanging around his neck was a cardboard sign which read: Tax Evading Super Scum.

Gabby and Chris looked at the image. Gabby had seen it at about the same time as every other over-enthusiastic user of Twitter and it was now top of all trending lists, racking up retweets like numbers on a pinball machine, flashing across screens and tablets and phones around the world as fast as the pixels could load.

'It's like the moon landing,' said Chris.

'What?' said Gabby.

'Everyone everywhere is looking at this right now.'

'What a sad indictment of the human race.'

'Welcome to my world.'

It had started much like any other day for Peter Robb.

His was the most household of household names. When you saw the shop front, 'Peter Robb' in curly gold letters, you also saw the man, dressed head-to-foot in his own clothes, the shock of blonde hair, the cheeky wink with which he signed off his TV adverts. Amongst UK businessmen, perhaps only Richard Branson was quite so strongly identified with his brand and so instantly recognisable.

Robb had a shop on every high street and, as often as his hectic schedule would permit, and certainly at least once a fortnight (he insisted on that), he would visit one of them. Appear without warning. It wasn't a formal inspection. All that was bollocks. The only thing he was examining was the ambience and you couldn't pin that down with a tick-box check sheet. Each visit was different. Sometimes, he'd not introduce himself and just buy something – although that was becoming more difficult now that he was so frequently on TV. Sometimes, he'd sit down with the manager and grill her – it was usually a her – on all matters Robb. Other times, he'd make for whoever appeared to be the shyest or newest member of the team and engage with them. He'd flatter a shy girl, encourage a young one. He'd often speak to the lads on the team since they were usually the minority. Most of them were hopeless but every so often he'd meet one who didn't make him despair for the male of the species. The name of the game was motivation: he wanted everyone to believe that team Robb was the team to be on. He wasn't a cynical guy – he did genuinely believe in his brand and his merchandise – but he wasn't a stupid one either and he understood that making it about something bigger than money made economic sense too. 'The money's not great but it's a great place to work' was a common verdict among staff and not one with which Peter Robb had a problem.

Television was a strange beast. You could be on the news regularly. You could be the commentator of choice for stories about the decline of the high street or on branding in retailing. You could even be the star of your own advertising. But these were all discrete worlds – segmented, to use the language of the marketers. 'More people have a pair of your knickers than ever watch Channel 4 News' was how one of his Comms team had put it. But get yourself on a reality TV show and the dynamic changes. Suddenly, he wasn't a brand, he was a bloke. People who'd never met him talked about him, online and offline, as if he were a personal friend, such was the false intimacy of a certain sort of television. Had he known quite how much it would change his public profile, he may have said no. It was too late for that now.

True, Mrs Robb had been concerned but he hadn't listened. He hadn't wanted to. Yes, he wanted to sell more T-shirts but, in truth, to be famous was what his larger-than-life personality demanded and he'd always indulged that part of himself. 'It's not just me,' Betsy had said. 'What about the kids? Do you want paparazzi camped outside their schools?'

On the day of his death, Peter had had his driver drop him outside the shop and then go and find somewhere to park. They'd done it a hundred times before. But it meant he entered the shop alone. It was one of the larger stores, the seventh largest to be precise, and he was delighted to see it so busy. Of course, the marketing men had all sorts of slogans, all sorts of stories to tell, all sorts of visual merchandising tricks and all very fine it was too. Peter paid them very good money to come up with it all. But, in truth, his success boiled down to two things. His clothes were fashionable and cheap. In straitened times, 'when the economy was up the proverbial without a paddle' as he liked to put it in the plain-speaking interviews in which he specialised, those things had a bigger appeal than ever.

He was in need of a new suit, so the plan was to select one of the higher-end models and buy that. He'd see how far he could get before anyone recognised him. Before the show, he had, on a number of occasions, made it as far as the till and even flashed his platinum-coloured store card bearing the name Peter R Robb before being identified. Since the show it was a lot rarer. Of course, the material and stitching in his suits weren't of a quality you'd expect a man of his status to wear, but he always had the clothes touched up by a decent tailor and seldom wore a suit more than twice (pretty much the shelf life of everything in the shop if truth be told). Point is you couldn't put a price on the public relations value in wearing your own clothes. And, as he got richer, the PR value grew bigger.

There was a new design that he'd fancied since he'd first seen the scamps. He'd come to this larger store because he was reasonably confident they'd still have one in his size and happily they did. There had been a lot of people about, younger females mostly as usual, but frankly he hadn't taken much notice of them. He'd been absorbed in the hunt, enjoying the process of the shop, just as he hoped all his customers would. And anyway, it was relatively quiet in the men's suits department – it always was.

A young male assistant was hovering. Peter liked that. Most staff may have been female but he preferred to see a man in men's suits. The assistant, stick-thin, tall and chinless, was close enough that the customer could talk to him should he wish, but not so close as to smother. All good. Peter helped himself to a suit. He chose the bluest of the three shades of grey, holding it up like a trophy in the general direction of the assistant. With the other hand, he pointed at the changing room. The assistant nodded and made an expansive be-my-guest gesture, with his arms. Peter liked the friendly informality.

It was a suite of changing cubicles, designed to Robb's own specifications. The cabins were a decent size with a slightly-tilted, flattering mirror and there were sofas, plants and pot-pourri in the waiting area. If you wanted someone to feel like they were a million dollars in your clothes, you didn't want the first time they put them on to be in a poky, smelly, dark shed. So many retailers got that wrong in Peter's view.

He heard a kerfuffle as he was buttoning up the fly – a feature which, while inconvenient, gave the suit a classier feel. He thought perhaps a stag party had come in to buy suits for the wedding. It wasn't uncommon at Peter Robb prices. Then, suddenly, the kerfuffle was right inside the changing suite and it wasn't just male voices. You could call Peter Robb flash, you could call him cheap and tacky, you could him a control freak, you could even call him Del Trotter without the dress sense – and the media had called him all of these down the years – but you couldn't call him a coward. He pulled the jacket on and stepped out of the cubicle.

There were dozens of them. They were onto him like a pack. A rail of clothes fell over. Even as he was being swallowed whole by the mob, he found himself thinking 'someone had better pick that up'. Yes, even in his final moments, there was still that attention to detail.

# 3.5.

### Clothes giant murdered
### By Blair Henry

Peter Robb, whose clothing stores can be seen on every high street in the country, has been found stabbed to death.

His murder is the third in a series of killings of senior corporate bosses of firms with controversial tax affairs. In Mr Robb's case, he himself had an exemplary tax profile. On the face of it. He was domiciled in the UK where he lived and worked and where he paid full UK tax on his salary. However, Mr Robb limited his tax liability by not actually owning the company that bears his name. Instead it is registered to his wife. She has never worked for the organisation but lives in Monaco, a tax haven. It is estimated that this strategy has saved the Robbs at least £250 million in tax.

Mr Robb's death follows those of Stufff owner Jack Sender and the CEO of Boomer's Coffee, Zak (aka Brian) Thomas Brown.

It lasted about fifteen minutes and in that time Blair Henry had, he would later admit, drafted an article. Fortunately, he had not hit 'send'. Jessica Gann was at her Aunt Debbie's. Gavin Henley was running. Gary Shad was meeting his brief. Cherrianne Dixon was counting the page hits accumulating on the website.

To be precise, Jess was claiming to have a bit of time between shifts but not enough to go home. 'Just wanted to see my favourite Auntie.'

It wasn't true. Jess didn't want to go back to her flat, was how it was. The smell of mould made her want to heave. The place was cold, even in spring, and, when your home is cold, it's always on your mind. You can't enjoy the summer because the winter's to follow. She was actually casing Aunt Deb's joint and was realising she'd been mistaken to have ever thought there might be room for her. Everyone was getting bigger and needed more space, not least the fucking dog. Now, she was no expert but Tyson was like none of the dogs she walked. He was twice the size for a start and his paws were even larger – like a werewolf. Although he got taken out a couple of times a day, it just wasn't enough. He had energy to burn and in a little two-up, two-down, there wasn't a lot of space to burn it. You could only shag the furniture for so long. The boys, Luke and Lewis, who used to take him out, were less and less interested and both of them were now ginormous as well. Just their extended legs took up most of the living room. They were computer-gaming throughout her visit. She got a grunted 'orright' from one of them and a 'yo, Jess' from the other. She wasn't sure who said what as neither of them looked up for a split second. Since her last visit, they had melded into an ogreish single, black T-shirted, two-headed creature with slumped, angular shoulders and four smelly feet. The great beast Luk-ewis. Nothing moved but its long fingers. The pair, if they ever uncoupled from the sofa, were presumably sharing a bedroom. She shuddered to think what that must be like.

Aunt Deb was chatting away as usual but she too was lost in her screen. Whenever she paused for breath, she'd answer a text or catch up on a bit of shopping. She registered next to nothing of what Jess had to say and was tapping away with a long burgundy-painted fingernail at her iPad for the duration. It was like having a conversation with a senile woodpecker. The iPad's screen looked like an ice rink. I would go fucking mad if I moved in here, Jess thought. It was roasting hot for a start, the heating blasting out and half the windows open.

'You look like that Swedish model,' Aunt Deb was saying.

'Do I?' said Jess. She was hesitant about pursuing this line. She and Aunt Deb looked very much alike. They'd both been served the same bucket of top-quality Gann oestrogen during puberty which had given them much the same shape, the same boobs and the same lips. So, when Aunt Deb said to her, 'Jess, you look like that Swedish model', she was really saying 'I look like that Swedish model.'

The Luk-ewis snorted under its breath.

'Look.' Deb thrust her iPad in Jess's direction. 'Frida Gustavsson, she's called.'

Jess didn't think she looked much like her at all but she could see what her aunt meant. Frida was all ovals. She had a perfect vertical oval face with large horizontal oval eyes, deep and blue, and large horizontal oval lips, rich and red. A perfect version of Jess. Jess without the pasty skin, three zits and bags under the eyes.

'She looks more like you,' said Jess.

That was the reply Aunt Deb had been angling for. 'But I'm twice her age,' she said modestly, beaming like a child. Jess understood it. You might curse your looks at times but you didn't want to lose them. As she got older, she was beginning to understand that only too well. Aunt Deb had way too much up top to be a model for anything other than the majesty of the female bosom itself but Jess didn't say anything. She didn't need to, as first a flock of notifications filled Deb's screen and then the image of a bloodied Peter Robb. Killed, said the caption.

'Oh my God,' said Deb. 'I just bought one of his onesies.'

Deb looked first at Jess and then at her boys. 'Luke, have you...'

'Seen it,' said one half of the dreaded Luk-ewis. 'Lame,' said the other half.

Jess reached across and prised her aunt's iPad from her hands. The fingernails tried to grab it back. It was like disarming Edward Scissorhands. Jess snapped the screen protector shut.

'What?' said Deb, still like a child but now a sulky one.

'Mum's had her fucking incapacity stopped,' said Jess.

Gavin Henley was standing on Moonshine Point, hands on hips

like a teapot trying to belly-breathe. He'd just spent the equivalent of Denise Gann's employment support allowance on two pairs of running socks. Breathable fabric. He wished he could buy breathable fabric lungs but you couldn't buy everything. Oddly enough, this fact of life pleased him. He may have been drowning in the green stuff but somewhere deep inside his scarred psyche was the notion, cherished, that something was better if you worked for it. Gavin loved how, through hard work, his muscles were expanding and his cardiovascular performance improving. Jogging was thus not only the road to wellbeing but the road to self-knowledge too. In through the nose came fresh sea air, out through the mouth came a catalyst to wisdom.

Gavin could hear the deep blue stuff doing its thing against the rocks down below. He didn't go too close to the edge today. Too much of the white stuff the night before. He relished danger but he wasn't reckless. Instead he did a few stretches against the bench, working the calves and the ITB. He needed to get the old lactic acid moving. Or so he'd read anyway. He windmilled his arms a few times to ease a muscle spasm he'd felt in his upper arm.

Gav saw the picture when he sat down to consult his watch. He fancied the climb up to Moonshine had been a Personal Best and had been delaying the pleasure of finding out. But his smart watch was so clogged with messages it was as if someone had died. The sensation in his upper arm had not, he realised, been a muscle spasm but his mobile phone which, strapped to his arm, had been repeatedly vibrating. It was quite a relief. He'd feared, albeit for only a second or two, that it was the early warning of a heart attack. Instead, he leaned back on the bench, stretching the spine and shoulders, and allowed the feel-good endorphins to break over him like the waves down below. The image of the battered body of Peter Robb, a man whose chutzpah he admired but whose clothes were for the plebs and chavs, did nothing to spoil that good mood. In fact, it enhanced it. It wasn't, after all, anything for him to worry about. And someone dying while you were living always delivered that special feeling.

Gary Shad's brief was flicking through a thin manilla dossier like it might explode. He looked too young to get served in a pub, too young to fucking shave even. He had a downy top lip and chin. Was that supposed to be a goatee? Cheap suit. He wasn't actually even a lawyer. He was what they called an accredited representative: the spade-worker. 'Now, let me see,' the kid said. 'There seem to be several charges. The Ferrari.' He examined the photo, a hard copy (what a waste of public money), and whistled. 'Nice car. A substantial quantity of Apple computer equipment. They did a section 18, it appears.'

Gary was only half-listening. He pulled his vibrating phone from his pocket and began to scroll.

'I hope that iPhone is demonstrably yours, Mr Shad,' said the kid.

Gary nodded but he didn't look up. 'They're saying Peter Robb's dead,' he said. He wasn't sure why. To show he didn't give a shit, presumably.

The kid put the folder down pointedly. 'Can we just stick to offences you're actually charged with, Mr Shad.' The kid sipped from a bottle of mineral water he'd brought in with him. 'Unless you want to confess something to me... usual duty of confidentiality, of course.'

Gary snorted. 'Very funny,' he said but this time he did raise his sleep-depleted eyes. The kid might look about ten but there were no flies on him. Perhaps he wasn't such an arse after all.

'That looks like one of his suits,' said Gary with a nod towards the kid's over-shiny attire. Partly, he was being friendly and partly some testosterone-filled cesspool inside him needed to regain the upper hand in the rapier-like wit stakes.

'It is,' said the kid.

Cherri had found the original photo and forwarded it to Chris.

'Some mob of fans, mostly prepubescent girls, apparently jumped the guy,' said Chris.

'He does random inspections of his shops,' said Gabby.

'That's it. They'd seen him on Celebrity Tiddlywinks or something. Someone snapped it and posted it. Someone else Photoshopped it, added a bit of blood and...'

'Robert est ton oncle,' said Gabby.

'Tout à fait,' said Chris.

'How many of them out in internet land think it's real, do you think?'

'Most of them at the moment, probably. This particular moral panic is still only ten minutes old.'

It was a really well faked photo. Chris had seen a few and this was one of the best. He could imagine it being used in a Photoshop masterclass in years to come.

'They say a picture is worth a thousand words,' said Gabby. 'Well, Marcel Proust didn't ...'

'These days nobody can be arsed to read ten words, let alone a thousand,' said Chris. 'Everyone can see a picture.' And DS Caton could see quite clearly where this particular internet meme was going. It would be like the skeletal bodies at Belsen, the Vietnamese girl on fire, the Dust Lady on 9/11, the child drowned on a Greek beach, it would be an image that changed the news. The big difference was, of course, that none of those others had been flipped, brightened, touched up and resampled on a computer.

'I give it another five minutes,' said Chris.

'Seven,' said Gabby.

'Done.'

'What's Tiddlywinks?'

Chris stared at Gabby, not for the first time. 'Did you just make a joke about Marcel Proust?'

For Peter Robb, his death lasted a lot less than even a quarter of an hour. He was out for barely a minute but, by the time he opened his eyes, the world had changed.

'Sorry, Mr Robb', said a girl with an enormous serpent of a po-ny-tail. She could only have been nine or ten.

From his slumped position against the wall, it was her eyes his met first. She looked terrified, eyes like soup plates, and he remembered what had happened. A solicitous shop assistant was holding his hand. Nobody else said anything as he looked around at the sea of faces: the unblinking, eager eyes, the goldfish mouths. It was television without the screen and he suddenly didn't like it at all. He felt a drip of heavy, cold sweat trickle down the back of his neck.

Looking back, perhaps he made the decision then. Later, he had no idea where the notion had come from. Nobody other than his accountant had ever mentioned Peter Robb's tax affairs to him. But sometimes you just knew. Or rather, sometimes he just knew. That was difference between success and mediocrity. Peter Robb had never needed a focus group to tell him what he ought to be doing. And he didn't really need to see the photo of his 'dead' self either.

The first phone call was to his wife. Betsy took it rather better than he'd imagined.

'You mean I don't have to live in snotty old Monaco any more. Fantastic. Not London. It's full of money-launderers. How about Paris?'

Good choice. Cheap move too.

# 3.6.

'The tabloids are beginning to get interested' was how the Head of Press put it. That was the understatement of the year.

A nightclub killing was never not news but, while Sender's company was a household name, Sender's, in his own right, was not. The same applied to Zak Thomas Brown and he'd been inconsiderate enough to die overseas, reducing the news value at a stroke. Peter Robb was a different story. His name could be seen on every high street. Moreover, while two deaths could be a coincidence even on the parallel planet that was the British media, three could not. Of course, Robb had only been internet dead and then for less than the time it takes to drink a coffee. (Analysis would later reveal that 12 minutes and 47 seconds had passed between the first post of the Photoshopped image and it being outed as a fake on a rival platform.) But, in that time, the hallowed phrase 'serial killer' had returned to the public currency. Media subs, who had taken it out of storage, scrubbed it up and set it in big bold capitals, weren't going to be denied on a technicality. And, even in 12 minutes, the world can come up with a lot of puns on 'tax man' and 'axe man', many of which demanded a better, more public fate than that to which Peter Robb's inconvenient survival appeared to condemn them. Of course, strictly speaking, the source of the blows to the heads of the dead men had not been clarified. An axe was possible but, according to Corrigan, improbable. 'We suspect a blunter instrument.' Again, a technicality. Half the head's missing? It's an axe.

You could delete tweets, but you couldn't delete a state of mind. Two deaths, three deaths, who cared? There was a killer on the loose. Dominic Mason was reminded of a song by Pulp, his favourite band as a kid: Jarvis Cocker's breathy vocal as he led a reluctant melody through the minor chords before the tune finally resolved in a simple and inevitable way on the major. 'Something changed,' sung Jarvis. Something had, indeed, changed.

Dominic sat at the breakfast bar, spooning up cereal with his right hand while scrolling and swiping his way around his iPad with his left. Their kitchen still resembled something from a show home. The only item out of place was the stern grey air-tight barrel in which Dominic kept his own special muesli mix (cornflakes and toasted nuts being the secret ingredients). There wasn't even a kettle. They had a boiling-water tap which delivered, as the brochure put it, hot water at the perfect temperature for your morning cuppa. This was, to be precise, 98°C. Dominic had, no doubt, rolled his eyes, when Heather had first insisted on it. She claimed that an appliance delivering two temperatures of hot water and two types of cold (one filtered for drinking) was 'essential'. Dominic still doubted that but he had to admit it was, like so much of modern life, agreeably convenient.

Neither he nor Heather were big on cooking. They ate out a lot and had a good cleaner. But that would all have to change if they got pregnant. Both the eating-out and the cleaner. He wondered if Heather had thought that far. He suspected that she probably had but felt confident that she could persuade him that a cleaner was 'essential' even if she, Heather, was at home on maternity leave and he was the sole earner. She had probably figured right. To be honest, once the pregnancy came, he'd probably agree to anything. As it was, he could feel the sacks under his eyes, the fatigue in his legs. His thighs felt as if he'd been playing squash every night. He hadn't. He'd just been trying to get his wife up the duff. During her fertile period, it was at least twice a day, usually more. The missionary position with a cushion under her bottom was, according to some magazine or website Heather had read, the best position to get pregnant in. A couple of months in, they'd switched to doggy style, sometimes to a variation thereon that his wife called the 'Magic Mountain'.

'Is that mountain or mounting?' he had asked.

'I don't know but it's essential,' she said. 'Very scientific. Amanda Roachford swears by it.'

'Isn't she in your book club?'

Dominic wasn't sure he liked the idea of Heather and her coven discussing his futile attempts at knocking her up over Pinot Grigio and Jane Austen. But that was nurses for you. Blasé about bodily functions, especially other people's.

'And Amanda has had endometriosis. Her periods were like the battle of the Somme.'

Dominic scowled. 'Really? First World War jokes?'

'Get over yourself, Mr Fast Track,' said Heather. 'No danger of a battle of the Somme today.' Dominic could see another punchline coming over the top as certain as a doomed squaddie. 'Sperm counts have fallen 50% in 50 years, today's men haven't the balls.'

'That may be no bad thing,' said Dominic, civil service smooth. He quite fancied his wife when she was in this mood but he wasn't saying anything. Balls as small as currants in more ways than one.

'The other thing is no more alcohol for you.'

He thought he liked doggy style but, a further three months into the process, his leg muscles were beginning to protest and he was gagging for a pint.

His wife's attitude to sex had changed. She'd always been, well, sexy. Before they were married, what she said and the way she said it had had him very interested indeed. She'd always had copious supplies of the chiffonny, lacy, frilly, stringy, effectively transparent, virtually invisible undergarments that men liked. The first time she'd undressed in front of him she'd been wearing stockings and suspenders and he'd only ever seen them in the movies. He felt like Dustin Hoffman. Now it was more like a trip to the supermarket. 'Dominic, I need your seed' uttered in much the same tone as 'Dominic, I need a lift to my mother's' or 'Dominic, I think I have piles'.

'Now, have you been playing with yourself?' she'd demand.

'Of course not.'

His dick was sore enough without that, but he didn't say anything. Once or twice he'd ventured a rumbling yawn and a 'well, I am rather tired.'

'Oh come on, Dominic,' she'd reply. 'Five minutes of your time is all I'm asking.'

She'd woken him up at 3.30am. Unimpressed by his observation that it was the fourth time that night, she'd said: 'Come on, I'm sure we can get it harder than that' and placed his penis in her mouth, looking every bit like a busy nurse taking a quick temperature reading.

At least the 'tax man axe man' gave him an excuse to work late.

'What's it got to do with you?' Heather had said. 'Are you in the police now?'

'No. But I am the liaison point between... well, I'm not supposed to say, am I?'

'I'll wait up,' she said. 'Or perhaps we can do it more in the morning.'

With this thought, Dominic found himself looking back nervously over his shoulder. His wife was sleeping in – it was fine for her, she was on a late again – but well... he hastily knocked back the last of his tea and tiptoed, sock-footed, upstairs for a shave. Very quietly indeed.

Dominic shut the front door gingerly behind him. He was trying to get his mind back on his work. Not something he'd ever had any problem with in the past. And, as it happened, his job slapped him round the face.

'What the fuck is this?' A familiar voice. Uncommon utterances for the 'hood.

Dominic spun round to find his neighbour stalking around his, the neighbour's, car. Dominic's house was at the end of the close. The next door neighbours' house was at right angles to his and Heather's, so that effectively their two drives joined the road at much the same point. They had been neighbours for several months now but Dominic had no idea what his neighbour's name was. It wasn't that they never spoke. They did. That was the problem. They'd now spoken far too often for Dominic to ask his name.

'I think it's Wilf or Walt or something,' Heather had said.

'Walt! Have we moved to the Midwest?'

'Well, have you got any better ideas? You met him first, he must have told you his name...'

'Well, I think he did but...'

They'd taken to calling him Walt, anyway. Between themselves. Walt was suited and ready for work but he was crouching to look under the chassis and squinting to finger apparent dents on his Audi like a mechanic inspecting a write-off.

'What's the...?' Dominic began and then he saw the windscreen. Couldn't understand why he hadn't spotted it sooner. Distracted by Walt's bad language and unusual behaviour perhaps. Painted in red paint – well, you couldn't say painted – splashed on the windscreen contemptuously were the four letters: TESS. Tess? An ex-girlfriend? A current lover? Had Mrs Walt – seldom seen and also, so far as the Masons were concerned, nameless – exacted some sort of revenge?

'What happened?' asked Dominic.

'It must have happened in the night. Were you in last night, Dom?'

The whole forgotten-name problem was exacerbated by the fact that Walt knew Dominic's name very well indeed and used, unbidden, its diminutive on every possible occasion. Come in for a glass at Christmas, Dom. (That had never happened.) You a commuter too, Dom? (Asked while both were standing on the train platform with their briefcases.) What are you driving then, Dom? Dominic hated being called Dom and, while he was clearly obliged to plead guilty to not remembering everything that had passed between him and his neighbour, he'd certainly never suggested he call him 'Dom' which, to his ears, always sounded like 'dong'.

'We were, mate, yes. Got back about nine myself. Heather a little later. Didn't see anything. Was she parked here then?'

'No, we were out. Back at about 10.30.'

'Kids at closing time, perhaps?' Dominic ventured. There was no way Heather could have come in without noticing it. Plus, there was a pub round the corner but, their road being a cul-de-sac, there wasn't a lot of passing traffic. Not a convincing theory.

'They've punctured the tyres. Dented the doors. I think they've had the bonnet up...'

This really was not the sort of thing you expected. There was hardly a house valued at less than a million within a mile radius. It was hard to see this as a random attack. Dominic was sure that Walt had been targeted. Walt's house was set back a couple of hundred yards but he always parked at the road end of the drive. Not keen on reversing perhaps. The drive was narrow, the previous owners having been keen gardeners who had maximised the space for lawns, beds and borders.

'I should have driven it in,' said Walt, as if reading his mind.

'Anything I can do to help?'

Walt had resumed his circling of the vehicle and was shaking his head slowly from side to side, eyes intense, the odd-tutting sound from under the breath. He gave the impression of having forgotten that Dominic was there. He had a very smart double-breasted suit on and a decent tie, clearly silk. This was also, Dominic found himself thinking, one of at least three cars owned by Mr and Mrs Walt. (At the end of the narrow drive was a wider parking area and a state-of-the-art double garage.) It occurred to Dominic that it was quite probable that his nameless neighbour was very well-off.

Dominic watched as Walt took his phone out and began photographing the damage. Walt poked at the phone as if it might explode – the tell-tale sign that Walt was a generation older – and then held it up inches from his ageing eyes to inspect the images over the top of thin-framed Cartier-branded spectacles. Dominic took his own phone out and a couple of searches confirmed his suspicion.

'Your tax affairs in order, mate?' Dominic heard himself asking.

'What did you say?' Walt was suddenly very much aware of Dominic and was looking at him as if Dominic had just attempted the Magic Mountain on him.

A question on his tax affairs was more offensive to the average suburban Englishman than a windscreen of red paint and any number of envy marks. Dominic wondered where it had come from. Such boldness.

# 3.7.

'Estimated tax evaded: £3.4 billion.'

'Er, £2.7 billion, you win again. Lucky.'

'Talent, Josh. Talent.'

Pip watched with a mixture of horror and fascination as Tommy and Josh played their card game. Tommy was winning, obviously. He suddenly seemed to know as much about finance as he did about football. It seemed to have happened overnight, as if he'd taken a knowledge pill. Pip could only be impressed. It took her days of study to master a topic for ten year olds.

'What's it called?' Pip asked.

'Tax Evaders Top Trumps,' said Tommy.

'Estimated tax evaded: £4 billion,' said Josh.

'£4.2 billion,' said Tommy. 'Sorry.' He took the card from his friend. 'You should have gone for estimated total wealth with this guy,' he said. 'He's loaded. Or number of houses. He has 15.'

'Where did you get it?'

'Off a stall in the North Laine.'

'I think it's macabre.'

'Don't worry, your dad's not in the pack,' said Josh.

'It's not that. It just feels like... well, pack is the right word. It feels a little like mob rule. Two men have been murdered.'

'It's just a bit of fun,' said Josh.

'And it's tax avoidance, isn't it? Which is not illegal.'

'It's all smoke and mirrors,' said Tommy. 'But forgetting the legal niceties, if you look at it in terms of the bigger picture, these people wouldn't really be any worse off if they paid a bit more tax and the rest of us would be much better off. I mean, how many kids you got in your class, Pip? 25? 30?'

Pip looked at him sulkily and munched a Dorito.

On the other side of town, Debbie Gann was watching a similar game with a similar expression on her face. And she was reacting in much the same way as Pip, although her drug of choice was chocolate.

'Cheat!' shouted Luke.

'They're all cheats,' said Lewis. 'That's why it's called Tax Evaders Top Trumps, lame brain.'

It made a change from computer games, Debbie thought, nibbling a square of sugar and cocoa heaven. At least the boys were talking.

After a fashion.

'Can I play?' she said.

Ever since the greatly-exaggerated reports of his death, Peter Robb had been walking on clouds. He felt as if there was nothing he couldn't do. He'd seen the Tax Evaders Top Trumps and they confirmed his decision.

Like most businessmen, he'd long hoped to make his name immortal. He'd plastered his own name up in every shopping centre in the country, for God's sake. He could complain, and frequently had, about how businessmen didn't get the respect they deserved, how they contributed far more to the economy than, say, actors or footballers, but riffling through the pack of Top Trumps, he could feel that argument turning sour in his mouth. His son Aidan had had the World Football Stars Top Trumps and Peter could remember, on one of his rare visits, playing it with him. The game focused on how many trophies the player had won, how many goals he had scored, his international caps. Peter had known then that it was this sort of fame he craved. He'd have loved his son to look up to him with the same undiluted worship he reserved for David Beckham. But now, whatever he did in business, he'd be remembered as that guy who played fast and loose with his tax. His Wikipedia entry was already saying as much. 'Peter Robb is a UK businessman best known for his eponymous chain of high street clothes stores' the entry had used to begin. Now it said: 'Peter Robb is a UK businessman best known for a faked photo on the internet drawing attention to his tax affairs.' The Wikipedia editors had not marked this page as 'in need of attention' and why should they? It was perfectly true. His nitpicking over his tax liability was on the verge of destroying everything he had worked for and that was not going to happen. He could give away the majority of his wealth and still be a very rich man. Of course, in business you had to focus on the bottom line but the truth is a guy can only spend so much.

And there was another reason – a ridiculous, ridiculous reason that had made him realise just how far he'd moved away from what really mattered in life. The thing was this: he actually loved his wife. That may have been rare amongst his contemporaries but it was big fat fact all the same. He didn't want her living in a tax haven, bored out of her mind. He wanted her living with him. Had he realised that fifteen, twenty years ago, he might actually have been around to see Aidan grow up. Still, that was then. That was before he died online. There was no use crying over spilt milk, the point was to make it right and that's what he was going to do. Walking on clouds, you see, he could see it all.

'Mr Robb, we're ready for you now,' said the floor girl. She couldn't have been more than about 22 but had her blonde hair in a 70s style he knew well – the pageboy cut made famous by Joanna Lumley as Purdey in the New Avengers but also worn, back in the day, by his wife Betsy. Purdey was armed with a clipboard loaded with a ream of A4 pages. He knew her from somewhere. Was she on the production team for the reality show or had he seen her on a previous appearance on the news? He knew her frowning little face better than he knew some of his own office staff and that couldn't be right. Wronger still that he needed her to remind him of his wife. He sat down in the proffered chair and a powder puff hopped and skipped its way across his sticky forehead. 'Thank you,' he said.

Peter tightened his tie. It was one of his silk range.

He looked up and saw himself on a monitor, the slightly anxious glance to the side that always made you look shifty. On another monitor, the presenter was winding up the previous item. Purdey held up two ink-stained fingers and mouthed 'two minutes'. Usually, before news appearances, he'd been prepped to within an inch of his sanity. This time there had been none of that. Nobody in his office even knew he was going on. Oh, he knew what he was going to say all right but there was no script. He didn't need one. He could see it as clearly as skywriting in a perfect blue firmament.

Dominic sipped his pint. He had half an eye on Roger Wilkins' thick-set form. His former colleague, now at the Treasury, was looking in leaden-footed vain for an opening in the mass of civic humanity that engulfed the bar. Mason was glad he'd got there early and got his own round in.

The television in The Red Lion was tuned to the BBC News channel, sound down, subtitles on. Dominic was watching with another half an eye. He found the speech recognition software that churned out the live subtitles hilarious. A few weeks earlier, a serious item about a new DH initiative to raise awareness of 'colorectal cancer risks' had instead identified the 'co-director's pants at risk'. The Richmond House mob had been furious. He'd also seen an item on the most popular coffee in town – Boomer's frappaccino, apparently – turn into a discussion on Fred Pacino, Al's lesser-known brother, presumably. Dominic's personal favourite was the supposedly amusing sign-off on 'playing the slots on Brighton pier' which had become 'playing the sluts on Brighton pier' – an unfunny funny saved by a vowel. He couldn't excise the smile from his lips, especially as the software appeared to be up to its old tricks. Wilkins appeared with a pair of beers.

'What's amusing you?' he asked. 'The special advisors got another drinking competition?'

'No, it's the subtitles,' said Dominic. 'They're claiming that Peter Robb is about to pay his taxes live on air.'

'Pay his taxes? Hail his taxi, more like. Cheers.'

Dominic had a dilemma. To drink or to service his good lady. Of course, both were possible but he was past the age when that sort of multi-tasking came easy. What's more, Wilkins was downing his beer like an alcoholic at closing time.

'Didn't you use to be at Health?' Dominic asked with a grin.

'Yes, but I was never on message,' said Wilkins. He really was hitting the beer.

'What does the Chancellor make of Sender and Thomas Brown?'

'I think he thinks that now they're dead, he's going to get even less tax revenue.'

Dominic half-laughed but his attention had been drawn once again to the subtitles. 'Robb really does appear to be paying his taxes,' he said.

Wilkins looked in the same direction. It was a long, thin hostelry. A number of others had also stopped drinking momentarily, their eyes drawn to the big wall-mounted screen. The sound went down a notch, a hubbub replaced by a rumble. 'Bloody hell,' said Wilkins, he was poised in mid pint. 'Turn up the sound,' he said, to himself at first and then he turned to the bar – Dominic had never seen the treasury man move so fast – and shouted: 'turn up the fucking sound.'

This was a sentiment that a number of other punters echoed and suddenly all the attention in the highly-ceilinged, wood-trimmed room was trained on the TV. It was like the final of the 100m, Usain Bolt going for the world record.

Peter Robb was waving a cheque.

'A cheque? Some of those younger Spads won't know what that is,' Wilkins whispered.

Peter Robb was talking about righting moral wrongs and about undoing immoral decisions. He had, that much was clear, not only paid several years of back taxes live on air but also announced a new charitable foundation. To a room of politicos and civil servants it was televisual dynamite, their sort of reality TV. Comfortable in their new suits and old opinions, half of Whitehall had flocked round the telly. The grey army. Peter Robb was shaking it all up. Complacency up in smoke.

The interview was coming to a close. People were hushing each other: 'Ssh, ssh'.

'I bet he says it's the right thing to do,' said Dominic.

'Sssh.'

'That's all they can say,' said Wilkins. 'They've no ideology any more.'

'Here we go,' said Dominic, 'he's about to say it.'

The camera zoomed in on Robb. His nose was enormous and had, Dominic noticed for the first time, probably been broken at some point. His skin, in high definition, looked like hessian. There was a messianic gleam in his eyes.

'Regardless of whether it's legal or not, it is immoral not to pay your taxes,' said Peter Robb. 'It diminishes the individual and society.'

'I didn't see that coming,' said Dominic.

'Sssh.'

'If I don't pay so much tax, I can send my child to a public school where the only lesson he'll learn is that money buys you advantage,' Robb said. He looked into the camera lens like a pro – the interviewee taking over the interview. 'If I do pay my tax and send him to a good state school, the lesson he'll learn is that together we can do great things. What do you want your child to learn? It is,' he paused, dramatically, 'as my own son would put it, a no-brainer.'

There was the briefest beat of silence as the interviewer, like everybody in Whitehall's local, groped for the right words.

'Peter Robb, er, taxpayer,' said the newscaster which was, under the circumstances, pretty damn good. Dominic drained the best part of a pint. Like Peter Robb, his decision had been made.

'Bloody hell,' said Wilkins. 'He's just surpassed any politician I've ever worked with and it took him all of five minutes.'

'He could be Prime Minister,' Dominic said.

# 3.8.

'They're having a fucking Cobra meeting?'

Corrigan was on the phone to Mason again. 'I'm trying to calm the public down and the Prime Minister decides to have a meeting of the national crisis committee. Very calming.'

'I can see how it might appear,' said Mason.

'It was fake,' said Corrigan. 'Nothing has changed.'

'Didn't you see the TV last night? The public mood has changed.'

'And you need to be seen to be doing something. Never mind if it interferes with a real investigation.'

'The Robb photo may have been fake but two people have been killed,' said Mason.

'I hadn't forgotten,' said Corrigan. 'But three times as many as that will die on the roads today alone. You're creating panic here. We need to keep this as routine as possible.'

'There are a number of issues emerging which are very far from routine. You know about TESS.'

'Tax Evading Super Scum. Yes, we're aware, you can reassure Cobra. Tell me, is that what they call the law of unintended consequences?'

'Well, Robb didn't invent the term but he may have stoked the fire. Are you aware people are selling these badges online, writing TESS on people's windscreens and spray-painting it on their houses?'

'We're collating all local reports of incidents of this nature, yes.'

'Mostly we're under pressure from a number of,' Mason coughed, 'our better-off citizens who feel they need better protection. Just giving you a heads-up.'

'Appreciated,' said Corrigan. 'Let's keep this channel of communication open.'

Corrigan sunk eager teeth into his doughnut and felt the jam leak out in a slow ooze. His tongue whipped the sugar from his lips. The chief inspector had a lot on his plate and not just the doughnut. He now had a small team in France and a third looking into the Peter Robb business. It wasn't 100% clear whether any crime had been committed in that regard but nobody could deny the chaos. He had a killer whom he really didn't understand. Sender and Thomas Brown had both been killed by well-aimed blows to the head – clearly the work of the same man. The standard definition of a serial killer was three or more murders over a period of time. This killer had committed two. Was there a third body out there somewhere? If not Peter Robb, then someone else? Or was the killer keeping his options open, implying a third would follow at some point if... well, if what? Perhaps it was already over? Had Sender and Thomas Brown been purely personal (but, if that was the case, why go to the trouble of all those letters and numbers?) Or was the killer himself now dead? Both the scale of the police operation and the complexities of the case appeared to be running out of hand.

On the plus side, Mason was proving very useful indeed, keeping him, Corrigan, one step ahead of a Commissioner who was becoming increasingly jittery, no doubt fearing for his knighthood every time Number Ten called. Commissioner Walters had already been summoned to Downing Street for no better reason other than to be seen walking up there – pictures in the papers, feeds on the telly. He never looked right. The prime requirement of the Commissioner's job was not to sweat in full uniform whatever the time of day or year. Walters singularly failed this requirement.

Corrigan was also distracted by a selfie his daughter had sent him of her cleavage, followed two minutes later by a text saying 'sorry Dad, meant 4 Damian.' Who the bloody hell was Damian? He had texted his wife to that effect. Who is Damian? But any action on his part would have to wait until the evening. The question was: would Damian be quite so patient? Corrigan turned his phone off. He needed some thinking time.

He surveyed the office with its half-hearted decoration and physically-impaired furniture. In many ways, working conditions had improved little since he joined the Force.

Corrigan used his tongue to extract the rest of the raspberry jam from the heart of his doughnut before demolishing it in two greedy bites.

'Can someone make me a tea?' he shouted through the open door.

He went to lean on the wobbly filing cabinet and then thought better of it. Instead, he perched on the edge of his desk and watched as a blonde-haired man walked proprietorially in the direction of his office, the entreaties of the young WPC scurrying along at his side clearly falling on deaf ears. The man was about the same age as Corrigan but dressed like a twenty-something computer student with a well-gelled hairstyle to match. To the DCI's surprise, the man invaded not just Corrigan's office but his personal space too, eventually coming to halt with his nose barely a foot away from Corrigan's.

'I'm sorry, guv, I tried to explain,' began the distraught WPC but Corrigan waved her away.

'DCI Cardigan?' said the man. He had an accent Corrigan couldn't place – regular, machine-like. Not German but that ballpark.

Corrigan eased himself up from the desk and, in rising to his full height, repelled the space invasion, the man taking a step back like a retreating fencer and removing his rhomboid horn-rimmed glasses to peer up at Corrigan inquisitively.

'DCI Corrigan,' said Corrigan and extended his hand.

The hand was ignored, the glasses returned to the aquiline nose.

'I am Lucas Forsberg.'

Corrigan nodded slowly. He recognised the name. He'd had a pair of researchers all over corporatesponger and similar websites, identifying other business leaders with opaque or controversial tax arrangements. But he obliged Forsberg to plough on all the same. Corrigan had learned a bit in his time as a copper. Forcing those who felt that they needed no introduction to give one was an effective technique for deflating the self-importance of the high and mighty. His first Super had said 'they may think they're better than you and I but, if you punch them on the nose, they bleed'. He often imagined that punch.

'I am the Chief Executive of MöblA.'

Corrigan knew all about it. In the last year for which records were available, the Scandinavian furniture giant had made UK sales of about £1.2 billion and paid just over £8 million in corporate tax – barely half of one per cent. The scam was to force down reported profits by obliging MöblA UK to pay royalties and licence fees to a holding company abroad to secure 'permission' to use the logo, name and designs of MöblA. Clever. Corrigan had the idea that Forsberg himself was Swedish.

'Pleased to meet you,' said Corrigan. 'We have one of your filing cabinets.' He gestured towards the item in question.

'Ah, the skåpP,' said Forsberg.

'Yes, it took two officers two days to assemble it and it falls apart if you put more than three files in it.'

Forsberg appeared to take no notice. 'My friends are terrified,' he announced.

'They have your furniture too?' Corrigan wondered aloud. He really had better things to do.

Forsberg again carried on regardless, naming a couple of actors, a celebrity chef and someone Corrigan had never heard of, who, according to Forsberg, was 'a popular vlogger'. A vlogger sounded like one of Forsberg's pieces of furniture.

'And they are terrified because?'

'Because of your complete incompetence, they are terrified to come as my guest at Beautiful Homes exhibition in Olympia. A crazed killer is stalking the business world and the famous British police take no action.'

'I see.'

'I demand additional protection for myself and my guests.'

'There is a major resource issue, Mr Forsberg. Police cutbacks have been quite significant over the last few years.'

Forsberg snorted. 'We don't pay you to tell us there is nothing you can do.'

'What you pay and to whom seems to be one of the issues here, Sir,' said Corrigan, tailing off.

'Can't you protect us?'

'You are a very rich man, Mr Forsberg. Can't you?'

Forsberg turned his back on Corrigan and looked at the filing cabinet. 'Birch veneer,' the Swede muttered in a wistful tone so leaden and laden he made the remark sound like a line from a Bergman film. Corrigan had seen Bergman's Seventh Seal one night on Channel 4 and, while he'd fallen into a scotch-induced slumber long before the end, he had grasped the general idea: nothing escapes Death. It was a philosophy Corrigan, and all sensible men he assumed, shared. Death had been depicted in the film as a sinisterly-cloaked chess player, Gary Kasparov with a scythe, and Forsberg had the same mannered gestures. His hand descended into the side pocket of his loose-fitting, light cotton peacoat-style jacket. Forsberg was, even Corrigan could see, painfully stylish if a bit of a ham. He produced a pack of playing cards which he tossed onto the desk like a man chucking in his hand, having already bet the farm.

'You have seen these?'

Corrigan assumed that he wasn't suggesting a game and picked the deck up. It was quite cheaply done – a flimsy cardboard box with the cards themselves made of the same coarse material. They didn't have the traditional rounded corners of playing cards. 'Tax Evaders Top Trumps' said the box and inside a full deck in the style of the famous game. Corrigan flicked through the cards.

'Quite a rogue's gallery,' he said – and it truly was. The head of the world's leading car manufacturer looked like one of the Krays, the bloke from that cardigan company had just stepped off the set of the Sopranos. He happened upon Forsberg's picture.

'I am Cristiano Ronaldo,' said Forsberg.

Corrigan nodded slowly. This interview was becoming more Bergman-esque by the minute. 'How so?' he enquired.

'I have the Top Trumps ranking of number two – the same as Cristiano Ronaldo.'

Corrigan nodded again, the card confirming the assertion. 'And who is Lionel Messi?'

'Comm-N is number one. Warren Ruff.' Forsberg pronounced the surname of the head of the global internet brand like a yapping chihuahua.

'I see,' said Corrigan. 'Well, thanks for bringing these in. We'll look into it.' And he was genuinely grateful. The Detective Chief Inspector could see the significance. It may have looked like a bit of market stall crap, but it was effectively a hit list.

Corrigan extended his hand but once again it was not accepted. The look on the Swede's face was one of such profound gloom that, had Forsberg been playing chess with Death, Death would have resigned. No wonder alcoholism was the national sport in Forsberg's country.

'I have over 350 stores in 43 countries,' said Forsberg, capturing once again the most wistful of tones. 'How many stores does Mr Ruff have?'

'Well, he effectively owns the internet, Mr Forsberg. You own a lot of MDF.'

Forsberg looked at Corrigan over the frame of his glasses, piercing blue eyes beneath a landscape of frown lines. There was a moment's stand-off. The sun cut low and harsh through the window, causing the dust to dance in the air and both men to squint.

'You could call a private security firm,' said Corrigan. 'Secur4U are usually available and always tender competitively.'

'Ja. Or I could just go to your very fine London Zoo and get a couple of baboons,' said Forsberg.

The Swede walked over to the window. The view wasn't one of London's finest, mostly buildings of dirty glass.

'I walk around London, Sergeant, and I still see the same magnificent city I fell in love with as a student,' said Forsberg mournfully. Corrigan anticipated a but bigger than his old Auntie Elsie's.

'But something has changed. Your train companies are run by the Germans and Dutch, I believe.'

'Yes, well, owned...'

'And your energy by the French and Spanish?'

'You could say that.'

'And the Chinese own your nuclear power.'

'Well, that sounds a bit... are you sure?'

'This used to be the greatest country in the world, Sergeant. Why did you give it all away?'

Corrigan joined Forsberg at the window. A bus made a little staccato progress.

'Chief Inspector,' Corrigan said in the absence of anything else. 'Chief Inspector.'

But the Swede's attention had been drawn to an enormous Comm-N poster opposite: an ad for some new technological device, apparently, the Comm-N Touch. Corrigan wondered what it was but he knew better than to ask.

'The skåpP is an excellent cabinet,' said the Swede, returning his thoughts to the interior of Corrigan's office. 'I have several myself. I imagine your officers failed to follow the instructions. I will fix.' And, with that, he began opening the various drawers of the filing cabinet, chuntering gutturally under his breath. The cabinet tottered and creaked as it always had done. Forsberg handed Corrigan the half a dozen files which made up the piece's entire contents.

As Corrigan looked vainly around the office for somewhere else to put the files, the distraught WPC reappeared in the doorway, armed this time with a mug of tea. 'You were after tea, guv?'

'Thank you. Can you bring some for Mr Forsberg?' The furniture mogul had levered the filing cabinet over onto its back and was now crouched over it with muttering intent.

The desk phone rang. Corrigan put the files on the desk and sat down. It was Mason again.

'How did the Cobra go?' asked Corrigan. There was much rattling and the squealing of metal on metal coming from the filing cabinet. Corrigan was impressed as Forsberg produced his own Allen key.

'Are you on a building site, Chief Inspector?'

'My furniture is being repaired.'

'We had to keep the Cobra short. It was all hands to the pump at HMRC.'

'What do you mean?'

'Tax payments have gone into overdrive. I don't think Revenue and Customs have ever had so many and for so much.'

Corrigan sipped his tea, appreciatively. 'I'll send you over a revised budget,' he said.

# 3.9.

Brighton fancied itself as a bit rad. It made Cherrianne laugh every time she encountered it. Could you really call designer coffee, hipster beards and overpriced scratched vinyl of interest only to flaky old white men rad? The politics was so mixed up.

The rents in this town are an absolute disgrace – thank God for my fixed-rate mortgage.

I'm right behind the squatters and the strikers – yes, quinoa and hummus wholemeal wrap to go, if you please, Tarquin.

I'm 110% opposed to global warning – but, of course, I can't cycle up this hill and I need the 4x4 for when I visit ma-ma.

That being so, it was no surprise to Cherri that when she arrived at the station, the four letters TESS, which were now trending like Kardashians, were painted on the pavement outside in screaming white. A fair impersonation of the Helvetica Neue font, Cherri reckoned. It was one of her favourites and she'd designed the corporatesponger interface around it. Each letter was enormous. Fifty thousand picas high.

The bread guy was moaning. The workmen trying to clean off the graffiti were in his way and, he claimed, putting off his customers. He had a barrow for his wares – a quaint affectation that implied the artisanship of a bygone age – which he'd moved about twenty yards to the left, much to the chagrin of the procession of commuters whose path he was now partly occupying. So they were moaning too. Cherri waved at the bread guy. She'd been known to purchase the linseed-topped gluten-free panini. They tasted so good.

She smiled to herself as she imagined how her Auntie Rita would react to a linseed-topped gluten-free panini. How much you pay? You bafan girl? (Bafan was her Aunt Rita's insult for everyone.) Cherrianne wouldn't be telling her aunt about the panini. Cherrianne wouldn't be telling her aunt about lots of things. She still remembered how her aunt had freaked when Cherri had told her she wanted to buy a motorbike, booming 'no, no!' for what seemed like an hour and a half. But it was Rita's big heart and bigger arms that she needed, a large plate of rice and peas and a larger serving of wisdom.

Were the graffiti merchants making a point about the bread man and his tax affairs or making a general comment about Brighton and/or its commuters or were they just savouring the air of anarchy? There was something imprecise about it, something out of control that she didn't like. The mob worried her. You couldn't be black, be female or be androgynous – and Cherri was all three – without being a little worried about the mob.

She looked up at the Departure board. She wanted the train to Victoria to change for Brixton. But her attention was distracted by a kerfuffle outside M&S. She realised how wired she was. Three young white men in hoodies and jeans were tight round an older man in a suit. For a moment they were a single mass, all arms and elbows. A well-polished shoe was scuffed, a lapel flicked contemptuously, a cheek chucked. The older man pulled himself free and something hit the ground with a metallic ping and spun to halt. A coin. No, a badge. She knew what that said.

TESS, again.

They'd been trying to pin it on him. And she knew what TESS was supposed to mean. Not 'Text and Email Support Services'. Not 'of the D'Urbervilles'. But 'Tax Evading Super Scum'. The older man marched away, a hasty panicked look back over his shoulder as he passed through the ticket barrier and then stopped to catch a panting lungful of breath. Nobody seemed vexed. Most probably, most people never noticed. Like the three monkeys.

Cherri was more than androgynous. Some would call her 'non-binary' although she had never used the term herself. The thing was that she was attracted to men but she liked – sometimes – to be mistaken for a man herself. She loved being able to duck into the Gents toilets when there was a queue at the Ladies. She welcomed buying clothes in the Boys dept. Cheaper. More colours. She wore boxer shorts and felt more comfortable in them. But there was more to it than all that. She didn't like the categorisation, the precisely-labelled boxes into which people and especially women were put. She felt that men had more freedom in this regard. But, at the same time, she wouldn't want to be a man. As she was, she felt like a free spirit. That was what non-binary meant to Cherri. She felt that at heart everybody was like that. All individuals, all different. Yet the lure of the group was strong in the human being. Very strong. Too strong? She looked at the three boys with their silly badges, overgrown boys in the boots of men, rock boots with buckles and skulls. They had another victim in their sights now: a waddling man who looked more like a school caretaker than a tax dodger (although Cherri knew you couldn't tell by looking.) His only evident crime was being in possession of a suit. He emerged from their attentions covered in stickers.

'Tess,' one of the boys shouted after him. 'Tess!'

The lure of the group was presumably to do with clarity. We all want answers and, whether it's Facebook or religion, the group seems to provide them. Perhaps Cherri just found clarity a little dull. She didn't fit in and she liked it. It was all there in the expression, fitting in. 'Fitting in' was about changing yourself – filing off your square edges to fit into the round hole. Left to their own devices, people were all non-binary – nuanced and complex – but groups tended to a self-righteous simplicity.

Her mind went back to a pub conversation in the early days of corporatesponger, Dan holding court. He was saying that companies and corporations were psychopaths. Or rather that their behaviour was psychopathic. 'Yes, Dan,' everybody was saying. 'Yes, Dan.' A company's raison d'être was to feed itself with money. 'It's not some theoretical thing', Dan said. 'This is not academic. It's the law. Companies have a legal obligation to their shareholders to maximise profit.' This meant that, if it wasn't illegal, they had to do it. Pay workers as little as possible. Extract or treat raw materials as cheaply as possible. Strip assets. Relocate. Disregard environment and community consequences. 'Corporate social responsibility is not just the biggest load of PR bollocks,' Dan concluded. 'It's not, even with the best will in the world, actually possible.'

If that was true, then the individuals at the top of the company weren't really the problem. Their scheming and conniving to avoid paying tax was just a symptom. The cause was the machine: free-market capitalism in which businesses' first duty was to their own survival, not right or wrong. The 'tax man axe man', as some were calling him, may have firmly placed the issue that Dan and Cherri had been concerned with for years on the map but he'd done it in the wrong way. The medium was the message and the message of the murders was that this was about greedy individuals when really, since much of what most corporates did was legal, it was about government. Lax tax regimes. A lack of regulation.

So why did Sender and Brown and Robb and all the others do these immoral things apparently so willingly? They didn't start out as bad men. Sender was a bookworm, wasn't he? A guy with a massive library who yearned for somewhere cheaper to buy his books. Robb was a talented designer. Zak Thomas Brown just wanted a decent cup of coffee. Surely the real point of what Dan was saying was that the machine corrupts the individuals in it. Following the will of a psychopathic entity, the corporation, makes psychopaths of us all.

And now Dan, her Dan – the funny, generous guy with a scooter that sounded like a hairdryer, had turned into the living proof. Corporatesponger was a business too. Valued in six figures. That wasn't some notional paper value but real hard cash offered by an American investor. And, as the crisis escalated, with each dead or later undead CEO, corporatesponger was snowballing – more attention, more hits. 'A growing asset,' as the money men put it.

And that was why she had found the paint and brushes, stickers and badges in the office stock cupboard. She'd only been looking for paper. It wasn't Helvetica Neue that she'd recognised on the station forecourt, it was Dan's big bold handwriting.

# 3.10.

From the master bedroom window, Jessica watched Gavin. He was out on the cliff again. It was hard to see how close he was to the edge but it couldn't be far. What was the matter with him? It was definitely 'His Lordship', Mr Gavin Henley Esquire. She had a pair of binoculars that she had taken from the space he liked to call the 'observatory' – actually, the loft – in which he had installed a telescope for stargazing. She'd seen him standing there before and wondered, not for the first time, if it was anything to do with the rows with 'Her Majesty'. They'd recently 'celebrated' their second wedding anniversary. That was paper, wasn't it? How many 'I vill fucking kill you, you are fucking dead man's could a paper marriage take?

Jessica sometimes asked herself whether she felt a bit sorry for Her Maj. Second wives always got it in the neck. The first Mrs Henley from Blackheath had never been satisfied with her slice of the pie. Then there was Pip, the daughter from the first marriage, a student who blamed Her Majesty both for her parents' divorce and for her father's move to Estuary Sands. Hard to say which she hated her for the most. Jessica had heard Pip castigate her stepmother for both and in terms that might have made even Jessica's own mother blush (but probably not). The pair were downstairs, going at it like alley cats even now, and that was the reason Jess was plugging in the vacuum cleaner.

'Where's Dad? What have you done to him, you witch?'

Jessica could hear it all through the state-of-the-art insulation, state-of-the-art floorboards and state-of-the-art carpets.

'I do nothing. He out. He have to work to keep your stupid fat face at university.'

Jessica had two other jobs, one of them was at The Smugglers', a pub on the wrong side of town (was there a right side?) that had seen better days but the brawls were nothing like this. Blokes swore a bit, went red and then either laid into each other or walked away; women got under their adversary's skin like a scalpel.

'Perhaps you like stuff fat face with big bag of Doritos while you wait.'

Got right under the skin and stripped it off.

Princess Pip's house, the one that His Lordship had bought her when she got her place at uni, had caught fire. It had been a dramatic night. Jess had been the one who called the fire brigade. Podgy Pip had been carried from the blaze by a fireman. (Jess hoped he hadn't done his back in.) Nobody seriously hurt. Pip had spent the night in hospital and, after a couple of nights on a friend's couch, had moved home. She was now threatening to move her stuff out of storage and move home 'for good'. Jess wondered how that could be good in any good sense of the word.

'This not your home. You never fucking live here. You move in my house over my dead body.'

'Let's see what Daddy says, shall we? I shall also need a new laptop, a new phone, some new books, new clothes, new furniture...'

'Ha. Ask him where is cash? Ze darling Daddy. Idiot is going to pay ze tax. In my country ve don't pay ze tax. Vy he not buy property in London like normal person?'

'A property in London would be nice but all I want is a little house near to my dear stepmother.'

Silent seething was audible even through the state-of-the-art insulation, state-of-the-art floorboards and state-of-the-art carpets.

'And I'm glad he pays his taxes,' Pip went on. 'You'll just have to wait for your yacht.'

Wait until your opponent is off their guard and then land the killer blow.

'And ze idiot Daddy say he go give charity,' said Her Maj wistfully.

'Well, he's already a major donor to the national society of sponging Russian tarts.'

'Zu fucking bitch.'

'No, you're a fucking bitch.'

'Zu fucking bitch bitch.'

'You're a fucking bitch with a PhD in Fucking Bitchness from the University of Bitchdom. Bitch.'

Then it went quiet. A few moments later, there was the muffled crunch of Doritos being eaten. Was this hellish home better or worse than her own hellish home?

Jessica looked at the lawn, freshly-cut, the shrubbery for which hollyhocks and sunflowers were planned, the gazebo, the decking, the putting green, the barbecue – all electric, the crystal blue pool. She wasn't against all this bling. She'd have some of it herself when she won the lottery. Do it large. But you didn't need to be that MP for Brighton, that green woman, Caroline something, to see that this house in this place was like socks in sandals, just plain wrong. Estuary Sands was Lady Gaga at the all-England bowling club, a blot on the landscape.

Jessica dragged her gaze back into the house. It was every bit as substantial and screamingly inappropriately state of the art as the garden. Still, asking why was not her job; her job was to clean the place. She looked at her vacuum cleaner, waiting for her impatiently on the landing. She looked at herself in the two full-length mirrors. Her outfit was not flattering. The jogging bottoms, grey and stained with polishes, oils and paints; the old T-shirt; the hair up in a bandana and the Nikes. She hoped she'd still got something. Maybe it was nothing more than optimism, but so what? You couldn't buy that. Eat your heart out, Frida Gustavsson. The smile flickered across her lips again. A little self-satisfied that smile, and that made her smile some more. Not all saggy. Not yet. Still looked like a supermodel in the eyes of her mad old Auntie.

Jessica returned to the landing and fired up the Dyson. She liked the landing. It was like a hall. It was so wide and the carpet so deep. Bastard to vacuum but gorgeous to look at. This was also where Lord and Lady Regatta hung the paintings that they'd paid too much for to allow all and sundry to see. His Lord Highness had informed her he didn't want them being 'eyed up by every artisan and brickie'. There were still plenty of both on the estate with everything being so new. Jessica liked one or two of them – the paintings, not the artisans. And not the Damien Hirst sculpture style of thing. She used to like art at school, wasn't bad at it, and she knew the difference between culture and fashion. Loved fashion, for sure, but wouldn't pretend that it was anything more than dressing up.

She turned the vacuum cleaner off. She never really got anywhere with this carpet and Her Majesty never really noticed. She wasn't likely to be anymore observant today what with her and Princess Pippa at it hammer and.

As the motor died, Jessica became aware of singing, a child's tuneless la-la-la-ing. The sprog was at the top of the stairs. On the second stair down probably because Jessica couldn't quite see her, only her little hands on the landing. She was playing with a Barbie doll. Jessica didn't really think this was a suitable toy for a child of three-and-a-half and found herself raising her eyebrows like her own mother. She amazed herself sometimes, how old school she was. In the sprog's tiny fingers, the naked doll was an anorexic giant with boobs as pointy and plastic as the sprog's mother. The sprog crawled up onto the top stair and bobbed to her feet, waving the doll at Jessica as if she had just found something that everyone had been looking for. She padded along the carpet in designer Burberry booties and a bright pink DKNY dress. She was only dressed because Jessica had dressed her, the sprog. No sign of the nanny this morning.

'Hello sweetheart,' said Jessica.

'Mummy's crying.'

That was a new development. There had been no tears when Jessica had arrived, just a 'thank God zoo are here, Roberta can't comm.'

The sprog wobbled by the Damien Hirst, chubby little Barbie-free hand clutching air. Now, if she pulled that over, there really would be tears. Damien Hirst was the plastic tits of the art world, so presumably Her Maj liked it. Liked the price tag anyway.

Her Majesty had been flapping about trying to get the sprog something to eat when Jess had arrived. You'd think she'd never been in a kitchen before. True, hers was big enough to service a football team – something Her Majesty was rumoured to have done herself in a previous life if Shelley Dabrowski were to be believed – but, all the same, she should have known where the waffles were kept.

Jessica guessed they didn't have waffles in Russia. (Did that make her a Tsar – or a Tsarina – rather than a Majesty?) Not that Her Majesty ate much apart from raw men. Still, the sprog must have got her waffles habit from somewhere.

Her Majesty's name was Malvina. She was six feet tall, stick-thin. (If she was a mail order bride, it must have been a bloody big envelope, said Shelley Dabrowski.) Quite what His Lord Highness, who wasn't a bad-looking bloke and was clearly loaded, saw in her, Jessica hadn't the foggiest. Even a blind man could tell that her tits were fake: too high, too pointed, too far apart.

'Roberta says zat she can't comm because she is traumatised,' Her Majesty had said.

Her Majesty's tongue whipped words into a guttural shape. Traumatised had emerged in four spat syllables.

Traumatised by what, Jessica was not sure – the constant rows, the fire at Pip's, the missing waffles.

'If we'd got an illegal immigrant for ze nanny like everyone else, zis wouldn't have happened. But Gavin insisted on a British nanny. Vould be good for ze language development of ze daughter. Well, if you have lived in ze fucking war zone, zoo are not going to be traumatise-ed by lizzle domestic, are you?'

'You might be.' You might be in this house, is what Jessica meant.

'Can you make zer waffles?'

'For your daughter?'

'Da, I'm far too fucking upset to eat.'

'Yes, Mummy's very sad.' Jessica said. She got down on her haunches as the sprog stumble-stopped before her. 'We all cry when we're sad, don't we, darling?'

The sprog held up the doll and made crying noises. 'Mummy's crying. I don't like it.'

'No, sweetie. But she'll stop crying soon. Why don't we go and put some clothes on Barbie?'

'Barney's sunbathing.' She set the doll face down, spread-eagled on the carpet.

Jessica smiled. 'Barbie's sunbathing.'

'Barney.'

'Barbie.'

The kid looked at Jess as if Jess were utterly insane, as if, rather than the name of a doll, Barbie was a Mongolian or Martian word. Victoria, they'd called her, the sprog. Tori, for short. Jessica thought that quite funny. 'They're all fucking Tories up there, aren't they?' That's what her mum had said when Jessica had told her she'd be working there.

'I'm just cleaning their house, Mum. I don't suppose there'll be any political discussions.'

'They're in our constituency too, Estuary Sands. This place will go the wrong way. Why else do you think that cunt of a Prime Minister visited the hospital?'

'Mum.'

Jessica didn't have anything against Anglo-Saxon language but keep it in proportion.

Jessica led the child by the hand towards her bedroom. 'Come on, Tori,' she said. 'And bring Barney.'

The kid waddle-walked beside her. 'Barney, Barney, Barney,' she said. 'Barney, Barney, Barney.' She held the doll by its hair and it nearly dragged along the carpet. 'I like Barney.'

Tori's room was anaemically neat for a toddler's. The result of having a nanny running after you, Jessica presumed. After all, she had to find something to do, young Roberta. Tori wasn't yet old enough for Latin and prep school, wasn't a prodigiously early reader devouring

Ivanhoe and had shown no genius for the piano. In fact, Tori was a pretty ordinary kid with mousey hair and a dirty nose. She was another of her mother's disappointments. You should never give up on your kids, should you? But Jessica frequently felt as if Her Majesty already had so far as Tori was concerned. If Roberta wasn't around, it was always Jessica she turned to. Take Tori for a walk, da? Take Tori to ze shops if you're going, I headache. And once even: can you clean up Tori's vomit? No, Her Majesty was not built for childcare.

In fact, it was a moot point whether Her Majesty was really built for any form of human interaction at all. She may have had the mother of all spats with her stepdaughter and she may have been sitting in her enormous kitchen-diner sobbing. But it would be a mistake to assume that these two events were directly linked. She was probably crying because her Botox appointment had been cancelled or something.

Bundle in the constant rows with Gavin himself and you found yourself wondering what the future was for the couple. Actually, thinking about it, perhaps Malvina was crying for this very reason. Divorce would cost Gavin Henley but it wouldn't ruin him. Malvina might crawl out of it a few hundred thou' richer but, whatever they said in the Daily Mail, the truth was she'd be going right back to Shitville with her tail between her legs.

All that, and despite a diet of sea air and waffle incense, she had crow's feet and bingo wings.

You'd expect to feel more for a woman you'd spent so much time with, even if you were just the cleaner, but Jessica didn't. She looked inside herself. There was no compassion. So perhaps she was the heartless one.

Tori's little wheedling fingers had managed to ease open the door on her pretty pink toy cupboard. (The sprog's room was about the only one that wasn't basically black and white and blingy.) Jessica returned Barney to his rightful home between the Play-Doh and Princess Tiara. The cupboard was packed with toys, neatly so, and Jessica spotted the gap immediately. Downstairs the front door slammed (Pip?) and she heard Her Majesty crashing about in the kitchen. Perhaps she'd fallen off her authentic imitation 70s leather-topped bar stool. Jessica got it, or thought she did: the real reason for Her Majesty's tears, anger and general bitchiness to the max. The large Hello Kitty duffle bag which, the last time Jess had seen it, had been stuffed full with bundle after bundle of £10 and £20 notes, had gone.

# 3.11.

Ron was impressed by the level of industry for a Saturday morning.

He was focusing on striding purposefully. The old head was a little heavy, the nearest he'd had to a hangover for years. Friday night at The Smugglers. Vic's merry band of no-particular-place-to-goers had been discussing the murders. It had not been an edifying spectacle but it had been impossible to walk away from.

You live by the sword (Vic Hooper).

It's shocking. An appalling indictment, really. But we only even notice because they're rich. How many are killed in the Middle East every day? (Tommy the student).

If you can't do the time, don't do the crime (Wilf McCauley).

I don't agree with it, right – but they don't care about ordinary people like us, do they? Why should we care about them? (Hovis).

What murders? (Ruby Tuesday).

The ignorance didn't surprise him. Nor did the moral ambiguity. But it was odd to hear it expressed. Scrape away a little and the Great British sense of right and wrong was scratchcard thin, with all sorts lurking underneath. The whole discussion, if you could call it that, had lasted barely ten minutes but Ron had been thinking about it all the way home and, once he got there, had found himself pouring a triple scotch. At least, he hadn't been called upon to recount it blow for blow to Eileen. She'd have been appalled. She'd have had a thing or two to say.

'The world is built on moral ambiguity, love.'

'Well, not in my classroom.' Eileen was smiling as she looked up from her marking, red pen in hand. It was a wand of morality, that red pen.

'Especially Biscuit Town.'

'You're going to mention the wife-selling again now, aren't you, Ronald?' Sometimes she called him Ronald as if he were a child. Especially when she considered his argument suspect.

Every local knew Biscuit Town was the site of the last known incidence of wife-selling in Sussex – and most, even the wives (although not Eileen), found that quite amusing. (The sale in question had been for the knock-down price of half a crown and a pint of ale making the pub in question – now a bookmakers, a kind of conjugal Poundland.)

'I wasn't actually,' said Ron. He was reading one of his local history books from the library. It was the book of his dreams – a big, fat one with all the facts.

'This town was built on slave money.'

'Stern and Feltman were Quakers. They founded the school.' Eileen, not looking up this time, was the one resorting to familiar lines now. Tick, went the red pen. Tick, tick, cross.

'A good half of the Victorian part of the town was built with slave money, love – compensation to the former owners on abolition. Including Lyon House.'

'Lyon House? But that's National Trust.'

'It is now.'

Ron enjoyed running this conversation in his head. But he knew it had never actually happened. (He hadn't had that much to drink.) He'd never really got the better of an argument with Eileen (or discussion, as she called them). Only in his dreams. Ron fancied himself as a bit of a local historian, but he was beginning to see things in a different light – and it wasn't just the hangover. If you let it, history had a tendency to become all dates and statues. He'd never really looked at it with a policeman's eye. There had never been a lot of justice, had there? Not a lot of fairness.

Unfortunately, for a man concentrating on walking, the foot-shaped stickers all over the hospital floor showing the routes to the various wards and departments were being replaced. Then, at the spot where you usually needed to sidestep a bucket beneath a leak in the flat roof, Ron noticed scaffolding had been erected and men were cheerfully removing mouldy grey ceiling tiles.

Both renovations were very welcome. Many a visitor had complained about the feet coming to a halt halfway along the top corridor of A wing. Depending on how his mood was swinging, Ron found it alternately disturbing or amusing that the steps stopped by a permanently-open window as if they were inviting the visitor to jump. Sometimes jumping was exactly what he was minded to do. On other occasions, the gallows humour tickled him. Today ...

He arrived at the 'Where To Go' desk to find Mrs Graham already seated behind it.

'Morning, Gill. I didn't know you were on today.'

'It's all hands on deck, Ron. Haven't you heard the news?'

'What news?'

'Well, there's the government's revised budget that you'll have heard about, but also we've had a massive gift – a major charitable donation to the hospital.'

'So we won't be entertained by the dripping roof today?'

'No, they're redoing the entire area, including the café.'

'I see.' Ron looked around. It really was quite impressive. Plenty of men. Plenty of plant, paint and tiles. Clearly, the aim was to get the work done over the week-end. Usually it took a month and a half to replace a washer.

'Did you not see outside as you came in?' Gill continued. 'You know the Italian garden? They've replaced the cherub statue.'

'There was a dripping tap in Eileen's room,' he said, aware he was talking across her but unable to stop. 'Kept her awake all night. Took them ages to repair it. I had to...'

Gill rearranged the leaflets on the 'Where To Go' desk in a business-like fashion. She was wondering how to reply, Ron knew that. You were supposed to talk about your loved one in the immediate aftermath of his or her death. They called it 'sharing your grief'. This was considered to be healthy, one of the acceptable routes through the five stages of grief. But then, after an appropriate interval – the socially-correct duration of which was not at all clear but was presumably related to a number of factors including age, nature and length of terminal illness, general character and gender of loved one, general character and gender of mourner and all sorts of other random cultural bollocks, you were supposed to shut the fuck up and get on with your life. Ron was failing the etiquette test. Gill's arm went for the china cup on the desk and finding it now devoid of tea, jerked back to her side.

'Do you want another cup?' Ron asked.

'You need to go to the other end...'

Ron nodded. Their café, he could see, was closed for its long overdue refurb.

Oh, it wasn't Mrs Graham's fault. She had been more understanding and sympathetic than most. It was just fucking society, wasn't it? He watched as three T-shirted workmen wrestled a pallet of gleaming new white ceiling tiles into the middle of the room. He wanted to smash every single one of them – the tiles and the workmen. Instead, he was going to drink some tea.

'Back in a minute,' he said, taking Gill's empty cup with him as he went.

A woman with a clipboard bristled past, all hairspray and skirt suit. He recognised her as one of the hospital managers. Following behind were more of this seeming army of workmen wheeling trolleys chocker with materials. As he walked through the hospital, he became aware of more little jobs in progress and, in several departments, waiting rooms of individuals, turning the pages of magazines without really reading and playing with their mobile phones, the evidence not just of a backlog of jobs but of a backlog of patients also being addressed.

He took a detour – up a flight of stairs. And, at the end of the corridor, more workmen and more patients. He recognised the receptionist. He recognised the young consultant with the open-necked shirt, emerging from his room with a sheaf of notes and calling a patient's name. He recognised the nurse with the headscarf. She was white but she was married to a Muslim, he remembered that. She was leaning over addressing a seated patient as Ron arrived and she spotted him as she rose.

'Hello, Mr Newton,' she said automatically – the reflex smile.

And then the smile cracked like a pixellating screen as her brain flagged up an awkward chronology.

'Busy, this morning,' Ron observed. 'And a Saturday too.'

'Mr Newton, are you...?'

'It's OK,' said Ron. 'I'm just here for my Friends of the Hospital shift.'

The smile reappeared. 'That's very community-minded...'

'Thought it was odd when they asked me to come in on a Saturday, but now I see.'

The nurse surveyed the assembly. Another consultant – a new face – appeared and called a name.

'Just a quick question,' said Ron. 'Are you prescribing Revanex?'

The nurse looked left and then right, up then down and, in the absence of anywhere else to look, replied: 'yes'.

It was the reply he wanted to hear and the reply he didn't want to hear. The china cup, Mrs Graham's cup, was no longer in his hands. Instead, it was in half a dozen pieces on the shiny, clean floor between two pairs of sensible shoes, his and the nurse's. The nurse said something to him but he didn't hear her. Just as he hadn't heard the cup shatter.

As he retraced his steps in search of tea, Ron felt like he was in a bubble. He'd temporarily lost his hearing once, following an explosion in a building he had been staking out, and it felt a little like that. Other people passing in the corridors looked like fish, mouths opening and shutting meaninglessly, but he was the one in the goldfish bowl, going round and round, round and round. When that building had exploded, his first thought was that he had been shot. It felt a bit like that too.

The five stages of grief were supposedly denial, anger, bargaining, depression and acceptance. Feeling detached, feeling on the edge was not one of them. In truth, Ron knew he was stuck. The five stages of grief had become like a hospital in which the fucking direction signs were absent: an impenetrable mess of a maze. He'd never done denial. As an ex-copper, he couldn't deny the reality of death or kid himself that it was anything but arbitrary. He'd accepted that Eileen was going to die from day one of her diagnosis. Perhaps, if he'd not accepted that, perhaps if he'd done a decent bit of denial, he'd have fought a lot harder to get her prescribed Revanex. That thought was like a bullet every time it went through his mind. But accepting death was not the same as accepting the loss that results from death and he was nowhere near that. The bed, the house, his life – they were all so empty without her. In the maze of grief he was wandering back and forth between anger and depression, going round and round, round and round.

He burned his hand on the tea vending machine and then found himself with three cups to carry when he only wanted two. No tray. Steam coming out of the machine; smoke coming out of his ears. He left the third cup in the machine, someone else's problem. This wasn't Ron Newton. He knew that. Leaving it to someone else was not Ron Newton's style. 'Come on Isaac, let it go,' they'd say. His ex-colleagues. He never did. Never let anything go. But, right now, he didn't feel much like Ron Newton. He pulled the sleeves of his cardigan down over his hands to provide a little protection from the heat of the cups and carried them, one in each mitt, back to Gill seated at the table.

Gill looked up at him. Was that contempt in her eyes or paranoia in his head? Ron Newton was a man who coped with whatever life threw at him and, here he was, struggling with two paper cups. Ron slumped into his seat. Gill was talking about the work they were doing in the hospital. She was talking about all the money. Ron looked at her and had that goldfish bowl feeling again. He could hardly hear her and she was out of focus, blurred like when you looked at something through water.

'Are you crying, Ron?' Gill asked.

'What did you just say?'

'Are you crying...'

'No, before that.'

'I said do you remember the fire when Colin rescued that girl? Well, the donor, the big donor to the hospital, is her father. A Mr Henley...'

Ron let the tears come. He was crying like a baby in public. He had never done anything like this before. He allowed Gill to fish him out first one, then two, and then three, double-ply paper handkerchiefs from her handbag. 'Ron,' she said, 'Ron...'

And Ron didn't have the faintest idea whether he was crying with sadness or happiness. He was just so fucking delighted that they were prescribing Revanex and that nobody else would have to go through what he had been through. He said as much to Gill and he knew as he said it that he sounded like one of those idiots on TV – 'I don't want anyone else to have to go through what I've gone through' – or like those bloody self-righteous cancer women, Debbie Gann and Ruby Tuesday, down the pub. Glib, vacuous, self-delusional. But in the moment he said it, well, it wasn't closure, it wasn't acceptance, but it felt a little bit like it and for that moment he wasn't in a fishbowl but on planet Earth with the sane people and with the sounds of drills, male voices and of ceiling tiles being removed.

Gill patted Ron on the top of his hand. They were seated side by side at the Friends' desk.

'Oh, and I took your cup into the kitchen,' said Ron.

'Thank you,' said Gill. 'It's going to be a busy day.'

# 3.12.

Standing on the edge of the cliff. When was it at its most exciting? At night when you could hear the waves crashing against the rocks below, or during the day when you could see all the way down, imagine yourself falling and wonder what would go through your mind. Night or day, he loved standing there. Flip flops were best. You could feel the big Nothing gnawing on your toes. The adrenalin rush through his body was as powerful as any tide. To be a footstep from death made him feel alive. It was his morning coffee, his pick-me-up, his nightcap. This was why he had always loved his job. You were always standing on the edge. You needed to know exactly where you were, where the terrain was firm and where it was crumbling beneath your feet. But was something seismic happening in the world? Was it all about to fall down?

One false step and, shark or not, you were swimming with the fishes.

Gill had found Ron's crying more disturbing than she would ever have guessed. She had, like most people she presumed, an instinctive trust, a confidence in the emergency services which amounted to, if she were honest, a sort of blind faith, something almost religious, a notion that they were better than other people – level-headed, unemotional, selfless. Silly, really, when she examined it properly. Childish. Deluded. Were all English people labouring under that misapprehension or just her generation? She had stopped believing politicians but somehow her faith in doctors and nurses, police and firemen, had persisted. Perhaps because of Colin. Perhaps because she knew her son was made of the solid old stuff. Seeing Ron cry was like seeing Colin cry. And that wasn't right because to cry, when she thought of Colin, was what she, the silly old woman, was supposed to do.

Gill had offered to walk back over Moonshine Point with Ron after their shift and, in keeping that promise, she was beginning to realise how fit Ron Newton still was, slight limp or not. She tried to suggest they stop for a little sit-down on the bench but nothing much came out when she tried to speak. She was already seated – a flop down, really – and stretching her calves out in front of her before words finally emerged.

'I'm not really wearing the shoes for hill-walking, Ron,' she said, between breaths.

Ron, a handful of paces ahead of her, stopped and turned. 'No,' he said, taking a look at her outstretched legs. 'I always struggle in heels too.'

It was good to see him smile, good to hear him complete a sentence. It was the first he'd managed since they'd left the hospital.

Ron came and sat down beside her. 'I sometimes stop when I'm walking home but I don't sit down,' he said. 'Worried I might not get up again.'

Gill didn't say anything. She was still catching her breath. Ron, for all his size, seemed to have already caught his and was looking to get moving. Men had a way, when they were itching to get moving (or avoid a conversation or both), of moving forward in their seat and looking left and right like birds of prey.

'It's that bloke again,' he said.

Gill looked up and followed her companion's pointing finger. A little further up the slope and dangerously close to the precipice was a jogger – well, she presumed he was a jogger – in black lycra.

'He's a bit close to the edge, isn't he?'

'I've seen him before. He's new. Estuary Sands. I don't think he realises how unstable the cliff is here.'

'Hasn't he heard about the accident, the little girl?'

'Thanks for walking me,' said Ron, with a grin. The big man had regained his composure and was up on his feet already. It was an action that he completed like an oiled piston and that she increasingly completed like a rusty hinge. Gill decided to stay put for a little longer.

'I'll just have a little...' They both smiled. 'Good bye, Ron.'

She watched him walk away. You could just tell he was ex-army or ex-police, something in his bearing and gait: the set-back shoulders, the efficient heel-toe movement of the feet. He stopped to exchange a few words with the jogger. Gill looked out to sea. There were a couple of container ships and a viscous black murmuration of starlings doing their swooping and diving thing: thousands of birds as if as one twisting and turning, transmuting from one mathematical shape to another. It was quite uncanny the way they moved in such perfect harmony. She could watch this display all day. It made her feel free – and less like a rusty hinge.

Ron had moved on and the jogger was descending towards her at quite a pace when Gill recognised him.

'Mr Henley,' she shouted.

He came to a reluctant halt. The English would go to great lengths to avoid seeing each other, but there was an instinctive understanding of when the game was up, and then all politeness was unleashed with a fanfare of trumpets and a troupe of jugglers. That line between convincingly and unconvincingly not seeing someone was very thin indeed but, like swooping starlings never flying into each other, everybody seemed to know exactly where it was.

'Good afternoon,' said Mr Henley through the most radiant of smiles.

'Lovely day for a run.'

'Or for a walk,' he said.

'Look at those starlings,' said Gill. 'Isn't it magnificent?'

Gavin hadn't really noticed them before. Too focused on his Fitbit, his heart rate, his safe-exercise zone and the nagging twinge in the back of his calf.

'It really is,' he said, looking up at the steel grey sky. And he really meant it.

He found himself doing something that he'd never have expected to do.

'May I?' he asked but it was a rhetorical question. And then he was seated on the bench beside the fireman's mother (he hoped he would remember her name at some point), the pair of them watching the birds.

'Wish I had my binoculars.'

'They roost in the trees,' said Gill, after a moment. 'Used to be more of them before they...'

She was going to say 'built Estuary Sands' but she didn't, and Gavin appreciated that. He used to think that this linguistic pussyfooting was a sign of weakness. While the English were dancing around not saying what they meant, Gavin Henley was in there closing the deal. But he wondered if he still believed that. It was an odd sensation for Gavin to be wondering what he actually thought about something. Ambivalence. He couldn't remember feeling it before. It wasn't as unpleasant as he would have imagined.

'It's one of the reasons I bought here,' he said. 'Not the starlings exactly, but the nature, the sense of freedom when you're up here on the cliff.'

'You need to be careful, Mr Henley. We may say solid as a rock, but it's not true. These cliffs have never been solid.'

Again, Gavin was aware of what was not being said. Over the years, so he'd been told by his property investment broker, Moonshine Point had been becoming less of a point and more a stump: crumbling into the sea like the chalk that it was. There had been heavy erosion in the 60s and 70s and the coastal footpath had been moved back thirty or forty yards. But matters had settled themselves and, by 2000, even the protective fence had been taken down. That was the official line. However, over the last six months or so, things had started moving again, with 65-million-year-old chunks the size of boulders crashing to the beach below. Gavin knew that this, rightly or wrongly, was being attributed to the multi-property, swimming-pool-rich, basement-heavy, flamboyantly over-endowed gated community in which he was now resident called Estuary Sands. The argument was that the heavy building work had set the cliff off again. It was possible, of course. He'd considered suing the developers over it and had even taken legal advice.

'Free as a bird,' said Gill.

'Free as a bird,' echoed Gavin.

He had wanted to live in a gated community. Who wanted to live with the plebs, with their aches and pains, their state pensions and benefits and their ugly, fat little children? But now he lived in a gated community, he wasn't so sure. Gavin watched a lot more television than he would ever have let on and there was an advert he liked. He couldn't actually remember what it was for. It was some sort of cheap aspirational crap that anyone with actual money, actual success and an actual life wouldn't buy in their worst nightmares but the first line of the voiceover, delivered in husky male American, was 'every habitat is his natural habitat' and that chimed with Gavin like a supper gong. Gavin's profession didn't rely much on marketing; the suits and the cars and the exclusive memberships were subliminal advertising of the most seductive kind, conspicuous consumption, a medium with the clearest message. But that didn't mean he didn't understand how marketing worked. Gavin knew very well when someone was spinning him a line, trying to awaken inside him a craving he didn't even know he had. But he also liked to think that he knew himself well enough to recognise a genuine response when he felt one. To be at home in every habitat felt like a primeval male need to Gavin, something that connected the Silverback Gorilla with James Bond. Living in a gated community was the very opposite of that. What's more, it was a form of cowardice, a denial of the reality of the world in which you lived, no better than Downton Abbey, organised religion or a round-the-world cruise. Gated communities were for politicians who didn't have a clue how the other half lived and had never got over their public school matron. They were for suckling kittens, no place for sharks – especially not for sharks getting an attack of conscience.

'Have you seen Mad Men?'

Gill wasn't sure what he was talking about. Mad men sounded like one of those rock bands that Colin used to go and see – or a description of them, at any rate.

'It's a television series about advertising in America in the 1960s. They have this title sequence of a man falling out of the window, tumbling down very majestically and never hitting the bottom.'

'Can't say as I have,' said Gill.

'It's all very classy, New Yorker-style artwork. It's not real people.'

There was a long pause during which Gill wondered if he'd finished and that she'd perhaps missed the point or misheard. Or not heard at all. She could watch the birds swoop all day but she ought to be getting back to her mother and Dimmy. Susie had offered to cook but all the same. Well, it was good intentioned but you couldn't call her timid potterings with microwave and packets cooking.

'It's about success, I suppose, the series. And the value of it. The main character is very successful but never happy. And it's perhaps because that at which he's successful has no real value.'

Gill looked at Mr Henley. She tried not to judge people but she had judged him. She wasn't about to revise her judgement but in his silly, self-important lycra, he did seem like a lost soul.

'On behalf of the Friends of the Hospital, Mr Henley, can I say how grateful we are for your donation.'

He nodded. 'How's Colin, Mrs Graham?' His name and hers had come back to him from he knew not where but they were as vivid and sharp as the picture in his mind's eye of the comatose fireman in the hospital bed.

# 3.13.

Had it made the world a better place?

That was, at heart, the theme of several TV programmes, dozens of newspaper, magazine and online media articles, innumerable blogs, posts, status updates and indeed more than a few real conversations around real tables, real kettles or water coolers or real pints of craft ale.

To a large extent, it depended where you drew the line. Everybody agreed that more money for schools and hospitals was a good thing. Most agreed that more for the military and the genuinely unemployed, disabled or incapable was too. (The key word in this particular branch of the discourse was 'genuine' as there was a widespread feeling that impersonating unemployed, disabled or sick people was a popular and profitable pastime. This feeling was especially keen amongst those who had never actually met anyone doing it.) Most also thought that the growth in what had, in Stern & Feltman's day, been called 'good works' or 'patronage' by the rich was to be welcomed and many liked to see the nation's charities better provisioned. But all that was, as one philosopher had put it on BBC2's Newsnight, 'after the fact'.

The mere presence of a philosopher on Newsnight – and one who wasn't French – was an indication, if not of how much things had changed, then of at least how much events had shaken up sleepy old England and its somnolent establishment. How to react? It wasn't just the Director-General of the BBC asking himself that question. Turning no further than the corporation's appointed 'correspondent' on whatever was the matter in hand was clearly insufficient (although BBC News did hastily rebadge an underused Religious Affairs editor as its Head of Ethics.)

The professor of Moral Philosophy, from one of the redbrick universities, posed the question as to whether the moral character of an event should be defined by its outcome or its intention. He argued that results-based ethics were frequently applied in times of war. But was the nation at war? the presenter had asked. The war on terror, the professor suggested. And anyway, he said, sipping at a glass of water, the principle was frequently used during peacetime too and cited an example from the 1985 Miners' Strike. The presenter was quite red-faced by the time the debate ended. The Guardian asked whether it was the first time consequentialism had been discussed on national television.

As well as the tectonic plate spinning at macro-level, smaller, specific changes and developments were analysed, unpicked and put back together again. In Biscuit Town, the Stern & Feltman factory that had been slowly rotting for so long was earmarked by the Council for housing: live-work units, social housing, perhaps some sort of gallery or public space. When the plans, which preserved much of the character of the factory and even found a place for the old charabanc in a cavernous vestibule area inspired by the Tate Modern's Turbine Hall, won a prestigious architecture competition, the rest of Britain was reminded of the town and the origins of its iconic nickname. BBC South Today even had a short item on the history of the Almond Crisp, complete with seafront shots, sepia photographs and stock footage of the inside of the eastern European establishment where the biscuit was now manufactured.

Something even grander was happening in the capital. A wealthy overseas 'investor' who, to avoid tax, was sitting on half a dozen properties in various prime central London locations, had signed over, in the words of his lawyers, 'control and effective day-to-day management' of the buildings to a housing association. One of these was round the corner from Dominic Mason. The exact term of the arrangement was not in the public domain for 'commercial reasons' but that didn't stop the tenants from queueing up. Some more cynical commentators speculated that, since several similar buildings were now being squatted, then an organised management arrangement was probably best for the anonymous owner anyway. The squatters were justifying their acts by revealing the sort of information that many London property owners wanted kept quiet and, again, the tax aspect – #immoralifnotillegal – was frequently part of it: the lever that was crow-barring open so many doors. In the wake of the runaway commercial success of the Tax Evaders Top

Trumps (an image from which seemed to illustrate every news story and magazine feature on the topic), the squatters had produced their own property Top Trumps deck.

There was increased demand for accommodation because of the student fees holiday. The Chancellor had waived tuition, accommodation and all other student fees for a year and had given every indication that the holiday would continue so long as he was in office and the taxation revenue continued to come in. Many said that the speech, which was well-argued and rather old-fashioned, emphasising the benefits of education for its own sake as well as for the economy's, had fired the starting gun in the as-yet-undeclared post-election party leadership race. For Pip Henley and her friends, the fee holiday was accompanied by news that her university was to build two new halls of residence on a brownfield site near campus. For Pip, there was the added thrill of her teaching practice school getting a new site and half a dozen new classrooms.

But could some other event 'before the fact' have precipitated the same behaviour and attitudes? That question receded with time. Especially with Peter Robb springing up every five minutes on every network to proclaim the brave new world and to prove with every zealous proclamation that anyone and everyone could change. It wasn't right but Time had always been a healer (and the Old Father, like everyone else, had a truncated attention span these days). Of course, it wasn't like that for everyone. The media appearances and videos of Zak Thomas Brown's widow Rachel featured her alternately apoplectic with rage at the failure of French and British police to capture her husband's killer or inconsolable with tears at her family's loss. But, gradually, even her access to the mainstream media was curtailed. Her unwillingness to leave the Cayman Islands may have reduced her ability to fully prosecute her case.

The fact of two brutal murders was not fully forgotten but, as it became incorporated into the national debate, it changed its nature, acquired a symbolic dimension, not as profound as JFK's assassination or 9/11, but something tending in that direction. One incident which demonstrated this – and perhaps too the futility of Rachel Thomas Brown's rage in the face of the zeitgeist – was the artwork

'Poetic Justice' which recreated in plasticine the Sender and Thomas Brown crime scenes. It was like hardcore Wallace and Gromit. When the widows were asked to comment, Gabby Garnier's statement said that art ought to elevate emotionally, spiritually or intellectually and that, if people felt this work achieved that, then it was art. Rachel Thomas Brown's lawyers' tightly-argued four-page response called for the art gallery to lose its public funding. It was particularly ill-timed because the gallery had just received an enormous bequest following the sudden death of Archie Kray, another well-known tax exile. 'Poetic Justice' was shortlisted for, but did not win, the Turner Prize.

Could the emergence on the scene of a non-mainstream politician have had a similar impact? Even the most political of anoraks such as Dominic Mason and Roger Wilkins were compelled to concede that it was an entirely theoretical debate since there was no such politician on the horizon – or, at least, there was no such politician likely to achieve a position of influence within a narrow two-party system that tended to squeeze out marginal opinion. What had made the change so seismic was that, for so long, the political class – whose once uneasy stand-off with increasing inequality had blossomed into a rigidly-observed non-aggression pact – had said that it could not be done. ('Life's unfair. Nothing can be done. It's globalisation,' had long been Roger Wilkins's summary of the prevailing political orthodoxy. His verdict thereon: 'Pretty poor show if that's the best we can come up with after 100, 150 years of democracy.')

Yet it had happened within weeks, for this wasn't so much a change of regulatory environment – although that, as the more pedantic of commentators liked to point out, was going to be necessary if the change was to become permanent – but of attitudes. It had, for some politicians, notably the Chancellor, been a revelation. He could now talk, as he was fond of doing, of the British sense of fair play without provoking universal eye-rolling. It was impossible to overestimate how much better the English seemed to feel about themselves (and, as Dominic had heard the Chancellor say on at least two occasions, to overestimate the effect of such a feel-good factor on the government's poll rating.)

But again, that was all, 'after the fact'. The Chancellor was happy to benefit from the change of mood but he could never have initiated it. The general consensus of the British intelligentsia was that no other politician could have done so either. (The political question was which politician, or which clothing chain owner turned politician, would profit in the long term.)

The media, particularly television, had long been considered more influential than any focus-group-fawning politician. So could a programme like the one Tommy Lockhart had been talking about on the night of the fire have changed the nation in this benign way? Perhaps a better one: higher production values, more interesting guests, screened at primetime? Again the smart money said probably not. The audience for documentaries and current affairs had dwindled. (To paraphrase the off-the-record opinion of a leading television executive, political documentary could never compete with celebrities eating grubs in their underpants or stupid people hurting each other for a lot less than an actor would want to be paid.) And television was no more willing to challenge the received wisdom on the tastes of its paymasters than were the politicians.

Could a satirical novel have been the wake-up call? Were any bookmakers drawing up odds on the various alternatives to bloody murder, this would have been the longest shot of all. Jonjo McCain, the UK's leading satirical novelist, hauled his bloated intellect onto both Channel 4 News and Newsnight to argue for his profession although his appearance may, of course, have been satirical. The presenter (Kirsty Wark this time) cited the decline in book sales as one of the factors mitigating against McCain's case. McCain argued that his daughter reading the 870-page-long Harry Potter and the Order of the Phoenix inside a week was proof that folk would read if given the right stimulus.

'They could order their satire on Stufff,' McCain concluded with a cheeky smile.

'And read it over a Boomer's coffee,' trumped Kirsty. It really was a hilarious proposition when you stopped to think about it.

Because, of course, for all that had happened, Stufff continued to stuff package after package, Boomers continued to boom. Despite its founder's untimely demise, Jack Sender's business remained, in the words of its mission statement, 'the hub for everything'. Nor did the death of Head Barista Brian stop people wanting coffee, and oceans of it.

Because the downing of their CEOs had done little damage to the institutions themselves, one history don compared the deaths to the assassinations of tsars in nineteenth century Russia. The deaths did not, on the face of it, much change the institution of Tsardom or the experience of the serfs (emancipated or not) and were widely considered by all right-thinking analysts from Marxist-Leninists to British television historians to have been a political mistake but, argued the don in his first-ever appearance on television, the deaths did change the spirit of the age and pave the way for more fundamental change later. (He was up against one of those right-thinking British television historians arguing more accessibly that a more appropriate historical analogy was the witch-hunt.)

Although the discussion reached large numbers of the population, it would be wrong to think it engaged all. Even at the height of it all, a survey of Stufff customers found that the majority did not know who Jack Sender was. Most folk just enjoyed the prospect of shorter hospital waiting lists, smaller class sizes, new roads, improved railways, affordable housing. Had a new status quo been arrived at almost by accident, another paradigm for another generation or two of Brits to accept with the usual shrug of the phlegmatic shoulders? A new normal?

One commentator, who was fond of taking 'the long view', suggested that the two deaths would one day come to be seen as the 'political crime of the century', 'bigger even that 9/11', as 'with two blunt blows' they had killed off a political consensus that had existed since Reagan. 'Benjamin Franklin said that "in this world nothing can be said to be certain, except death and taxes",' the commentator wrote. 'The killings of Sender and Thomas Brown reminded us of this.' He concluded: 'these two men will go down as durable footnotes in history, their achievement in death far more valuable than anything in their selfish lives.'

Nobody could argue that it had made the world a worse place and, whatever way you cut it, nobody could come up with a scenario that achieved the same happy result but by a less unpleasant route. And that disturbed the few folk who actually thought about these things. The philosopher said it kept him awake at night and it certainly disturbed Dominic Mason – at least when he wasn't, to her delight, banging his wife senseless.

# 3.14.

The papers were full of Vladimir Ilya Chuchumashev who had stumped up the cash to rebuild a run-down housing estate that he passed on his intermittent journeys from the airport. (He said that it reminded him, and not in a good way, of his late mother's dwelling in Belarus.) The outgoing was a not inconsiderable sum. But the political left were pointing out that such were the inequalities in the country that it was the equivalent to someone on the minimum wage of a thousand pounds or so. Hardly generosity to crow about. Mason's boss was old school. Still liked to have all the newspapers open on the table.

'They're calling him VIC.'

'The Mirror tried to doorstep him in Belgrave.'

'They'll have a wait. He's only there for a long week-end in August.'

'They could headline it "Is Vic there?"' quipped Des Westmoreland, an overweight career civil servant whose scruffy appearance often caused others to underestimate the sharpness of his mind. But he was showing his age with this reference. A sea of blank faces.

'Is Vic There' Des began.

'Hit in the 80s.' Even blanker.

'Department S, one-hit wonders.' Des was on his own.

Heather would have heard of it but Dominic Mason wasn't paying a lot of attention. He had other things on his mind.

The Head of Press – a party appointee – interrupted the banter by hurling the Daily Mirror down in disgust. 'A grand's a fortune for millions of people in this country.'

'Is that something we really want to crow about?' Mason had

asked. It was his parting shot. The clock on the wall was counting down to the appointed hour. He made his excuses and left.

Infrastructure projects like Chuchumashev's were the latest in a long line of community-minded gestures from the corporations and individuals whose own tax affairs were, they and their advisors were eager to stress, absolutely within the law but who wanted, in these difficult times, to give something back to the country and the great British people who had given them so much. Charitable donations, ex gratia payments, local sponsorship initiatives that went way beyond the usual. Companies that would normally insist on oversight of the precise ROI on every penny 'given' were suddenly offering both public and voluntary sectors effective carte blanche with significant sums and no strings – apart from the fanfare of trumpets and waterfall of press releases and media appearances that accompanied the gesture. Public spirit was suddenly the only drink in town.

It had always amused Mason, a very silent and personal amusement, that the Cabinet Office building had, until the reign of Charles II, been used for cockfighting. (Plus ça change.) It had also been used as a theatre, for real tennis (by Henry VIII) and even as a bowling alley. Imagine all that going on behind its stern stone: a facade of austerity for the public while, inside, the rich were making whoopee. Well, you didn't need to be Private Eye to see the irony.

Mason had been enjoying the theatre while anticipating a little cockfighting to follow. He'd heard from Roger Wilkins that something more substantial was in the offing, that the revised budget had just been the beginning. It really was a succession bid, no doubt about it. There would be a full reappraisal followed by considerably less austere public spending on roads, hospitals, schools and, more radically, social housing. There were even plans for the regeneration of the North (basically defined as everything the wrong side of Luton). Internally, the Treasury were calling it 'Windfall Budget 2 - this time it's personal' but, of course, that wouldn't be mentioned. Nor would the precise reason for the sudden bounty.

'You remember that story about George Best,' Wilkins had said. 'In bed with Miss World in a sea of money.'

'And the waiter delivering the champagne said: "George, when did it all go wrong"?'

'That's the one. Well, that's the Chancellor right now. Rolling around in a sea of money. "It would" and I quote, "be criminal not to spend it".' Wilkins went all gooey-eyed and looked like he'd been on the champagne himself. He allowed the whisky to swirl around the bottom of the glass, the meniscus clinging and spinning. Wilkins was not a natural whisky-drinker. Lager was his usual drug of choice. But he would occasionally betray a longing for something more.

'Someone said: "but what about the austerity programme, Chancellor?"'

Wilkins paused melodramatically.

'And he said?'

'And he said: "austerity posterity".'

'I thought it was ideological, ' said Mason. 'To roll back the state.'

'It was – but if you had to choose between a narrow, mean, small-minded, penny-pinching little theory designed to take money from the poor, give it to the rich and prevent the state from ever giving it back again and being the most successful Chancellor of all time, what would you choose?'

'Won't hurt his leadership chances at all,' said Mason.

'Indeed,' smirked Wilkins, polishing off his double single malt in double quick time. 'I think we should bump off a few reluctant taxpayers on a regular basis. My round?'

Mason was a state school fast-tracker. He was also a former AAA Borough Schools 400m champion. His dining-out story was that he had beaten, at the age of 12, the athlete and national treasure known as the Waltzing Welshman. (The nickname was the result of Strictly Come Dancing but he had become an eligible celeb years before by winning bronze in the Commonwealth Games 4x400.) As any athlete would tell you, the fastest track is the inside lane but, of course, being a fast tracker didn't mean you were on the inside in the civil service. Those on the inside were actually from the other side of the tracks. Mason had learned that.

But from which side of the tracks was Wilkins? The British establishment wasn't a unitary thing. It was more complicated than just whether you were part of it or not. There were inner circles and outer ones. But even these weren't fixed. They were more like the rings on Saturn, visible at times, not at others, made up of thousands of small particles of almost nothing. You might not be on Planet Elite but you could still be in its orbit, its gravitational pull.

Mason's old friend was now sporting a beard that made him look alarmingly like George V. Perhaps he was getting ideas above his station. Or perhaps he just knew his station very well. Wilkins was minor public school and Oxford. To him, the people who ran the country weren't just people stationed further up the governmental food chain. He had, as a child and a younger man, rubbed shoulders with them. He had seen them. Watched them, no doubt. Observed. Like animals in a zoo. He didn't dine out on schoolboy athletics but on tales, often second-hand, of the Bullingdon and White's. If Wilkins was, like Mason, on the wrong side of the tracks, then it was only just: close enough to feel the whistling breeze of the gravy train as it raced past.

As a kid, Mason, had he thought about his place in the world at all, would probably have believed that Britain was a meritocracy. Wilkins had never had that luxury. Perhaps Dominic ought to be grateful for that. Wilkins would always been aware of the invisible hand. (A hand up, not a hand-out.) But it was all academic. Wherever exactly his friend was located, be it in the outer reaches of the exosphere or the very heart of the machine, there was absolutely nothing that he could do to help Mason now. Wilkins would never have received the call that Mason had received earlier that morning. And that was a difference between them. Stratospheric.

Dominic was at his desk now.

He picked the phone up once and then hung up again. Should he use his mobile? He glanced at his watch, the second hand circling with Swiss precision. Heather's engagement present. He still had a little time. And what would she say? As a nurse, she'd presumably welcome the serious investment in the NHS but what about the rest... It wasn't yet 11am but he could do with a whisky or two himself. He had a strong sense of something else circling. Vultures. He got up, put his jacket on and, with a roll of the shoulders and several long, deep breaths, strolled out of the office.

Sooner or later, the thing that made you rich will make you poor. And it looked to Mason as if his time had come. For the second time that morning he got into the lift, for the second time he nodded amiably to a bloke on reception he didn't recognise and for the second time he emerged onto Whitehall. An hour and a half earlier, a spring in his step, he had headed south, cut up King Charles Street past the Churchill War Rooms, down the Clive Steps into Horse Guards and Her Majesty's Treasury – a five-minute walk. This time around, he started out in the same direction but continued down to the junction, turned and crossed Westminster Bridge. South of the river. No chance of bumping into anyone who mattered in government, south of the river – unless you counted the Department of Health which, of course, you didn't.

He knew Ellis, the Chancellor's top special advisor. King Spad. Everybody did. Eton, Oxford, Institute of Fiscal Studies. Mason had been at some meetings with him – largeish ones – and he'd been CC to some of his emails – widely-shared ones. So, when he'd been summoned for a one-to-one, it was a surprise but not a big one. And, at first, quite pleasant. This was what had happened to Mason before. He'd get noticed and then get an approach. Mason was formulating his polite rebuff as he skipped down the steps past the bronze statue of the enthusiastic taxer of India, Clive. But it hadn't been like that. Not at all. With the result that he was now scurrying past St Thomas's Hospital towards Lambeth North like a fugitive, like one of the rats you're supposedly never more than six feet away from in London. No, Mason's smoothness, his facility for networking, was about to get him in trouble – best case scenario: only with his conscience.

They said it was an ill wind that didn't blow someone some good. The inverse of that would be something like it was a benign wind that didn't blow somebody some harm. Dominic Mason was about to find out.

He wondered how many people were involved in this. A handful at the very most, with the Chancellor presumably one. What he knew he could be certain of was that he was the only civil servant. The others would all be the Chancellor's place men. They could have used the usual informal channels to communicate with the police.

They could even have used the security services. But they wanted a civil servant in case it all went tits up. In his career, Mason had blown a bit of smoke but never anything like this. He wasn't the trusted aide, he was the fall guy. The patsy. The cockfighting had started and, instead of watching from the sidelines, he'd been sent into the ring, armed not with sharp spurs but a naff hat.

He had purchased a bright red 'I Heart London' baseball cap from a street vendor. Extortionate price and he couldn't even charge it to expenses. Now he put it on, pulled it down almost over his eyes, walked into a down-at-heel-looking phone shop and bought a cheap handset and a Pay-As-You-Go Sim. Then he made the call.

## 3.15.

Dan read Blair Henry's latest piece. The scribe had appointed himself the unofficial recorder of all that was happening in the wake of the 'tax man axe man'.

The trouble was that it was all such terribly good news. And who wants to read that? No wonder his editor had taken to burying it.

Blair had done what every journalist wanted to do. He had written a story that had changed the world. You had to take your hat off to him for that. The 'tax man axe man' had not made it easy with his Bs and his Ms and his complicated numbers written on mirrors or in snow! (So needlessly complicated in fact that Dan had wondered if he were a geek – an angry techie, maybe.) Blair's investigative journalism had cracked the code and found the link while the police were still cordoning off the crime scene. Without him, who knows how many times the murderer might have struck.

But things had evolved. In part thanks to Peter Robb, a crime story had become something far bigger, a cultural game-changer, the catalyst that sparked the revolution. Once you got past the reason for the sudden swelling of the public coffers – and everybody knew what the reason was but nobody was saying – then 'rich man pays tax' or 'rich man makes song and dance about charitable donation' wasn't really news.

To Blair this wasn't fair. And Dan was getting a little fed up with hearing him go on about it. They had been speaking regularly on the phone ever since Blair's first story – Blair looking for new meat, Dan eager to feed it to him. But the public was tiring of the diet and Blair, to paraphrase Cherri, was becoming a miserable China, Ukraine, Nigeria, Turkey. He was particularly peeved that the attention on social media that had once been his was now focused elsewhere.

'Look at this Scootergirl,' he had complained. 'Robb deserved to die. Her tweet says. With a picture of a Bangladeshi sweatshop. This is incitement.'

Dan wasn't sure about that. 'Well, it's not journalism,' he said. 'But then she's not a journalist, is she? She's an agitator.'

'Have you seen her stuff on "Fashion Sister"?'

'Can't say I have,' said Dan. 'It's for teenage girls to talk about clothes, isn't it? Wouldn't have thought it was your scene, Blair.' Dan didn't say that he'd actually built 'Fashion Sister', won an award for it. He hated anything that sounded like boasting. Wanted people to recognise his genius unprompted.

'She's trying to turn it into a wing of Class War or something. Posts about low pay, poor conditions, shoddy-quality merchandise, exploitation of models, exorbitant profits.'

'Well, the fashion industry is pretty disgusting. Take a look at the fashion industry corporates listed on our site.'

'Whatever,' said Blair, sounding exactly like a teenage girl himself. 'My fifteen minutes of fame are already over.'

'Your fifteen minutes?'

'Yes. In the future, everybody will be famous for fifteen minutes. Andy Warhol said it. Well, the future's here.'

'Who's Andy Warhol?'

'A pop artist.'

'What's pop art?'

'A pseudo-naive form of art that drew heavily on comic-book style representation. Popular in the 1960s.'

'What's the 1960s?'

'Are you taking the piss?'

'Of course I am, Blair,' said Dan. 'You're taking yourself way too seriously. So maybe your fifteen minutes are up. At least you had them.'

Dan mugged as he said all this, pulling faces, and Cherri was unable to stop herself giggling. It was all water off a duck's back to Dan. She'd challenged him about the paint and the stickers and he'd brushed it off – described it as just a bit of fun – but, when she told him about seeing the bullying at the train station, he had accepted her point and the next day the stuff had all gone. That was the thing about Dan, he liked a laugh and wanted corporatesponger to be famous, but his heart was in the right place and he knew where to draw the line.

Cherri understood what Blair was upset about. She knew what contemporary news values were but she hoped that they would eventually change along with everything else. She certainly enjoyed reading Blair's good news stories and was glad the world was changing for the better.

# 4:
# 'I Can't Enjoy A Cake. I Just Taste Self-Loathing And Guilt.'

# 4.1.

Corrigan sat down as if all the air had been let out, of both him and the room. He felt featherlight and he couldn't quite breathe. In all his time as a copper, this was the most unusual request of all. Mason hadn't introduced himself and it had taken him a moment or two to recognise the voice.

'I think we can meet that new budget and considerably more. There's been an unexpected revenue surge...' Mason's voice trailed off in a manner that concerned Corrigan. He sounded like someone with a gun to his head.

'Right,' said Corrigan. 'Are you all right? You sound a little strange.'

Mason coughed. 'They want you to go easy.'

'What?'

'The matter we have been discussing. The case...'

Corrigan knew which case Mason was alluding to.

'Just play it long, they suggest,' said Mason cryptically.

'I don't...'

'It's an ill wind.'

Dominic jettisoned the baseball cap into the Thames as he crossed Westminster Bridge. He leaned over the side, allowing a timely gust of wind to remove it. It was smartly done. The plan was to slip the phone into a waste bin but, of course, there weren't any. National Security.

He could have chucked the phone in the river too. The bridge was clogged with tourists, all more interested in their Big Ben selfies than anything he was doing, but it only took one. Dominic hesitated, removed the Sim, hesitated again. What the fuck was he doing? All this James Bond bollocks. He had been planning to go back to the office but he changed his mind and descended into the Underground at Westminster station. He suddenly felt very resentful, very angry – neither were emotions he felt very often and they had an odd effect on him.

# 4.2.

Chief Inspector Corrigan had given himself the afternoon off too. Now he was sitting in his living room with his second cup of tea.

He really didn't know what to do. Of course, he'd been told to do nothing. That would have been difficult at the best of times but given that this was, in his view, the most ridiculous, dangerous and immoral 'suggestion' ever to come out of Whitehall, it was next to impossible. He'd tried the TV. He'd tried the newspapers. Beyond those matters directly pertinent to the job, Corrigan was not a big consumer of either and he'd forgotten how vacuous, unprincipled and populist they could be. It was amusing to watch them flailing in all directions. In the absence of any values to ground them, the media couldn't decide how to handle it all. Conflicted was the social workers' word. For once it was appropriate. Articles about the beast and the monster sat alongside good news stories: housing crisis solved, higher education crisis solved, NHS crisis solved, refugee crisis solved. The army were apparently dancing in the street and the Met and other police services were finally seeing a sensible level of funding too. Moreover, the media could hardly ignore the change of behaviour of the super-rich, especially since their tax affairs were all over social media and being discussed in every bar, club and bingo hall. They preferred to save words like 'sponger' or 'scrounger' for benefit claimants and migrants but those were the words now in the public domain. In many ways the British newspapers had never looked more tired or more out of touch and the TV wasn't a lot better.

'If a newspaper editor doesn't understand the mood on the street, a politician has no chance,' he said to the BBC News channel which was still flickering away but with the sound turned off.

'Talking to yourself, Dad?'

It was his daughter Sophie standing in the doorway. Corrigan looked at his watch automatically.

'You home already?'

'Looks like it. Do you want some fat water?'

Corrigan allowed his eye to examine his daughter from foot to head, again this was something automatic, something he couldn't control, the primeval parent deep within. He sensed the phrase 'isn't that skirt a bit short?' forming on his tongue and swallowed it. First rule of policing: don't fight battles you can't win. 'Fat water?'

'It's water with coconut oil in it. It helps you burn fat.'

'Exercise burns fat,' Corrigan said, sounding like the gym instructor he surely would have been, had he not joined the police.

'I'm fit enough,' she said with a deliberately demure smile. His little girl was getting bigger and he didn't like it. Her hair was that cascade of thick, dark glossiness that her mother's had been when they met.

'Did you get your application forms?'

'I did indeed, Daddy Dear.'

Sophie had finally capitulated and, after months of digging in her too-high-for-school heels, had agreed to go to university. Following the massive increase in higher education funding, her main objection – the cost – had been kicked into touch. As Mason had said, it's an ill wind.

Sophie hurled her schoolbag onto the sofa and arranged herself beside it, kicking off her heels and folding her legs beneath her. She was clinging onto her water bottle as she had once clung onto her favourite doll. Click, the sound was back on the telly. Click, the channel was changed. Corrigan turned to his daughter to object but she already had her tablet on her knees. Girls used iPads and computer tablets in the way women once used knitting.

'What are you doing here anyway?' She didn't look up, didn't pause in her precise, punchy typing.

'Needed a bit of thinking time, Sophie.' Corrigan made a little show of finishing his tea. He wasn't quite sure why he did this so pointedly – perhaps in the hope that his daughter might offer to make him another? (Modern justice was built on the triumph of hope over experience.)

'The tax man axe man?'

Corrigan looked across at her levelly.

'Don't give me that look. I read the papers.'

'Do you?'

'Yes, I read online, dinosaur.'

'I didn't realise they covered current affairs in Just 17.'

'What's Just 17?'

'Isn't it a girls' magazine? I don't know.' Corrigan didn't have a clue where he'd plucked it from. He'd dredged it up like a clue at the bottom of a silted-up river.

Sophie shook her head as if dealing with a wayward five-year-old. Her fingers continued to dance without pause.

'Just 17 shut down in 2004 according to the Wikipedia,' Sophie said. 'Dinosaur Daddy.'

They sat in silence for a moment, Corrigan watching the TV with both eyes, Sophie with barely one. It was an American sitcom with fresh-faced kids in improbably-large and impeccably-clean, well-furnished houses. Pretty much every line generated near hysteria. Corrigan got about one joke in ten. And were jokes about masturbation, vomit and cat faeces (and, on one occasion, all three) really suitable for his seventeen-year-old daughter? But the dinosaur kept his mouth shut: a Tyrannosaurus sucking a jelly baby. There was far worse online. And she was, whatever else, an intelligent kid.

'How's Damian?' he asked conversationally.

'Who's Damian?' she replied, again not looking up. He couldn't see her properly beneath the hair but it really did sound as if she'd never heard of him.

There was another pause during which Corrigan accepted the inevitable. If he wanted another cup of tea, he would have to make it himself.

'Daddy Dear,' Sophie began. It was that questioning voice. It sounded expensive.

'Yes?'

'You after whoever's behind the Tax Evader Top Trumps?'

Corrigan was aware that he was once again giving her an incongruous look and that she was once again shaking her head wearily.

'Well, you don't have to tell me. Tax Evading Super Scum is all over the internet.'

'What about it?'

'It's just there's this girl posting images of the cards and little comments. Look...' She patted the sofa next to her in a gesture Corrigan found sweet and disconcerting at the same time.

'She's called Scootergirl.' Corrigan's daughter moved text and images around on the screen as if she'd been born with an iPad attached to her index finger. Facebook appeared, Twitter, YouTube. He knew those ones.

'What's this?'

'Instagram, it's an app that let you post photos in various places.' Scootergirl was on them all.

'And this site?'

'"Fashion Sister" is a portal, Dad. You can create scrapbooks to share. You can dress virtual models in actual, like, clothes. But mostly, it's a chat forum, a bit like Facebook but for fashion.'

'Right.'

'But this is the strangest of the lot. Scootergirl doesn't do any of these things. She posts about sweatshops in the clothing industry.'

'OK,' said Corrigan hesitantly.

'The point is, Dad, that if Scootergirl is, as she claims, 14 years old, then I must be 57 and you 290.'

He smiled. He did feel about 290 at times.

'Is she even a "she"? It's a bit freaking NMS, isn't it?'

Corrigan had no idea, but he agreed anyway. He eased himself up from the sofa with a sudden sense of purpose.

'Where you going, Daddy Dear? Garn a nick 'er, guv?' She said this last phrase in a heavy cockney accent.

'No, to make some tea,' he said.


Heather Mason rolled over in bed and checked the clock. A little early. She was on lates again and had been for a while. Her body had, it seemed, been getting used to the schedule so she was a little surprised to find herself awake. Probably a noise then? The trouble with sleeping during the day was that sometimes even triple glazing, a tall hedge, half a dozen small trees and a substantial drive couldn't keep the outside out. It was probably Walt or whatever his name was with his new car, some souped-up thing which was way too powerful for him and which he seemed incapable of driving quietly.

She stretched and then stopped in mid-extension. That noise sounded like it was coming from downstairs. The front door closing. Someone was trying to do it surreptitiously but it was audible all the same. Footsteps on the stairs. Heather reached round and eased the baseball bat out from beneath the bed. Dominic thought the precaution a little unnecessary but it made her feel safe. As a nurse, you saw all sorts of shit that a civil servant would never see and would only read about in judge-led public enquiries. She pulled herself up onto her knees, flicked the hair from her eyes. Footsteps in the hall. She raised the bat over her shoulder like a pro. The door handle turning. Her hand tightened on the bat but, in truth, she was already relaxing.

'Dominic?'

Dominic walked in to see his naked wife wielding a baseball bat. It was surprisingly arousing.

'Nice welcome.'

'What are you doing here?'

'I thought we could hit a home run.'

'What?'

'Aren't we making a baby, Matron?'


In the kitchen, Corrigan put on the kettle, waited a moment for it to begin the noisier phase of its boiling routine and then adjourned to the back of the kitchen, by the enormous double-door fridge and furthest away from any teenage ears.

He wrestled his mobile phone into life and eventually found the screen that displayed his list of numbers. If Sophie played her iPad like a concert pianist, he was a one-armed, tone-deaf beginner wearing a boxing glove. So bloody small and fiddly, he wanted to scream but didn't. DS Caton was clearly surprised to hear from him.

'Guv?' he said, not totally unlike Sophie's cockney impersonation.

'Chris,' said Corrigan, calling Caton by his first name. 'Straight to the point: can you step up what you're doing on the investigation side? It's, well, there are a number of reasons. My hands are a little tied. Low profile. Report directly to me.'

'Of course, guv.'

'First thing: there's this person online, Scootergirl. She's on websites like Facebook and the usual, and also on one called "Fashion Sister". Posting the Tax Evader Top Trumps all the time. Sophie reckons she might be an adult posing as a kid.'

'Sophie?'

'My daughter. And she should know. She lives online. Can you check it out?'

'Definitely. I've got someone who could do that.'

'The less I know about that side the better, but results to me, and me only.'

'Will do, guv.'

'Thanks, Chris.'

He hung up. He was lucky to have Caton out there. Just as well he'd suspended him.

Corrigan finished making his tea and returned to the living room. The TV was still on and Sophie was still on 'Fashion Sister'.

'Homework time, Soph?'

'You got me bang to rights and no mistake, guv'nor,' said Sophie in her cockney accent.

'I think you've been watching too much of The Bill.'

'What's The Bill?'

# 4.3.

Chris had a spring in his step. Far from being off the case, he was back on it with a vengeance. He couldn't understand why so little was happening in London. It was as if they were just going through the motions. Still, whatever was going on behind the scenes at the Kremlin, he was, to all intents and purposes, back on active duty and, what's more, operating semi-autonomously. Whatever the guv's exact reason for deploying him in this unorthodox manner, it suited him fine.

He sat in his car eating an apple and watching as the ferry approached. He was a little early. As the big-nosed vessel neared, he turned off the prattle on the radio, preferring the hubbub of a ship putting into port. A handful of blokes in wellies were unfurling ropes and generally readying themselves on the quay. To his side were the ranks of cars waiting to go to France. People were returning to their vehicles. Doors slammed. Engines started. An unmoved old boy continued to lean against his bonnet, reading the paper. Nice car, an old Cortina, almost a classic. The old boy glanced up and then looked back down again. Seen it all before. Plenty of time.

The English Channel was almost a millpond, the ferry's bow cutting up barely a ripple. Some kids on the upper deck were jumping up and down excitedly. This made Chris smile. Did these kids realise they were approaching Newhaven? It really wasn't anything to get too fired up about. He might have been jumping with joy, had the ferry been travelling in the opposite direction. As a child, Chris had, oddly enough, never been taken to France by his mother and, knowing his origins, he'd always been keen to go. It wasn't until he was 18 – a day trip to Boulogne – that he made his first visit. He hadn't quite jumped with joy, but he'd been full of anticipation as if going to meet a distant relative or something for the first time. He spent a fair stretch walking around the town, taking it all in, speaking the lingo and not just getting pissed like his mates. On the approaching vessel, there were three boys and two girls – all holding onto the railings and pointing and screaming, anorak hoods flying like flags, their voices lost in the noise of seagulls and the rumbling piles of scrap metal lining the shore. Still, he had a rookie's enthusiasm today. He was excited to be here. Why shouldn't they?

He had been working with the tiny black girl from the website, Cherri. He'd got her to look at all the traffic to corporatesponger in the weeks before the killings started and she had confirmed his suspicions. That had almost had him jumping with joy too – what was happening to him?

'Any place with particularly high levels of traffic, possibly a single user?'

'One or two,' Cherri had said, nearly as excited as he was to be 'on the case'.

'Where?'

'You're staying in Biscuit Town, aren't you?'

'I was.'

'Well, that's one of them. That's the main one, in fact. Multiple visits, I reckon, although I can't be sure, from the same machine.'

So here he was. Now, he'd got Cherri on the 'Fashion Sister' thing. She was proving very useful. She said she knew all about the site because someone she worked with had been involved in setting it up. Knew something about the back-end or something. 'Fashion Sister For The Fashionista,' she had said.

'What?'

'I think it might have been their slogan. Anyway, leave it with me.'

Chris was happy to. It didn't feel like proper police work, playing with a phone. Chris was an analogue copper.

A couple of the guys portside were winching frantically and the ferry opened up like a whale. The metal gates slowly parted and locked into place before disgorging car after car from the boat's belly. Chris took a final crunch of apple and tossed the core into the sea. Beside him engines began to rev, although the Cortina owner read on.

In the terminal building, things were a little quieter. Most of the outgoing passengers were in their cars. A restless posse of foot passengers, all rucksacks and bags, stood by the exit waiting for their cue to board. Chris knocked on the office door and invited himself in.

An Asian guy, Indian or Pakistani, looked up from his screens. He had a bank of them – most were CCTV, but a couple were old-style cathode tube computer VDUs. Chris took in the scene. Corrigan had taught him that. He was a great believer in first impressions and their value in policing. One of the screens had a model Ferrari racing car parked on top. On the desk were several coffee cups in various states of undress, half a dozen clipboards and a small neat bookshelf of printed timetables. The wall, a study in off-white chipped paint, displayed a chart of the English Channel and a whiteboard with tide times and various scribbled notes. 'Albion Forever' in big blue marker pen was the only one Chris could actually read.

Chris noticed that one of the CCTV cameras appeared to be

trained on the Cortina.

'Nice car,' said Chris.

'Lotus Cortina Consul. Mark II, I'd say,' said the guy, genuine awe in his voice. 'Lovely motor. Must be fifty years old.' He spun his chair round to face Chris directly. 'How can I help?'

'DS Caton – Metropolitan Police.'

Chris showed him his warrant card. The guy was overweight with a white shirt that was too small for him, brown chinos that were too short for him and a hastily-assembled tie that was too childish for him.

'Sponge Bob,' said Chris, nodding at the tie.

'My son's idea of a joke,' said the guy with a smile. He gestured at the seat beside him, briskly removing the parka draped over it to allow Chris to sit down. 'Howard Chowdhury. Port Manager.'

'It's about your manifest,' said Chris, not sitting. 'I need your passenger records.'

'OK,' said Chowdhury hesitantly.

Chris hoped it wouldn't come to a full inspection of all the records, but he had found that suggesting upfront that something highly intrusive and time-consuming might be necessary often prompted more immediate cooperation.

'We're looking for a man we believe may have travelled to France recently.'

'It's not about that coffee man? Terrible...' Chowdhury paused to take in the gallery of coffee cups before him.

'I can't tell you that, Sir,' said Chris. He pointedly took the photo, provided courtesy of Biscuit Town nick, out of his jacket pocket. 'Have you seen this man?'

Chowdhury hardly needed to look at it. 'Yes,' he said. 'I don't have a great memory for faces, Sir, but I do remember a fine machine. He was driving a California T.'

'What?'

'A Ferrari California T. Burgundy.'

'When?'

'Couldn't say exactly, but it was a few weeks ago.'

Chris suggested some dates – the days leading up to the Thomas

Brown killing.

'It could have been. I just remember him because of the car – not the sort of motor you usually see on a ferry, and not the sort of driver you usually see in that sort of car, if you get me, Officer.'

Chris nodded. 'Can you check the records? We believe his name is Gary Shad.'

'Very fishy character.' Chowdhury didn't so much laugh as say 'ha ha'.

'What?'

'Shad. It's a fish. Ilish in Bangladesh. Herring family.'

Chris watched him write the name down.

Back at the park in Biscuit Town, he pulled up in the same spot, the one he'd waited in with Gabby. It offered a decent view. He couldn't see Shad. Nor could he see the women's exercise class. Both absences were, in their way, disappointing. He could, however, see a few dog walkers. He also recognised at least one of the dogs. Chris hoped that it wouldn't recognise him.

'Dimmy,' shouted Gill. She watched him half-hobble, half-run back in her general direction. She sometimes wondered if he was half-blind as well. You certainly couldn't say he was taking the most direct route. It was amazing how he seemed to be able to forget how old and decrepit he was from one step to the next. But then, each time that arthritic back paw landed awkwardly, it would all come back to him. Ouch. Gill felt the pain herself, even from fifty yards.

She was aware of someone else heading in her direction and rather closer. Was it that homeless man who sometimes slept in his car? Said he was from Spain but looked blank whenever Camila spoke to him. It was possible he just couldn't hear Camila, of course. This man looked younger and taller. His jacket looked like it had been sleeping rough even if its owner hadn't.

Chris stopped in his tracks. The woman looked like a local in a reassuring overcoat and appropriate shoes, but now he wasn't so sure. He thought he recognised her. Probably mistaken. It was just her expression probably – a lot of people looked anxious as he approached, as if he had 'copper' tattooed on his forehead.

'Hello, I wonder if you can help me,' he said, flashing the warrant card.

She read the card, looked at him quizzically, looked at the card again and then back at him with a smile.

'Hello Chris,' she said, brightly, as if she had last seen him about ten minutes ago.

Chris pressed on. 'I'm looking for a local man...' he said. His hand was groping around in his jacket pocket but he couldn't quite locate the damn picture.

'You don't recognise me, do you, Chris?'

Chris stopped searching. 'I'm sorry, Madam, I don't.'

'Gill Graham. Colin Graham's mother.'

Gill was so thrilled to see Colin's childhood friend, albeit that he was big and scruffy and looking at her if she were a fruitcake. It was almost as if Colin himself had strolled up in the Brighton kit that Cliff had bought him. Cliff being Cliff, it had been about two sizes too big but Colin had loved it.

'It said 10-12 years on the packet,' Cliff had protested.

'He's only eight,' Gill had said.

'Is he? Well,' Cliff had shrugged, his eyes twinkling in that irritatingly attractive way, 'better that way than the other.' Gill's hard stare had elicited the explanation: 'I mean, if he'd been 10 and I'd bought a kit for an eight-year-old. I mean, at least he'll grow into it. Come on, Gill, girl, it's hardly a hanging offence.' It wasn't, of course, but, to Gill, not knowing your kids' ages was an offence of sorts. As was not turning up when they were lying in hospital in a coma and with that she realised that, of course, the big lump of beefcake in front of her wasn't Colin, couldn't be Colin and that in a moment or two she would have to explain why.

'I thought you lived in Brighton...' said Chris.

'No, no, never left here. Different house now. Well, two different houses...' Was she really going to get into this? 'Well, how are you, Christophe?' She was grateful for the distraction of Demetrius who had finally made it back to her side and was looking up, tongue lolling, in search of a welcoming pat on the head.

It had been a long time since anyone had called Chris Christophe – his mother had eschewed his given name as long as he could remember – and, as a result, he was able to place the voice with eerie precision. He did know her. He and a boy called Colin had been at playgroup together and Colin's mother, this woman, Mrs Graham, used to collect them sometimes and, when she did, she'd take them back to Colin's house and serve Victoria sponge cake – not a treat he ever had at home. 'Another slice, Christophe?' she'd ask and he'd always say yes. She'd been one of those adults who got down to your height, squatting to address you as an equal. She was doing it now, to put the lead back on her dog. It was technique he would use with kids himself – had he got it from her?

As he looked at her, he began to recall features too. Her eyes were different colours, one a shade or two greener than the other, and it made her look ever so slightly cross-eyed. The glasses were different from those she'd worn twenty-odd years ago, of course, but she still peered over the top of them in the same way: a bit like a friendly witch.

'Mrs Graham,' he said as she rose, a little creakily, to her feet.

'You've joined the police,' she said.

'Yes.'

'You're so similar...' Gill was determined not to cry.

'How is Colin?'

She had known it was coming. She swallowed and continued to swallow, pulling the tears back. 'Christophe, I actually need to go. The dog needs...' What did the dog need? The dog didn't need anything. She needed a good cry. She pointed at her house. 'I live there, number 5. Why don't you come...'

'Yes, when you've a little more time,' said Chris. 'I'd love to ...'

'But sorry, before I go, what was it you actually wanted?'

Chris had forgotten all about Gary Shad, but this time he found the photo in a different pocket.

'Have you seen this man, Mrs Graham?'

'It's Gary something. He walks his dog here.'

'Seen him today?'

'Well, no. But I wouldn't expect to. Can't your colleagues tell you more about it that I can? I heard he'd been arrested.'

'And freed,' said Chris.
'Really? I heard he'd been charged.'

## 4.4.

Gabby was lying on top of the neatly-made bed in Mrs Caton's tiny box room, watching a spider making its wriggly way across the ceiling. She would have screamed at this once. Certainly, she'd have demanded that someone remove the offending beast. But here she was, hands joined behind her head, head on the pillow, casually watching it. The cracks in the ceiling plaster were not unlike a giant spider's web.

She had put in a call to Louisa, her PA. Even the new lower-maintenance Gabby could only survive for so long on the small bag she'd brought from London. As a model, Gabby had prided herself on never sweating, not even glowing, but the turtle neck she was wearing was nose-nudging evidence that this was no longer the case – if it ever had been.

Louisa had sent a suitcase which was standing in the doorway where the TNT driver had kindly put it. They'd used their standard alias – Kate Moss – and it had generated the standard response from the driver: 'You've got the same name as that model'. Gabby would usually reply, 'yes, it's funny. Unfortunately I've never been sent any of her cheques.' That always got a laugh. Nobody had ever said, 'but aren't you Gabby Garnier?' It was hiding in plain sight.

She was lying on the bed because she had discovered, completely unexpectedly, that she had no desire to open the case. She'd got used to travelling light and incognito, and clearly liked it more than she had realised. She found herself fretting about how much it must have cost to send a big, heavy suitcase. She'd never worried about that sort of thing before. She'd had great trunks shipped halfway across the world and never batted an impeccably-shadowed eyelid. Was she becoming normal? She wouldn't say it was fun exactly, but it was interesting. She was rediscovering parts of her that had been lost in a sea of wealth. This had left her in a reflective mood, thinking about what had happened since Jack's death. Her first 'arrest'!

Lying beside her on the fading silky counterpane was an old copy of 'Brighton Rock' that she had been reading. She'd spotted it sandwiched between a Franco-German dictionary and a book on accountancy in banking – a shorter, thin volume between two tall, fat tomes.

Gabby had seen the film eons ago, remembered the black and white Catholic guilt that ran through it. This was a classic Penguin paperback version, the plain orange and white cover. However, any value it might have had as such had been reduced by the scribblings on the cover and frontispiece. An S had been added to the title so that it now read 'Brighton Rocks'. A rather different sentiment. And inside, in a pencil hand more chaotic than the ceiling spider's best efforts, the young Chris had written: Chris Caton, North Road, Brighton, Sussex, England, Great Britain, United Kingdom, Europe, Earth, The Solar System, The Milky Way, The Universe. There were several spelling mistakes but Gabby was impressed that he had included both Great Britain and the United Kingdom – an early sign of a policeman's attention to detail.

It was cute. Chris could have only been young when he wrote inside. But an inappropriate book for a child, surely. A sign of a disturbed one? You'd have thought that a child's mother might have spotted that from the first line: 'Hale knew, before he had been in Brighton three hours, that they meant to murder him.'

'Zere are so many books, I don't know what I 'ave,' Mrs Caton had said when Gabby had shown it to her, but it was clear that she'd kept it deliberately. It was a good read too. She wondered if Chris knew it had survived.

Gabby could hear Mrs Caton's radio playing downstairs. It was an old model, not a digital one, but it did have presets and one of them was a French station from Normandy. Mrs Caton played the radio loud.

'I am not going deaf,' Mrs Caton had insisted. It was a self-delusion not uncommon in ageing French women. Her own mother too denied being afflicted by greying hair or bagging skin or fading hearing. 'I play ze radio comme ça because in English I need to 'ear every word to understand and in French ze reception is, 'ow Chris say, a crock of crap.'

Even the French radio was talking about what had been going on in the UK since the murders began. France, of course, prided itself on its civic culture and great public works, and the presenters were clearly jealous that suddenly all this seemed to have come like a gift from the heavens to small-minded, selfish little England. New outposts for both the British Museum and the National Theatre were being mooted and this is what the French presenters were discussing. One of them admitted that the British Museum was perhaps the finest in the world. Brave.

Gabby was confused. All these good things were, in some way, the result of Jack's death. The more she found out about what had been going on at Stufff, the more immoral it sounded, but did he deserve to die? No crime had been committed and, even if it had, she was opposed to the death penalty in any circumstance and certainly not for a dodgy tax return.

Mrs Caton had not been a lot of help on this one. 'Jack was generous,' Gabby had said. 'I've all the material things money can buy but your little house here is more comfortable than any penthouse or villa.'

'Don't be so bloody ridiculous,' Mrs Caton had said, showing an uncharacteristically good grasp of English vernacular.

Mrs Caton was surprisingly unconcerned about the moral aspects. Instead she'd explained the three best ways for a company to lower its corporation tax. Gabby couldn't remember them precisely and wasn't sure she really understood them anyway. But there was something about charging services from your subsidiary in one country to your subsidiary in another. It was called 'transfer pricing'. You could also load debt from one subsidiary onto another or borrow from it. All these would reduce the apparent profit and thus the tax due. The most ridiculous one was companies charging other parts of the company to use their 'intellectual property'. Boomer's was a good example of that. She had read more about it on the internet. Boomer's UK effectively paid a royalty on every cup of coffee it sold to the Boomer's subsidiary in some tax haven – all for the right to use the logo and offer customers the chance to 'size up to a big Boomer'. Absurd. She was slightly relieved that Jack's scams hadn't been quite so blatant.

'What's the difference between tax evasion and tax avoidance?' Gabby had asked.

'That is very facile en théorie,' said Mrs Caton. 'One is illegal and ze other is not. But very difficult to answer in ze practice.'

'A grey area?'

'Une zone floue, oui. But, yes, a grey area. And gris is such a difficult colour. You will know zat, ma petite, in your line of work.'

'Close up, one shade of grey looks pretty much like another.'

'Before you know, you have crossed ze line.'

'How do you know all about this?'

'I was an accountant. It's like asking a footballer how he knows to kick. Not all my clients were... ow you say?'

'Does Chris know?'

'Chris doesn't know a lot of things,' Caton mère had said cryptically. 'Do you think zat I am a mad, crazy French woman?' she had said in English, and then in French: 'do you think that I have gone mad, locked up in this little house in the hills?'

It had crossed Gabby's mind, yes – but she didn't say anything.

On the radio, they had moved on to discussing the proposed improvements to rail and road.

'They promise you will be able to get to Birmingham more quickly,' said the female presenter in that just-got-out-of-bed voice that was de rigueur for women on French radio.

'Have you ever met anyone who wants to get to Birmingham more quickly?' said the male presenter.

Gabby steeled herself for a quip about Marseille, France's equivalent of Birmingham, but it never came. Instead the female presenter said she'd never been to Birmingham at all and didn't know where it was. What were they talking about? Gabby remembered a trip to Birmingham for The Clothes Show live at the NEC. It had been hilarious. One of the girls had had this new laxative tea which turned out to be a little too effective. But it seemed like another lifetime. Gabby ran her finger over the cover of 'Brighton Rock' and smelt the pages. Suddenly, she felt about ninety and started thinking about children. Where had that come from?

She levered the suitcase up onto the bed and clicked it open. This too reminded her of the catwalk and living in hotels out of bags. Was this ache because she wanted to go back to that, when she was young and life was simple? Was it just because it all felt so long ago?

As well as some clothes, Louisa had thrown in a note – understanding but concerned – plus some post. She wasn't sure she much wanted to open any of them. One of the letters was from Jack's lawyer's. She recognised the crest on the envelope. That could only mean hassle.

On the radio, Mrs Caton had switched over to the UK news. There was a politician on. It was presumably someone from the opposition – although he sounded a bit like Peter Robb – and he was saying that there was one guaranteed, sure-fire, 100% legal, 100% moral way to reduce your tax liability: pay your workers more. Gabby understood that idea perfectly.

Jack had paid a high price for his hubris. Her sense of melancholy was metamorphosing into anger: anger with her husband and anger with herself for not taking the teeniest, weeniest bit of interest in what he had been up to. She had just lain on the glorious beach, reading.

She looked at the book; she looked at the lawyer's letter. She opened the latter.

# 4.5.

Dominic Mason seemed to be looking at screens more and more – was this the way government was going? Was this the way the world was going? Everyone seemed to be glued to their screens. Heather had been known to consult Twitter during foreplay (which Dominic took as a sign that he should get on with it). But this life mediated by a screen, was this living?

He was young, born into the internet age. And he knew such thoughts were a kind of treason against his generation. But he felt increasingly detached. He'd always fitted in, like the smoothest peg. But now he was aware of only friction (and not just in his baby-making with Heather).

He was in the Press room where the TV was tuned to Al Jazeera showing Peter Robb in the Bangladeshi capital, Dhaka. Peter Robb was on telly all the time, suddenly. He was the latest soap. The businessman was outside one of his factories. The dusty brown street, the stark concrete façade of the building, a couple of ancient motorcycles, half-a-dozen cycle rickshaws, the latter like miniature versions of the covered wagons seen in Westerns. There was a small fire at the roadside, a single wavy plume of black smoke. That was a bit Wild West too. It was hard to tell what was going on. A bit of cooking? Burning rubbish? Nobody was taking any notice. Most passers-by didn't even look. The incongruity had Dominic transfixed for a moment. He couldn't remember the last time he'd seen a naked flame. It really was another world.

A minibus creaked across the screen. It was heaving with passengers. Two white-shirted men were sitting in the roof rack. It had a slogan painted on the side in fat Bangla characters. The font was the only thing that was fat in the whole scene, apart perhaps from Peter Robb's head. The minibus exited right, to leave centre screen a colourful mob of factory workers, mostly women in saris, carrying Peter Robb aloft on a chair. It was like a moment from a Jewish wedding. Robb was beaming like a triumphant football manager.

'It's like a scene from Ghandi, isn't it?' said someone. There were a handful of other Cabinet Office officials watching with Dominic – some flicked through their phones, some scanned the papers, but all had a watching brief on the telly. Like the men in the roof rack, the civil servants were all white-shirted and jacket-less. There the similarity ended.

The sound was down. Dominic couldn't see the remote control to turn it up. He wasn't about to look for it anymore than anybody else was – rooting around for the lost remote was so domestic, so plebian, so un-Masters of the Universe. What a bunch of ... Dominic didn't want to think about it. He cringed and was aware of his eyes closing tightly as if remembering some mortification. He felt disgusted with himself but he still didn't do anything. Instead he read the captions rolling along the bottom of the screen: Robb ends outsourcing ... Massive wage rise ... Robb: if you want to pay less tax, pay your workers more.

'Has everyone forgotten about Zak Thomas Brown and Jack Sender?' someone said. 'It's all Robb, Robb, Robb.'

'No arrests. What are the police doing?'

Dominic tensed. 'Their best, I'm sure,' he said through pursed lips.

Des Westmoreland could usually be relied on to find an interesting angle and so it was. 'There will be more joy in heaven over one sinner who repents than over ninety-nine righteous ones who do not need to repent,' he said.

'You think they're sinners?'

'He that is without sin, let him cast the first stone,' intoned Des, sounding more sonorous and reverential by the minute.

Someone laughed a false laugh.

'Are you going to quote the Bible all day?'

'For everything there is a season,' said Des.

'You remember that Rana Plaza disaster?' It was a woman's voice. There were so few senior women in the department that Dominic recognised it as Tina McCauley without turning round. She had a slight Irish brogue. 'The building in Dhaka that collapsed in 2013 after they'd illegally added extra storeys ...'

'That was a garment factory too, wasn't it?'

'Some of it was,' said Tina. 'Several household names, every single one of which had a Corporate Social Responsibility policy.'

'Yes, but it's all outsourced, isn't it. The manufacture.'

'Can you outsource responsibility?'

There was a pause. 'Question,' Tina announced. 'How many died in Rana Plaza?'

There was some shuffling of feet, some turning of newspaper pages and some frantic screen swiping but there was no reply. This was from a group of civil servants armed between them with umpteen degrees and decades of service to the British state. They could have told you how many people died in Moorgate or King's Cross, in the Birmingham or Guildford pub bombings, in 9/11, in 7/7, in umpteen multiple shootings in the USA, even in incidents in Paris, Norway or elsewhere in Europe. Dhaka, until now, had not been on their radar.

'1,219,' said someone who had found it on his phone.

'Exactly,' said Tina.

'That wasn't one of Robb's factories, was it?'

'No, but that's not the point I'm making.'

'The rich and the poor meet together; the Lord is the maker of them all,' said Des.

Dominic turned back to the screen. The camera angle had changed slightly and he couldn't see if the fire was still burning.

On the other side of London, Jess was also watching Peter Robb being feted in Bangladesh. It was on the big screen in the grand hall where she had got a couple of days' work at the Beautiful Homes Exhibition. She had half an hour for her lunch and was wishing she'd brought something with her. Half an hour wasn't enough time to go out, get something and get back. So she was sipping cold tea which was all the venue itself seemed able to provide. She hoped the fare would be a little better once the paying guests arrived tomorrow.

There was some excitement over at the MöblA stand. It was one of the biggest displays in the room and all the casuals were hanging around. Jess had been hoping for a grand Swedish Smörgåsbord – or at least some meatballs. But there was no food. The attraction was the head honcho of MöblA, who was in the house and, alongside his workers in their distinctive coloured uniforms, was assembling filing cabinets. He seemed to be in an unofficial race with at least three of them.

Jess watched for a bit, sipped her tea and felt her stomach rumble. When the MöblA man finished, he leapt to his feet with a flourish as if it really had been a contest. He was quite short for a Scandinavian – blonde with glasses and what they used to call designer stubble.

'Not bad, eh,' he said to the crowd. He looked at his watch. 'Four minutes 37.'

There was a ripple of applause. 'It should be an Olympic Sport. Assembly of the skåpP cabinet.' He surveyed the audience but it was already breaking up. Watching a multi-billionaire build a filing cabinet was all very well, but where was the grub? Jess hesitated and, as she did, the MöblA guy's gaze met hers. Was he beckoning to her? She wasn't sure. A stunted hand movement, as if he had a spasm in his fingers. But then he hopped down from the raised platform on which he had been working and walked towards her.

'Frida Gustavsson is in our next advertising campaign.'

'Pardon,' said Jess.

'It is a secret but I can tell you because you are surely her sister.'

'I'm sorry, Mr ...'

'Forsberg. You don't know me but, of course, you know my furniture very well. You were probably conceived in a MöblA bed.'

'Well, I don't know about that,' said Jess.

'Är du svensk?'

Jess had no idea what he had said. It sounded like the name of a footballer. She shrugged.

'I asked whether you were Swedish but clearly the answer is no.'

'It is,' said Jess. 'The answer is no.' She was wondering if he was trying to chat her up. If so, it was time to swipe left.

'Only Sweden has Swedish gooseberries.' If so, the Swedish had strange taste in pick-up lines.

'We say this. Only Sweden has Swedish gooseberries. But it is clearly not true. You are the Frida Gustavsson lookalike.'

'My aunt says the same thing.'

'Are you a hostess?'

'No, I'm a casual – behind the scenes. I'm supposed to go back now.'

'You work for me. On my MöblA stand. As a hostess.'

Jess hesitated and looked around. She'd been assigned to someone called Aleksy, a big guy with a bigger clipboard. She couldn't see him but she could see a MöblA suited man wheeling a trolley of food onto the platform. Forsberg spotted the guy and made the same flourishing gesture as he'd made when he'd finished the cabinet. 'First we eat,' he said.

'OK,' said Jess.

Elizabeth Robb was also watching her husband on the television. Although, from her hotel balcony, she realised, she could probably see the whole fine procession live. When they had first arrived, she had stood on the balcony and it was like a front-row seat at the festival of humanity – the noise, the bustle, the ancient engines, the rage of colour, the heat, the dust. Quite overwhelming. Exciting and terrifying at the same time. She chose not to do it again because she found the hordes of over-familiar foreigners disconcerting and even a little frightening.

She knew you weren't supposed to think like that, but she did and that was that. She couldn't help what she felt. She wished she didn't but she'd been born cautious – the product of a lower-middle class upbringing. Her father was in and out of work so often, sometimes you could hear the trapdoor to poverty creaking beneath the carpet. Her mother's sister had died young of whooping cough and so her mother had always been a bundle of nerves, never letting Elizabeth or her sisters do anything. She'd cried for a week when Elizabeth went to university and it was only down the road. It was at university that she'd met Peter, the son of a tailor, and, as it turned out, hitched herself to his stellar ascent. It had been far from obvious at the time. Peter had dyslexia, undiagnosed until he was in his twenties. She wished she had Peter's bravery of spirit. The hotel was nice though. She was glad that Peter's new-found social conscience didn't require them to live in a mud hut.

Everything you wanted was on tap. The handsome Bangladeshi staff were in stark contrast to those stuffy old souls in Monaco. It was like being on a second honeymoon. The puppy fat she had had in her teens had returned in her 40s but Peter didn't seem bothered – he didn't even need Viagra anymore. So that was something to be said for a social conscience. She doubted it would last. Like Peter's passing interests in astronomy, yachting and opera, it would be a fad. Fashion lived and died by its fads and her husband was nothing if not a product of his industry. His social conscience would be as transient as the mullet haircut or armadillo shoes. Still, she would enjoy it while it lasted.

First and foremost, her husband was a businessman. He knew that making money was about spotting trends early. He'd spotted a new one and would abandon it once it ceased to be lucrative.

She turned the TV off. For the first time in many a year, she had chosen her outfit for the evening as much for how she would look stepping out of it, as for how she would look in it.

While she was waiting for Peter, propped up on a soft assortment of multicoloured pillows and cushions on a bed the size of a tennis court, she sipped the peachiest of Daquiris and enjoyed her iPad. Peter returned just as she was getting bored with reading about his antics.

'I got a lift back on a scooter,' said Peter, as excited as a schoolboy.

Elizabeth puffed up a cushion and created a space on the bed beside her. Peter scooted over.

'Are you playing with fire?' she asked him.

'Is that what you're calling yourself now,' said Peter. 'Fire?'

Peter had a Cheshire grin from ear to ear but, when he looked at Elizabeth, she wasn't smiling at all. She had that grey foreboding just behind the eyes. Would she never relax? Would she never feel safe?

'What am I going to do, Betsy? Hire Secur4U or recognise that there's a new game in town and play to win?'

Elizabeth shook her head. She placed the iPad in his hand and showed him post after post from someone called Scootergirl.

'Who gave you a lift back?'

'Well, it wasn't a girl if that's what you mean, Bets. This is Bangladesh. It was a thin man in a bright pink shirt. Sumon. One of my supervisors at the factory.'

Elizabeth was aware that she spent too much time inside her head but she ploughed on anyway. 'Do you think she (or he) was behind ...' She pointed at Scootergirl's most recent post.

'My death?'

'Yes.'

'I don't know.'

Peter read through some of the posts, nodding occasionally, emitting the odd verbal exclamation of what sounded like approval. 'She's very interesting, your Scootergirl' he said eventually. Elizabeth was pouring her husband a cocktail. 'Interesting posts. Thank you, darling. Mostly accurate. Clearly a very intelligent child.'

'She's not my Scootergirl,' said Elizabeth. 'And who's to say she's a child?'

She put her own cocktail down firmly and with an implied finality. Peter did not want her not to pick it up again.

'I don't like people writing these things about you,' Elizabeth said. 'I worry.'

Peter rolled off the bed and pulled his telephone from his jacket pocket.

'What are you doing?' Elizabeth asked.

'Calling the police.'

Elizabeth smiled. 'Then you can come over and play with fire,' she said.

By the time she left at the end of the day, Jess had doubled her money. The next day she'd be working on the MöblA stand wearing the female version of the MöblA uniform, looking after Mr Forsberg's personal guests. He wasn't a bad guy – surprisingly human. Very pleased with himself. Reminded her of her mum when she'd successfully built a MöblA bedside unit.

She plugged her headphones into her phone but, instead of her music, she tuned into the iPlayer. She wanted to hear more of what Peter Robb had been saying.

# 4.6.

Gabby said goodbye to Chris and turned off the phone.

It was happening now. The life which had been on hold since Jack's murder was beginning again. She had been floating on a cloud, really – a soft cocoon of quaint old seaside towns, rolling green hills and the balmy honey of the French language. Anglo-Saxon reality, that big awkward guy with the fat wallet, had come calling. The hallway was dark and cramped and she suddenly felt like she had very little room for manoeuvre. Gabby looked at her suitcases sitting by the door. By her standards, this was still travelling very light indeed.

Perhaps she wasn't going back. Perhaps there was still hope that she could move forward. She really didn't know. She walked back into the prettier living room.

For a while back there, she'd been in the eye of the hurricane that was her husband's death and relatively safe, but she and it were out of sync now and the wind was beginning to toss her and her emotions around like cheap confetti, like long flowing shampooed locks in a wind tunnel. Where was Mrs Caton? If she couldn't have her mother, she wanted her mother tongue.

'Mrs Caton,' she shouted. 'Do you have a number for a taxi?'

Mrs Caton appeared, carrying an old Filofax in tastefully-worn brown leather. She handed it to Gabby. It was crammed full of notes tightly written in Mrs Caton's classic, round hand and, as Gabby opened it, dozens of business cards tumbled out onto the thinning carpet.

'You'll find one there,' said Mrs Caton. Mrs Caton, seemingly reading Gabby's mind, was speaking French. 'Now where is my son?'

'Biscuit Town. He said he'll back soon. I think he is going to walk on the pier. Some problem with the case.'

'Why is he spending all his time in Biscuit Town? I don't like Biscuit Town.'

'Well, I don't think he's on holiday, Madame Caton.'

'You defend him now,' said Mrs Caton, before adding melodramatically: 'but you are walking out of his life.'

'I'm just walking back into my own, said Gabby.

'Bof,' snorted Mrs Caton. 'If you take over your husband's business, you will be exposing yourself to the same risks as your husband.'

To Gabby, this was beginning to sound like a cracked record as Mrs Caton repeated her principal argument for the fourth or fifth time.

Gabby was hands and knees on the floor, picking up the cards. She found one for a local taxi firm.

'I just need to do some paperwork,' said Gabby. 'To do with my inheritance of the estate. I'm not moving to America. I'm not taking over the firm.' Going through all this in conversation was actually helpful to her. It clarified her own thinking.

'You will not come back,' said Mrs Caton, achieving some melancholic top notes that a soprano would have been proud of. 'Who will I speak French with? Tell me that.'

'England is full of French people and Chris speaks excellent French,' said Gabby with a straight face.

Mrs Caton snorted once again. She was, in this quaint little room with its porcelain and doilies, a bull in a china shop. 'You sound almost like you believe that. Perhaps you'll start an acting career,' she wailed.

Gabby changed the subject. 'Chris says he bumped into Mrs Graham...'

'Mrs Graham. Mrs Graham!' Mrs Caton was in that borderline state between overacting and genuine hysteria that gave French women of a certain age such a reputation. 'Who, in the name of God, is Mrs Graham?'

'The mother of someone called Colin, I think – Chris's childhood friend.'

'Oh, mon Dieu,' said Mrs Caton and collapsed into a Georgian-style wooden-framed armchair, its high back leaking stuffing like Mrs Caton was now leaking tears.

'Francine,' said Gabby. She really did look distressed. This was what nineteenth century novelists referred to as 'a touch of the vapours'. 'I promise I'll come back very soon. Je vous promets.'

Chris was sitting in Brewed Awakening, contemplating a second cup of coffee. He was feeling sorry for himself. The world may have suddenly become a better place, but he had so wanted to be a small part of that happening and it wasn't turning out like that.

The reason Howard Chowdhury, port manager at Newhaven, had recognised Gary Shad and his impressive motor was that Shad had stolen it and had been taking it to France to flog it. It all predated the Zak Thomas Brown killing and he had, as Gill Graham had informed him and as the Biscuit Town wooly backs had confirmed, since been charged with it – a happy accident of his and Gabby's arrest of Shad, admittedly, but very far from the main prize. He wanted to go back to Corrigan with something solid. He wanted to prove how useful he was and, perhaps even more importantly, prove how much more useful he could be, given a longer leash and a greater capacity for using his own initiative. And now to make matters worse, he'd lost Cherrianne Dixon, his geek girl. That's why he was killing time in her coffee shop in Brighton. (And it was a lot better and cheaper than Boomer's – that he did have to admit.)

'I'm in Brighton, catching up with the geeky girl I've got investigating the website,' he'd told Gabby on the mobile.

'A geek girl?' And Chris had wondered whether that had been a note of jealousy in her voice or just a bad connection.

'Trying to, anyway.' Chris had said.

'Message her on Facebook.' Gabby had said. Probably not jealous then.

Chris was playing the conversation in his head for the second or third time and it wasn't getting any better. The truth was that Gabby was going and he was going to miss her. He couldn't really say any more than that. Did he fancy her? What sort of question was that for a grown man to ask – even of himself? He wasn't in high school now. Yes, he probably did 'fancy' her but then so, probably, did half the men on the planet. It wasn't really about that, was it? But if it wasn't about that, what was it about? Chris didn't have a clue. He realised that he was even worse at talking about his feelings with himself than he was with someone else. He looked at his watch.

Cherri wasn't in her office. Nobody had been. Corporatesponger was locked. She wasn't answering her phone or replying to texts. He had taken a walk along the front, all the way to the Marina. He'd eaten some cockles and watched a man gut a fish. It had affected him, the fish gutting, in a way that the far worse things he'd seen on the job had not. He'd been leaning against the wall, eating his seafood with a cocktail stick, enjoying the wind in his hair. A couple of kids had been crabbing and the fisherman had been reading a book. Suddenly the end of the rod had dived down like a buzzard and the fisherman was up and all action. The taut line, the bent rod, the silver fish wriggling on the hook. One minute, the fish had been slip-sliding happily through the water, the next, to its dead-eyed amazement, it was in the palm of the fisherman's hand, being sliced longwise from throat to tail. Silver to silver to red. It reminded Chris how quickly life could be taken away in a way that 150 crime scenes – so business-like with their cameras and chalk, exclusion zones and white-coated professionals – had not.

He was on edge already and no man enjoyed a lesson in his own stupidity.

'Message her on Facebook,' he said, aloud this time, and began poking around on his phone. But the act of booting up Facebook and searching for friends made Chris feel even more juvenile. Modern life was infantilising him. Modern life was turning him into someone who couldn't cope without his 4G security blanket. Ten years ago, he wouldn't have known that Gabby was going until he'd got back home and she'd gone. Nice and clear. Black and white. Adult and manly.

He found Cherrianne Dixon's page. She didn't share much with those who weren't her 'friends' but one of the half a dozen images she did share made his blood run cold. He'd seen it umpteen times before, all over the internet. He felt just like that fish as it squirmed its final squirm in the fisherman's hand. This he had not been expecting. Cherri was Scootergirl. There she was, bold as brass, sitting on a bloody scooter. She had a hoodie on, true. You couldn't really see her face or the big hair but...

No wonder he hadn't heard from her. No wonder she'd disappeared. For a moment Chris just looked at the image. Then he clicked to the 'Fashion Sister' website to check he was right. He was. Absolute rookie's error. Why hadn't he checked that for himself before? Because, as usual, he'd been happy to leave the boring stuff to someone else while he got on with the serious police work of roughing up suspects.

He looked at the Facebook page again and it was so bloody obvious. The girl worked for an organisation that existed to generate, develop and amplify hatred for corporates? Why had he assumed she'd be on his side? Because she looked about twelve years old? Because he was a stupid fucking idiot, infatuated with an unattainable supermodel, also like a fucking twelve-year-old.

He was on gardening leave because he was only fit for gardening leave and, with that, he picked the phone up and brought it crashing down on the table like a suspect's head in The Sweeney. The phone may have been smart but he wasn't. The screen and, along with it, the image of Cherrianne Dixon in a pink hoodie shattered into a dozen angry pieces.

Gabby was standing by the cab with her own suitcases and looking at Mrs Caton's. The cab driver was doing much the same thing and with increasing impatience. Francine Caton's case was a bijou, old-fashioned one, leather with bolts – a classic of its type but totally impractical for actual travel in the actual world as actually was. Gabby was trying, for the third time, to get Chris on the phone.

'I'm sure he's just out of earshot or on the front where there's no coverage,' she said.

'Why are you calling Chris? I am the mother, he is the child,' said Mrs Caton, looking every inch the child. 'I can make my own decision.'

She had just announced that she was coming with Gabby to America.

'If you take over Stufff, you will be exposing yourself to the same risks as your husband.'

As Gabby repeated her vain attempts to call Chris, so Mrs Caton repeated the same phrase over and over. They were getting nowhere fast.

The cab driver looked at his watch extravagantly. The time-piece nestled in his hairy forearm like a white egg. 'If you want to get that flight, it's now or never,' he said.

Leaving her case on the ground for the driver, Mrs Caton got into the taxi cab – legs surprisingly agile, spine unexpectedly supple, rouged lips and a moue like a duck's bill. Gabby was French enough to know that, with a face such as that, further discussion was pointless.

The cab driver was placing Mrs Caton's case in the boot. Gabby, battue, handed him her cases and walked round to the other side of the vehicle.

# 4.7.

The problem with number three Estuary Sands (house name: 'The Schooner') – well, one of a number of problems – was that it was so big that it was relatively easy to avoid someone. That, Gavin had concluded, was what Pip was doing with him.

She was seldom home for long and, when she was, she was locked in her room. They'd passed once on the stairs. She'd given him a wide berth. (It was the sort of staircase where that was more than possible.) They'd been in the same room for breakfast – again, a single occasion. She'd left clutching her bowl of Bran Flakes. He resolved to sort the situation once and for all. Gavin had, and Pip as a recent guest would not have known this, a master key to all the rooms in the house. He planned to occupy her bedroom until she returned. He reckoned she couldn't have been intending to go far or for long as she hadn't taken a coat.

Her room was more like a hotel room and one in which the guest was not intending to remain for more than a night or two. There was a pile of boxes and, on top of them, an open suitcase out of which she was living. She wasn't using the ample wardrobes although there were a couple of baggy cheesecloth-type tops hanging on hangers on the wardrobe door.

This taste for hippy chic was something Pip had probably got from her mother who had still been a flower child when, for most, the flowers had long since wilted. Gavin had met Greta at a party neither had much wanted to go to. There'd been a big concert at Wembley which is where both of them would have preferred to be. Instead they'd been in a garden in Harrow with a bunch of arseholes and shandy drinkers and a band playing limp Rolling Stones and Beatles covers. With Bruce Springsteen playing down the road, it was like watching the cub scouts play on Cup Final day. He and Greta, whom he'd never met before, but who was wearing a Springsteen T-shirt and had the sort of sad, sultry eyes that someone called Greta should have had, walked through north London in the general direction of the venue hoping to get an earful of The Boss. It was a long walk. You couldn't hear much until you were virtually on top of the stadium.

Gavin liked the upbeat rocky Springsteen – Born To Run, Born In The USA – while Greta preferred the more acoustic, meditative stuff – The River, Thunder Road. It seemed like a funny little nothing at the time, a fine topic for a teasing conversation on a summer's afternoon in London when they were both enjoying getting high on each other, but later, when Gavin was veering in one direction towards Guns And Roses and Greta in the other towards Joni Mitchell and Suzanne Vega, it would mean everything – the symbol for the different directions their lives had taken. Greta despised Gavin's materialism. He hated her dumb, 'good in everyone' sentimentality. Well, he'd had the last laugh on that one. His lawyer, a wicked misogynistic cunt who cost a fortune and played harder than a brick football, saw to that. Materially, she'd got bugger all. Result: his ex was living in a rat-hole of a flat which, with its lumpy, stunted sofa, was way too small for Pip to share with her for longer than a night. Greta had been done up better than the most smoked, most pickled kipper. (You think there's 'good in everyone', Greta? Well, not in me and certainly not in my lawyer.) She now referred to Gavin as the merchant – as in merchant banker. When Tori had been born, she'd sent a Congratulations card to 'the merchant, the slapper and the sprog'. Challenged by Malvina as to the acid epistle's provenance, Gavin had claimed that he couldn't read the writing.

On one side of the bed, which was neatly made (possibly by Jessica), there was a laptop and a book. On the other was the only real mark of Pip's occupation of the room, the one personal touch: her atlas, propped up against the wall. It was a big old Reader's Digest one, that he and Greta had given her for a birthday or Christmas when she was little. It had been damaged in the fire; the cover was smudged with black and the top corner looked like it had had a bite taken out of it. Gavin wondered if she'd put it there deliberately in anticipation of just this eventuality. Had he been in her position, it was the sort of thing he might have done. Water-tight attention to detail was what won you the prizes whatever the game.

He sat down on the bed and opened up her laptop. Well, why not?

If he was going to get charged with the offence, he might as well have the pleasure of committing it.

Still open on the desktop was an episode of Mad Men. This tugged at Gavin's heart in an unfamiliar way. Why was Pip watching this? Had she discovered it for herself – not likely since he could imagine the average dickhead student wetting himself about it – or had she heard him and Malvina arguing about it? Malvina had described the show that he considered achingly cool (and had been heard to describe, after a drink or three, as 'the most beautiful nihilism') as 'Western bullshit'. It was the word 'Western' that had done it. It was the moment that Gavin realised his wife had been born in the Soviet Union. It made the gap between him and Greta seem like pretty small beer really. Jesus, they both loved Rosalita, seven minutes of the most sublime Springsteen.

Anyway, Gavin had been reduced to getting his fix of Mad Men late at night, watching it on streaming like some old pervert with his porn. It struck him as sad on more levels than he could manage to separate in his mind that his daughter, two rooms along, was doing much the same thing. Lonely was the word if one word were enough. She was as lonely as he was.

Also on the desktop was a folder called Photos. There were perhaps twenty images in there. A few included Pip and her friends. There was one of half a dozen fresh-faced students, a couple of whom he recognised as tenants who had shared Pip's – his – house. But, mostly the photos were family. There were several of the three of them – Gavin, Greta and Philippa – in their younger, happier days; one of his and Greta's wedding; one that he hadn't seen for ages of him and Greta kissing in a hot tub somewhere (Vietnam?); and one of him and Pip ice skating. He'd forgotten about the ice skating. It was at Broadgate, the pop-up ice rink in the city. Dusk was descending and the twinkling lights on the ice gave the image a cinematic effervescence. Pip was holding his hand and the photo of the pair of them slicing up the rink, which must have been taken by Greta, was close to perfect. They looked fantastic, he like a Hollywood actor, a rip of muscle beneath the arm of the T-shirt, she like a teen model, Kate Moss or someone. His trailing blade was angled, sending up a shaft of icy white sparkles as he and his beautiful daughter arced round like a couple of pros, Torvill and Dean. They both looked so happy it was enough to make you cry – and Pip, as pretty as he'd ever seen her, was holding his hand so tightly he could almost feel it. Lastly, there were a couple including Malvina – one of the four of them (Gavin, Malvina, Pip and Tori) in which they looked about as relaxed as a family of rabbits in a tiger cage and one of Malvina by herself. It was the one Gavin still had on his phone: Malvina tall, slim and gorgeously pre-botox in which her brand new tits just looked so fantastic you wondered if you had a 3D screen.

She didn't look like that anymore and when, a few moments later, Pip walked in, Gavin was back in Broadgate.

Pip didn't scream. She'd seen the open door. 'So now you break into other people's bedrooms as well, do you?'

'I've got a key,' said Gavin. 'And it is my house.'

'Broadgate,' said Pip and for a moment they both looked at the picture, full-screen, on her laptop. She allowed her bag to drop to the floor and, shuffling it shyly from her shoulders, hung her jacket on a rogue coat hanger. She folded her arms across her chest as she lowered her gaze towards him.

'I'm going to have to password-protect that now, aren't I?' She was being businesslike; she wasn't in the rage Gavin had been expecting. He knew that today's generation sometimes went to concerts, the cinema and even parties with their parents (imagine his father at Bruce Springsteen) but breaking into your kid's bedroom and looking at her stuff, they were surely still capital offences just as they had always been.

'Sorry,' said Gavin. 'I just wanted to talk to you and there wasn't much else lying around to pass the time.'

'Yes, well, I'm not staying long.'

'Can't we find some way back, Pip,' he said. 'I mean, it hasn't always been like this, has it?' He moved over to allow her to sit down on the bed. The result, as he moved the laptop, was to draw their attention, once again, to the screen image. She ignored his offer and positioned herself by the window instead, three-quarter profile.

'You're offering to take me ice skating.'

'We could,'

'The nearest one's Gosport.'

'There's one in Brighton over Christmas.'

'It's a lovely idea, Father, but I'm afraid I won't be here at Christmas.'

'You feel isolated from it all up here?'

'In here,' said Pip. 'Inside this prison.'

'The gated community.'

'I call that the outer wall.'

This sort of dialogue reminded him so much of his daughter at the age of that skating photograph – pouting, selfish, spoilt rotten and feeling guilty about it – but he thought it better not to say. Instead, he slid over a little further, offering even more space on the counterpane which was, like most of the furnishings and fittings in the house, in the tasteful, neutral colours of a top-end hotel. (No wonder she treated it like one.) This time Pip acknowledged the gesture and shook her head slowly. She looked at him with pure contempt – but whereas, when he'd seen that sort of expression before, it was because he had just royally screwed the scowling individual (or was just about to), in this case there was nothing to be done. He looked at the picture instead.

'I thought you were just selfish and ambitious,' said Pip, 'but it seems that you're even worse than that, you're empty. Now everybody has a social conscience, you want one too. Well, it doesn't work like that. You can't just say you care, you have to actually care.'

'I've given money to the hospital,' said Gavin. 'I've given money to the factory redevelopment.' But he knew that wasn't the point.

'Now Mr Big is Mr Generous. Are you thinking, Father, that if you give enough money, they'll name the town after you? Well, I've got news for you, there's already a town called Henley.'

'And that's full of wankers.' He muttered that really – trying to lighten the moment but without a lot of conviction.

'It's all a bit of a joke to you, isn't it?'

'What is?'

'Anything that isn't about money. Well, I tell you, money can't buy you love, Dad. Now you may think that's an old song, a silly song with a naive sentiment, but it happens to be true. You can't change the way people feel with money.'

Gavin couldn't agree with the last bit but, again, he knew better than to say it. Instead he said: 'You can move into the factory redevelopment. As one of the major backers, I'm sure I can swing it. Your friends too...'

'Once upon a time, I would have jumped at that.' She was folding up the hippy tops and putting them in the case as if she was about to leave. 'Just like I did when you bought the house. Not now. You just don't get it. There comes a point when it doesn't matter how much money you've got, if you're an empty, cold-blooded reptile, you're an empty, cold-blooded reptile.'

'An empty cold-blooded reptile who remembers taking you ice skating.'

'Dad, unless that factory redevelopment is going to be finished tomorrow, it's too late because I'm moving out.'

'Do you have to?'

'I can't bear another day with that bloody woman.'

'Me and you both.'

'Fucking hell, Dad – all for a pair of plastic tits.'

'It wasn't like that,' said Gavin. But it probably was.

# 4.8.

Mason sat very still, taking as much of it in as possible. The study was not a grand room – small, poky and in need of a duster, in truth. Grey shadows crept along the walls in the spring sun. The carriage clock, which stood on the mantlepiece between two glazed figurines of white knights on chargers, had stopped. The wan yellow paint and criss-cross lattice work on the glass-fronted bookcases and on the banquettes in the window bays gave the impression of a golden cage. This was the heart of government, Mason's first visit to 10 Downing Street, but it felt like the lions' enclosure at London Zoo.

There were five of them in the room: Mason; Ellis, the PM's king Spad; another of the PM's men; the Chancellor; and the Prime

Minister. The two big beasts were standing, circling the room and each other as voices boomed and bellowed, gestures became more warlike and faces reddened. The subject was serious enough anyway, but there was far more at stake than the tax take. Mrs Thatcher, hanging over the fireplace, watched the proceedings with a gleam in her grocer's eye.

On the dining table, five untouched coffees in matching bone china cups on saucers. On the small coffee table, by which Mason was seated, was a chess board with a game in progress. Mason assumed it was the famous match between the PM's team and the Chancellor's in which a single move was made each day. His ears could not avoid the discussion (it was the frankest of 'frank exchanges of views') but, as it continued, his eyes were increasingly drawn to the chess board. Black had numerical superiority and was attacking on several flanks but, unless Mason was mistaken (and he hadn't played chess since childhood), white had a killer move which would checkmate in two moves. Of course, he wasn't sure whose turn it was.

Mason had expected something explosive like this ever since the one-to-one with Ellis. Ellis himself appeared calm, remaining seated throughout and occasionally checking his phone. He had a pile of papers which he'd placed beside the chess board. He didn't read or examine them, but he would touch them from time to time as if for good luck. Mason knew exactly why he, Mason, had been summoned: he was to be sacrificed if needed, the civil servant who would carry the can if the skullduggery came unstuck. The Chancellor would have been hoping, like Mason, that Mason didn't have to say a word but if he did, if the PM called on Mason to speak, the Chancellor wanted to hear it. That was the insurance policy. If Mason changed his story later: well, the Chancellor would reason smoothly, he (Mason) had been compromised. (The Chancellor was very fond of the idea that people had been compromised.)

'We're meeting the PM. I'll do the talking,' the Chancellor had said to him on the phone without even introducing himself. In response to Mason's heavy silence, he added: 'You'll get your reward in heaven.'

'But I already have a job in the Cabinet Office, Sir,' Mason had said, singsong – of course he would go along with it all, but he wasn't having anyone, even the Chancellor, thinking it was all hunky dory.

Mason assumed the PM's other aide was the sacrificial lamb from the other side. He had the air of a well-behaved schoolboy who unexpectedly finds himself waiting outside the headmaster's office. The youngest man in the room, he flinched frequently throughout the exchange, screwing up his eyes with pain.

'So I had Commissioner Walters in,' the PM had begun. 'I told him he was taking way too long. Told him it wasn't good enough. I asked for the full breakdown: numbers of officers, lines of enquiry, et cetera, et cetera. He played absolutely everything with a straight bat. Constantly apologised, agreed that everything wasn't good enough. And smiled at me throughout, as if we were playing a game. No, as if we were in a play, playing parts: me pretending to be angry and him pretending to be apologetic.'

The Chancellor had simply shaken his head at all this like a wise, old sage – there's nowt so queer as folk, you can't get the staff and I don't know what the world's coming to, were just three of the meanings tangled up in this most commonplace of gestures. It was very annoying and it was at this point that the Prime Minister had left his seat.

Office had greyed the PM's hair and added several kilos to his backside. Although they were contemporaries, he was beginning to look older than the Chancellor who carried, as time's scar, only the beginnings of a monk's bald patch. The PM was the ageing silverback, the fading alpha-male facing a challenge from within his own pack. As the PM began to pace the room, you could see the gait of an old man.

'I know you want this fucking job,' he said. 'I know you've wanted this fucking job since we were at prep school. But you want it ten times as much now, don't you?

'Seeing as it's mine.' The PM was looking out of the window. To say something like that to the Chancellor in front of low-life like Mason was to escalate the conflict to just short of nuclear within five minutes.

The Chancellor was knocked off his guard although not, since he was still seated, off his feet. He called the Prime Minister by his Christian name. 'I am the loyalist member of your cabinet,' he said, sounding as wounded as he could manage. The remark could have been true without actually making the Chancellor any more loyal to the PM than a cat to a goldfish.

'I ask myself who benefits,' said the Prime Minister, 'from a sudden vast influx of tax revenues and the answer is obvious, Chancellor.'

'The country benefits, Sir.'

'Don't fucking call me Sir. Don't pretend to respect me.'

'Nobody likes the idea of a killer at large.' The Chancellor got out of his chair and raised himself to his full height. He was three inches at least taller than the Prime Minister. They had almost identical suits on. Mason had seen their almost identical wives and could imagine them in their almost identical prep school uniforms with their almost identical ambitions. How annoying for the Chancellor – everyone thought he was the one with the brains and the PM the one with the charisma. It was unfair that the spoils should go to the one with the least insincere smile. The Chancellor joined his boss at the window, just an inch or two behind, a perfect spot for sliding a stiletto between the ribs.

'But it's an ill wind,' said the Chancellor, quietly. 'Even my father has paid some tax.'

This seemed to break the tension. The PM turned to face the man who was supposed to be his best friend in politics and he was smiling. Mason knew the Chancellor's father by reputation but the PM clearly knew him a lot better than that.

'Old Willard has paid some tax, has he?" chirped the PM. 'Last time that happened, it must have been collected in Groats.'

Now it was his turn to call the Chancellor by his Christian name. 'I'm getting a little sick of hearing that phrase, "it's an ill wind". There's no such thing as a free lunch. I'm old-fashioned like that.'

'If you're a graduate from the school of hard knocks, I'm a Bangladeshi trawler fisherman,' said the Chancellor, turning away. The PM put his hand on the Chancellor's shoulder and spun him back round again.

'You knew Brian Thomas Brown, didn't you? You were in the same college. Was he Rhodes? I fucking remember you like a pair of dandy highwaymen, dressed like Adam Ant with an expenses account. What a pair of queens. What happened? Did he not recommend you for the fucking Netball Blue or something. And you've harnessed the same resentment against him as you do against me...'

'Are you accusing me?'

'I'm accusing you of stoking a fire. I'm accusing you of being an utter twat. Why do you think you're Chancellor?'

'Because you appointed me.'

'Yes, more fucking fool me. But do you think it's your skill or talent? Don't make me laugh. There are three men sitting in this room right now who could do a better job than you do.' Mason could see the Chancellor's eyes narrow. He was concentrating on keeping them focused on the PM and not allowing them to turn towards Mason, Ellis and the schoolboy.

'There are probably mice in the bloody kitchen could do a better job.'

Mason found himself thinking of the cartoon mouse Ratatouille and it was all he could do to keep the smile from his lips. He concentrated on the chess pieces.

'You're here because you're a member of the party – the richest and most successful political party in the history of the world. But let me tell you this, since you're such a fucking financial expert, there's an election coming up and we don't have any money.'

Mason could see that the Chancellor was genuinely stunned by this. His 'really?' was neither sarcasm nor play-acting but the best reaction he could muster to an uppercut straight to the jaw.

'No chance of your becoming PM if we're not in government, is there, you prawn?'

'Don't call me that.'

'You are a fucking prawn. You've always been a prawn. You were born a prawn. You bloody prawn.'

Mason could see the Chancellor metaphorically pulling himself up from the canvas, the nose bloodied, the eye turning purple and closing. The PM did not need to spell it out. Since all the party's donors were now paying their tax and doing other fine deeds, they didn't have the money or the goodwill left for, ahem, 'charitable and political donations'.

The Prime Minister walked over to the dining table and downed a coffee. 'Stone fucking cold,' he said.

He allowed his substantial arse to rest on the edge of the table as he surveyed the room. The Chancellor walked back to his seat next to Ellis with a stride and a swagger, but the whole room could see that he was limping.

'What do you think you're doing, anyway?' asked the Prime Minister in the level, hyper-reasonable tone of a schoolmaster teaching idiots. 'I didn't come into politics to spend money on hospitals and schools. Did you? That's what I came into politics to stop the other lot doing.'

He looked up at the portrait of Margaret Thatcher.

'I want this bastard caught. I want us to go back as close as we possibly can to that nice old country that dear old John Major was prattling on about: the warm beer, the county cricket grounds, the dog lovers and the old fucking dears on pushbikes.'

He necked another cold coffee, then walked across the room to the coffee table. The old man's gait had gone. With a dramatic sweep of his loose, simian limb, his chubby hand moved the white queen down the diagonal, three, four, five squares, the move that Mason had spotted. The black king's undoing was a move away. The Prime Minister examined all four faces around the coffee table, one after the other, before walking away.

At the door he turned. 'In other words,' he said, 'where the rich are rich, the poor are poor and everybody knows their place. OK?'

'Yes,' said Ellis. 'I wouldn't put it like that in your conference speech, though.'

# 4.9.

As soon as she met Rachel Thomas Brown, Gabby realised what had been missing from her own reaction. Perhaps she really was the ice maiden she'd so often been cast as in fashion shoots. Or perhaps she was just in tune with more accurate and honest feelings. Rachel's emotions were all reality TV: big, bold and vengeful.

As well as sorting out all the probate issues, Gabby had always intended to visit Rachel when she went to the US. She'd never met her properly but their paths had crossed once at a political fundraiser. They'd exchanged business cards and shortly afterwards Rachel had sent Gabby her congratulations on the opening of the first of Gabby's cupcake stores. The shop happened to be in Boston, Rachel's home town, and Rachel had sent Gabby a photo of it, complete with the girlish caption: 'Look what I saw – clever you XXX'. She was being anything but girlish now.

Gabby had invited her to the shop. The pinafored staff, so excited at the proprietor's presence they could barely breathe, had put the women upstairs to give them a little privacy but, Gabby realised as they sat down, the nature of the venue was ill-suited to the meeting it was to host. With primary-coloured, primary school decor, twee handmade wooden fixtures and fittings and drapes, mobiles and toy windmills, the idea (Gabby's) was that the shops should look a little like cupcakes themselves. But, with the two widows alone in the middle of the upstairs room, at a sunshine yellow table in powder blue chairs, it felt odd – like an empty creche. They were both sitting there, looking at their cupcakes and sipping green tea.

Rachel was hitting out in all directions. She intended to sue pretty much everybody including, it seemed, the entire French state and anyone who'd ever bought a croissant. 'You know what the French are like, Gabby', she said over and over. Gabby wasn't sure whether Rachel actually knew that she, Gabby, was French. After all, a good half of the elite WAGs had accents. Perhaps she just meant that everybody knew what the French were like. The phrase 'cheese-eating surrender monkeys' inevitably made an appearance. The police were in the firing line for the melting of evidence, the striking translators for failing to get the report over to the British police and the hotel for not spotting that Zak hadn't returned from the slopes. Gabby nodded and made the odd sympathetic noise, but Rachel clearly didn't require her to say much. Gabby knew from personal experience just how difficult it was for the super-rich to find anyone at all to talk to. When every single relationship is underpinned by money, the only people you could trust were others in the same boat – and there weren't too many of those. Gabby had been lucky to have her fellow models. There had been, perhaps still were, one or two genuine friendships there. Rachel clearly had nobody and she and Gabby now had something unique and ghoulish in common.

'I'm angry with myself as much as anything, Gabby. Zak was so regular.'

'Regular?'

'He lived by a routine. In absolute everything. He went skiing every year at the same time of year to the same place and went out on the piste everyday, at exactly the same times. You could set your watch by him.'

'Meaning that everybody in the resort would know at what time he'd be on the slopes.'

'He used to go for a morning ski, the way some people go for a morning jog. Always on his own. He'd pay them to open the drag lift specially for him.'

'I'm sorry,' said Gabby.

'They think they're invincible, don't they?'

Gabby could hear in Rachel's voice the gradual change of register from anger to exhaustion as she realised that, when you looked at it, it wasn't particularly surprising that they hadn't yet found the killer. It wasn't human error, it wasn't the stuff of lawsuits, it was just bad luck. Gabby wasn't a religious person, but the arbitrary nature of death did make her wish that she was. It had happened to be Jack and Zak, but it could have been any of several hundred similarly placed men. Just very bad luck, the karmic opposite of the very good luck that had made them rich in the first place. What goes around, comes around. She didn't say that though. She sat still as a Zen master.

'Your shop is adorable,' said Rachel. 'It's like sitting in a cupcake.'

'Thank you,' said Gabby.

The two women looked down at the daintily-decorated table top, all flowers and icing-like swirls of colour, and then up at each other.

They were both smiling, sincere smiles no doubt, but they were locked in a battle of wills. Who would eat the cupcake first?

'What will you do without Jack?'

'I don't know. Nothing for a while.'

'I can't do nothing. Never could.'

It became clear that there were no flies on Rachel – and she'd acted before there were any on her husband. As soon as she had heard of his death but before it was publicly announced, she had called her broker and sold a vast tranche of Boomer's stock, buying it back again a few hours later when the share price plummeted on news of its founder's demise. So, while Rachel may have been angry and sad and everything in between, she was expert in the complexities of the Statutory Residence Test and knew precisely how many days she needed to spend on the Cayman Islands. Gabby wasn't going to waste too much energy feeling sorry for her.

'I went to one of Jack's warehouses.'

'I can honestly say I've never set foot inside a Boomer's coffee house.'

'I wish I hadn't. I'd always thought that modelling was a cattle market but it was a walk in the park by comparison.'

'I always thought it was a walk in the park,' said Rachel, 'modelling'. She was unable to keep the note of jealousy from her voice.

Gabby had been shown round by a supervisor who seemed keen to stress how Stufff extracted the last pinch of labour from every worker every minute of every day. Her guide, a man with slick-backed hair and a cheap moustache, knew full well that she was the boss's widow, so presumably he emphasised the points he thought she'd want to hear. She could see that there was a deep seam of insecurity at the heart of every big business. School bullies (I'm talking about you, Celine Vincent) would hit you until somebody stopped them, even if the point of their bullying, to make you scared and to make you cry, had been long since achieved. Well, you couldn't generate too much fear, could you? Always good to have some more in the bank. All of this, this brutalisation of the staff, like all the accounting wheezes, was about extracting a little more pointless profit. Because, when you already had too much money, you could never have enough. How could you know?

'But they're just hamsters in a cage,' Gabby had said.

'Hamsters in a cage with access to very cheap consumer goods, Mrs Sender,' the supervisor replied. 'And when you factor in the staff discounts ...'

'They were like hamsters in a cage,' Gabby said to Rachel.

'We're all in a cage of sorts,' said Rachel.

Gabby looked across the table. Rachel was not an easy woman to like but she was very glad to have met her. She picked up the shocking pink, fondant and cream-topped cupcake before her and devoured half of it in a single bite.

'I thought you'd crack first.' Rachel Thomas Brown looked happy for the very first time that morning.

'I didn't crack. I just realised I actually wanted to eat the cake.'

'I can't enjoy a cake, Gabby. Even one of yours. I just taste self-loathing and guilt.'

# 4.10.

Peter Robb was dying for a pee. He had been since the plane had touched down. Increasingly, it seemed that, as soon as his ageing body was placed in a situation in which it was unable to urinate, it suddenly desperately wanted to. Should he just bark like the Pavlovian dog he was? He didn't like it. More than losing your greying hair, more than fading eyesight, more than the aching in the lower back and the need for a 'good night's sleep', it was the constant peeing that symbolised decline, the elements regaining control, the inevitable return to the bawling ball of piss and shit that you were as a baby.

Betsy's capacity for worst-case-scenario mindfucks was such that, were he to mention it to her, the dominoes collapsing in her head would have him dead and buried inside the week of galloping prostate cancer. He'd never want to worry her like that and especially not now when she was so happy. Like the girl he'd married, really. She had him - Peter Robb – which was all she'd ever really wanted. Well, him and three sacks of duty-free comestibles, consumables and fragrances which she was wheeling in front of her on an airport trolley. Of course, when she had been living in Monaco, they'd never been together long enough for her to really notice. Now they were together so much more, it was less easy to hide. He blamed the amount of coffee at the office, the quality of the local water, the poor facilities in some public places (the implication being that he never actually used said facilities, which was a complete lie) – but Betsy wasn't daft. Touchingly naive at times. But not daft. So he crossed his metaphorical legs and resolved to hold it until they got home.

'I want to go to the toilet!' It was a little boy wailing and a mother with more luggage than Betsy consoling. I know how you feel, lad. A girl, presumably the big sister, was slurping a milkshake or similar through a thick straw, sucking up the dregs and making a noise like a draining plughole. She wasn't helping any either.

'Baggage reclaim,' Peter announced. But Robbins was already leading them off in the right direction without any prompting.

Peter had been employing Robbins for a few months now. He was a good lad, ex-Marine, efficient, presentable, unobtrusive and with the key skill of laughing just the right amount at the weak jokes of Robb and his business associates (even the particularly feeble but common one about Robb and Robbins – less a joke than the simple recognition of a coincidence). He would never pry but he had commented, just a casual observation after Robb had spent the best part of five minutes at the urinal to produce a thimbleful of piss, on his father-in-law's prostatitis. 'Not cancer,' Robbins had said. 'Just an infection. Tablets cleared it up.'

In the early days following the epiphanous event that Peter still referred to in his own mind as his internet death, the feeling persisted, and it wasn't just Betsy's fretting, that his actual life was in danger. Robbins would accompany Robb into the public toilets. After the prostatitis remark, Robb had suggested that his bodyguard just wait outside. Increasingly, he would even give Robbins the slip – jetting to the john unaccompanied. It was just plain embarrassing, that's all. The guy was a Marine, decorated in Afghanistan, trained to kill and here he was traipsing around after some old geezer who couldn't piss straight.

He wondered whether there would be any press at Arrivals. They couldn't get enough of him. He wasn't complaining. On the contrary. But he did want to get his bladder home before it exploded. He expressed his concern to his wife.

'You never told the journalists we'd be on this flight, did you, Peter?'

'Not explicitly, but it was pretty obvious from what I said at the factory – and flights from Bangladesh aren't like the number 93 bus, there's only a couple a day.'

'Sounds like the 93 bus to me,' said Betsy with a smile.

The wait for the luggage seemed interminable although the clock suggested that, if anything, the baggage had been discharged with more alacrity than usual. Robbins found another trolley, loaded it up and led the way. As well as his legs, Peter now had his fingers crossed too – hoping that the driver would be on time. As they emerged into the Arrivals hall, Peter's eyes were drawn to the iconic image of a stick man on a bright yellow background with the same honed instinct as a Palaeolithic hunter's to his prey. There was no press, no scrum, no huddle of microphones – and he, for once, was pleased. He followed his wife and bodyguard to the exit. The driver wasn't there. The driver and Robbins would have been texting but it was still a tricky piece of timing to get to the set-down area at just the right moment.

'Won't be a minute' Peter Robb said, just loud enough that he could claim with honesty to have said it but not so loud that Robbins or Betsy would have registered it. And he peeled off towards the relief of that yellow sign.

The conveniences were surprisingly quiet. The cubicle at the far end was occupied but the urinals were empty, just as Robb liked it. Moreover, the urinals were disinfecting and cleansing themselves, the sight and sound of which increased his need to pee and, in the event, he pissed as near to normal as he had for a long while – his own personal Niagara pleasing him as much as a new product line, that he himself had initiated, becoming a best seller. Was this what happened as you aged? Eventually the achievement of which you were most proud was not soiling yourself.

Just as he was having a good shake, he was aware of the entrance door opening behind him – but there were no footsteps, no apparition at the edge of his vision of another man. Robb coughed and zipped himself up. When he turned, the new arrival was still standing in the doorway. Robb registered him – he was short and black with dreadlock-style hair – but he tried not to take any notice. Or, at least, to affect not to. Instead, he washed his hands at the middle basin and opted for the automatic dryer rather than the paper towels. The young black lad – and he was very young – continued to stand in the doorway. As Robb turned to leave, he could see that the lad was fiddling nervously with something in the pocket of his pink hoodie. The kid looked terrified but despite this, or perhaps because of it, Robb could feel his chest tightening.

'Excuse…' he said – no louder than he had when announcing his intentions to give his wife and bodyguard the slip. He coughed again, clearing his throat which was also feeling noose tight.

He had the pocketed item in his hand now, the black kid. It could have been a knife. It almost certainly was a still scabbarded knife. Robb was seeing and thinking in slow motion. Time enough to register the item, to define it, to respond to it. It was still scabbarded. If he moved now, he had a very good chance. He may have been older and less fit than his assailant, but he was considerably larger and momentum was probably, almost certainly, all that he needed. The door, after all, was not shut. It had banged to and the latch bolt was sitting, resting against the strike plate. The Arrivals hall outside and safety were less than five yards away.

'You don't recognise me, do you?'

Robb shook his head. Now was the time. A single lunge with all his might. Now – while his assailant was focused on speaking, not on stabbing.

At this moment, there was the flush of a toilet and the cubicle door at the far end opened. Another black man emerged. He was three times the size of the boy in the doorway with the knife and had tattoos crawling up his shaven head where other men wore beards and sideburns. He walked towards Robb, hands outstretched like a wrestler. The odds had tilted drastically to Peter's detriment.

# 4.11.

Chris was walking along the seafront in Biscuit Town. During the course of the investigation he'd spent a lot of time here and a lot in Brighton. It was odd how it was in this place – and not his home town – in which he felt more comfortable, more familiar, more at home, really.

He had been to Biscuit Town as a kid. That was true. He remembered his mother telling him. The beach was safer, apparently. And there was a funfair. Chris could see the funfair at the far end of the prom. He racked his brains but he couldn't quite remember going there. All the same, there was something evocative about Biscuit Town, something almost magical. The place seemed out of time, out of this world, and yet it reminded him of his childhood. Perhaps that was the effect of all these old English seaside towns, symbols of the past.

He'd been to the local museum. He'd called at Gary Shad's place and found it – surprise, surprise – deserted. Traffic to corporate-sponger may have continued to increase but there were still disproportionate levels from this small town even now, not just in the period leading up to the killings. Cherri had told him that before she went AWOL. That Shad was a con and car thief did not reduce the possibility that he was also a murderer. In fact, as any policeman would tell you, it suggested the opposite. The port manager at the Newhaven ferry had claimed to recognise Shad from the motor – that was his sincerely-held belief, anyway – but perhaps he actually recognised him because he, Shad, was a frequent user of the port. Chris's plan was now to return to Brighton and once again see if he could get a lead on Cherri. She'd left her home but someone must know where she had gone. Were there relatives, perhaps? But instead, he found himself walking away from the beach towards the park where he and Gabby had first arrested Gary. It was too late for the exercising mums but a good time, late afternoon, for dog walkers.

He turned the corner and a great Golden Retriever appeared and started yapping at him. Chris was not generally scared of dogs and this time he recognised the big, old thing, anyway. Did Mrs Graham call it Dummy? Surely not.

'Dimmy,' came a voice from behind the trees.

'Dimmy!' The voice emerged. It belonged to Gill Graham.

'Hello,' said Chris. 'I thought it was a good time for dog walking. He's a bit vociferous this one, isn't he.' Dimmy had stopped barking, but he was still squaring up to Chris like a guard dog.

'I think he remembers your antics here that other time,' said Gill. 'Haven't you got something for him to chase?

'Heel, Dimmy,' she commanded. Dimmy, unsurprisingly, did not heel. He did, however, amble in her general direction.

'If you've got something he likes to chase, I'm happy to take him for a walk,' Chris said.

'That would be very welcome, thank you,' said Gill. 'But, first of all, why don't you come for that cup of tea we were talking about?'

'I can't say I knew your parents very well – it was you and Colin who were the friends – but we would always speak. Your mum had a very strong accent.'

'She still does,' said Chris.

'She would always say "bonjour" or even "bonjour, mes amis".'

'She still does.'

'Full of joie de vivre, she was. And she lives up on the Downs, you say.'

Chris nodded.

'Very quietly.' Gill Graham's house was a 1930s semi-detached. It was a lot tidier than his mother's, the fixtures and fittings far newer, double-glazing. There was also evidence of some kids – grandchildren, presumably.

'I never actually came to this house.'

'No, it's my mother's. There are four generations of us in here now. Well, sort of.' She made a gesture, half pointing upstairs with her thumb, half raising her eyebrows. 'I moved in when Mum became poorly and Susie, that's Colin's wife, and the kids moved in after his accident. Mum's since moved herself into a home but... well, it's complicated.'

'It's nice to be able to support each other,' said Chris. 'I do remember Colin and I do remember you but, I must admit, I'm very confused about my childhood. Where did you live?'

'We lived next to you – well, a few doors down. By the playgroup.'

'But we lived in Brighton.'

'No, your memory really is playing tricks, Chris. You lived, like us, in North Street. Right here.'

'My mother definitely said Brighton.'

Gill leaned forward and poured the tea. She'd rustled up some biscuits too, but they were children's biscuits really, too creamy and sweet, and Chris had the impression that she didn't entertain too often. His host picked up a cup herself and pushed one in Chris's direction. No saucers. 'Your father's death must have been very traumatic. Perhaps you have post-traumatic stress disorder. I'm no doctor but...'

Chris nodded. Truth be told, Gill Graham looked absolutely exhausted and, given what had happened to her son, very much like a candidate for PTSD herself.

'Well,' he said. 'I've never had any real symptoms of that.' This claim was not entirely true since Chris had been angry for as long as he could remember, but he didn't have any precise PTSD symptoms (or none, at least, that any doctor could diagnose, and one or two had certainly tried).

'Don't people sometimes repress difficult childhood memories?' Gill suggested.

'I have heard that.' And Chris would have been quite prepared to buy that too. It explained his own paucity of memories well enough. It just didn't explain his mother's insistence on Brighton.

'Of course, I remember the day of your father's ...' Gill paused and sipped a little more tea.

'Actually,' she said, rocking forward in the armchair, a high-backed, thick-cushioned French-style one with wooden arms. 'I do have something else that might remind you of your childhood.' She jerked forward twice more to build up the momentum to rise from the chair. The coffee table between them prevented Chris from assisting. 'Getting old,' she said, as much to herself as to Chris.

She was gone rather a long time and Chris was beginning to think about going to the kitchen to find her when she reappeared with a small thin packet. She handed it to Chris. More biscuits.

'The Almond Crisp,' said Chris.

'Do you remember them?'

'To be honest, I don't. I know from the town museum though that they were the most famous of Stern & Feltman's biscuits.'

'That's right.'

'But don't they make them in Romania now?'

'They do. They're not the same. But these are a packet of Stern & Feltman originals. When they closed the factory, my mother bought a whole crate of, I think, 24 packs.'

'Can you eat them?'

'We had some last Christmas and they were lovely. A little crisp on the edges perhaps, but then they're supposed to be crisp.' Gill smiled and scored open the packet with a long thumbnail. 'They're not called Almond Softs, are they?'

'Just as well,' said Chris.

'Here,' said Gill, helping herself and pushing the packet across the coffee table towards him. 'Everybody used to eat them and I'm sure you did. We definitely would have had a packet when you came to tea with Colin, I'm sure.' The biscuits were thin and oval-shaped. They looked rather like flattened French Madeleines, with caramel crisp edges. He really couldn't remember eating them.

As Chris leaned in to help himself and as Gill, waiting for him, sat with her poised biscuit over her teacup for dunking, a key turned in the front door lock and a boom of voices bounced in.

'Susie and the twins,' said Gill, placing her biscuit on the table.

Two boys raced into the room, their mother's voice hot on their trail, and, seeing an unfamiliar face in the armchair, skidded to a halt. They were aged about ten maybe. Not having kids of his own Chris was poor at this sort of guesswork.

'Jake! Ryan!' shouted the pursuing voice. 'Oh, hello.'

'Chris, this is Colin's wife, Susie, and the twins. Susie, Chris used to know Colin.'

'It was a long time ago,' said Chris. 'When we were younger than Jake and Ryan.'

'How do you know our names?' demanded an astonished child.

'That's Chris's job,' said Gill. 'He's a policeman. So you'd better be on your best behaviour.'

'Wow,' said the child.

'Do you want fish and chips with us?' said the other.

Susie was trying to escape from her coat without putting down the parcel under her arm. 'Hang up your coats and go and get some plates,' she said.

'Would you like some?' asked Gill.

'Don't let me interrupt,' said Chris, 'but I'll nibble a chip if you like.' The aroma was already choking up the room like a swarm of locusts. It smelled fantastic, reminding Chris just how hungry he was.

'Five plates,' said Susie to her sons' shadows.

Jake and Ryan returned in seconds, armed with plates, knives, forks, vinegar, salt and ketchup, all of which they began to distribute around the coffee table with the dexterous accuracy of nightclub croupiers.

'Napkins, please,' said Gill.

'Serviettes, boys,' said Susie.

'Did you shut the kitchen door, Ryan?' asked Gill.

'Dimmy's asleep,' said the boy.

'They're an impressive team,' said Chris as the greasy parcel was unwrapped and its steaming golden contents dealt out to the various plates.

'They wouldn't be quite so impressive if we were having salad,' said Gill.

'What?' said Jake, reappearing with enough paper napkins/serviettes to service an army.

The coffee table was replete. The boys were now showing impressive restraint, waiting for the word to dig in.

'I've just realised I haven't eaten my Almond Crisp,' said Chris. He picked it up and dunked it in his tea and, as he lifted it to his lips, its sweet, nutty, butterscotchy smell merged with the salty, sea-fresh salute of the fish and chips to create a rich nosegay that took Chris right back. 'Cod mixed with custard,' he said, aware of the hint of wonder in his voice.

The Grahams, who had fancied Chris a little odd for eating a biscuit before his fish and chips, clearly thought he was stark staring bonkers now.

'Cod mixed with custard,' he repeated. 'That's what we used to say Biscuit Town smelt like. Cod mixed with custard.'

'You're right.' Gill picked up her biscuit and smelt it. 'You kids did use to say that. Cod mixed with custard. The smell of the biscuit factory with the smell of the sea.' She turned to Susie. 'The fishermen used to bring the boats in just downwind from the factory. In the summer, when the wind was in the right direction, you could eat that smell.' Back to Chris. 'I'd completely forgotten.'

It was the smell, the one he had been trying to tell Gabby about, the one he associated with his father and the chocolate. And there was something more. 'I remember it at night,' said Chris. 'As a kid, I remember lying in bed at night and basking in it.'

'Gross,' said Jake.

## 4.12.

Cherrianne watched as the big man crossed the check-tiled floor of the toilets and wished she'd never left her aunt's. Head like a tattooed medicine ball, he wore sweats, jogging pants and, incongruously, a pair of brightly-polished black brogues. They must have been size 14 or 15 and his outstretched hands were equally enormous. Peter Robb's bodyguard.

She suddenly felt very silly indeed, no older than the little boy she resembled. A knife. In an airport. She was in serious trouble. Ever since she'd discovered that Scootergirl or boy or whoever had stolen her picture – the one Dan had taken of her on his Lambretta – for their online avatar, she had been freaking. Total spin-out. They'd pulled it off her Facebook page, anyone could have done it. Was it someone who knew she worked for corporatesponger and wanted to implicate the site in murder? Or did someone know she was helping the police? DS Caton had made it blates clear that he was no geek. Had someone hacked his phone? Or was Caton himself the creep? She'd seen enough TV crime dramas with that particular twist. It must have some grounding in reality. Whoever it was, was a pro. Dan had set up the back-end to 'Fashion Sister' and she knew all his passwords. Dan! What a derp she'd been. She hadn't told him yet because she knew he'd go ballistic, especially as he was now, against her better judgment, engaged in some sort of financial talks with a supposed angel. She'd accessed Scootergirl's 'Fashion Sister' account as admin – so fly, she'd thought, when she'd done it – but, while from the outside Scootergirl's profile looked pukka, in the back-end there was nothing. The email address was dead, possibly even a dead alias, no mobile number, no address, no real name.

Given all this (coupled with the inflammatory content Scootergirl was actually posting), Cherri had very good reason to think that Robb's life was in danger. Very good reason to track him down and meet him the moment he arrived in the country. From her research, she was certain that Scootergirl was the person who had created the image of a bloodied and apparently-dead Robb that had gone viral. The version attached to Scootergirl's 'Fashion Sister' profile was the earliest and highest res version of the image she could find. Given what had happened since, Cherri saw it not as a bit of internet fluff, not as a meme, but as a forewarning of what was to come. But now, to any objective airport security guard or policeman, the only nutter was her – carrying a knife and looking like the internet troll in question. Derp!

Quite why she'd grabbed Dan's fishing knife on the way out, she couldn't quite remember. To protect Robb? She'd had it all planned in her head. Find the right terminal. Wait. Watch. She thought she'd got so lucky when he went into the toilet. Now she couldn't remember why and realised that everything she'd done had been in panic.

It was all she could do, not to scream, as the bodyguard advanced. But she'd always managed to pass for male in the men's toilets before and even at this moment, even as she was in the middle of the biggest mistake of her life, she didn't want to fail the sex test. The man's hands were like buckets, a strangler's hands, hands that could kill. She watched as he put them under the tap. He washed them thoroughly, using a blob of soap from the dispenser. Then he dried them with a paper towel, rubbing down each finger in turn, like a surgeon preparing for an operation. And who was going under the knife!? It really was all she could do, not to scream. Her grip tightened on her knife. Perhaps this was why she'd brought it: to protect herself.

The guy was right there now. His clean hands reaching towards her. She was frozen, like a vampire victim. She looked at Robb. He looked as scared as she felt. Well, that's no surprise, is it, Cherrianne Dixon?

'Scuse, bro,' said the bodyguard, taking the door handle and moving to open the door.

She stepped back to let him pass. He exited and the door shut behind him.

'Oh,' said Cherri, unable to keep the utterance rising in her throat at bay. At least it wasn't a scream.

She was aware that both she and Robb were breathing heavily, both rooted to the spot.

'You really don't recognise me, do you?' said Cherri.

'No,' said Robb. He too had found his voice.

Cherri pulled up the hood of her hoodie. 'Now?' she asked.

'Scootergirl,' said Robb – and his face broke into a smile.

There was a pause in which Cherri felt the bubble of tension finally burst and dissolve. Robb walked over to the sink and began to run the water. He leant against the pedestal and splashed it all over his face.

'You've come to kill me, have you?' He was laughing now. Cherri wasn't sure why. 'Well, you'll need to take the knife out of its case.'

'No,' said Cherri. 'You need this to protect yourself.' Peter Robb was still leaning. He was doing some breathing exercises – in through the nose, out through the mouth. She put the knife down beside his hand.

'I don't think so,' said Robb. 'The nastiest things being said about me online are by you.'

'There's a lot I need to tell you about that.'

'First, there's something I'd like to ask you, Scootergirl. (Or can I call you, scoot?) I'm setting up a foundation to improve working conditions. Not just in my factories, not just in textiles. Everywhere. Here in the UK too. I'd like to talk to you about it. But not here. I don't think you're allowed in the Gents.'

Robb reached inside his jacket. For a beat Cherri thought that all that bullshit was just to soften her up for the coup de grâce. But all he pulled from his pocket was a small elegant leather wallet from which he removed a business card. 'Come and see me,' he said.

He picked up the knife and, holding it correctly by the scabbarded blade, returned it to Cherri. 'We can go fishing if you like.'

Cherri tried for the third time to say something but she couldn't. Robb had his hand on the door handle now and, within a matter of seconds, he too would be gone.

'And don't worry about me. I've got someone to protect me. He's called Robbins. Ex-Marine. You'll like him.'

When Robb had gone, Cherri went and sat down in a cubicle where she counted to ten to calm down. That didn't work, so she counted to ten again. And then she started writing code in her head. Should she have told him that she wasn't Scootergirl? And that Scootergirl was not the sweet little kid he obviously thought she was, but a professional hacker, the blackest of black hats, with malice in mind?

Er, probably.

# 4.13.

Lee White was next in line for the search. The way they did it was semi-public, two other inmates in the same room. He always tried to avoid being in there with a woman. It was so fucking shameful for her. Stripping down to your pants, pulling your top up to your bra strap.

The idea of it being done to his Jen made his blood boil. He knew what he was capable of when angry. They couldn't win, you see, the women. If they were wearing sexy knickers, it was all over the building within minutes. Hangar the size of half a dozen football pitches and a rumour traveled from one end to the other quicker than a Shay Given goal kick, got into every nook and cranny like a jet-propelled mouse. If they had the big baggies, the 'Bridget Jones's', that was just as bad: 'Susan Smedley had a sack on her arse'.

Lee nodded at the security guard, tossed his backpack onto the table. You had to try to take it in your stride. Lee didn't actually know the guard to talk to. They bussed them in, but he knew this lad was a local. Toon fan. He'd seen the bobble hat. The guard didn't nod back. He made a gesture to take your top off. Lee lifted it just above his breeks. The minimum. He didn't make it easy for them. Forced them to man-handle him in a way that would make any decent human being feel bad. Then he assumed the position against the table, the sort of cheap femmer crap you wouldn't even give house room, metal legs and splinters. Three tables in a row made this, the barest and greyest of rooms, look like they were setting up a soup kitchen or the world's most depressing jumble sale. He spread his legs. He'd never actually been searched by the poliss, but he'd seen it on the TV often enough.

'If you can't do the time, don't do the crime,' Lee said, not for the first time in this position.

'Doing t'job,' the security guard muttered, ashamed of himself as, indeed, he should be. Lee wondered if he, like Lee, had had a father who had done a proper job.

'That's what they said in Belsen,' said Lee with a big broad grin that conveyed the opposite message to his words.

He picked his bag up. It had made it safely through the scanner. The scanner looked ancient, probably rejected by the airlines in the 80s, spewing radiation. Lee slung his pack back over his shoulder and stepped out into the dawn. The morning shift were arriving.

He turned and walked backwards for a pace or three, as he often did, just to take in the size of the enormous machine in which he was the tiniest of cogs. You had to admit it was impressive. Indian chiefs had their headdresses, generals had their pips and stars, the boss class big offices and bigger chairs, Jack Sender – the late Jack Sender – used the sheer scale of his warehouses to intimidate his staff. 'Stufff – where the customer is king' said the sign above the entrance.

The late Jack Sender. Lee said it twenty times in his head. They couldn't own what was between his ears and, if he wanted to think that the company was the biggest heap of shite since Sunderland was invented, that was his fucking birth right. Some bloke had been sacked for making the joke out loud.

'Don't be late again,' the supervisor had said, hiding behind his little blue badge like a proud blackboard monitor.

'What, like the late Jack Sender?' the guy had said.

Third strike and he was out. Must have been English to have made that joke. Not one of the Eastern Europeans. Third strike was the official jargon – like Little League in which, Lee imagined, the late Mr Sender was probably frequently struck out. They called him a book lover but Lee reckoned he was just taking revenge on the human race for his shit childhood – that's why he treated his employees like children. 'Released' they'd call it, when they sacked you. They said you'd been released. Well, they were right about that.

Lee checked that the wardrobe was still on the back seat. He knew it would be. Who the fuck was going to nick a flatpack wardrobe? But it was automatic. The result of living where people had fuck all for too long. He had picked up the wardrobe on the way to work, the MöblA warehouse outside Newcastle, and wouldn't be sleeping until he'd assembled the thing. Half an hour according to the Swedes in their bright white advertising.

He liked coming out after the night shift, enjoyed watching the sun suck the dark and dank out of the moors, rendering the bleak beautiful. Finding beauty in the bleak was a philosophy he tried (and failed) to apply to life. The journey back took him past the farm. Couldn't avoid it without adding a petrol-guzzling fifteen miles to the journey. He turned the engine on and waited for the automatic choke to finally wake up. Handling an old car was an art, he told himself, especially a Montego. In truth, it was the sort of shit heap that a teenager would have as his first motor (good for shagging in the back). It wasn't a family car unless you had a family of dogs. When he was a kid, his dad had had a proper car.

He remembered the farm well. During the strike, he had all but lived there. Uncle Lenny he'd called him, the farmer, although Lenny was actually a cousin of his mother's. Lenny may have owned a few fields but he wasn't really a farmer, still part of the community. 'We all work the land,' Uncle Lenny had said to Lee's dad. 'You just do it a quarter of a mile underground.' Lee's dad had laughed at that. Of course, it wasn't the only time he'd heard his old man laugh, or even the last time, but it was a time he remembered.

Lenny was gone, best part of ten years now. Moved to York. The road was much the same though: a long never-ending sweep of a bend that cut back through the countryside as it circled the inclining escarpment on which Uncle Lenny used to graze sheep. Sometimes, when the bend was thick with mud, the wheels on his dad's old Cavalier would grip and spit dirt and Lee could imagine he was in a stock car race. The roads were a lot cleaner now. The route straightened out and Lee accelerated past the farm entrance, a new gate but the same stone wall, riddled and green with bracken.

Easing his foot down, Lee realised how much his legs ached, the calves. It was like he'd been playing football for a week. He didn't seem to get used to it and, no matter what shoes or trainers he wore, his bones always ached. Ten hours was too long without a proper break, it was as simple as that. There was nowhere to rest in the warehouse but, if you wanted to leave, you had the full search routine. What with the search on the way out on top, you could add an hour to the day that way and, since they didn't pay you for waiting to be searched, reduce the hourly rate accordingly from piss poor to fuck all. His dad wouldn't have put his hoggers and helmet on for the hourly rate he, Lee, was prepared to accept. He was ashamed. Just as well his dad wasn't around really.

He lived in his dad's house and now, with his mother moving back in, it was as if they'd come full circle. In other words, his entire life had led precisely nowhere. Ironic thing was that, by the standards of the village, he was doing OK. Own house, own car. He wasn't on drugs, wasn't an alcoholic. He was a bit overweight, but not obese or diabetic. He was a real local success story, really.

Jen had taken Lee's old girl up the hospital. Jen needed to know the routine: what drugs when, what could his mother do, what couldn't she – and there was no sense from his mother. One minute, she was close to tears at being unable to open a jam jar and, the next, she was talking in rabble-rousing (and highly coherent) tones about the pit strike, cursing Margaret Thatcher and lauding Anne Scargill. The pair of them out, Lee reckoned he had about an hour to get the wardrobe up. Living out of suitcases wasn't dignified for an old woman and was only adding to her confusion.

Sometimes Lee wondered if she even knew she was back in the family house she'd lived in for so long. He was amazed how well she'd hidden it, her confusion. It had been a bit of joke between him and Jen, before – the hairdryer in the fridge, the Christmas tree she'd put up early November – but now he could see that they'd been tips of a very big iceberg, an iceberg that was freezing parts of his mother's mind. You couldn't disguise a fall down the stairs though or the inability to use a mobile phone to call for help. Neither his mother nor he and Jen had the money to pay for professional care, so her moving in was the only solution.

Kaylee had moved into the box room. It had been a price she'd been prepared to pay to have her gran around, but Lee wondered for how long. He hated the idea of his daughter's good memories of his mother being tarnished with new ones of her absent-mindedness and perhaps of her even forgetting who her granddaughter was. She'd always been so good with Kaylee, just the right side of spoiling her rotten, and the perfect outlet for the inevitable clashes between Kaylee and Jen, a mother and daughter who resembled each other right down to the beauty spot on the right cheek and the dimple on the left one when they laughed.

Lee pushed the flatpack up the stairs, sliding it along the carpet. Fortunately, the back bedroom, where he'd put his mum, was right at the top of the stairs. No need to twist the package around to get it along the landing. He slid it in through the door. By throwing everything else in the room on the bed, he just about had enough space to work. The recess to the side of the long-gone chimney would, he had already established, take the wardrobe with a couple of centimetres to spare. Downstairs the kettle boiled and he descended, suddenly desperate for the caffeine hit he'd been denying himself. He hadn't stopped at the old ice-cream van that an enterprising ex-miner named Micky had taken to parking outside the Stufff factory for half an hour at every change of shift for the sale of tea, coffee and cash-and-carry bullets and chocolate. Too poor, right enough. Embarrassing. He knew and liked Micky Wells too. He was a canny lad. Sometimes couldn't avoid his eyes and had to wave as he drove past. Fuck, it didn't bear thinking about.

He laid the pieces out on the floor and counted the nuts and bolts and little plastic screw caps. Wielding his Allen key like a tiny gun, he dived into the diagrams for the kostY wardrobe. KostY? Costly, more like. Every line and every dot counted in the MöblA diagrams. It was about making exact matches and always making sure you had the piece in hand up the right way. The instructions said it was a two-man job, but there wasn't a lot he could do about that.

He wrestled with planks that seemed to have a mind of their own and to be heavier outside the pack than in. He started off cautiously but, within twenty minutes, was bludgeoning screws and nails into forced submission. Once you'd done it once, it became easier to do it again – like, according to the men who'd done it (he never had), adultery. It looked a lot like a wardrobe, his construction – so why wouldn't the pole, the hanging rail, fit across inside? He contemplated the problem as he downed the now icy dregs of coffee.

He looked at his watch. An hour.

He took the pole at 45 degrees, held it in the approximate position and began to incline it to the horizontal. When it was at about five, ten degrees, it became wedged. The two sides of the wardrobe were about a centimetre too close. How? Pieces the wrong size or assembly error? He could snip the end off the rail with a saw. He had one somewhere. Or he could tap it into place with the hammer which he already had.

He was sitting inside the wardrobe, perched on the small shelving unit that he still needed to bolt into place. He was sitting there, like a man building a cell around himself. Was he really going to go all the way downstairs for a saw? And to cut the pole – well, it was a kind of admission of failure, wasn't it? So he tapped the underside of the rail on the lower side, trying to get it as close to horizontal as possible. Tap. Tap, tap. Still not straight enough to take a coat hanger. Tap, tap, tap. Two bolts at the bottom pinged out. The right side fell away, scraping a protruding bolt down the wall and pulling out a ribbon of plaster, as the top fell on Lee's head. He sat there rubbing his forehead, thinking how funny it would have been, had Laurel and Hardy had access to flatpack furniture, and then he heard Jen's key turning in the lock downstairs. He wasn't crying, but the blow on the head had brought tears to his eyes and he thought about his old man again. Lee had really only known shit. He'd never really been able to look after his family properly, not really. His dad had though and how fucking terrible it must have been to have seen that taken away. He couldn't forgive his dad, but he could understand it. The room must have been about the size of this one. An outhouse on Lenny's farm. Had his father known there would be a gun in there or had it been chance? And, if Lee had a gun in his house, would he have done the same thing by now? God knows, he'd been tempted often enough.

'Back, pet,' shouted Jen.

'Just putting up the wardrobe,' he said, pulling himself to his feet. 'You putting the kettle on?'

As he got up, Lee's phone tumbled from his pocket. A single text message. The supervisors at Stufff telling him how many minutes he had wasted on his shift that day. Fourteen, apparently. About the time the unpaid body search he'd been subjected to in order to leave the building had taken. They were quits and then some, really. But it wasn't really the time that Stufff owed him that hurt, it was the dignity, the respect. His father had been cremated but, if he hadn't been, he'd have been spinning like a top. Lee put the phone on the window sill, took a deep breath and picked up the wardrobe assembly diagram again.

# 4.14.

He ran his finger along the perfect join. The side of the wardrobe and the top were locked together as if welded, as if someone had used extra industrial-scale bolts. Lee was impressed.

He perched on the small drawer unit. This too was solidly in position and he was able to allow it to take his weight and sit on it without fear of collapse. The doors were nestled neatly in position, an even five millimetres of light between the two, all the way from top to bottom. He could see out with comfort. There weren't many residents of his village, male or female, who could get inside a kostY wardrobe and shut the door – all too fat, too disabled or too stoned. Lee hoped nobody would accidentally lock the door as the unit was so secure. It was cosy inside, in fact. Like a safe hiding place in a childhood game. (Coming, ready or not.) Or a bedroom fort fashioned from blankets and boxes. Perhaps it would be better if somebody did lock the door.

Lee was tired and, in the half-light, was suddenly very aware of it. He had been up pretty much all day (his night) and pretty much all night (his working day). The wardrobe had been on his mind all the time. He had set off to work as normal but had been unable to leave the task uncompleted.

As far as Jess was concerned, this could be the 'Impossible Dreams' Show or the 'Life On Mars' Show. The vast spectacle had all fallen into place very quickly. The previous evening, the hall had still looked like an upmarket car boot sale, but now it was luxury in vision, a hundred West End stage sets. Of course, you could see the joins backstage but out front it was the heaven of a TV advert made real, all logos and lighting and glittering temptations. Every stall and stand seemed to have a special 'Beautiful Price for Beautiful Homes' exhibition-only offer on everything – provided, of course, that you bought everything. The smaller items, the impulse purchases, remained as competitively priced as ever. In fact, their luxurious surroundings permitted a small mark-up, Jess reckoned. She had calculated that, on the MöblA stand on which she was working, there were precisely nine items she could afford. Still, she looked a million dollars. Or, as Mr Forsberg had put it, a million Krona. (Was that more or less than a million dollars?)

The exhibition was sponsored by a national newspaper and there were complimentary copies everywhere. Jess's job, or one of them, was to remove the discarded journals from the MöblA stand to ensure that the display rooms remained pristine. One copy on the coffee table was acceptable; half a dozen strewn over the leopard-print sofa was not. The same applied to empty glasses. Jess was to get full glasses into hands at every opportunity (a decent Prosecco, according to Mr Forsberg), to ensure that the coasters were suitably adjacent on whatever items of furniture the visitors happened to find themselves by, and to then whisk the glasses away as quickly as possible once they were abandoned. Knocking back the dregs was not permitted, Forsberg had said with a smile.

'You are impressed I know the word "dregs",' said Forsberg. 'Dregs is like the Swedish "drägg". Dregs is from old Norse, when we dominated your little country.' He laughed long and loud. One of his secretaries came over to see if he was feeling all right.

Jess couldn't help but be amused by him. In his own mind, Lucas Forsberg was clearly hilarious. Too much Prosecco? Could you be drunk in charge of a child's scooter? Forsberg's transport of choice for the exhibition was a kick scooter. It wasn't made by MöblA, but it may as well have been with its creamy colours, exposed steel and curvy platform.

'They have everything here,' said Jess for want of anything else to say. Forsberg seemed to have adopted her.

Before he could reply, she targeted a young couple wandering into the most expensive of the three MöblA kitchens on display. They were discussing fan ovens. 'Prosecco?' she asked and had the glasses in their hands before they had even registered her.

'Thank you,' said the man, flipping a foppish fringe back with long slim fingers.

'Help yourself,' said Jess. She placed the bottle on the draining board next to the guy's elbow while at the same time pulling the fully priced-up brochure into clearer view. Unlike some of the more upmarket brands, MöblA made sure the potential customers knew exactly what they were paying. And, as regards the bubbly, she wasn't leaving them much – just the dregs of the bottle.

The man jerked his heavy fringe in the direction of Jess's employer.

'Is that Lucas Forsberg?'

'It is,' said Jess, nodding in the same direction. Forsberg was absent-mindedly spinning the front wheel of his scooter with the toe of his suede-shod foot. 'Would you like to talk to him?' They were, after all, admiring the most expensive kitchen.

Forsberg pushed himself off and rolled a couple of paces in their direction, his corduroy slacks whistling like Venetian blinds. He couldn't have heard them. Business men had a sixth sense, Jess presumed. He came to a halt perfectly with no more effort beyond that initial push. It was smooth, a gesture that said his furniture was smooth.

'The Beautiful Homes show is like an ice cream parlour with too many flavours, is it not?' he said.

This wasn't the hard sell but the girl of the couple, painfully thin with hair like a model, like Gabby Garnier's, got it. She smiled and nodded.

'I hope you find what you need,' said Forsberg. Need was a MöblA word. Furniture to meet needs.

The girl raised a twig of an arm and pointed. 'There are knives on that stall in the same leopard skin as your sofa,' she said.

Forsberg laughed.

'The blades,' said Jess. She'd seen them too.

'If you have the knife, then you will be wanting the sofa too,' said Forsberg, showing two fine gleaming rows of teeth. They were all giggling and then, with one foot on his scooter, he was away again. Still laughing. He pointed at the sofa as he scooted past it and then executed a spin turn which resulted in the scooter coming to rest hard against the side of the sofa, and Forsberg himself sliding into a sitting position on it. Jess and the couple gave him a little round of applause. Forsberg continued to sit on the sofa, making to get his breath back. The human touch. He was sharp as a knife, smooth as the sharpest blade, Forsberg. Jess distributed glasses and tidied papers. The couple finished the Prosecco and began pricing up their kitchen.

Jess followed another couple into the bedroom area, but they were out again before she could offer them a glass. She put her tray down and straightened the duvet cover. It looked as if someone had spent the night. As she leant over to smooth down the pillows, Forsberg was behind her.

'The MöblA king is as wide as the Scandinavian landscape,' he said.

Jess looked back over her shoulder. She felt vulnerable all of a sudden, alone in the bedroom with him. She smoothed down her cocktail dress as she jumped up, wobbling on her stilettos. Where was his scooter?

Lee had fingered the guy in the corduroy as Forsberg and now he was sure. He was less sure of the Swede's intentions. He'd surprised the girl, that much was clear. She worked for him, that was clear too. Given his own experiences, Lee could guess exactly how people like Lucas Forsberg treated their employees. Forsberg was number two on the Top Trumps deck (Jack Sender would have been 'only' number 8, apparently) and the girl wasn't bent over like that for the post-shift body search.

Lee readied himself, one hand on the door, one on the blade. Then he pushed all his weight down through his feet, flexed his knees and was out into the daylight. The bedroom was lit, like all the MöblA 'rooms', by LED spots fitted on top of the 'walls'. Lee felt like he was jumping into the sun. The girl, tall lass, straightened herself and pulled away from Forsberg. Suddenly, she was between Lee and his quarry. Not where she was supposed to be. The knife was above Lee's head, at his side, above his head. He'd thought this bit through. The knife just had to keep moving. Like a piston. But the girl was in the wrong place. Her cream dress was flecked with red. She was gone and Forsberg still had no idea what was hitting him. Lee would never have guessed that he could move so quickly. Adrenalin had turned him into an athlete. He stabbed Forsberg twice, three times. Stab, stab, stab. He hoyed the lime green knife – price from £19.99 to £89.99 for the full multi-coloured set – upwards in a last gesture.

Lee hadn't been able to decide what colour to get. Bright green was Kaylee's favourite colour but the leopard skin version matched a pair of Jen's knickers. (Obviously, given his intended use, it would have been daft to get the full set.) In the end he thought the green would make more of a statement.

The knife caught in the lights and dripped blood, spinning like a deadly boomerang. Feet. He was aware of feet. People in the bedroom. He'd already plotted his escape. Round the back of the wardrobe there was a plywood corridor to a side entrance. Five minutes to the Tube but, in truth, he wasn't expecting to get that far. Forsberg was on the bed. The girl was on the floor. He hoped she'd be OK, but he didn't think she would be and, as he took one final look back over his shoulder at her motionless body, his right leg was suddenly pulled away from him as if on wheels. As he keeled over backwards, he saw a child's scooter roll off into the wall – that was what had upended him – and then a security guard's tunic as a lump of flying human landed on his tightening chest.

Lee rolled to the left and the bed collapsed under the security guard's beer-gut-fuelled momentum. Plan B. Lee grabbed the scooter and kicked off into the auditorium, brushing past a dozen onlookers and a screaming secretary who tried and failed to take him down with a clipboard. Lee himself screamed with the exhilaration of it all. He was riding the Rolls Royce of kick scooters, the Ferrari, the Aston Martin, and its friction-free ball bearings took him from nought to twenty in the blink of an eye.

# 5:
# 'It's Jaws All Over Again.'

# 5.1.

Chris Caton was looking at a press cutting. It was faded with the years, the paper yellowing and rough, turning back to bark. It told of a local man, Chris's father Anthony, being shot dead on his doorstep. His mother had labelled the cutting, writing the date and the source, the Brighton Argus, in the top corner in blue fountain pen that now looked brown like dried blood.

There was a photograph, a halftone, but it was now faded and poorly printed on cheap newsprint in the first place. He was examining it with his mother's magnifying glass but it didn't provide any additional information. The image was just a grey blur really which, when examined under the magnifying glass, turned into a series of black dots of various sizes on a white background. So closer examination did not make things clearer. Quite the opposite.

He was not in shock. That would be going too far. But he would plead guilty to confusion, a catch-all confusion in that he was confused about what exactly he was confused about (or at least, most confused about) and confused about why. He was surviving on a diet of tea and stale toast, working his way through the provisions in his mother's fridge and larder. He'd eaten half a jar of the Reflets de France jam made with Corsican clementines in a single sitting.

The bloody attack on Lucas Forsberg, still touch and go, meant that he was confused about the case. His suspicions about Gary Shad were not completely allayed, yet at the same time...

Lee White had been caught in the act with Forsberg and was an employee of Stufff. He hadn't yet had a proper conversation with Corrigan but it was clear what the politicians thought. The Prime Minister had been all over the media. The usual condolences to Forsberg's family and hopes for a speedy recovery, followed by a virtuoso segue into the Sender and Brown deaths (fleeting reference back to the usual condolences there too) and 'these three cases' and 'a difficult period in British public life' now 'being behind us'. It was the sort of national address that, had it been made by the French president, would have ended with a heartfelt 'Vive la France' and a rousing Marseillaise. Case closed. Normal service will be resumed as soon as possible.

But if he was being truthful, it was not, for once, work that was uppermost in Chris's mind. Gill Graham was under a lot of stress with her senile mother and her comatose son. Had that had an affect on her memory? Was she perhaps senile herself? There wasn't any other evidence for it but Chris might still have given the notion house room, were it not for that glorious sensation in his nostrils with the fish, chips and dunked Almond Crisp biscuits. Olfactory memory was primeval, wasn't it? Related to the survival of the species. Otherwise some fungus or bacteria would have got the human race years ago. There was a solidity, a reliability about it, that he knew, both as a human being and as a policeman, wasn't always there with other sorts of memory.

So what if his mother had made up the whole Brighton business and they'd never lived there? That his mother was capable of fabricating such a tale and playing it out with such authenticity did not surprise him. She'd always been perfectly self-contained. The question was, why? To protect him? From what? And how was it protecting him?

Now that he came to analyse it, there wasn't a lot of Caton family history but what little there was was very clear. His father's death was like the family's 1066 – the one big thing with not a lot else of significance for years either side. His dad, a train driver, drove the London-Brighton train, ergo they lived in Brighton. They lived in North Road. One afternoon, two gunmen had knocked on the door. His father had opened it and they had shot him in a case of mistaken identity. Round the corner, in North Gardens, at the same house number, lived a known member of a local gang involved in drug dealing and armed robbery. He left town within 24 hours of Anthony Caton's murder. Shortly afterwards, the Catons, Francine and Chris, moved to London. Chris had not, as he'd explained to Gabby, been told any of this at the time. He'd been a teenager before he learned that his father had not abandoned him.

The thing was that, as a kid, Chris had always been very sure that it was he who had been abandoned, not his mother, he who his father did not love, not his mother. This certainty was largely down to another of those solid nuggets of family history. His parents had got together as a result of a genuine holiday romance, a lightening love affair after which nothing was ever the same. En vacances in Brighton with some French school friends, Francine had been swept off her feet by Anthony. At the time she was, she would always say, 'une âme perdue' and he was a tall, handsome Englishman speaking a little French in the most 'suave' accent. The consequences were inevitable, the way Francine told it. Her friends returned to France; she did not. Within a week she and Anthony were married. There were several subsequent tales that underlined that theirs was a true love match – magic moments, holidays and so on – both from before and after Chris was born and it was hard for him, on hearing them, to believe that they could ever have fallen out of love. Even as a young boy, he could tell how much his mother still loved his absent father, pined for him. So, if the father had left, it could only have been to get away from his child. In essence that was how Chris saw it. It was self-analysis. He'd never had any therapy. But that was how it was.

Later, on learning his father was dead, he was angry but his anger had no legitimate outlet. Understanding entirely why his mother had not told him at the time, he couldn't be angry with her, so who could he be angry with? The killer? The drug-dealing, armed robber who'd split town? He didn't have a name, a face. There was nothing in the cuttings. So he couldn't even picture the bastard and as for tracking him down? Well, he had once tried to find out who had owned the house in North Gardens at the time and turned up only an absentee landlord. Not a sensible idea anyway, tracking someone down for revenge. So all that anger... well, did he really need Sigmund Freud or one of his disciples to tell him where all that had gone? Anger had been the story of his life of which the present, albeit interrupted, interval of gardening leave was only the latest chapter.

Chris sipped some tea and made some more toast. He had found his old copy of Brighton Rock on the bed in Gabby's room and that had compounded his confusion. Exactly what he was doing in Gabby's room was another source of confusion. He told himself that he was just making her bed and tidying the room up for when Mum would return, but that was utter bollocks. He'd never voluntarily made a bed or tidied a room in his life. So why start now? Especially as, if anything, he was angry with his mother, rather than eager to please her. After all, she had buggered off just at the time he really needed to speak to her. And that was very confusing too. Normally she was reluctant to go into the nearest village and here she was hopping on a plane to America. That eager traveller sounded more like the woman Gill Graham had described than like the reclusive woman who had brought him up. It was understandable that the murder of your husband might change your disposition, so had she changed back to the impulsive thing his father first wooed? And if so, why?

She'd always affected that her reclusive nature was, at least in part, down to the English reserve and thus she was disinclined to intimacy with a people who were so clearly terrified of it. It was odd then to hear Gill Graham describing her as the life and soul of the party. 'Joie de vivre' was not a quality he'd attributed to his mother, any more than he'd ever attributed it to Vlad the Impaler.

Inside the copy of Brighton Rock (or should that be Brighton Rocks), he had written Chris Caton, North Rd., Brighton, Sussex, England, Great Britain, United Kingdom, Europe, Earth, The Solar System, The Milky Way, The Universe. The proof was there, in his own hand. They'd lived in Brighton. So what was Gill Graham on about? Obviously batty. It was the only possible conclusion. Perhaps they'd visited? Perhaps they'd had friends in Biscuit Town. Perhaps his mother had never mentioned them because she had subsequently fallen out with them. Highly likely. Or they'd dumped the widowed Mrs Caton? People never knew how to speak to someone whose loved one had been murdered, Chris had seen it time and again.

Chris tried to remember writing in Brighton Rock but he couldn't. He remembered the book though and it made sense that his mother should have kept it. It had been one of his favourites, although he'd never read it all. Dipped in and out. Frightened him to death at times. It was about everything that was nasty beneath the surface. Had that made him want to be a copper? He was aware of the famous film with Richard Attenborough and the more recent remake, although he hadn't seen either of them. Nobody to go with. There was a stab of self-pity in that thought and that always stirred his anger. He hated self-pity in himself. He looked at the book, trying to use its familiar feel, smell and images to take him to a calmer place. He placed it on the table, next to the press cutting. With his fingers he made sure the two items were perfectly square on the table, aligned and set against each other. He noticed his hands were shaking a little. His heart went out to the child who had scribbled that long address. He wondered if writing it – Earth, The Solar System, The Milky Way, The Universe – had made the child feel insignificant. Irrelevant. A speck. Mortal like Pinkie.

# 5.2.

The tabloids were in no doubt. 'Well, they never are,' was how Dominic Mason had put it. But sometimes the news agenda was beyond management.

After their litany of state-subsidised failure, the private security company Secur4U (whose last appearance in the news had been when they'd lost a high-security prisoner on a pee break) couldn't publicise their success widely enough: at one end of the exhibition hall a murder scene, at the other a hastily organised press conference at which a beaming head of Secur4U PR played the mobile phone footage of Lee White's attempted escape on the scooter on a loop. It was one of those clips they would be playing until Domesday. A global manufacturer of toilet tissue had been running a competition to see who could stack the highest pile of toilet rolls in 30 seconds (the world record was 29, apparently) and White, after slaloming through half a dozen entries, had finally been brought down by the instability of the attempt from Jackson of Thamesmead. Meanwhile, alongside loops of the blood-stained MöblA bed and the ambulance, siren screaming, arriving at the hospital with a bloodied Forsberg 'between life and death', the BBC news channel were also playing the beaming PR. Photogenic smile, a hint of cleavage. Loops upon loops. Twenty-four hour rolling news, 24/7 pressure.

Corrigan was losing track of just what the powers that be wanted and he probably preferred it that way. For now he was following his own instincts, his own tried-and-tested ways of working and the question uppermost in his mind was a simple one: what the fuck is going on? He sped along the corridor as if he himself was on a kick scooter.

'Doughnut,' he shouted.

'Yes, guv.'

'Tea.'

'Yes, guv.'

Uniforms peeled away to do his bidding.

The dossier was thin but compelling. White had been caught, if not exactly red-handed, then certainly with mitts a crimson shade of pink. There were at least three people who had seen White wield the knife (although one of them, admittedly, was an employee of Secur4U) and the weapon itself was covered in his fingerprints. His departure from the scene of the crime had also given every impression of a man on the run, albeit by means of a child's toy. It was odd though that White's fingerprints appeared nowhere else on the NPC or IDENT1, meaning he had no previous at all. There was the odd exception, like the GP Harold Shipman or the civil servant Dennis Nilsen, but most serial killers were known to the police, albeit often for fairly minor offences.

Bradley Coombes-Walker, a square-jawed bulldog of a man who saw himself as Corrigan's natural successor, had been champing at the leash, unable to understand why Corrigan appeared to be dragging his heels. He had furnished his superior with a full biog of Lee Kelvin White within half an hour of the suspect's arrest. Married, one kid. A life on and off benefits but now working for Stufff. Six months at the Northumberland fulfilment centre. Coombes-Walker had handed over the document as if it were a killer's signed confession.

He even had the answer to Corrigan's question about the MO. How come the first two murders had been so smooth and this attack so brutal? 'Getting more and more angry, guv. Angry that the Robb business has diverted everybody. Wanting to get caught to get us focused back on the issue.'

'That sounds like two somewhat incompatible reasons. You sure you're not having your doughnut and eating it, Bradley?'

Corrigan still had questions for everybody. What about Zak Thomas Brown? Where was the link? What about Robb?

He'd even texted Caton.

Actually, as he ate up the corridor with commanding officer size strides, Corrigan realised that he knew exactly what the powers that be wanted and that was why he had found himself so reluctant to jump to conclusions. They wanted it sorted. Quick confession. Keep the suspect banged up until everyone had forgotten or, failing that, until after the forthcoming election.

Corrigan didn't need to speak to the attending officer. His, Corrigan's, intentions were clear enough in the speed of his feet and the set of his forehead. The officer unlocked the door and there he was: the 'tax man axe man' elect, sitting at the desk like a little boy hoping to get his homework back without too much of a bollocking. Corrigan trusted his first impressions. He never let them distort an investigation but he always remembered them. He had an 80-90% success rate with them even when, as in this particular case, the facts demanded a certain conclusion.

Corrigan took off his cap, a gesture that he felt implied an openness on his part. He removed his jacket, pulled back a chair, hung the jacket over the back and positioned himself in it opposite the suspect.

Corrigan looked across at the audio-recorder. 'I'm waiting for another officer,' he said. 'To commence the formal interview.'

He was leaning forward in the chair, open body language, a getting-down-to-business, shirt-sleeved posture. Lee White pulled an awkward smile, the sort of embarrassed expression you got when someone asked – 'excuse me, Officer' – for directions in the street.

There was a tension-charged pause, nine months pregnant. White cleared his throat, looked around the room.

'Why no numbers?' asked Corrigan.

'I'm sorry, Officer, I ...' White looked genuinely bewildered. Corrigan pulled his mobile phone from his trouser pocket and placed it pointedly on the interview table: a gesture that said 'I've got all day'.

'Yes,' Corrigan pushed on. 'Why didn't you leave any numbers behind?'

'What, you mean like a phone number?'

Edgar Corrigan was still laughing when the tea arrived. The attending constable placed the cup and saucer gingerly on the interview table and backed away. Corrigan stopped him with a heavy palm on the forearm.

'Doughnut?'

'Coming, guv.'

'You want a brew, Lee?'

White was silent but nodded a barely-perceptible nod.

'And another cup,' said Corrigan. He waited for his colleague to leave, waved him away impatiently. White's eyes, moving at last away from the phone on the table, followed the retreating constable out of the door. Both men were listening for the lock to click again.

'You're right, Lee. It's police cutbacks. We now ask all suspects to leave a phone number at the crime scene.'

Corrigan resumed his business-like attitude, leaning forward, arms resting on thighs, hands clasped affably in front of him. He was grinning broadly. 'Then we call you back, Lee. Sometimes we have to put you on hold, of course. Play a bit of music.' Corrigan picked up the phone and waved it about a bit as he hummed the 'Z Cars' tune. 'Please hold, your crime is important to us,' Corrigan intoned in a robotic voice. 'Please continue to hold. Your crime is important to us.'

All the time he was speaking, Corrigan kept his unblinking eyes trained on White's. The DCI believed that, if you looked at someone long enough, you could read them and White, frankly, was a Janet and John book. He repositioned the phone on the table top.

'You haven't a fucking clue what I'm talking about, have you, son?'

White didn't reply. He just blinked a few times as if to make up for the lack of activity in the eyelid department from Corrigan. The policeman pushed his cup of tea towards the suspect.

'Drink mine,' he said. 'I can wait.'

Lee White hesitated for a moment and then helped himself to a sip. Corrigan could tell by the way he pursed his lips prepared for the heat that he hadn't sampled a lot of Met tea in his time. 'Thanks,' said White, unenthused by the lukewarm offering.

'Why did you attack him?'

Lee White took another gulp and let his cuff run across his mouth. 'Because his furniture is crackin' shite.'

'You're telling me, son.' And this time, when Corrigan laughed, White joined in – not a lot, but it passed for a chuckle. The policeman's first impression was that, if this kid was killing a string of CEOs in a hate-filled rage against corporate tax evasion, then he, Edgar Corrigan, was a sumo wrestler.

The second tea appeared. And the doughnut. Corrigan pulled it in half. 'Very jammy or less jammy?' he asked, offering a portion to White.

'I'm on a diet, Officer, my wife, our Jen won't like...'

'She's not going to go a bundle on the murder charge either, is she, son?' Corrigan ate one half of the doughnut in a single bite and, again, offered White the other half.

'It was flat-pack rage then?'

White nodded. 'Is he dead?' he mumbled.

'Intensive care,' said Corrigan. He studied White's face for a reaction. 'They don't think he'll make it.'

White's expression dropped to the floor like a medicine ball.

Corrigan's mobile began to bounce on the table. Corrigan looked first at the half of a very leaky doughnut in one hand, then at the sugar-coated, sausage-like fingers on the other and then at White.

'It's just a text,' said Corrigan. He hated to sound so helpless, but at least his occupied hands had saved him from the indignity of not knowing how to use his phone in front of a con.

Lee White picked the device up and tapped it into life. He held it up for Corrigan to read. It was from Northumbria Police. They'd been all over White's laptop. 'Solid link to Robb. IP data places known associate of Scootergirl in suspect's village.'

Corrigan let the remnants of the doughnut drop to the table and slowly licked the sugar off his fingers. The size of his stomach, he was a bloody sumo wrestler.

'Why did you use a scooter?' he asked.

'I just found it. It was there. I didn't bring it with me.'

'You've heard of "good cop, bad cop", have you, son? Well, I was the good cop.'

# 5.3.

The Chancellor had been walking around like Churchill with the blackest of black dogs, according to Wilkins. The arrest of Lee White had not suddenly change the game in the way Peter Robb's internet death had but, slowly and surely enough, normal service was being resumed.

The media managed to have it both ways – luxuriating in the gruesome detail from the Beautiful Homes Show and hollering for the death penalty at the same time. Horrified by blood while baying for it. 'Isn't this terrible – and here are another 20 pages of it,' was Dominic's summary. He felt that the British media had got its mojo back. It knew how to do Gory.

Most of the newspapers led their print version with a still either of blood all over the MöblA king-size bed or of Forsberg's scooter abandoned by White in his escape attempt. Their websites ran the various bits of mobile phone footage until the internet could bear no more. For two whole news cycles, there was no other story in town and, by the time the nation emerged suitably stimulated by the bloody pageant, it felt itself to be dirty and unclean, like an alcoholic who had fallen off the wagon – and it needed someone to blame.

'They're twiddling their thumbs at HMRC,' Wilkins told Mason. With Dominic on baby-making duties, they hadn't met for a while but both felt the need to get together and compare notes in the light of the new situation, each beginning to realise how much he relied on the other's input and analysis in these interesting times.

Wilkins explained that, while business year-ends continued to arrive, the tax take did not. Figures were constantly being revised down. At the Treasury, they were doing the same with the budget – revising it down – hence the Chancellor's mood. This didn't come as a complete surprise to Dominic. He'd seen the Head of a leading housing charity at what was supposed to be the launch of a massive social housing initiative. After the fantastically upbeat video, presumably made before White struck, came the most ponderously pedestrian of presentations from the sour-faced CEO who regretted that they may not be able to do as much as they had hoped.

'You're lucky I'm here,' said Wilkins. 'I've got to come up with a new budget across all departments.'

Dominic sipped his pint. The pub lacked its usual hustle and bustle. There were customers, but it was all a lot more like a wake than a celebration. The sound of a packet of crisps being opened boomed like a small bomb.

'Why not just give him the old one from before Sender got killed,' Dominic said.

Wilkins lipped his lips. 'You don't think he'll recognise it?'

'Do you? And, if he does, just tell him that his previous work couldn't be bettered.'

Wilkins was beginning to see why his chum had been so often compared to Teflon. 'You are smoother than a Jensen gearshift, aren't you, Dominic? Do you really think the Chancellor is that vain?'

Mason smirked. 'Don't you?' he said.

Wilkins took a long draft and then wiped the foam from his top lip. 'At least we're back in a game we understand.'

'Not quite,' said Mason. 'The PM is happy as a pig in shit.'

'Really?'

'Tax take may be down but party donations are up and, with an election coming...'

Wilkins raised his glass, tilting it towards Mason as if in a toast. 'So it is business as usual.'

'The bottom line, maybe. But a jolly PM is not something we're used to. He asked me about Heather yesterday. Remembered her name.'

'Remembering names is basically what being a good politician is about, Dominic.'

'Wanted to know if I'd be putting in for paternity leave anytime soon.'

'And will you?'

'Let's hope so.'

There was no news as such – Heather wasn't pregnant – but his attempts to bring about that happy situation continued to be a much-needed distraction.

DCI Corrigan had explained to him that Lee White could not possibly have committed the first two murders. There was CCTV footage from the Northumbria Stufff centre placing White in work 250 miles away at the time of the Sender killing. 'What about Zak Brown?' Dominic had asked, clutching at straws.

'How the fuck was he going to get to France and back between two shifts in a 1992 Austin Montego Estate?' said Corrigan. 'Even if he could afford it. Come on.'

'Robb?'

'White's daughter has a "Fashion Sister" account which she uses a lot, but that's all.'

'Why are you telling me this?'

'Because, right now, the State is complicit in fitting this bloke up,' said Corrigan.

Dominic considered mentioning the Birmingham Six and the Guildford Four and pots and kettles, but he didn't. He liked Corrigan and needed him to feel that their chain of communication was not becoming a weak link.

'This is a police matter, Chief Inspector,' he said. 'Government is disinterested. As well it should be.'

Corrigan's silence spoke volumes.

Dominic had felt slightly nauseous when he had put the phone down, as desperate for his pint as Wilkins usually was and that couldn't be good. This was shit that would hit the fan eventually and, when it did, he would be covered. What could you do? Except keep the wife happy.

But, as Mason drank with his friend, Corrigan was watching his investigation melt into the ether.

With White in custody, Commissioner Walters had told the Chief Inspector to wind down the whole team. Public sector budgets were getting haircuts like an army of appearance-conscious skinheads and Corrigan had already lost several men to various disturbances as various projects hit the buffers. A Central London housing project had been all but abandoned with the result that a dozen or so homeless people had holed themselves up in the mega basement of a nearby 'iceberg home'.

'Iceberg home?' Corrigan had said.

'More beneath the surface than up top,' Bradley Coombes-Walker had explained, throwing himself into the new case with the same enthusiasm he had brought to the White interrogation.

Right now, he, Corrigan, also had more beneath the surface than up top. He was boiling with rage but couldn't think straight.

'They're claiming squatters' rights on the grounds that it's a non-residential property,' said Coombes-Walker.

'Is it?'

'It's a house, but it's not been occupied for a couple of years. The owner is abroad.'

'Tax exile?'

'No idea, Sir.'

'Whose house is it?'

'That artist, Sir.'

'What artist, Bradley? I do believe there is more than one.'

'The one who made the plasticine models of the Sender and Thomas Brown murder scenes.'

Corrigan smiled a flat smile. 'Which sold for several million, if memory serves. Ironic that he's now come running to us then.'

'Not actually running, Sir. He called from Bermuda. His staff found...'

'Yes, I get the picture.'

Corrigan allowed his gaze to run down the case notes. He wasn't really reading them. He wasn't really interested. 'Perhaps we should question him about the murders since he knows all about the crime scenes.'

'Bermuda is a Category 2 territory for extradition purposes, Sir,' said Coombes-Walker, pulling a face like a builder sizing up a bathroom renovation.

'I was being sarcastic as you full well know.'

'Yes, Sir,' said Coombes-Walker. To Corrigan's ear, sarcasm wasn't entirely absent from his understudy's sing-song voice either.

'You really think this is more important than whether Lee White killed Sender or Brown?'

'Lee White's a cold-blooded murderer, Sir. That I do know.' The implication being that, if you were guilty of one murder, you may as well be guilty of three. It was as close as Coombes-Walker would go to insubordination. Corrigan waved him away impatiently. 'Don't take too many officers,' he shouted to the flapping door.

Corrigan's tea was cold and there were no doughnuts, so he sat motionless at his desk for what seemed to him like several minutes. He had a folder on his desk with many of the press cuttings from the murders. It was very old school, Corrigan knew that. But, when he was thinking, he liked to flick through actual physical papers. It helped lubricate his mind in a way that virtual material did not.

Sender despatched.

Coffee King found dead.

Sinister link between corporate killings.

Jack, Zak and the tax man's hack.

Blair Henry was the byline he came across most – the guy who'd figured out what the letters and numbers meant. He tapped a number into his mobile phone and got Henry immediately. A journalist with time on his hands. It confirmed Edgar Corrigan's suspicions.

'Mr Henry? It's DCI Corrigan from the Metropolitan Police. I'm heading up the investigation into Jack Sender and Zak ...'

'I know,' said Blair Henry.

'And I know you're very interested in this case and have done a lot of valuable work on it.' Corrigan could butter like a Parisian sous-chef. 'I think I may have something for you.'

'Right?' Henry couldn't help but sound intrigued. Desperate for a bite.

'Can you get me on live television?'

'Possibly. I've got a good friend on Channel 4 News. But you'll have to give me a bit of a hint.'

'I will, but you have got to get me on live.'

# 5.4.

Whatever Scootergirl's real motivation – be it mischief, malice or murder – Cherrianne knew she had to find her, or him, as quickly as possible.

Once again, she logged onto the back-end of the 'Fashion Sister' website and used the details of an existing administrator called Jackie3 to give herself access to the site's analytics. This would enable her to follow live page by page whoever was visiting the website at the exact time they visited. Then she changed Scootergirl's profile picture from the image of Cherri on a scooter to a simple image she'd created herself in a heavy black font on a white background. It said simply: Imposter.

Her heart was beating like jacked-up hip-hop. She knew that 'scoot', as Peter Robb had called 'her', would spot the change and be compelled to investigate. What else could they do? And the only way to do that was to log onto Scootergirl's profile page on 'Fashion Sister' where Cherri and her real-time analytics would be waiting. She felt like a hunter, a hunter with a handful of cherry muffin. She sipped water, forgoing coffee in kindness to her already pounding heart. 'Fashion Sister' was busy but nobody was following 'scoot'. Cherri had deleted umpteen of her quarry's more recent posts to reduce the number of other users who would see the new image. It was for Scootergirl's eyes only.

Her hands were unsteady on the keyboard of her laptop – another wodge of juicy muffin would help. She looked around her. She'd chosen to work in Brewed Awakening, sitting in her favourite window seat in her favourite coffee shop. Had she done this at home, she'd have been terrified, expecting a bloodthirsty axe-wielding Scootergirl to break into her tiny flat, Jack Nicholson-style, at any moment. Instead, the early evening quiet in the coffee shop helped her to kid herself that what she was doing was quite normal, quite safe, the everyday behaviour of a Western consumer. What was it that made her so brave? The knowledge that she was doing the right thing or the prospect of an ego-massaging, high-profile position with

Peter Robb?

Brewed was one of the few coffee shops that stayed open late and at this time, after the post-work rush and before the arrival of the evening crowd of recovering alcoholics, clear-headed clubbers and older theatre-goers channelling San Francisco, it was a relaxing place, the clientele a handful of loners like herself delaying the inevitable return home with a short shot of wakefulness.

Behind the bar, Wilson was cleaning the coffee machine, buffing it with a black cloth, making the chrome shine like a Chevy fender. 'You want a coffee there, Cherri?' he asked.

'No, I'm good.'

'Coding?'

'Of course.'

She watched her screen as if it might explode. 'Fashion Sister' was filling up for the night. There was a lot of traffic and a lot of heat being generated by what Jennifer Lawrence was wearing to a film premiere in Leicester Square. One post suggesting that old ladies shouldn't wear short sleeves made Cherri smile. Jennifer Lawrence was, what, 25 years old? Cherri finished her muffin.

'Another muffin, dude?' That Wilson was sharp-eyed. Cherri sipped her water.

'Go on then,' she said.

And then it happened. The page she was monitoring had a visitor. The IP address appeared and a little timer started counting the duration of the visit. Within two seconds Cherri had copied the address and was using an IP location finder site to identify where the visitor was coming from. The information from the location finder site caused her to freeze inside as if Jack Nicholson really was pounding on her bedroom door with an axe. The visitor was from Brighton. She inhaled deeply and moved back in her chair a little, trying to relax muscles which everywhere felt tense. Where was that second muffin?

'You OK, Cherri?' said Wilson, sliding the muffin and his own stick-like fingers into view.

'Thanks,' she said. 'Sorry, mad girlfriend bug, right now.'

'Tell me about it,' said Wilson. 'Pay laters.'

Cherri stuffed a lump of muffin into her mouth and she clicked back to 'Fashion Sister'. Had the image been changed back? No. But something else had happened. The Brighton visitor had gone, replaced by someone allegedly from China.

This confirmed Cherri's worst fears. She'd been expecting whoever was using the Scootergirl account to also be masking their IP address to hide. The first visit, from Brighton, suggested that, in their anger, the imposter had forgotten, initially, to do this. They had now masked their true location. Where was Dongguan, anyway?

Ping. You have one new message, said her screen.

Cherri clicked automatically, her impatience mirroring that of Scootergirl logging onto the site without masking. Neither of them, Cherri realised, neither she nor 'Scoot', were exactly steady old hands when it came to this black-hat computer trickery.

> You are not Jackie3

Cherri didn't reply.

> Jackie3 lives in Edinburgh. You live in |

The sentence hung there incomplete, the cursor flashing on the screen. Had Scootergirl been cut off, Cherri wondered. She looked around the 'Fashion Sister' admin window for some sort of guidance and realised, nearly choking on her muffin, that she'd made a rookie's error. Because she'd logged in with an actual administrator's details, the admin panel listed her as online. There in a little box it read: Online Now: Jackie3.

Shit. The metaphorical door was crumbling under a mad Jack's raging blows. 'Here's Johnny!'

> Are you in Brewed Awakening?

Cherri snapped shut her laptop lid. She looked around the coffee shop. Nobody had noticed. Wilson had turned his attention to mopping up behind the counter. As she breathed deeply, the rich, deep, dark smell penetrated her lungs. She was waking up and smelling the coffee. She was in serious danger. Scootergirl, who had tried to kill Peter Robb and God knows who else, was in Brighton and knew where she was. She heaved her laptop into her bag without bothering with the protective neoprene cover and was up and out of the door before Wilson could shout 'muffin'. But as she stepped onto the pavement, the hustle and bustle of the city, the wind funnelling up the narrow street, the street lights speckled with the beginnings of rain, she wondered whether she'd made another rookie's error. She was now alone. She consciously stopped and stood on the pavement, letting her feet feel the concrete beneath, getting balanced. She looked first one way and then the other. A perfectly ordinary Brighton night.

She turned round and went back into Brewed Awakening.

'Thought you'd done one,' said Wilson.

'Sorry.' Cherri was fishing in her purse for some change.

'And you haven't even finished it.'

'No. I suddenly remembered something, but it's coming on to rain so it can wait.' She picked up her muffin and moved away from the window seat to a chair at a table by the counter from which she could see the door. Wilson watched her.

'I can't stand the rain, against my window,' he sang and Cherri was impressed. He had a decent voice.

'That's right, dude,' she said and took a bite of muffin. 'I'll have that coffee too, please, Wils. Flat white.'

If she'd made a newbie error, so had Scootergirl. Since she, he or it had at first visited without cloaking, they would, assuming they were a registered user, appear in the user log.

Cherri logged back in. There was nobody from China now. Nobody on Scootergirl's page. Was Scootergirl coming after her? Cherri reminded herself that she was safe in the cafe. She navigated to the list of recent visits to 'Fashion Sister' but, apparently, there had been none from registered users that night. Given the amount of traffic on the site, Cherri knew that that was impossible. Scootergirl had obviously wiped all the data. A hammer to crack a nut that was, but quicker than finding the needle in the haystack. Scootergirl had clearly been concerned that Cherri might get there first. Cherri had got inside Scootergirl's head.

Wilson brought her coffee and she managed to accept it like a sane person but, inside, she was anything but. She felt she could feel her brain working, the cogs spinning and grinding. She scrolled down through the list of visitors from previous days. Panicking, she had no idea what she was looking for, but suddenly she saw a name that caused her to calm down. Dan Mann.

Dan was a visitor from a few days earlier. He obviously still did a bit of work for 'Fashion Sister'. Cherri didn't know that. And he was still the registered Super Administrator. But why hadn't she thought of him before? Dan would know what to do (and he would know how to find the hidden data on 'Fashion Sister'. Scootergirl would not have been able to hide her presence completely.)

Cherri took a hit of coffee. She found Dan's number on her phone and was about to call him when suddenly, the 'Chinaman' was on Scootergirl's page again. She sipped her drink and watched as her 'Imposter' profile pic was deleted and replaced with another. She read the new one, it too was text only, and she drank coffee, hoping that it would lubricate her mind and tell her what she should do. The new profile pic read: Meet You At The End Of The Pier.

# 5.5.

Chris had too many things on his mind and the case was not top of the list. 'The wrong man', Corrigan had said and he'd agreed, but the wrong man he was thinking about right now was not a 35-year-old Stufff employee from Newcastle, but his own father. Was his father, as he had always believed, the wrong man, truly the victim of mistake identity? He had to entertain the possibility that he was not and the notion was not a welcome one.

Mrs Graham had told him where Colin was and a complex bundle of motives was propelling him towards the hospital. He wanted to see his old friend and wish him well, regardless of whether Colin could hear it or not. Injured in the line of duty – he knew something about that and respected it. Even from Trumpton. Especially from them really. He remembered seeing a warehouse blaze once. Absolutely terrifying, a series of little explosions like random fireworks, and just so hot – but there were Barney and Cuthbert with their hoses, taking it all in their steely stride. But he also wondered if it might stir some memories. He had only very vague souvenirs, all faded and frayed, of life before he and his mother moved to London. His dad and that bar of chocolate, its shiny squares and the shinier silver foil wrapping. A play group and a big toy garage which must have been before he started school, so before the age of five. A paddling pool which wasn't in London and, since they never went on holiday, could only be from, well, he'd believed Brighton but now he wasn't so sure. There was also one of Colin with a comic. Just sitting there, cross-legged, reading it and laughing. That may have been at the nursery school too, thinking about it. He could do with some of that easy uninhibited laughter himself.

There was nobody around Colin's room at all. No nurse to talk to here and the nurse on the main ward had just waved him through. The security in the average hospital appalled him. He'd been called to one of the big London teaching hospitals once, after a bloke with a machete had been spotted strolling down a corridor on the tenth floor. The tenth floor!

Anyway, no point knocking when you're visiting a man in a coma, so he just walked in. He'd visited injured colleagues in hospital before and the room was much as he'd have expected it to be – the machines (state of the art for once), the smell (cleaner than clean – again, better than usual), the daytime television – but he was too late. The metal-framed bed, sitting in the middle of the room, was empty. Clean, made – but empty. Chris reacted like a burst balloon. His head a screaming whirl of sensations. He felt himself deflating – shorter, smaller.

Chris allowed himself to slump into the plastic-padded chair beside the bed.

On the television, a daytime soap.

As he gathered his breath, an odd battering of emotions rained slowly down him. Nothing was very precise. Nothing had been for a while. He was an impulsive cop at the best of times. Dedicated, committed but impulsive with, as Corrigan had put it on a number of occasions, 'authority issues'. He acted as an alternative to thinking, was probably the truth of it. Taking it easy had never been easy. Sleeping had never been easy. Sleeping at his mother's had been worse. Sleeping at his mother's with the knowledge that she may have been feeding him a line of bullshit his entire life close to impossible. He suddenly felt very tired indeed. He'd lost colleagues before. He remembered a funeral. Early on in his time on the Force. The vicar had said that PC Gilbert – knifed in the chest while out on the beat – was 'at peace'. Chris had been anything but at peace that day. He'd been raging. Took it out on some plonk later in the day. But, with time, he'd begun to wonder. He, Chris, was clearly anything but 'at peace' and wouldn't 'at peace' be a lovely place to be. To not have all this shit inside you. Well, anything that enabled you to turn off the hate and the loathing like a switch couldn't be all bad. Even when he was asleep, he was dreaming. Pulling himself from the chair, like a rusty nail from a plank of driftwood, he felt like he'd been awake his entire life.

He watched the TV for a moment, didn't have the foggiest what was going on and then turned it off by simply pulling the plug from the wall.

The sheets were clean. This was a fresh bed. He laid down on it. It felt good. He slipped his shoes off to get a bit more comfortable, reaching around, but without sitting up, to slide them under the bed. Then he rolled under the sheet and pulled it up, covering himself from head to foot like a corpse – all ready for the coroner to lower the sheet for identification. The slow nod of the next of kin. The practised grimace (but secret satisfaction) of the officer in charge. Peace at last.

Chris had no idea how long he had been laying there. It was possible that he had dozed off. However, he was wide awake and about to get up again when the door opened. He froze, the absurdity of the situation in which he found himself suddenly crystal clear. His reaction, which included closing his eyes like a child who thinks that, if he can't see you, then you can't see him, made him smile inside. Absurd indeed. But, at the same time, he was trained to keep his head and his nerve had got him out of far stickier situations than this. Was it a nurse? No, the footsteps were too substantial. A man. A male nurse? (He hadn't seen any.) A doctor? Whoever it was fell into the chair in much the same way as he had. A heavy sigh suggesting a certain age? Then there was a tinkling sound and the settling of a cup on the bedside table. A cup of tea? A slurping sound. Yes, a cup of fucking tea. Who was this guy? For what felt like an hour but was probably a minute, nothing was said. Tea was slowly supped.

Then: 'I don't know what to say, Colin. We hoped it wouldn't happen but you and I both know that it usually does.'

Chris didn't recognise the voice. But it was definitely an older man. A visitor who had entered the room to find the subject of his visit shrouded and apparently dead. Chris was aware that he was holding his breath. He couldn't breathe properly without causing the sheet to quiver. He eased a little breath out of the side of his mouth and sucked a little back in. Eyes closed, he focused on stillness. Would the visitor lift the sheet? Well, there was nothing he could do about that.

'You've heard about the murders, I suppose. Can't imagine your visitors have talked about much else since the donation. All these new machines... If I hear someone say it's an ill wind again, I swear I'll...'

There was a cough and more tea slurping. And slurping was the word. It sounded more like a cat lapping from a saucer than a man drinking from a cup.

'All these new machines haven't stopped you from dying though, have they, Colin, son? Too little. Too late. Just like my ...'

Chris was aware of the visitor rising from his seat and beginning to pace the room. After a few steps he stopped.

'It was one day when I was playing bowls and the utter fucking futility of the game just struck me, you know. The utter futility of everything, really.'

Chris couldn't say what it was but there was something about the way the man paused before he started speaking again, something in the new tone of voice – a little lower and measured, and something in the more considered sentences that Chris had heard before. It was that moment when you knew a con was about to confess. Chris concentrated on breathing through a little gap in his lips, the corner.

'Had my bowls in the bag and I was walking over here to come in and see the wife...'

A half shuffle. A step. 'We'd just beaten someone so easily I'd hardly noticed I was playing. Proof is I can't even remember who it was. Walked through the Italian garden and I don't know why. His stupid fucking grin, that gravity-defying blanket that preserved the little mite's modesty... I don't know. I raised my bowling bag above my head and brought it down. Smashed that bloody statue to bits.' The speaker paused as if revisiting the spectacle. 'I had a lethal weapon in my hands. Complete and utter impulse. And I'm not a man given to impulse.'

Lucky you, thought Chris.

'I looked around. Nobody there, so I just walked on like nothing had happened. Like I've seen a thousand cons do. Over-innocent, a bit swaggering and big in the walk. Not quite whistling, but you know what I mean. They call it "the pimp roll" in America. I sat beside her bed for an hour and I couldn't stop thinking about it. Had to walk back past it on the way out. Returning to the scene of the crime as you're never supposed to do.'

Chris had heard less interesting confessions, but not many. After a few more steps, the bloke sat down again.

'Did you know I got a Bravery Award? I took a bullet and still tried to complete the collar.'

Another copper! Chris was listening intently again.

'There was talk about a Queen's Police Medal.'

A QPM for smashing a statue?

'Back in the early 90s.'

OK. Off on a tangent. Old guy, it happens.

'But it never crossed my mind not to try to complete the arrest any more than it crossed your mind not to go back into the house for that girl. It's the code, isn't it? The compact between us, the state and the public. Then, somewhere, it broke down. Somewhere along the line they stopped honouring it.'

There was some more tea cup activity.

'It was great for a while.' A little wistful.

What was?

'All this money suddenly appearing. But now they've got the wrong guy. It's not that Geordie lad. And that's bad because I've never knowingly let an innocent man go down and never would. And it's bad because now everything will go back to normal again. No more donations to hospitals. No more anything. So I don't have a lot of choice, do I?'

The padding in the chair exhaled as the man got up again.

'One more and I can die happy.'

Footsteps. Receding. He was heading towards the door. Chris processed his options without being aware that he was processing them and stayed put beneath the sheet. One more what? The door didn't creak as such, but there was a click and a wheeze as it opened and then the reverb – sounds bouncing in and around the room – as the outside rushed in.

'Brighton won again,' the man said. 'That's three in a row and the new lad from Italy scored two – that must be ten or eleven already for the season.' Pause. 'He's only 19.' And then the door shut.

Three seconds later Chris swung out of the bed. The bedside table had acquired an empty cup and a saucer half full of tea. He used the edge of the sheet to pick them both up and slide them into the cupboard in the bedside table. No time now, but fingerprints might be needed later.

He was in his socks. Valuable time lost finding his shoes and wrestling them onto his feet. He sprinted out of the door and through the ward outside. The nurse clocked him but, before she could object, he'd gone. No lift waiting but one was coming up. Two floors away. Wait or run down the stairs? Stairs. Lobby at the foot of the stairs. Double doors. Was the main entrance left or right? Footprints on the corridor floor in pink.

Chris half ran, half walked the corridor, circumnavigating a trolley of equipment, a bed (empty), a man on crutches wearing headphones the size of bean cans, a pair of barely-mobile pensioners – 'sorry' – and a gang milling around the 'Where To Go' table. He crashed into a man who chose that moment to thank the woman sitting at the desk and step back.

'Sorry, sorry,' said Chris, leading with the shoulder but not quite moving quickly enough to start an incident.

'Chris,' said the lady behind the 'Where To Go' desk.

'Mrs Graham,' said Chris – he recognised the voice before he saw her. Her head was bobbing around like a chicken's.

'Have you been to see Colin?' Gill tried to make eye contact with him from her seated position.

'Haematology,' said one of the many people who were making this task more difficult. She looked first one side of the burly enquirer's fawn corduroy jacket and then the other. Even at this distance, DS Caton didn't look well, even scruffier than usual. As if he'd just got out of bed.

'One moment,' said Mrs Graham.

'But he was after me,' said the man in the fawn jacket, an exasperated hand flicking up to straighten hair that was no longer there.

'Mrs Graham,' said Chris. He was ducking and diving to make eye contact too. 'Do you know anyone who drinks their tea from a saucer? Might be an ex-policeman.'

'That's Mr Newton, I just saw him go down there. Ronald Newton. He looked rather flustered.' In fact, Gill thought, the pair of them, both DS Caton and Sergeant Newton, appeared to be in a terrible state. Is that what hospitals did to policemen?

Chris looked in the direction Gill had pointed, a narrower corridor, obviously not for patient use at all. In fact, it looked like the way they took the bins out. There was a notice on the wall about the correct disposal of sharps. He'd seen one upstairs. The name Ronald Newton was familiar to him. Perhaps the Bravery Award? Although it was presumably way before his time. By the time he looked back over his shoulder, the information table, Gill Graham and the crowd were no longer visible. It may have been cowardly not to tell her but then when did it become brave to tell an elderly woman her son was dead?

The man in the jacket stepped forward again and Gill once more lost sight of the detective. 'Are you both quite all right?' She angled her head, craning first one way and then the other, but he'd gone.

'Haematology,' repeated the man in the fawn jacket. There was still no question mark, still no 'please'.

Third floor, B wing, said the location plan on the desk in front of her. 'Sixth floor, C wing,' said Gill.

She composed herself to answer the next query, a pleasant-looking young girl clutching a familiar blue appointment letter.

'Can you tell me where ...'

'No,' Gill screamed and jumped out of her chair, her pounding heart rising like a bubble in boiling water. She had just realised exactly what it was that could have made the two policemen so distraught and so reluctant to speak to her.

'Colin!'

## 5.6.

Chris ran out of the hospital into the 1990s.

The corridor had been lined with big wheelie bins in a variety of colours, the entrance itself just a couple of industrial rubber door flaps. It was the engine room of the hospital, the back door, not a patient entrance. The corridor spilled out onto a side street. A couple of cars had sped by – could one of them have been Newton? He could have been parked here. Chris could see that parking in this street and using the side entrance would enable you to avoid paying for the hospital car park. Or could he live in the area? Assume the latter for now and check. Chris had slowed down and started walking, fishing his mobile phone out of his pocket and texting Corrigan.

It was fiddly. He'd seen other fingers tap-dancing across mobile phone keypads – Gabby's, for example – but he was a neanderthal, a hunter and pecker. Couldn't decide whether he preferred the screen upright or horizontal, whether to use fingers or thumb. Result: he was all fingers and thumbs. 'Sorry,' he said, nearly flattening an old lady carrying a basket. She fenced him off with an elbow.

Address for ronald newton. Used to be onion here. In pursuit.

Send. He entered a narrower street and, as he looked up from his phone, time stood still. Christophe Caton is five years old. He is kicking up the leaves in his big-tongued turquoise and white, velcro-fastening training shoes. He wears baggy cargo-style jeans, a baggier white T-shirt that says 'Kid' on it and a browny-purple flannel shirt with big checks. He is holding his daddy's big hairy hand

– well, holding a finger really. Dad has big, black, brightly-polished shoes and he is not kicking any leaves. Down the road – four trees away, then three trees away, then two – is nursery school. They walk past Colin's house and then past the house with the cat sitting in the window under the shabby lace curtains and then past the house with the grumpy lady who always has lots of Tesco carrier bags and shouts at everybody as she tries to make her way along the packed pavement outside the nursery. And then Chris is at the nursery school and he sees his friend Colin. Colin pokes his head out of the toy train in the playground and shouts, with unbridled joy, 'Chris!'

Chris walked down the street in the direction of the nursery school. The nursery was on the corner. On the other side of the junction would be the park. Of course, everything was smaller and, at times, a little disorientating. He was looking down on front garden walls that he used to look up to. The house with the cat had, assuming he had identified the house correctly, been painted a pastel blue and generally done up. It sported not shabby lace curtains but crisp clean Venetian blinds. He could see right through the house to the French windows at the rear: the bare floorboards, the leather sofa, the flat-screen TV. There was no cat. But, when he counted the trees, it was surreal. The imperfections in the bark, the whorls and whirls, the pollarded branches, they all looked familiar. Was that possible? Even the way the roots caused the pavement to buckle in places seemed to him fixed points.

It was definitely North Road, the street he'd lived in as a very little boy. He felt like the policeman in that TV series who gets shot and goes back in time. Except, of course... He stopped in his tracks. It wasn't him who had been shot. He retraced his steps to number 12. This was the house he had lived in. There were a couple of mountain bikes in the front garden beneath a wooden shelter. There were grey-green blinds in the living room window, flying at half mast. The lights were off. The residents were presumably at work and school. It was a very average terraced house in any small town but that doorstep, the original if that bevelled worn shape was anything to go by, was the doorstep on which his father had been shot. Why had his mother misled him so? Why all that crap about Brighton?

When she'd finally told him what had happened to his father, she'd sat him down with the Brighton A-Z. She'd shown him the two streets and laid on the mistaken identity thesis with a trowel. He had always assumed she'd emphasised it so that he would understand that his father had done nothing wrong. But here in Biscuit Town, there was no North Gardens, only North Road, so no potential for going to the wrong location...

His phone made him jump, almost like an electric shock. He had to get back into the present. The guv had texted him an address. He stopped and took one last look up and down North Road and let it burn into his mind's eye. Whatever his father had or had not done, nothing would bring him back. There would be time for this later.

He ran to the end of the street. He remembered the road that formed a T-junction with North Road (although he couldn't remember its name) as equally quiet, but time seemed to have turned it into a major thoroughfare. Traffic on both sides of the road. A handful of kids in various football kits leaving the park, waiting to cross. The smallest bounced the ball with no great skill or attention and Chris had to quash the inclination to shout 'careful'. Is that what his father had shouted at him when they'd played ball in this park? He couldn't remember. His mind was running away a little.

He got lucky. A driver stopped to let a woman with shopping out of the car. Money changed hands. A minicab, then. On closer inspection, there was a sticker in the window saying 'Green Cabs'. The vehicle wasn't exactly green. It was turquoise and dirty white. Much the same turquoisey green, Chris realised, as the taxis in Brighton that the driver was presumably hoping to pass off as. Very enterprising. Chris flashed his badge and got in. He reeled off the address before the driver had had time to think.

'Where is that? Carter's Green,' Chris asked.

The driver was a balding, greying man. But his hair, what there was left of it, was still bushy and he wore it long. Chris met his eyes in the rear-view mirror. Late thirties. Dark eyes. Very heavy. Suit-style jacket but an overtight, open-neck checked shirt. Extra from a bad 70s movie.

'Round the other side of Moonshine,' he drawled. A very bad 70s movie. 'Couple of mile.'

They turned left at the top, away from the centre of town and the road began to climb.

'So who are we tailing?' the driver asked, chirpily, turning his head in Chris's direction rather than relying on the rear-view mirror. 'We're talking Carter's Green, so we must be talking cat up a tree, theft of a gnome or Jehovah's Witnesses after the hours of daylight.' Then he laughed a lot at his own joke, a deep throaty rumble. 'It's quiet,' he added eventually, by way of explanation. 'Carter's Green.'

They slowed. Stuck behind a JCB or similar digger. 'He'll turn off in a minute,' said the driver. 'It's the new development at Estuary Sands. That's where he'll be going. Very posh. Couple of footballers have bought apparently. Though why they call it Estuary Sands, I don't know, since the estuary is the other side of town. True, the beach is only a few hundred yards away. If you jump off the cliff.' Another long slow laugh. 'If you want to go a more conventional route, it's miles.'

'Once he does turn off, I really need you to step on it,' said Chris.

Carter's Green was on the other side of the hill. They turned off the main road into a much smaller road which quickly became single-track. 'Is there any other way out of the village?' Chris asked.

'Not by road.'

There were just a dozen or so houses, Newton's in the middle of them. They came to a halt and Chris hopped out, jettisoning banknotes behind him.

'Wait,' he said to the cab driver, turning to push another tenner through the open window.

He stood on what little pavement there was and took it in, allowing the taxi to park up. Pretty little cottage. He knocked. No answer. The front door was locked. Apart from a few parked cars, the street was deserted, so he walked up the side alley. The back gate was locked too and he wasn't sure he wanted to climb over at this point. The place looked empty but Newton couldn't have gone far. There were some footprints in the alley – boots – but Chris wasn't sure how fresh they were. Probably could have been made at any time that day.

Back in the street, the lady next door was emerging from her house – perhaps alerted by Chris's arrival.

'He's on holiday,' she snapped. In slippered feet, she was standing unsteadily on her weathered front step, supporting her frail frame on a Council-issue step rail. She'd had a purple rinse but was wearing gardening gloves and, next to her on the step, were a pair of green wellies. Chris admired her tiny but immaculate garden. No sign of gnomes. How would she get into those wellies? They looked too small to be responsible for the footprints in the alley, but it wasn't impossible.

'Yes, I know,' said Chris. He produced his warrant card with a flourish.

'Can't read that.'

'Detective Sergeant Caton, M'am. Metropolitan Police. I'm a colleague, well, a friend, of Sergeant Newton.'

'I see.' Her demeanour mellowed a very little.

'The thing is he's forgotten his passport,' said Chris.

'I see.' She was as stony-faced as any con he'd ever interviewed.

'He won't be able to get on the plane without it and he asked me to come and pick it up.'

'I see.' She considered the proposition. 'Not a lot of point in that, is there?' She wasn't wearing glasses but clearly needed them. Her piercing eyes were like lead shot. 'Since you haven't a key.'

'No. Do you know anyone who has?'

'I do.' But she gave no indication of going to get it. The only thing that moved was her head. She slowly leant forward to peer still more intently at Chris. 'The thing I don't understand is why he called you and not me.'

'Ah,' said Chris. 'That would be because I have a little blue lamp and siren and can get it to Gatwick in no time at all. His flight leaves within the hour.'

She nodded slowly. 'Hmm. One moment.' And she went back into the house, closing the door behind her.

Chris looked at the pansies, teasels and thyme. A sleek tortoise shell cat appeared, trotted proudly along the low standing stretcher-bond garden wall and disappeared up the alley. Chris watched its tail disappear and then looked up and down the street. He saw nothing and he could hear nothing. He looked at his watch. If Newton really was getting on a flight and was leaving within the hour, he was going to miss him. Mentioning Gatwick had been a gamble but, as she hadn't picked him up on it, perhaps he was onto something. She may have been doddery on her feet but there didn't seem to be anything wrong with her brain. In fact, she appeared worryingly perspicacious. He had visions of her either phoning Ron (although he suspected that the idea of calling a mobile phone, assuming Ron had one, would not occur to her) or, worse still, demanding to see Chris's putative police vehicle, complete with flashing lights and siren. Eventually – it was a little more than a moment – she emerged with the key.

'Just put it back through the letterbox,' was all she said.

## 5.7.

The cottage did not, on first impressions, look like the residence of a retired police sergeant. Pinks and pastels, patterns and laces, china cats and dogs, carriage clocks and antimacassars, Chris would lay a pound to a penny that it had been decorated by a retired member of the Women's Institute two decades or so earlier. Either way, it was suffering from neglect. Glass shelves laden with dusty chintz ran down the narrow hallway. Ahead, a staircase with faded patterned carpet. This area did not see a lot of sunlight. At the end of the hallway, an open door onto an empty kitchen, the only sound the big numbered wall-mounted clock pounding out the seconds between Chris and his quarry.

He entered the living room. The framed photos featuring big hair, high-waisted jeans and other 80s and 90s fashions were also dusty and there were cups and saucers everywhere. The room was mostly occupied by a folding dining table which had been opened up to its full size. On top, alongside a couple of take-away containers, used plates and several piles of papers, a well-thumbed deck of Tax Evaders Top Trumps, a one-third-full bottle of scotch whisky, strewn newspapers and books, was a computer – an old iMac. It was slot-loading in Bondi Blue, the classic iMac that Chris had craved as a student. It took him a moment or two to register that the screen was still awake. Chris felt his muscles tense. Was Newton still in the house?

There was no sound. Chris's ears were trained to the proverbial pin. He leaned into the computer as quietly as he could and moused open the computer's preferences. The Energy Saver widget was set to 'turn display off after 15 minutes'. In other words, the keyboard had been used at some point within the previous quarter of an hour. Newton must still be here, Chris realised, otherwise he would have seen him leave. He swallowed and felt himself tense a little more. He wasn't scared of Newton as such. In his right mind, the retired sergeant would not wish to attack a fellow officer. But he was not in his right mind.

Suddenly, a noise from the kitchen, the crash of a slamming back door. Chris chased the sound. He was greeted in the kitchen by the tortoise shell cat. She eyed him up and down disdainfully before brushing, tail like a periscope, past his leg. Behind her, the catflap rattled and settled back into position. Chris exhaled but he couldn't relax. Was Newton still upstairs? He retraced his steps and began slowly to climb the stairs. In the master bedroom, the bed was unmade. It was a mess. Like that bed by that artist woman that had won that prize. Sweaty disheveled sheets and newspapers all over the place. The Lucas Forsberg attack. Screw Loose, said a red-top headline. The second bedroom looked like it hadn't been used for years, the bed not made at all, just an empty divan. The doors were open to both the toilet and the thin galley bathroom. The bathroom window was open, but there was no way Newton could have climbed through that. Where the fuck was he?

Chris went back and checked the wardrobes. Downstairs, he checked the cupboards. He checked the small wooden shed in the back garden. He checked there was no cellar, no pantry, no scullery, no outside bog or any other opening sufficiently large to hide a human. It was perplexing. He went back into the living room and started a more detailed examination. He needed some clues and time was not on his side. There were several photos of the same woman but with a different class of schoolchildren in each picture suggesting that Ron's wife was a former teacher. Although the picture frames on the sideboard were generally dusty, Chris noticed that one had been polished and moved onto the table beside the computer, a certain pride of place. It was the same woman, much older, a recent photo probably. Then, next to it, the same photo on heavy vellum printer paper folded in half. Chris picked it up. Eileen Newton, it read, followed by the years of her birth and death: the order of service for her funeral. Ah.

As he replaced the document, the iMac screen went to sleep. Another quarter of an hour had passed. It was not conceivably possible that Newton was still in the house.

The bastard had somehow given him the slip.

His gaze settled on the monitor and there, yellow against the grey sleeping screen, was something Chris had not noticed before: a Post-it note. He pulled it off and the handwritten contents were in a very familiar form: 11.5 B 10.1 M.

Something at last.

Now he could wade through the stats maze on corporatesponger. co.uk himself or he could try to recoup a tiny drop of the buckets of time he'd lost by getting someone else on it. He texted 11.5 B 10.1 M to Cherrianne, adding 'who is it? Where is CEO? Urgent.' He had no choice, so he pretended nothing had changed. No mention of Scootergirl. The only alternative was asking Corrigan and frankly (and it had nothing to do with him being supposedly both undercover and not on active duty), that was not an option at all.

'Might as well ask the cat,' mumbled Chris.

The cat chose this moment to reappear in the living room. She swaggered across the carpet, hopped up onto the dining chair and then up onto the table. She threw Chris another haughty glance before proceeding to walk around the table top, inspecting the dirty plates and half-eaten take-away cartons in search, presumably, of a little light snack. She poked papers and books aside with paws and nose as she went and finally she marched straight over the top of the keyboard, causing the screen to wake up again.

'Shit,' said Chris.

The cat turned her nose up at some cold noodles and jumped back down onto the floor again. Chris resisted the urge to kick her.

There were a couple of web browsers on the iMac desktop. Chris booted them both up. As he'd expected, history deleted on both. He'd have to give Gatwick a try. But then he noticed the cat's meanderings had uncovered a fancy silver frame he hadn't seen before. But he recognised the logo and the date immediately.

Chris picked it up. A parchment-style marbled paper. The logo of the local constabulary was embossed. For Bravery, it said in copperplate type, followed by Newton's name and rank. It was dated the date on which Chris's father had died. Also in the frame was a photograph of a policeman in his smartest uniform. He had his helmet under one arm, the badge buffed up bright, and in the other hand he was proudly holding up the certificate that was now in the frame. It was a decent photo. Newton was a kindly-faced man with a boxer's ears and nose. There were flecks of grey hair around the temples and another larger patch on the crown which made him look a little like a badger. The picture was a good few years old now but it could be useful. Chris turned the frame over and took off the back cover. As he removed the photo, another item fell out, the flimsiest paper floating slowly to the floor. Chris could see what it was without even picking it up from the carpet, but he snatched it up anyway. It was a familiar press cutting.

As he read, he sank back into the chair. The only difference between this version and the one that he'd seen previously was that the latter had been labelled by his mother 'Brighton Argus'. This was clearly from the now-defunct local Biscuit Town paper, the Courier. So had his mother mislabeled the copy she had?

Purposely?

The implications took a moment to solidify in his mind and his conclusion surprised him. He really ought to be interrogating his mother, refusing to let her move until he had the truth. Was this why she had chosen to 'accompany' Gabby? But he found instead that his thoughts kept returning to Gill and Colin Graham. He ought to have said something to Gill at the hospital. The more he learned about his own father's death, the more he wished he'd known about it sooner. Although perhaps it wasn't the same thing. Either way, the wind had well and truly been taken out of his sails. As he sat, the cat jumped up onto his lap and was, before he had time to object, settled and purring.

Chris stroked the cat absently. 'What do you think, Puss?' he asked at length.

# 5.8.

**The Courier**

## SHOT ON HIS STEP

A man was gunned down on North Road as dusk was falling yesterday evening.

Anthony Caton, 33, was shot dead on his own doorstep in an apparently random killing.

Neighbourhood policeman PC Ronald Newton was nearby and heard the shots. He attempted to carry the injured man to Stern Road Hospital which is just around the corner but was then shot himself, apparently as the killers passed in a getaway car. Mr Caton, a train driver, died shortly afterwards. PC Newton was treated at the hospital for gunshot wounds.

A spokesman for British Rail said 'Mr Caton was an exemplary colleague who will be much missed. Like the whole town, we are at a loss to explain this barbarity.'

Police, who are looking for a blue and black Renault Espace, are examining the possibility of mistaken identity. They have also praised PC Newton's 'extraordinary courage under fire'.

# 5.9.

When Chris emerged from the cottage, the cab had gone. He had expected as much after all this time. It was getting late. There was just an hour of daylight left, maybe two. He had no idea of the tide times but there was only one way he knew back into town, and that was along the beach.

The road, and Carter's Green itself, petered out into pebbles, patches of ancient tarmac and potholes, a narrow unmade footpath led down to the beach. A sign reminded the unruly visitor of various activities that were forbidden on the beach including nudity, fires, alcohol, dogs and bicycles. There was a narrow ribbon of sand. To Chris's left, the cliff stood tall but was not much more prominent than the rest of the coastline. With a bit of luck he'd be able to get round.

The sand swallowed his trainers. Very powdery. Perhaps the tide never came in this far. He began to run. It was a toss up whether it was easier to run on the rocks at the foot of the cliff – leaping and tripping like an apprentice goat – or on the slip-sliding sand. He did a bit of both. In this way, he part jogged, part staggered, part jumped his way along. The evidence of erosion was clear. He came upon some ragged ribbons of police tape, strung around a handful of metal posts to cordon off an area. Danger: falling rubble, this sign said. It had been hammered deep into the sand but had still taken a major battering from the elements.

The strip of beach widened. It was deserted at first but, after a few moments, he saw in the distance a young woman in clear breach of the beach rules. No, not nude – she was wearing a tracksuit and a hairband or similar – but walking half-a-dozen dogs of various shapes and sizes in coats of different colours on leads of different lengths.

A Golden Retriever was tugging at its leash, keen to inspect the cliff at closer quarters. Chris was getting to know Mrs Graham's dog. He patted it on the head.

'Hello, boy,' he said.

'Woof, woof, woof,' said the dog, clearly very agitated. Uncharacteristically so, Chris thought.

'Dimmy, no, we're going back in a minute,' said the woman – in her twenties maybe, with a tired, un-made-up face. She had a half-dead cigarette hanging from the corner of her mouth like a gun-slinging gaucho.

'Hello,' said Chris, trying to give the impression of a man out for a bracing constitutional. 'How far to Biscuit Town?'

The girl removed the fag and stamped it into the sand. Smoking had become almost shameful. 'Only a mile or so,' she said. She was pretty when she smiled, dimpled with a slightly upturned nose and deep-brown pools of eyes. A bit Scandinavian-looking.

'You've got your work cut out,' said Chris, nodding in the general direction of the canines. The Retriever gave another tug on the lead and almost pulled his minder over.

'Dimmy!' she shouted.

As she stretched, her loose top rode up her arm and Chris saw the bandages.

'One of your charges get out of hand?' he said.

'No,' said the girl, training shoes digging into the sand to avoid losing balance. 'I had a bit of trouble with some flat-pack furniture.'

Another tug. Firmer still.

By now a couple of the other dogs were following Dimmy's lead and, when a big Newfoundland decided to join it, it was more than the girl could take. Her jogging shoes tried to grip on the shifting sand, failed, and she found herself on her stomach, arms out in front of her, still clinging onto as many dog leads as possible. The dogs themselves were several metres closer to whatever it was that was interesting them so much. As it advanced, the Newfoundland began to bark. The Retriever joined in. Chris picked up the two leads the girl had let slip and followed the dogs. One or two of them looked familiar. Chris prided himself on his memory for human faces but he was less confident with man's best friend.

'Fuck,' he said, the reason for their interest suddenly brutally apparent. He turned back and held up a flat palm like a traffic cop. 'Sorry, Miss...'

The girl raised herself to her knees and then to her feet, wrestling free from a tape of seaweed that had wrapped itself around her leg.

Chris produced his warrant card. 'Metropolitan Police,' he said. 'What's your name, Miss?'

'Jess. Jessica Gann. What is it?'

'I'm afraid your dog has discovered a dead body.'

'Shit.'

'I'm sorry.' Chris pulled his phone out of his pocket. 'No fucking signal.'

'There never is one down here,' said Jess.

'Can you go back to town? Go to the station or call the police as soon as you get a signal?'

'Can I see?'

Chris looked back. He'd seen enough to know it wasn't pretty sight. A couple of dogs were nosing the corpse, the others sniffing around the area. 'I don't think that's a good idea,' he said.

'I've lived here all my life,' said Jess. 'I might know who it is.'

'Come on then.'

They advanced together, cautious steps. Chris didn't offer his hand but Jess took it anyway. The body, which was slumped up against a rock, came into view. The position suggested the man had been sitting against the rock and perhaps had a heart attack or something, but that wasn't what had happened. There was a big boulder-sized hole in the back of his head. Chris led Jess round so that, rather than the back of his head, she'd see the front. She screamed anyway and the dogs started barking again.

'It's Gavin Henley,' she said.

'Are you sure?'

'I should be. I'm his cleaner.'

'Who is he?'

'He's in finance, some sort of banking or consultancy. I don't really know. His company's called needle something or something needle.'

'Threadneedle Investment?' Chris had heard of them from his research. They were the kings of the Swiss bank account, linked to many of the corporates and individuals who were in the frame for tax evasion.

'That's it.'

Chris looked at Jess. She was barely reacting. She looked at the corpse for a moment, shook her head and then began to gather up dog leads. In fact, she was responding much like the dogs. They'd lost interest as soon as they'd alerted the humans, the leaders of the pack, to their find.

'You don't seem very surprised,' Chris said.

Jess looked up. Up and up to the summit of the cliff. Chris followed her gaze. At this point along the cliff, there was considerable overhang. The top ledge was perhaps a metre or two further towards the sea than the cliff's base. It was quite precarious, tufts of grass and a scattering of tiny bushes hanging onto the crag for dear life. The chalk at the top was fresh white.

'I'm not. He's fallen off.'

That was clearly possible. There were a number of boulders and rocks around that could well have fallen recently.

'He's often out there, standing on the edge – after his jogs and stuff.' She paused, another look down at the body. 'Was often. I could see him from their upstairs windows.'

'There are houses up there?'

'Estuary Sands, it's a new luxury development. Well, quite new,' Jess winced. 'It's my fault, really.'

'What do you mean?'

'This cliff has been crumbling for years. Well, it had stopped for a while but the locals always warn new arrivals about it. Thing is, once he knew, he had to go even closer to the edge – you know, like a kid when you tell him not to do something and he just wants to do it more.' Her voice rose as if she were asking a question.

'Yes,' said Chris.

'It was like he didn't believe it could happen to him. Didn't believe anything could happen to him. He was into those daredevil sports. He had a jet-ski thing and a kite surfer. Went sky-diving. Perhaps he liked to dice with death. Like he thought none of it applied to him.'

'What do you mean?'

'Well, none of the rules. The rules of life, I suppose. You know, even gravity.' Jess looked at Chris. 'I mean, they don't believe anything can happen to them, do they? People like him.'

Chris returned his phone – still signal-less – to his pocket and removed his notebook instead. He made a few scribblings. An idea was hatching.

'Jess, will you go back and alert the local police?'

'I wish I'd never said anything about the cliff.'

'It's not your fault,' said Chris. He knew he needed to be businesslike. It would be dark soon. 'You warned him. He took no notice. You'd feel worse if you hadn't warned him and he'd fallen off.'

He didn't have time for too many words of comfort but these seemed sufficient. She smiled again. It wasn't the full beam of earlier but it was a ray of sunshine in the fading light all the same.

'I want to have a look round,' said Chris. 'And obviously someone needs to stay in case someone else comes by.'

Jess gathered up the dog leads. 'Dimmy, Bouncer... come on.'

'I'll give you my phone number,' said Chris. 'It's useless at the moment but it might be useful later.'

Chris watched as she and the dogs disappeared and then he set to work. It wasn't all chalk. There were plenty of stones and pebbles at the foot of the cliff too. Chris chose the darker, rounder ones. They'd been waiting thousands of years for their date with destiny. The sea was further out now than it had been when he'd begun to round the headland, suggesting to him that this top strip of sand was not likely to be affected by the tide. He found a spot big enough to be seen and near enough to the body. He took some photos before he left, the phone's flash winking in the twilight. It looked good.

# 5.10.

Dan, armed with rod and tackle box, was already at the end of the pier sitting on his fishing stool when Cherri arrived. The place was deserted. It wasn't exactly raining but with the sea foamy as a mad cappuccino, swirling around the pier legs, the air was damp with brume. Out at sea, a black lump of container vessel.

'I thought I could be happily fishing when your mystery date arrives,' said Dan.

'That's a good idea,' said Cherri. She was well pleased to see her friend. She'd missed him. He'd been in the office less than usual and standoffish and detached when he was there. He'd handed pretty much all his coding stuff to Conrad. But here he was, beaming just like in the old days, his Gap hoodie up around his head just like hers in that wretched Scootergirl photo.

'So who is it?' he asked. 'Your hot date?'

'Someone who's been using my image for their online avatar,' she said. 'And not in a good way.'

Dan nodded. 'And you're a bit wary of him? Which is why you want me here.'

He erected a little fishing stool for her too and gestured to her to sit down. 'The best thing about fishing is the snacks,' he said, opening his fishing bag. 'Haribo?'

'I've just scoffed two muffins,' said Cherri.

Dan put the Haribos back into the bag – Cherri was touched that he'd obviously brought them specially for her. He preferred savoury, helping himself to a packet of crisps. 'That happened to me at school,' he began, crunching away. 'My best friend at the time. He used a really embarrassing picture of me to create a Facebook profile for someone called Richard Head. And then he invited all our friends to be Richard's friends.'

'Richard Head?'

'And all the girls we knew. Dick head. Get it?' He chomped a big mouthful of crisps. 'It was mortifying.' And he looked mortified, half-chewed crisps hanging onto his lips – not like the confident Dan she knew at all.

'Well, I think this is a bit more serious than that,' she said.

'So it is a hot date, then?' And then, he was the old Dan again with the thousand-Watt smile, on and off like a light.

'Don't you take anything seriously?'

Dan smirked. He looked as if he was considering the question. It was getting darker and the stars were coming out. The end of the pier was just a couple of hundred metres or so out of the town but the light pollution was noticeably reduced. In the moments of silence, you could hear the structure creak, steel and wood singing in low harmony.

'What time did he say he was coming? It'll be closing soon.'

'Who says it's a he?' said Cherri.

Dan finished his crisps. 'You sure you don't want anything?'

'I'm fine,' said Cherri.

They sat for a moment. Dan was right, Cherri thought, the pier would be closing soon.

'I may as well tell you that I'm going to sell corporatesponger,' Dan said. It was difficult to squirm in a canvas-seated, foldaway fishing stool but that is what Dan was doing.

'No, you're not,' said Cherri. 'I refuse.'

'It's never going to be worth more than it is now.'

'What you going to do? Make more knock-off Top Trumps?'

'They were good, weren't they?' said Dan but, this time, the smile was less sincere. She really had no idea what to make of him.

They sat for some moments. Dan ate crisps slowly but steadily. Cherri couldn't take her eyes off her phone, every notification an adrenalin shot. She replied to a text from PC Chris. She'd been avoiding him but he didn't seem bothered and being in touch with him made her feel more secure. She might need a policeman before the night was out.

When Dan had finally finished (and he'd savoured every salty mouthful without ever given the impression that he was enjoying his snack), he sat there as if wondering what to do next – licking his fingers, fiddling with the empty bag. In the end, he folded the packet inside out and licked that too. Then he screwed the bag into a tiny ball and dropped it into his tackle box. A silent moment or three later (Cherri was still answering the text), he levered himself out of the stool and started putting all his gear away, stowing the floats and other paraphernalia, disassembling the rod and sliding it back in its travel case. Then he folded up his stool, packed that away and waited for Cherri to get up. She hesitated. He was clearly intending to leave, looking towards the promenade end of the pier. 'We'll get locked in,' he said.

'Scootergirl's not coming, is she?' said Cherri. It wasn't a rhetorical question when she began to ask it, but it was by the end. She turned and her eyes followed the departing Dan. 'And you were never intending to fish.'

Dan stopped. 'You're not allowed to fish off the pier anymore,' he said without looking round. 'Things change.'

Cherri stared. He was a hooded shadow. Three seagulls swooped and screamed at each other before disappearing into the dark.

'Scootergirl's already here,' said Dan. He turned to face her. 'And I think you know that.'

The truth descended on the pier like a helicopter, cutting through the air, booming noise and blasting wind.

'How did you know I was in Brewed Awakening? That message terrified me.'

'I saw you out of the bloody office window, Cherri – come on, you're getting a bit Bourne Identity here.'

Cherri turned her stool towards the sea, away from Dan. She didn't know what to say. For the first time since she'd come out that evening, she was aware of his fishing knife at the bottom of her bag. But it gave her no reassurance since she knew she'd never use it. Least of all on Dan.

'I know you don't like that picture,' said Dan. 'But I needed something authentic, something that nobody could reverse-search, so I just nicked it from your Facebook and then deleted it.'

'You turned me into a troll. How did you get on my Facebook page?'

'Cherri, you use the same passwords for everything.' That was true and she'd caught him out in exactly the same way.

'I uploaded the pic again as I assumed I'd deleted it by mistake.'

'But you don't like it.'

'No, I look like an American high school killer. But the idea of me having a motorbike makes my aunt freak and I wanted to send it to her.' She paused. 'For a joke.' Nobody was laughing now.

'Sorry, Cher. I just assumed you'd be OK with it. We've always been such a team and Scootergirl was agitating for what we believe in. Anti-sweatshops, anti-exploitation, anti-rip-off prices.'

'Pro-murder,' said Cherri. The helicopter had landed but the blades continued to whirl like knives. 'How could you think I'd be OK with it? You really don't see people as people, do you, Dan? Conrad is the high emperor of empathy compared to you. You may not have killed Jack Sender but, man, did you exploit his death. I presume you photoshopped the Peter Robb picture.'

'It was just marketing.'

'It was playing with people's lives...'

'It was playing, full stop. I might not take anything seriously, Cherri, but you take everything seriously. Way too much. You need to chill.'

Dan sounded angry. Cherri was aware of him behind her, aware of him putting the fishing gear down, aware of his footsteps, aware of his presence moving closer. She felt herself go tight tense across the shoulders, ready for the knife. Did he have a second one? She wasn't really expecting it now. Any pummelling Dan would give her would be metaphorical and she'd have to learn to live with it. He touched her on the shoulder with the faintest of fingertips as he walked past her and leaned on the railings, looking out to sea, not at her.

'I'm sorry I used your picture for Scootergirl.'

'Yeh, well, I've already put an end to that. As well you know.'

'Smart hack work. You always were better than me.'

'In so many ways, Dan. You've disappointed me so much. You know, if it had been a blind date, there was a time I'd have been over the moon to discover it was you.'

'What can I say? I can't apologise for being ambitious.'

'You can apologise for selling out.'

'What do you mean "selling out"? Corporatesponger will have more cash behind it and can do a better job.'

Cherri snorted. 'You sound like you believe that too. Like Comm-N will let you do anything radical.'

'It's not Comm-N, it's a local businessman. I think he made his money in the City. A guy called Gavin Henley.'

'Bullshit,' said Cherri.

She reached into the bowels of her bag and produced the fishing knife, kicking it across the boardwalk like a TV villain kicking his weapon towards the police.

'You'd better have this back,' she said.

'My fishing knife.' That, she could tell from the tone of his voice, had surprised him.

'Well, I thought I might need to defend myself.'

'From me? Come on, Cherri, we're mates, we're...'

'Don't say it, Dan. Take the dirty City money and go fish.' Cherri was gutted.

# 5.11.

Chris's car was where he'd left it. He collapsed into the driver's seat to drink the coffee he desperately needed. Probably wasn't the best thing for his pounding heart, but it helped in the short term. Needed some food really.

He reread the text he'd had from Cherrianne: Comm-N. Warren Ruff. Lives Manhattan Beach, Los Angeles.

Good work.

He googled Ruff. His tech company was in the news because it had paid less than £5,000 in corporation tax in the UK despite being one of the biggest tech companies in the world. Chris didn't fully understand what they did, but apparently the internet would collapse without it. (They were all over everyone's back-end, was how one commentator put it.) Whatever it was, £5K on a turnover of over £10 billion did seem a little on the low side. It was, as the newspapers were saying, less than most of the firm's UK workers had paid in tax and NI, less than Chris had paid. The scam here seemed to be to give employees bonuses in the form of shares which could then be shown as a cost. In this way, they'd managed to make an operating loss in the UK. You had to hand it to them.

Chris downed his coffee and clunked his ageing Citroën AX into gear. Back onto the A294. Google had also told him the time of the next flight from Gatwick to LA. It wasn't a lot to go on, but it was the best he had. And what else was Ron Newton going to do? Swim there?

Gatwick was, as expected, very busy. A stress factory was how Chris saw it, although he wasn't particularly familiar with airports. He didn't fly for work and, not having a relationship or a family, didn't fly for holidays either. It was more like a shopping mall than a transport hub – Marks & Spencer, WH Smith, Boots. He danced round islands of people and luggage, all wearing the same tired, bored expression, clinging onto their trolleys for support as much as security. Cases seemed bigger, heavier and more high-vis than the last time he'd flown. Was any amount of package deal heaven really worth this hell? There were children crying and adults not far from doing the same. Pretty much everyone seemed to be looking at their phone or talking into it. From more than one of the airline desks, the sound of raised voices.

A slight woman in a red blouse and skinny jeans appeared to be trying to wheel three trolleys. She shared a word with a couple of transport policemen who shook their heads heavily. They looked like they were about to expire with the tedium of it all. Well, it was policing of a sort. There but for the grace of God etc.

Departures. Upstairs.

Chris took the escalator two steps at a time. At the top, he stopped and looked around. A long corridor with a moving carpet, a procession of gates and numbers. Ron was sitting exactly where Chris would have sat, had he been wanting to keep an eye on as much as possible while keeping as low a low profile as possible. Off to one side, in an alcove between two departure gates, was a pair of vending machines and a banquette of four moulded seats. Ron sat at the end eating a packet of crisps and looking about as much like an old man temporarily abandoned by his children and grandchildren and off to Spain as was possible: will you look after the luggage, Grandad?

He was staring into space, munching absently. Beside him, an old suitcase in the classic style, a business man's carry-on made from leather rather than some grandly-named extruded plastic, and a smaller, square hand-held sports bag. Chris recognised its branding from the bowling green in the park. Big enough for four woods. Since the snapping of the photo that Chris had in his jacket pocket, Ron had added a lot of pounds and shed a lot of hair. The badger look had gone. The grey temple flecks were now thicker tufts that had taken over his ears and were migrating to his eyebrows. The flat nose was broader. He was turning into an inflated version of that bloke in the 'Carry On' films they always repeated, Sid James.

Chris went and sat down next to Ron – a single seat between them. He couldn't see Ron Newton running for it somehow, but he positioned himself in such a way as to make it more difficult. This made the body language more intimate than that of two strangers on a bench. Passers-by would presumably take them for father and son – the tiny, tiny proportion who even noticed. Ron Newton was not unaware that Chris was occupying some of his personal space. He looked across to him, half-smiled and offered him a crisp.

'Hello, son. You that lad from the Met, down from the Smoke?'
'Yes,' said Chris.
'Oh well,' said Ron in a tone of resignation but also some relief.

At his age, he didn't really want to be traipsing halfway across the world with a lot of heavy luggage, Chris could see that crystal clear all of a sudden.

'I always recognise a fellow copper,' said Ron, not without pride.
'I need your help with something,' said Chris.
'Of course you do. Can I finish my crisps?' He offered Chris another.

'It's about the case for which you got your Bravery Award.'

Ron stopped munching and, despite the older man's attempt to hide it, Chris could sense in the slight relaxing of the shoulder and the momentary confusion in the eyes, Ron's surprise and suspicion: this wasn't the case he'd been expecting to be quizzed about.

Chris got up and approached the vending machine. 'Tea?'
'Thanks.'
Chris began filling the machine with loose change. 'Sugar?'
'No, thanks.'

With a rattle, a rumble and then a rush of hot water, a cup of brown appeared.

Ron finished the packet of crisps and rose from his seat. Chris tensed but kept his energy trained on the vending machine. Ron simply folded the crisp packet in half, deposited it in the waste bin and resumed his seat. Chris handed him his tea and started over at the machine.

'You got 10p? I'm out.'

Ron groped in his trouser pockets. They appeared cavernous to Chris, like a magician's bag, Ron's substantial hand lost. He produced lint, paper (receipts, probably), tatty tissue and finally the requisite coinage. The vending machine struck up the same almost musical sequence before Chris got his cup of brown and also resumed his seat.

Ron took a sip, a deep breath, and then a second sip. There was an air of calm.

'It was a street shooting,' he said. 'Assume you know that. Very rare on the South Coast.' Ron laughed a little through his nose. 'Assume you know that too. In fact, it's the only drive-by incident I encountered in my career and I worked in London for a good while. The victim, Anthony Caton, opened his door and the gunman shot him at point-blank range. Two bullets. I wasn't far away. We still had beat cops then. I was in the park. Folk used to sleep rough there. I was checking...

'Anyway, by the time I arrived, the gunman was gone and Caton was on his knees, hands tight to his chest, shirt covered in blood. I could see it was bad. Well, the hospital's just round the corner, isn't it, so I tried to carry him. Well, I did carry him. He wasn't a big man. In my arms, like you'd carry a child or perhaps the missus across the threshold.

'A car comes back down the street and they shoot at us. Another two shots. I took one in the leg and we both went down in a heap. He's bleeding, I'm bleeding. The wife, Mr Caton's wife, appears with tea towels and starts bandaging. French and close to hysterical. Well, who wouldn't be? The ambulance arrived about three minutes later...'

Ron stopped. He took a long pause and Chris let him. They both sipped tea and stared straight ahead at the ground as if they were waiting for a bus.

'Well,' Ron said eventually, 'he died. I didn't. Simple as that.' More tea. 'I was lucky.'

'The papers suggested mistaken identity.'

'You've heard about that? Yes, there was a bit of talk about it. There was a theory it was the wife they were really after.'

Chris had to control himself; his hand was tightening around the paper cup and he didn't want to crush it.

'Or perhaps it was him they wanted, but to scare her. Apparently, she once did the books for some notorious Parisian crime family – I can't remember the name, three brothers, begins with A – and she got on the wrong side of them. I don't know if it's true. There was never a warrant or an extradition request or anything from the French police. The only real French connection we had was the car. It was a Renault.'

Ron turned to look at Chris. 'To be honest, a French copper I met over there told me most of that side of the story – about the wife. He may have just been trying to impress me. But I think they lost interest in her back in France. The Parisians, I mean.' Ron pronounced it Pareezians to rhyme with Friesians, as in cattle. Gabby would have approved. 'Some sort of spat with some firm from Marseille, or Sicily maybe. Or maybe both, I don't remember. One of the brothers was killed, anyway, perhaps two. As I say, I think there were three altogether. Sorry I'm a bit vague, aren't I...'

'On the contrary, you've been very helpful.'

Ron drained his paper cup and looked at his watch. Both men looked up at the Departure board.

'Well, am I getting this flight then?' Ron said. It sounded like a rhetorical question but Chris suspected it wasn't.

'Do you want to?'

# 5.12.

Edgar Corrigan was used to weighing things up, weighing up evidence, weighing up the likely outcomes from any course of action, trying, like a chess grandmaster, to see as many moves ahead as possible. But not today.

The message from the politicians had been very firm. It had been delivered to the country megaphone-clear through the news media and it had been delivered to Corrigan personally through both his Cabinet Office contact, Mason, and his Commissioner, Walters. We have the man. Close the case. Let's get back to normal.

Corrigan too would be clear. And he would be brief.

He was standing outside New Scotland Yard. The Met was planning to move out of its iconic 60s building. Would he, Corrigan wondered, be moving out sooner than most? New Scotland Yard was to be turned into multi-storey residential accommodation. The argument before the 'tax man murders' had been over how many of the properties would be 'affordable'. There had been just a handful in the initial plans and the joke around the Yard was that not even these were affordable on a copper's money. But then, in the brave new world that was now coming to an end, there'd been talk of turning it into something for homeless people. 'It's the appropriate use,' the opposition Housing spokesperson had said. 'We've ignored our homeless people for so long that the police are the only people who speak to them.' Corrigan had nodded so hard that he thought his head might fall off.

Corrigan had, of course, been positioned just in front of the three-faced revolving New Scotland Yard sign. The journalists loved the revolving sign and its many appearances on TV had turned it into a tourist attraction. Corrigan had been told the plan was to move the sign once New Scotland Yard had moved to its new premises. They were going to the old Whitehall police station on Victoria Embankment. The place was being refurbed by some fancy dan architects to meet 'modern policing requirements'. Would that include MöblA furniture, Corrigan wondered.

He had an earpiece and could hear what was going on in the studio. The idea was that he'd be interviewed live from the studio by the anchor. They were talking about the still-hospitalised Forsberg, the injured but now-discharged sales assistant and then Lee White and then 'we're joined from outside New Scotland Yard by the man who caught him, Detective Chief Inspector Corrigan.'

And suddenly he was being pointed at.

'I've been heading up the enquiry since the murder of Jack Sender,' Corrigan said.

'Presumably, Officer, you're delighted to have caught a man responsible for three gruesome murders.'

Edgar didn't take a breath, didn't cough, didn't clear his throat. It was all about not hesitating. 'He wasn't responsible for all of them,' he said. 'He's been charged with the attempted murder of Lucas Forsberg.'

'That's...' The sound of a news anchor being blindsided on live television was cacophonic. 'So there's still a crazed killer at large.' Out of the mouths of babes, thought Corrigan.

'This investigation is still active,' he said. Whether Corrigan could say the same about his career was another matter.

# 5.13.

Ron Newton sat uncomfortably in his seat, shifting position. But he didn't actually get up. He just pulled his two bags a little closer.

'You know that the Tax Man has struck again,' Chris said in a voice he hoped sounded conversational.

This time Ron froze discernibly. Then, with deliberation, he leaned forward: elbows on his knees, heavy hands locked together, eyes front and to the floor. 'Go on,' he said.

'In Biscuit Town. Victim lived in Estuary Sands, the new development. His name was Gavin Henley. The king of the Swiss bank account, they called him. Well, his firm anyway. Usual MO: blow to the back of the head. He was found on the beach.'

Chris paused to let Ron take it in.

'I say usual MO. I mean the original MO before the Forsberg business clouded the affair. We know it's not a single assailant...'

Chris mirrored Ron's posture and they both sat there. The screen on the Departure board cleared and then repopulated itself. The big clock above rolled on, looking down on them with complete indifference. 'Well, it was fun while it lasted,' said Chris.

Ron turned to eye Chris, like a poker player trying to read a bluff. 'What do you mean by that?'

'All this extra cash – I was up the hospital this afternoon and they've transformed the place.'

'Yes.'

'It's just been so wonderful to live in a country without austerity, where people have what they need.'

Ron remained silent.

'So I don't think there will be many awards going for this collar.' Chris laughed. 'I think most people would rather we didn't catch him – if it keeps the tax coming in. And, I may be a copper, but who can blame them? Terrible it came to this, obviously, but ...'

'I think of it like an insurance man thinks of risk,' said Ron, slowly. 'An insurer will basically multiply the likelihood of an event occurring by the potential severity of the results if it does occur. Criminals effectively make the same calculation: the likelihood of getting caught multiplied by the severity of the sentence. In corporate crime, especially this sort of thing, both figures are often close to zero. In some cases, if what they're doing is not even technically illegal – only totally immoral – then it is zero. They have carte blanche. By increasing the severity of the sentence this...' Ron hesitated, '... Tax Man guy will, to some extent, have acted as a deterrent.'

'Well, he clearly has. My guv has spoken to HMRC. It's been transformational. That was the word they used. Transformational.'

Ron nodded. 'As coppers, they teach you that, under any decent legal system, justice should be prompt. Currently it isn't. Corporate cases run on for ever. Their armies of lawyers and advisors literally buy time. This killer has cut out a whole bunch of middlemen and a whole lot of time – something people my age have not got a lot of.'

He coughed. 'The point is, isn't taxation a bit like insurance too? Well, it is called National Insurance. The more people pay in, the more security we have. The reason those poor bastards who have got nothing are getting nothing is that those rich bastards with everything are giving nothing.'

While he had been speaking, Ron had been pulling his luggage in towards himself, as if for protection, like a cowboy circling the wagons. He now had the bowling bag on his lap and was clutching the handgrip so tight his fingers were whitening. Chris slid his backside into the seat adjacent to Ron and put his arm round the older man's shoulder. Ron didn't flinch.

'It's a shame it wasn't transformational in time for my Eileen,' he said.

They sat in this way for several moments while Chris searched for the right form of words.

'The thing is that it's been transforming back again since we arrested the guy who attacked Forsberg at the Homes exhibition. Everyone thought we'd got him. Everyone wanted to think we'd got him. And all the bad behaviour came back. This Gavin Henley guy could have done us all a favour...'

'Transforming it back again. Exactly. That was the idea.'

Chris interrupted. 'In an ideal world, the killer would just stop. But we'd never catch him. So there'd always be the possibility of his striking again. But how do we get that sort of guarantee? That sort of assurance.'

Ron pulled from his capacious pockets a large white handkerchief and proceeded to wipe his damp eyes. Then he blew his nose.

'Sometimes, in policing, you just have to trust your judgement of the human character,' he said. He looked like he was ready to go.

'You're not going to be bowling on holiday, are you?' said Chris. 'And they'll sting you at the gate for something that heavy. I mean, it's hardly a handbag, is it?'

'You're right, son. Boring game anyway,' said Ron and handed Chris the bag.

Chris smiled, a smile that said 'we're done here'. Ron nodded and rose from his seat. 'So I'll be going then...' It was more like a question than a statement.

'You never told me where you were going,' said Chris.

'And you haven't guessed?'

'I've got my suspicions.'

Ron smiled his first proper smile for some time. Months, Chris would guess. 'And you haven't told me your name, son.'

'You're right. Very unprofessional. You should always introduce yourself to a fellow officer.' Chris pulled his warrant card from his jacket and handed it to Ron.

'DS Caton,' he read. He looked down at Chris, still sitting on the banquette and nodded. 'Who or what brought you to Biscuit Town in the first place, Detective?'

'Gary Shad.'

Ron let a slow grin spread across his lips. 'Gary bloody Shad. I might have known.'

The final piece of the jigsaw in place. Chris nodded back and then got to his feet. They shook hands, like a son seeing his father off on a trip – and to Chris, suddenly and unexpectedly, it did feel a little like that – but they both also knew what it really meant.

'You going to go away yourself, Chris?' Ron said. He gestured at the Departure board. 'Look at all these lovely places.'

Chris let his eyes run down the list of destinations – all of them warmer than the UK (and one of them hosting Gabby Garnier) – and chuckled. 'Maybe – but I need to make a call first.'

'See you, son. And thanks.' Ron walked off towards his departure gate with his carry-on. He was striding, really. Like he was back on the beat. Chris watched him go. Ron really was a big man. And he seemed to have grown six inches.

'Thank you, Ron,' Chris shouted after him.

Ron didn't look back but raised his hand in a gesture of acknowledgement that was so appropriate for his destination. So American. The hand signal for 'shucks, it was nothing'. He was already in the diner.

Chris picked up the bowling bag. It was heavier than he'd been expecting. He sat back down on the banquette to inspect what was, after all, a murder weapon. The exterior had been cleaned and smelled of bleach. The seams, coming away a little in places, were fibrous. No doubt DNA analysis would find traces of both Jack Sender and Zak Thomas Brown. But that wouldn't be happening. There were four balls inside. Getting on for eight, even 10 kilos, in total weight? In this bag with its easy-to-swing handle, they were as good as any cosh. He had seen everything now.

But then again …

What he did know was that Warren Ruff was a very lucky man. Or rather, an even luckier one.

He pushed the bag to one side and pulled out his phone. The

number was already programmed in.

'Hello?' said Gabby.

'It's Chris.'

'Hi Chris,' she sounded as if she were on the other side of the world, which she was. 'How's it going?'

'Good, thanks, Gabby. I've a few things I need to tell you but, first, can you put my darling mother on, we need a little chat.'

# 5.14.

'This is not a murder,' said Sergeant Marinelli. 'This is Biscuit Town. The only thing they murder in Biscuit Town is a nice cup of tea. Usually with an Almond Crisp on the side, nestled in the saucer.'

'That's how it used to be, Sarge,' said PC Penney. 'But now we've got this new thing called the twenty-first century.'

Lawrence Penney took a step back from the edge. Looking down from the clifftop made him feel queasy. It wasn't the dead body by the rocks below – that wasn't yet visible – it was the height. He hadn't got a head for them but wasn't about to let on. Instead, he swallowed and spat and ground the latter into the dirt with a heavy chalk-flecked boot.

Penney looked at his boss. The Sarge looked off into the mid-distance. Deep in thought but probably not about the case since he'd already decided there wasn't one. The point was that someone had to walk up to Moonshine and Marinelli had figured that, if he did it, he could justify chips for lunch. He was already dreaming of large chips with crispy bits from Gregory's, no doubt, the Sarge. Penney followed his skipper's gaze.

It was a beautiful day, rich golden sun and a decent breeze. The South Coast at its best. They said you could see France from Moonshine Point but Penney never had. The best he'd managed was Bognor. And, even on a day like today, all he could make out were a few ships and boats. One bloody enormous container ship that looked like a toy made out of big coloured bricks. Case or no case, he'd always enjoyed a walk up to Moonshine. Pleasant enough, even with the Sarge bending your ear all the way.

'Isn't that bloke fishing off a pedalo, Sarge?' Penney said. He still wasn't looking down. 'Is that legal?'

'Haven't a clue, son,' the Sarge wheezed.

Marinelli was a short man for a copper. Penney had been told that he had taken growth shots to get on the Force, back in the day when that sort of thing mattered. His prominent midriff – kebabs and fish and chips – permitted just a single, straining button to fasten on his fading tunic. This, plus his complexion and the short bushy moustache that he wore with all the strut of Tom Selleck in Magnum but none of the style, gave him the air of a minor Mexican drugs baron rather than a small town copper. He was still breathing like a broken hairdryer and that was after three stops for a rest on the way up.

'How far we walked, Lawro?'

'Stacy's flat to the top of Moonshine is 2.4 miles, Sarge, so I'd say about a mile and half. If that.'

Marinelli looked up at Penney with a sceptical eye. 'Most men would say about two and a half miles, Penney, but you...'

'It's pedometry, skip.'

'What?'

'Pedometry.'

'You can get ten years for that.'

'Stacy and I used to do a lot of walking, Sarge, and she had a pedometer to tell her how far she walked. It,' Penney coughed; the Sarge was looking at him as if he, PC Penney, were attempting to levitate. 'It counts the number of steps you've taken and if you know your average stride length...' Penney trailed off and for a thick moment the pair watched the pedalo fisherman toying with his line.

'I just remember she measured it once, her place, over the Point to Carter's Green.'

'Took her to The Peacock, did you, Lawro?'

Penney nodded. The Sarge shook a weary head. The spume-laden breeze was picking up, sufficient to bring a tear to the eye of both men.

The Peacock had long been the main attraction of the cluster of houses known as Carter's Green, The Peacock public house and the quaintest duck pond you'd ever seen. Technically the Green was still part of town, it shared the postcode, but it was a good six miles away by the coast road, a cab ride or, in Penney's youth, the number 17 bus. Walk from town over Moonshine to The Peacock and you'd really earned your beer by the time you got there. The walk was, as Marinelli's lungs were noisily reminding him, a bit too far and a bit too steep for the casual visit. However, it was popular with a certain type of jogger and walkers of the more hyperactive dog and it had been popular with Penney back when he and Stacy had been an item. He had even seen the occasional backpacker up there, looking for something off the beaten-track, and they'd once met a bloke in a leather outback hat who thought he was on the South Downs Way.

It was a beautiful spot but it was disintegrating. The cliff movement that had stopped by the turn of the century seemed to have started again. A little girl had been hit by a falling rock while on the beach. Geography field trip. ('Nothing like that in my day, Lawro.') There had been a hasty 'something must be done' discussion at a Council meeting, tagged on under AOB, but nobody had got round to actually doing anything. A fat bloke in a streaming sweat and a Brighton fun-run T-shirt had come into the station a week or so earlier to complain. Claimed he'd been hit by a lump of falling chalk too.

'Someone will get fucking killed,' he'd said.

And that was precisely what appeared to have happened. The dead man was Gavin Henley, a resident of the spanking new Estuary Sands development, which meant his back garden opened onto the cliff itself. No mile and half walk for Mr Henley to Moonshine.

Turning and looking back inland, Penney could see Estuary Sands, the back gates and the high walls, tall as Lewes nick and he understood why so many locals had complained about it being built on the cliff and had signed the petition against it. The sense of oneness with nature, the stark, weather-wrought beauty, the soul-lifting desolation – all were lost with a ribbon of pylons and three satellite dishes in view. Not that this seemed to bother the rabbits whose holes and droppings were everywhere. Surreptitiously, Penney took out a stick of gum and folded it into his mouth. The Sarge didn't much like his gum habit, regarding it as an effeminate alternative to smoking.

Fortunately, at least, the beach below had now been closed. Falling debris was one thing, but falling merchant bankers was another. Fencing and flags didn't deter the dog walkers though and it was one such who had found the body.

'Lunch time,' announced Sergeant Marinelli, burying his hands in his jacket pockets as he turned away from the cliff edge.

'Come on, skip, we haven't even seen the body yet. We need to find the point where it happened.'

Reluctantly, head down, hands pocketed, Marinelli leaned into the wind and allowed his constable to lead him up the path. The garden path, as far as he, Marinelli, was concerned.

'Couldn't he have jumped, skip?' said Penney as the pair drew level.

The Sergeant looked up at Penney but still managed, in Penney's opinion anyway, to give the impression of looking down on him. ''kin hell, Lawrence. Given the size of his house, the size of his car, the size of his bonus and the size of his wife's implants, I very much doubt it. This is hardly Beachy Head, is it?'

'They were tumbling like flies during the Wall Street crash,' said Penney, 'the bankers. And what with everything that's been happening. Maybe he broke his bank.'

'He certainly broke his neck.'

Marinelli walked off into the wind, big strides, leaving Penney chewing fresh air.

The shorter man turned. 'I tell you what, Lawro – perhaps he had his six-figure bonus in his pocket and some sharp-eyed mugger pushed him off.'

Penney shook his head. 'Don't think so, skip. SOCO found his wallet on him. It enabled the ID.'

Marinelli smiled as Penney caught up with him. He slapped his younger colleague on the back, a gesture not without something akin to affection. ''kin smart arse,' he said. 'Come on, let's get this done. That large cod won't eat itself.'

'If you look up there, skip, the cliff overhang is whiter. More freshly eroded?'

'Good spot, Lawro.' The pair accelerated, each wanting to get there first but not show it.

'It was an accident, son,' said Marinelli. 'A terrible accident. But one for which he was, in a small way, responsible.'

'What do you mean?'

'You see the film Jaws, Lawrence? Bit before your time, I suppose. But it's Jaws all over again.'

'Sharks off Bognor Butlin's, is it, skip?' Penney smirked.

'In Jaws, they're too scared to close the beach, right?'

'But the Council have closed the beach.'

'Don't be so literal, Lawrence. 'kin 'ell. This cliff, Moonshine Point, has been stable for years, hasn't it? Then they come along, these American developers with their poncy architects and their industrial-scale building site. Their JCBs, their bulldozers, their deep foundations and their full-size swimming pools, and more fucking concrete than a Qatari shopping complex. Not such a small housing development then.' Marinelli was getting into his stride, like when he was telling a story. 'And the cliff starts slipping and sliding again like a cow on a jet-ski. And the 'kin Council. Well, they don't want to know, do they? Even when that little girl gets hit. They aren't going to close the cliff that these bankers and footballers and soap stars have paid so much for a slice of, are they? No way. No, it's as plain as a jam doughnut, Lawro, Estuary Sands luxury housing has caused this accident.'

He paused for breath. A sudden gust of wind achieved the seemingly impossible task of prising the Sarge's receding Brylcreemed barnet from his scalp. The fibrous congealment waved for a moment like a giant rabbit's ear before flopping back down again and reengaging. 'And it ain't on the estuary and it ain't on the sands.'

Penney didn't reply. He mirrored his skip, hands deep in his pockets. Again he didn't want to look down. He looked the other way instead. He could see his dump of a home town: his old man's old newsagent's (now run by Koreans), the old factory (will that promised redevelopment happen now?), the school, the funfair (home of the Crystal Flyer), the football ground, the recreation area where his dad walked the dog. Biscuit Town had been crumbling for years and a gated community for the new rich on their doorstep was a reminder they didn't need.

'Oh, fuck,' said the Sarge – a different tone, suddenly full of authority. 'Get over here, Lawro. Look.'

Penney got over there but, rather than a look, the best he could manage was a cough. 'I can't look down, skip.' He directed his gaze downwards but in shame and directly at the chalky turf beneath their feet. 'Vertigo.'

Marinelli exhaled. 'By the body,' he said slowly. 'There are stones from the beach arranged as letters to spell out the word TESS. Deliberately done.'

Penney had read the papers, seen the news. 'Tax Evading Super Scum.'

'Like Sender and Thomas Brown.'

The Sarge's radio crackled into life with a whistle and rasp like its owner's windpipe. Marinelli was relaying information back. There was a pause. 'Of course, I'm fucking sure,' Marinelli said. 'Out.'

Penney wanted so much to look down – to see the body, to see the letters – but, try as he might, he couldn't quite manage it. He dropkicked his chewing gum but couldn't watch it fall.

The Sarge, hands once again buried in his pockets and leaning into the wind, had begun the descent. He was moving faster now. This was real police work.

'How come nobody spotted that down below,' hissed Marinelli. 'Those letters, 'kin useless...'

Something had clicked in Marinelli. Penney knew that but he couldn't find the same switch in himself, he couldn't get into gear. But this was what he'd joined up for, wasn't it?

He caught up with his boss and the two descended, leaning back from the direction of the footpath's incline, the path spitting up pebbles beneath their feet.

'Footballers, Sarge?'

'What?'

'You said footballers had bought in Estuary Sands. What footballers?'

'There's that one-footed, can't-head, spineless streak of piss who used to play for Brighton.'

'That narrows it down to about 300. Who, Skip? Names.'

# 6:
# 'Returning To The Scene Of The Crime?'

# 6.1.

David Dimbleby was beginning to show his age. No amount of make-up could disguise the bags under those eyes. Denise Gann knew a bit about that sort of problem. Perhaps he spent too much time on the telly, our David. Not enough daylight. Turning into a vampire. She, Denise, certainly spent too much time on the telly and was turning into a zombie. Still, tonight, they both had an excuse. The general election.

Denise could tell through her untidily-drawn curtains that it was morning. She couldn't really reach the curtains properly now – too immobile, but you try telling the PIP assessor that – and effectively had to drag them across while half-lying, half-leaning on the sofa. David wittered away grumpily. The TV cut back and forth between the new Prime Minister travelling down to London and the front door of Downing Street from where the BBC was expecting the outgoing PM to emerge 'at any moment'. Denise wondered if David was grumpy because he was tired, because the opinion polls had once again royally screwed up or because his team of toffs with their senses of entitlement the size of France had lost. Oh, she had nothing against Dimbleby as such. Quite liked him really. But you couldn't pretend he wasn't one of them. One of the establishment.

'They'll be locking up the silver at the Palace,' she said to nobody but herself. In Biscuit Town, how many people had stayed up all night like she had? Half a dozen maybe.

Jessica had gone to bed at ten although Denise was expecting her up soon for the early morning dog walk. Change of government or no change of government, those dogs still needed walking.

Denise liked having her daughter back home. Couldn't deny it. But she hated the circumstances. She'd lost her benefit and gained a daughter. No child should have to care for their mother at Jess's age. She should have been out enjoying herself. Denise and Debbie were at her age. Those Biscuit Town boys didn't know what had hit them. Denise knew her situation was in part her own fault. Terrible depression when, within three months in her late thirties, her marriage broke up, she was made redundant and she lost her looks overnight. Too much food, too much drink. Diabetes and a heart condition. The fat had eaten her soul. She'd slumped onto the couch in misery a decade earlier and now she genuinely couldn't get off it again. Not without help.

Her pleasure at the election result – the first decent thing to have happened in Britain in the twenty-first century – was tempered with self-loathing that she couldn't get up to celebrate it. Perhaps the new lot would sort out the benefits system. Or 'welfare' as the old lot liked to call it. Patronising fuckers. And then, perhaps, Jess would get her own life. And perhaps she'd even get a flat in that new development they were promising at the Stern & Feltman factory. Denise felt like a giant squid on the sofa as she extended one of her blubbery tentacles out towards the cluttered coffee table, hauled in a half-empty king-size bottle of Diet Coke and took a celebratory sip.

As the Chancellor, the ex-Chancellor, appeared on the screen, Denise heard a kerfuffle in the hallway, Jess wrestling with the mountain of coats, fleeces and woollens hanging at the bottom of the bannister. Her daughter's head appeared around the living room door.

'Put your beanie on,' said Denise. 'It might be bright, but it's bitter first thing.'

'Yes, Mum,' said Jess. She looked first at her mother and then at the TV. 'Who won?'

'We did.'

'That's nice,' said Jess with minimal enthusiasm, like a mother to a child who presents her with an unattractive painting.

'You off?'

'Yes, I'm going to the dogs.'

Denise watched her daughter depart. She was a pretty girl and had a nice figure, Jess. She ought to be out there. She ought to be doing more than walking dogs, anyway. It wasn't that, having messed up her own life, Denise wanted to live through her daughter – although she'd be a liar if she said that wasn't any part of her reckoning. No, she just wanted her daughter to live a little before life swallowed her up and spat her out as a zombie squid.

'Ours is an unequal country, Mr Dimbleby,' the soon-to-be-out-on-his-arse Chancellor was saying.

Denise allowed her attention to return to the screen. (You knew they were in trouble when they started calling David, Mr Dimbleby.)

'And, if our party is incapable of maintaining those inequalities, what is the point of us?'

Had he really said that? It was enough to make you choke on your Diet Coke. Or had she imagined it. She realised just how tired she was, eyelids like stone. And, when she emerged from a cavernous all-nighter of a yawn, the Chancellor had disappeared to be replaced by Peter Robb.

One of the few political faces out in public at this hour, Peter Robb had been doorstepped. He wasn't too upset about it. Quite the contrary. He was a political animal now.

He was using his flagship Oxford Street store for his ostensibly low-profile, but in truth anything but, meetings. There were a couple of decent rooms on the top floor, but he would need a new office for his new projects. Perhaps not in London. Perhaps in his home town. More politically astute.

Cherri had watched the election at her aunt's and taken the early tube in. She watched Robb live from the top floor window, looking down on his curly, greying locks and the scrum of reporters and cameramen thrusting and parrying around him. She couldn't figure out how to turn the wall-mounted TV on. It was the first time she'd been in a boardroom. She heard the lift rumble and then Peter appeared in the doorway. He wasn't alone. Both men were beaming.

'Cherrianne, you're already here.'

'Couldn't wait to get started.'

Robb turned to the other man. 'This is Cherrianne Dixon, who is going to be my right hand in the foundation.'

'Pleased to meet you,' said the man. He had stubble and copper-coloured hair styled in a simple, short cut with a gently-gelled bedhead. He was wearing one of Peter Robb's better suits, single-breasted, worsted, dark grey. He was as smooth as Wilson's finest flat white.

'This is Dominic Mason,' said Robb. 'Ex Cabinet Office. He's going to be heading up my political operation.'

'Looking forward to working with you,' said Cherri. That sounded suitably businesslike, she felt. She extended her hand.

'You'll have to hold on a little longer,' said Robb. 'He's got some paternity leave first.'

Cherri smiled as she and Mr Smooth shook hands. Easy come, easy go.

'The foundation will start off focusing on factory conditions,' said Robb. 'It's a bit of a personal crusade for Cherri.'

'I wouldn't say that,' she said. She could see the name 'Scootergirl' motoring into this conversation and wanted to head it off. 'So what did you say to them outside?' she asked.

'I called on the government to regulate business,' he said. 'I said the ethical businessman needs a sound regulatory environment, otherwise the ethical businessman is, by definition, a failed businessman. Currently, we operate in an environment that encourages business people to behave unethically. Regulate away the danger. Don't rely on fear of the Axe Man.'

'He doesn't really need me, does he?' said Mason with a lovely smile.

Cherri tried a smile of her own.

Peter Robb moved towards the window and looked out over Oxford Street and beyond to Soho. The sun was warming the city, coaxing it into life. A crane spun on its axis and a piledriver started up. He still had nightmares. But not about the future. They were all about the past. About his close shave. He truly had thought he might die but he'd never breathed that to Elizabeth. Yet here he still was. Glad to have Dominic and Cherrianne on board. He had never intended to go into politics but, then, he had never intended to exploit workers on three different continents. Life had a habit of creeping up on you. You think you just like fashion because boys who know about fashion get more attention from girls than boys who know only about football. But it becomes more than that.

Behind him, Dominic had turned the television on. Cherri watched. Dominic had detached the remote control from the side of the TV (why hadn't she spotted that?). He muted the sound and used the remote as a pointer to gesture at the screen. This was grown-up stuff. Cherri switched on her concentrating face.

'Is Forsberg OK?' asked Peter, turning back to his new recruits.

'I should think so,' said Dominic. 'He's just sold 150,000 MöblA beds to the NHS.'

Peter Robb had to support himself on the back of one the boardroom chairs because he was laughing so much. (Perhaps not so grown up then, thought Cherri.) In his younger days he might have worried that he'd piss himself with laughter, but there was no danger of that. There were some advantages to an enlarged prostate. He was already looking forward to telling Elizabeth about it – they had a couple of Forsberg's beds themselves.

'Now, the first question, Peter, is: should you accept a peerage if one is offered?' said Dominic.

The television was also on at the airport. Umpteen screens with flight details, but then one with the news. Chris was early, his attention darting back and forth between the Arrivals board and the election.

Estimated. Expected.

Gain. Hold.

Landed.

Gain. Gain.

Bags Delivered.

He was tying up a few loose ends with Corrigan.

'I'm frying bacon, Chris.'

'I think I can hear it sizzling, guv. Sounds delicious.'

'I thought I'd share that – since you saved mine. Bacon, I mean.'

Following his TV outburst, Corrigan had been summoned by Commissioner Walters. But, by the time the interview took place the following day, Henley was dead and Corrigan already had a man – Chris, of course – on the spot. What was supposed to be a bollocking turned into the Commissioner congratulating the Chief Inspector on his sharp work. The guv loved the story but, since there was nobody he could share it with except Chris, he had already told him it at least three times.

'The Commissioner had never heard of Henley, but I told him he had three or four of the Tax Evaders Top Trumps as clients and that therefore the offender was effectively...' – and here Chris braced himself for the familiar strained punchline – 'killing two birds with one stone.'

'I'm at the airport, guv. Made me wonder if I should take a bit of leave.'

'But you've been on gardening leave for months, Chris,' said Corrigan. He was turning into a proper little Michael McIntyre.

'You know what I mean, guv.'

'It's an excellent idea, Christophe. Enjoy, enjoy. My daughter is dancing around the kitchen, telling me the dinosaurs have lost the election.'

'Yes, a bit of an asteroid strike, guv.'

There was no reply, although Chris could hear his boss conversing with his daughter. Then Corrigan seemed to forget completely that he was on the phone as the pair of them, father and daughter, burst into a chorus of what Chris thought was a TV theme tune. Something about it all starting with a big bang.

On the big screen showing the news, a face now familiar to Chris and to many others from the Top Trumps deck appeared. Warren Ruff had dropped in at Comm-N's UK base. It was the 'non-permanent home to 2,500 employees', according to the ticker feed along the bottom of the screen. (Non-permanent? 2,500 employees? Must be the biggest prefab on the planet then. Or a big tent maybe, like they had at the festivals.) At an impromptu press conference, Ruff was announcing that he would shortly be visiting HMRC to 'restructure' the business's tax arrangements. There was a smattering of applause from a handful of travellers – most of whom were probably using Comm-N's products on their handheld devices. Others looked up from their papers, books, screens, shopping and yawning and joined in. Nearby, a sleeping mum pretended she hadn't been and jumped up, clapping enthusiastically. Her kids were dancing and shouting as if they were already on holiday.

Chris used the opportunity afforded by the kerfuffle as an excuse to hang up. 'Ruff's on the telly,' he told his boss.

He was downing his third tea at the moment the plane landed.

Chris's mother led, encumbered with no more than a vanity case. She appeared as light on her feet as a dancer, like on a good day in the garden. Ron Newton followed with a trolley piled high with cases.

Chris had asked Ron to chaperone Francine. Ron had been happy to do so – 'ah, the Big Apple' – and had flown up to New York after his holiday in Florida. Chris reckoned it was the best way to ensure his mother actually came home, given that he was pretty sure that Gabby had no intention of returning for a while.

'Salut, Maman,' he said and moved in for the kiss. Four bises. The full works. La totale.

He extended his hand to Ron. 'Thanks, Sergeant.'

'Another policeman,' said Francine. 'I should 'ave known. But he was ze perfect Eeenglish gentleman.'

'The two aren't mutually exclusive, Mother.'

'We had a nice little chat about France, didn't we, Mrs Caton?' said Ron. 'Eileen and I used to go there a lot for holidays,' he began to explain for Chris's benefit. 'I scattered her ashes...'

'Holiday clear your head, Ron?' asked Chris, taking over the trolley.

'Yes,' said Ron. 'Thanks.'

'What are you thanking him for?' snorted Francine, perhaps beginning to sense the pincer movement of a police trap.

'Your son is a quite amazing copper, Mrs Caton,' said Ron.

Liberated from his luggage duties, Ron stretched and arched his back. He'd caught the sun and was wearing a polo shirt rather than a collar and tie. Very casual by his standards. He felt ten years younger, a little of the American 'can do' attitude coursing through his veins.

'Works wonders, a holiday,' he said. Perhaps, he thought, he should just have taken a holiday in the first place.

'Mum, I'd like to formally introduce you to Sergeant Newton. He's the policeman who tried to save Dad's life.'

'Oh, mon Dieu.'

The trap sprung.

On the other side of the airport, in Departures, Malvina Henley was looking for her flight. She wasn't unhappy to be going home. Nyet, spaseeba.

Philippa Bitch had given her money. It was what the English called 'a pretty penny'.

Could you kill someone just by wishing it? Her mother and grandmother thought this. Stupid peasant women, really, but...

Had she cursed Gavin to death?

Did it matter? That was life, wasn't it? Death.

Malvina looked at Tori, holding her Barbie doll tight and looking around the airport. 'Baffled' was the English word. Tori was baffled. Malvina would have preferred to be boarding this flight alone but her mother would be pleased to have a grandchild.

'It is good to be visiting, but it is better at home,' Malvina said to her daughter in Russian.

Next time she'd find someone who had a house in London.

'Dan Mann? I'm Pip Henley. Your new boss.'

# 6.2.

Gabby wasn't avoiding Chris. At least she didn't think she was. But she had her own life and, as the widow of the late Mr Sender, it was suddenly a very busy one.

She'd got to know Rachel Thomas Brown better. Gabby's initial rushed judgment became more nuanced as they got closer. She'd been up to the Brown's seldom-used brownstone in Boston and, later, Rachel had come down to New York to see Gabby. She'd taken an adjacent suite and, for a couple of days, they'd felt as untroubled as two high school girls accompanying a great aunt on the grand tour. Shopping and sightseeing by day and then, with Francine safely installed in her bed, they'd while away the nights giggling and watching TV in one or the other's suite or slurping cocktails and attracting attention in the hotel bar. New York, New York. So good they named it twice.

She'd received the news at the Stufff offices in New York. She was trying to get her head round the enterprise, trying to understand, trying to figure out if it might be something she wanted to get involved with. It was an odd experience. A little like discovering that you'd been married to an alien. There was this whole part that you knew nothing about. You wondered what other aspects of your life were not quite as they seemed. You felt stupid. You felt angry. Sometimes it was too much. Abandonment plus anger plus isolation plus bewilderment. They all stacked up, one on top of the other, and you were all at sea, treading water in the stormiest of oceans with a five-ton rucksack on your back. She knew Rachel had had some of the same feelings, so the news wasn't a complete surprise.

But when Gabby heard that Rachel had committed suicide, she knew she needed to stick around – if only to say something, as the family had asked, at Rachel's funeral. (She'd underreacted to Jack's death, was she she now overreacting to Rachel's?) At least it gave Gabby a purpose for a short while. She was grateful for that, but she felt more alone than ever.

Ron Newton was one among the 5,350 (via post), 1,200,376 (via Twitter) and 5,784,002 (via Facebook) who sent the Thomas Brown family their condolences. Rachel was cremated like her husband. Their son, a pre-teen whose sang-froid under the circumstances amazed Gabby, kept their ashes on the mantlepiece in the Caymans, mixed together in a single Big Boomer coffee bucket.

It was a beautiful day over the South Downs as Chris rolled through the village and up the hedge-lined single track affair that led to his mother's cottage.

The journey had been taken up, as these things invariably are, with Francine recounting the things she had seen and done on holiday (Fifth Avenue, Broadway, the Brooklyn flea market) and Ron then doing the same (fishing in the Everglades, Miami Beach, sweating a lot in the humidity). Chris was happy enough with that. He was used to living life vicariously and he could bide his time.

He helped his mother upstairs with her cases. She'd invited Ron in but did not wish to delay her son.

'You must have work to do, Chris,' she said in French, through the side of her mouth. 'You always have work to do.'

'But you've invited Ron for coffee. How's he going to get home if I don't stay?'

'Oh, mon Dieu.'

Chris descended again and had the neglected coffee machine rumbling before Francine had unpacked even her scarf collection. Fresh coffee for himself and Ron; Ricoré for his mother. He could hear her cursing the fact that he hadn't opened the windows often enough.

Ron was hovering, a hesitant guest. Chris could see why. His mother's house was half museum, half junk yard. You didn't dare sit anywhere for fear of breaking a priceless heirloom or sitting on a squatting hedgehog. Chris ushered Ron out into the garden – it really was turning into a bright, sunny day – and parked him in a deckchair. Ron had the sort of build that suggested that, once in a deckchair, he wouldn't be getting up again any time soon.

He set two more chairs up and returned to the coffee. His mother was now in the kitchen, torn between trying to be a good host (opening a packet of Petit Beurre) and trying to persuade her son to leave (pretending there wasn't enough milk).

'I bought some yesterday, Mother. And some more of that Corsican jam you like. I ordered it online.'

Francine looked at him with a quizzical expression, lips pursed as if sucking very hard through an invisible straw, eyes trained sharp like a jeweller with a valuable specimen. 'You are not angry with me, Christophe?'

'Why should I be angry with you, Mother Dearest?'

Chris extracted a tray from beneath a pile of old copies of Paris Match and Courrier International, placed the three cups of coffee and the biscuits on it and picked the laden platter up with the gusto of the rudest Parisian waiter. Francine had little choice but to allow him to manoeuvre her into the garden.

'Lovely place you have here,' said Ron, trying to rise from the deckchair in a suitably gentlemanly fashion and failing.

'Chris has not cut ze grass,' Francine observed, perching on the edge of the metal garden chair that Chris had put out for her.

'It's a lovely day, I'll mow it later,' said Chris, breezily. He handed out the coffee and circulated the biscuits.

'Real coffee,' said Ron.

'This is a petit coin of la belle France on the South Downs, Ron,' said Chris.

'It really is a lovely spot, Mrs Caton,' said Ron.

They sipped their coffees. Chris was aware of his mother's suspicious eyes burning into him. He cleared his throat.

'Ron, I hope you don't mind. But can you tell me what you heard from that French policeman about my father's death.'

Ron looked at the younger man, a furrowed brow; Chris knew he'd been expecting this. He too cleared his throat and, after a moment, began.

'It was the most ridiculous thing, really, Mrs Caton. Funny really, if it wasn't about such an unpleasant business. The ideas people get. But now I've met you...'

The pussyfooting was understandable. Chris couldn't blame him for that. He'd have been the same. He felt a little guilty for putting Ron on the spot, but then Ron did owe him a little. Francine squirmed in her seat and sucked up coffee through those thin tight lips. Chris could almost hear the still formidable brain in her bony little head whirring. At length, Ron uttered the phrase 'mistaken identity'.

'Yes, he was mistaken for the drug dealer round the corner,' Francine snapped, grabbing at the opportunity to reroute the conversation in a familiar direction.

'No, that is not what my colleague in the Sûreté told me, Mrs Caton.' Chris could see Ron was getting into police officer mode.

Ron then recounted in more detail what he had told Chris at the airport. There was a lot of 'mon Dieu'ing.

'To put it bluntly, Mrs Caton, the theory was that you had been the bookkeeper for the notorious Albertine family, had got on the wrong side of them and fled.'

'Oh, mon Dieu.'

By this point both Ron and Chris were eyeing Francine every bit as intensely as she was scrutinising them. And they'd both interrogated enough suspects to know from her reaction that what Ron was saying was largely true.

'I think you need to tell me the whole story now, Mother,' said Chris.

He placed his now empty cup back on the tray and rose. Ron, eventually, with a little help from Chris, did the same.

'Thanks, son.'

'I'm going to give Ron a lift back and then I'll come back. I'll want the truth. But let me just tell you this. Please don't stress. I – we – won't be asking for this case, Dad's case, to be reopened. I don't want to hurt you.' She flinched. 'That's not what I want. I just want to know what happened.'

From his back pocket he produced the old copy of Brighton Rock(s) and opened it to the frontispiece where he'd written his address all those years ago. 'This might stir a few memories,' he said.

He looked at his mother. She looked like she'd seen a whole houseful of ghosts. She managed to look very old and very young at the same time. And, while she couldn't take her eyes off her son, at the same time she was refusing to make eye contact with him.

Chris led Ron back towards the car. He looked over his shoulder twice. The first time his mother was still rooted to her chair, the second she was standing, a little stooped, and collecting the coffee cups. He watched her polish off the last biscuit. What doesn't kill you, makes you stronger, thought Chris. His mother was as strong as an ox.

'Where do you want to go, Ron?'

'Drop me off at Gregory's. I fancy fish and chips.'

Gregory's was doing a fine old trade, Friday lunchtime on a decent sunny day. The owner, not called Gregory at all but Jorge, was scooping yet more twice-fried gobbets of sizzling, starchy heaven from the deep fat fryer. His wife, Ines, was deftly flicking slices of batter-kissed haddock into her fryer and, with the other hand, creating space alongside the cod in the warming cabinet. The queue was only four or five deep but, because of the design of the shop, it extended out through the door. Jorge liked it like this. The shop always looked popular, busy and bustling even when it wasn't particularly.

Marinelli and Penney had commandeered one of the four tables. Nominally, you were waited on by Ines or one of the stream of part-time girls but, in practice, you mostly went up to the counter and collected your own plate. Marinelli's standing joke faced with this indignity was to threaten to book Ines for wasting police time, to which she would respond by threatening to bar him. There was no doubt in anybody's mind as to which was the harsher sanction.

Marinelli watched Penney pick and poke at his food. Quite appalling behaviour in the Sergeant's view. He chomped away with even greater gusto.

'What's the matter, Lawro? Forget to vote?'

'No, just thinking about the...' – Penney lowered his voice – 'tax man axe man.'

'Still at large,' said Marinelli, with a gherkin belch.

Penney had been disturbed by his own inability to engage with real, hardcore police work when it had landed at his feet. And now that the investigation was over, he was equally disturbed by the casualness of his fellow officers about it all. About death. Murder. He was beginning to wonder if he was really cut out for the job.

'But it all took off after the Peter Robb non-killing, didn't it, skip? The killer didn't really need to actually kill anyone at all.'

'That is true, son. Very true. There's nowt so queer as folk.'

'Nowt so queer as folk? Every little ounce of Italian has gone from you, hasn't it, Sarge?'

'Every little gram, Lawro, yes. When in Rome...' He was wrestling with a particularly large piece of fish. Battered it may have been, but it came leaping alive in Marinelli's eager hands. 'And nowt so queer as internet folk, Facebook folk, social bloody media folk.

'Look,' Marinelli went on. He put his fork down. Clearly this point was going to be an important one. 'Would those people, the chattering classes, would any of them have noticed Robb if it wasn't for what had happened before?'

'Maybe not.'

'If our job teaches you one thing, it's that life's complicated. Black and white only exist in coffee shops. Everywhere else it's shades of grey.'

'Murder's not a shade of grey, is it?'

'Of course not. But you could think of Sender and Thomas Brown as collateral damage.'

Penney was about to protest when a familiar face appeared at their table. He and Marinelli clocked each other immediately. Blasts from the past. Raves from the grave. Oldies but goldies.

'Isaac!' Marinelli erupted gleefully through a mouth full of haddock.

'Pavarotti!' roared Sergeant Newton with similar enthusiasm.

Marinelli hooked a chair towards the table with an outstretched foot. 'Join us, join us. We were just talking about Sender and Thomas Brown.'

'How would you define collateral damage, Sergeant Newton?' said Penney, taking advantage of Marinelli being distracted by a particularly pulpous chip.

'Unwanted but unavoidable deaths in the service of a greater good,' said Ron, textbook.

The new arrival slid into his chair and leaned forward into the circle, conspiratorially. 'Why do you ask?'

'Look, Lawro,' said Marinelli, the chip chomped. 'It's like when you nick a couple of small-time drug dealers to make a point.'

'Pour décourager les autres, as they say in France,' Ron said. He gestured to Ines to bring his fish and chips to the table.

'It's like, how many celebs are in prison for sex crimes in the 70s?' said Marinelli, warming to his theme. 'A couple? Three? We know there were lots more. Tip of the iceberg.'

'But they don't think what they've done is immoral or illegal,' said Penney.

'You still talking about those 1970s celebs, lad?' said Ron with a smirk.

'Don't tell me you're on his side, Sergeant,' said Penney pointing a chip-loaded fork at his rotund skipper.

'I'm not on anyone's side, lad. I'm retired.'

Penney shook his head. 'That is a non sequitur.'

'I expect you use a pair of them in your garden, don't you, Ron?'

said Marinelli.

'We used to have this teacher,' said Penney. 'Mrs Newton...'

He stopped and looked at Ron. He had just put two and two together – something Mrs Newton had taught him to do. Newton was not an uncommon name but ...

Ron was nodding. 'My wife,' he said. 'Taught you, did she?'

'Maths. Primary school.'

'Makes me feel prehistoric.'

'And when we had tests, she'd leave the answers on her desk and then walk out of the room. She'd trust us not to look at them.'

'And did you look, Lawro?'

'Of course not. She was trusting us to know the difference between right and wrong, wasn't she? That was the point.'

'If you cheat once, you'll do it again and you'll never know what you could have achieved on your own,' said Ron.

'That's exactly what she used to say,' said Penney.

'It's a slippery slope that you can never go back up.'

'Exactly.'

'That was my wife,' said Ron.

'She was a fantastic teacher.'

Before Ron could reply, there was a volley of dog barking as half a dozen assorted mutts simultaneously caught whiff of Gregory's finest.

'Can she handle those bloody dogs?' asked Marinelli. Penney recognised the girl: tall and pretty. He'd seen her dog-walking before.

'Yes, she's sound,' said Ron. The three of them watched as Jess reined in leads and administered a series of short sharp scolds. 'Sorry,' she shouted through the open door to Ines who was, quite amazingly, in the process of delivering Ron's plate to the table.

Marinelli whistled. 'Blimey, what do you do to get that sort of service, Ronald.'

'You are nice and polite and not big fat bloody Italian,' said Ines.

Marinelli shook his head as if the victim of the most outrageous betrayal. Penney watched as the girl shoved, dragged, poked and cajoled her canine charges down the hill towards the beach.

'How does it feel?' said Ron.

'Well, even insults are better than being ignored,' said Marinelli. 'And I am fat and Italian.'

'No, I mean if PC Penney here had turned over that answer paper, he wouldn't have found any answers, just the four words: "how does it feel" and a big question mark.'

Ron looked around the table. He'd told this story before and this revelation always got a reaction. Marinelli took a sharp intake of breath, like he'd been rapped across the knuckles by his own teacher.

'Very black and white, my Eileen,' said Ron.

'The things that matter are,' said Penney. 'And I'm proud of myself that I never cheated.'

'Virtue is its own reward.'

'That's not really true in the real world, is it?' said Marinelli, who may well have cheated in the odd Maths test himself.

Penney looked despairingly at the two sergeants. Marinelli had scoffed his own chips and his untenanted fork was homing in on one of Penney's. Newton was licking his lips as he built himself an industrial-size chip butty with a thick slice of white, the butter running down his fingers.

The young PC shook his head. 'I don't know,' he said.

'I tell you what,' said Ron. 'Get the Tax Man Axe Man to kill not a tax evader but his damn dog, and then the British public will turn against him.'

Outside, one of the dogs barked, a single yap.

'One bark for yes,' said Marinelli, mopping up the fat with his own doorstep of heavily-buttered white bread.

# 6.3.

Gill came down the stairs carrying her heels – just an inch and a half, serious and, of course, black. She sat on the chair at the end of the hall and slipped them on. The day was a warm one. She wouldn't need a coat. A cardigan would do. This was a good thing because she didn't really have a suitable coat.

Opposite her, as she got back to her feet, was the three-quarter-length, wall-mounted mirror by the door into which she always took one final look before going out. She'd done it for years. The mirror had been stationed there for that very purpose. Hair repairs, make-up tweaks, removal of bobbles and pilling. But today she wasn't quite sure she could manage the sight of her own face without bursting into tears. Of course, she'd known this moment would come but she was worried about starting crying now when she was expected so soon at the crematorium.

Instead she just stood for a moment. The house was deserted and quiet. She wasn't sure she'd ever heard it quite so quiet in her entire life. Dimmy was out being walked. Susie and the kids had gone to the crematorium already. The only sounds were the carriage clock on the mantlepiece and a lawn mower somewhere down the road, perhaps three houses away, perhaps Mr Carpenter. A seagull screamed. She did what she'd been taught to do by Martha at the Mindfulness class and focused on her breathing. She checked in with the other sensations in the various parts of her body. They were tolerable. She still wouldn't be looking in any mirrors though. Then she opened the door and was assaulted by the sun. It slapped her round each cheek. Lovely day for it. Isn't that what Cliff would have said?

Gary Shad took a gobful of ciggie juice. New flavour. New York Cheesecake with Lemon and Lime. Not as good as it sounded.

'I'll almost certainly get a custodial sentence,' he said.

'You bloody idiot,' said Jess.

They were sitting in one of the shelters on the prom, looking out to sea. The tide was out and Jess was intending to take the dogs for one last walk on the beach before summer came and the local Plod got really heavy about the 'no dogs on the beach' rule. She'd tied their leashes to the bench but the dogs knew what was coming and the excitement was mounting. She was petting and patting each pooch in turn, telling them how lovely they were. Gary was doing the same, bless his jailbird heart.

'They were just asking for it, some of those fuckwits,' Gary was saying. The charge list had got a lot longer since Jess had last heard.

'There was some kid. Tweets about all the DJ equipment he's got.

All the records. All this rare vinyl. Never stops. Tweets his address, phone number, fucking inside leg measurement probably. Then he tweets he's doing an all-nighter, but he'll be using someone else's gear. Well, it's criminal, isn't it?'

'Yes, it is, Gary.'

'Well, I say music but you can't call a DJ a musician, can you? Pushing a couple of buttons. By that token, a fucking train guard's Eric Clapton.'

'Yes, Gary – but I don't think that's the point, is it?'

'No, I suppose not.' Gary stroked Demetrius on his head and Demetrius was almost purring like a cat, his snout resting extended on Gary's thigh. 'I suppose you can listen to music inside. I'll be able to catch up. And I'll take a load of books. Jess, can you ...' He trailed off.

'Can you hack it, Gaz? Prison?' she asked. Gary Shad wasn't half as hard as he made out.

'Ha. I got through Plane Grove comprehensive.'

'You did, indeed.' Gary had another toke. Jess stubbed out her cigarette. She'd taken just three drags. That was her target. Three drags. She was counting her smoking in drags now, not fags. Didn't really work, of course – you just took deeper, longer drags.

'I meant, French.'

'I'm sure we can sort something out.' Jess looked at her charges. 'I am, after all, a professional dog minder...'

'Thanks,' said Gary, miserably.

'Funny how we're the ones who are still in touch out of Plane Grove,' said Jess. 'Wouldn't have expected that when you were the king of the short-term exclusion.'

There was a pause as an older couple, out for a mutually-supportive struggle along the promenade, shuffled painfully past.

'I see Sheenah sometimes. Jacky Carstairs. Now Jacky Mohammed, of course. You know that? But I don't see them often.'

'Not so surprising to me,' said Gary, cryptically.

He looked at her. A worried expression she'd rarely seen before. Definitely not as hard as he made out. He shut and pocketed his e-cigarette. 'You got the real thing?' he asked.

Jess offered him her packet of ten. 'Don't start again before you go to prison, Gaz. Or you'll smoke yourself to death in there.'

Gary accepted the ciggie and the offer of the light. He took a lung-busting drag, just like one of hers.

'Jacky grassed me up to Mrs Newton once.'

'Good old Jacky,' smirked Jess.

'I looked at the paper on her desk. You know in the Maths tests.'

'Why doesn't that surprise me? You always did well in those tests.'

Gary laughed a truncated nasal laugh. 'The point is Jess, those marks were all me. I actually wasn't that bad at maths. The answers weren't on the back of the sheet.'

'They 100% were.'

'No, Jess. I can't believe you've never heard this before. The paper was blank.'

'Really?'

'Except she'd written the question: how does it feel?'

Jess allowed the implications of this to sink in. 'Wow. I did not know that.'

Jess looked out to sea. The dogs were all doing the same. They couldn't wait to get out on the big, vast glorious beach. Lucky bastards.

'She was good, Mrs Newton. She was very good.'

'She was. I felt terrible. You feel shit about yourself.'

'Of course, you do.'

'I've been feeling shit about myself ever since.'

'You were only a kid, Gaz. Give yourself a break.'

'Once you've done it once, it's a lot easier to do it again is all I'm saying. And you may as well do it because you can never wipe away that feeling anyway. The self-disgust. You can't undo it.'

Jess looked at Gary. She had been tempted to look at Mrs Newton's supposed answer sheet herself but she never had. Why not? It wasn't fear of Mrs Newton. She'd done far worse. Was it respect for Mrs Newton? Maybe. Or did she just know it was the wrong thing to do. Did she just know where to draw the line? A line in the sand. And if so, how?

'I moved to London after school, Jess. A few shitty jobs. Some legal, some not. Then I came back to Biscuit Town on a stag weekend. Bunch of arseholes. Big boozy bender. And we went to the Lucky Star. Well, it was the only club in town, wasn't it?' Jess patted Bouncer's nose, strategically avoiding the dribble around his jaw.

'And they were playing "Wishing On A Star" – always played it near the end. You remember? I was pissed as a fart and leaning against a wall in the entrance hall, drinking someone else's plastic pint of pissy lager.' Jess was busying herself, ensuring leashes were tight and collars secure. 'And you walked past with some bloke. I'd hardly thought about you for years. Only like once a week. Ha. And there you were. White dress. Dead tight. Heels. Your hair, like you had glitter in it or something, I don't know. You looked absolutely fucking gorgeous.'

Jess was listening to this, watching the dogs, ready with a poop bag. But her grip was tightening on the wooden armrest and she was gagging for another fag herself. Willpower, Jess. Willpower.

'And I was wishing on a star, Jess. To follow where you are. I followed you home.' Gary stroked Demetrius. 'Nice lad, your bloke. Didn't push his luck. I liked that. I might have had to deck him otherwise. Saw where you lived. Moved in myself about two weeks later.'

Gary was smoking in short sharp drags now. Like at school, when you were trying to keep a joint going.

Jess watched as Bouncer broke away from the pack, squatted and shat on the promenade. Jess had been expecting one of them to. Had to be one of the big guys, didn't it. She got up with her poop bag, scooped it up and deposited the Newfoundland's warm offering in the little black bin designated for that purpose. It was right to hand, the bin – the reason she sat in this shelter and not one of the others.

'It's a dirty job but someone's got to do it,' said Gary with a flat smile. He looked up at Jess as she resumed her seat.

'Why didn't you say anything before?'

'Shy.'

'Shy!" Gary Shad admitting to shyness was like his confessing to a penchant for cross-stitch.

'I don't know what to say, Gary.'

'I've been in love with you since I was five years old, Jess.'
The story was melting her heart. 'You bloody idiot,' she said.

# 6.4.

Chris was standing on a rock just outside what had been the cordoned-off section, Gavin Henley's body long gone. All that he had found remaining were a few torn fragments of police tape. He'd picked these up and put them in his pocket. Didn't want the police accused of polluting beaches and killing any innocent creatures who were daft enough to gorge on blue and white crime scene tape.

He wasn't quite sure what he was doing. Apart from avoiding his mother for an hour or two. He'd already chatted up the local detective who'd been charged with comparing Henley's head wound with images of those of Sender and Thomas Brown.

'Very similar – my report said odds on the same murder weapon. Round object.'

The detective, an owl-faced man who looked in need of a good meal, had told him that there had been some discussion about removing as evidence the rock against which Henley had been found slumped. It too had been covered in blood and it was technically possible he'd hit his head on that. But the view was that, on balance, it was probably not necessary.

'We're sure he was already dead when he hit it,' the detective had said. 'And it is a bloody heavy rock.'

'The letters? TESS?'

'We photographed them obviously. They've taken a couple of the stones used for prints but the rest, I think, we just chucked them back on the beach.'

Surveying the scene now, Chris had no idea which rock was the guilty rock, which stones had formed which letters. It was just a beach on a beautiful day. The sun was beaming, accentuated by the white sheen of the chalk face. Chris took his jacket off and slung it over his shoulder. Then he began to walk back towards Biscuit Town.

He saw the dogs before he saw the girl. That big hairy Newfoundland again. Nearly knocked him over. Then a couple more on tight, taut leads. Then the girl. Jess. They recognised each other immediately.

'Returning to the scene of the crime?' Jess said.

Chris laughed. 'I think they might be,' he said, gesturing at the sniffing, straining dogs.

She smiled. 'They're into everything. I can't understand how I missed seeing those letters. TESS.'

'Ah, that's the difference between the trained eye of the policeman and the beady-eyed member of the public.'

'What, the ability to see a word in stones the size of a swimming pool?'

'I don't think it was quite that big.'

Demetrius was rubbing himself against Chris's leg, almost cat-like. Chris chucked the animal beneath the chin.

'He likes you,' said Jess.

'I think he likes everyone, this one,' said Chris. 'He's Gill Graham's dog, isn't he?'

'That's right. You know her?'

'I was at school with Colin.'

'You're a local then?'

'Seems like it.'

'But you moved to London and joined the Met.'

'You've a good memory.'

'You showed me your identity thing.'

'I did,' said Chris, remembering. 'And I gave you my phone number.'

'So it's all finished here, is it? Back to London?'

'I don't know. Right now, I'm enjoying this wonderful weather.' Both of them were squinting, the sun reflecting back off the cliff like movie lighting bouncing off a reflector, Jess and Chris in the middle of the screen. Close-up. 'This beautiful beach.'

'Well, it's not the Bahamas.'

'No, but Biscuit Town has a certain feel... a kind of... a bit...' Chris wasn't sure whether this was nerves or if he really had no idea how to finish the sentence.

'Don't say it. Land that time forgot.'

'Well, I was going to say a place out of time but I won't argue.'

Demetrius had tired of Chris's attention and had wandered off. The other dogs seemed similarly eager to continue their constitutional.

'Well,' said Jess, gathering up leads and looking, for the first time, beyond Chris. 'The tide won't stay out forever.' She'd obviously spotted their canine impatience too.

'Do you want to come to Paris with me?'

'Sorry?'

'I've got some work and I'll need an assist...'

'Paris? You've got some poodles need walking?' Jess laughed. 'I've just acquired one of those...'

'Come on,' said Chris, trying to sound encouraging. In for a penny, he was thinking. 'I mean, your boss is dead, isn't he?'

'One of them, yes, but then there's the dog walking, the bar work, my mother...'

'The old portfolio career.'

'The old can't make ends meet, no matter how hard I try career.' Jess focused back on Chris again, shading her eyes from the sun so he could truly see them. 'I'll come,' she said. 'How long you going for?'

'However long it takes.'

'That is the perfect amount of time for my schedule.'

The funeral had gone well. Jake and Ryan had joint-read their poem in loud, clear voices and looked very smart indeed in their suits. Gill was proud of her grandchildren, proud of Susie and how she'd spruced them up and rehearsed them. She wasn't sure whether they would manage it. But they'd done themselves proud. She was fairly sure she wouldn't have been able to speak in public like that at their age.

Gill surveyed the crowd. Not the biggest funeral reception, but then not the smallest. Much as you'd expect really. In her hand, she had a glass of sherry, her mother's favourite tipple, so it seemed appropriate. Colin came up behind her and put his big arm around her shoulder. It made her feel tiny and her legs like jelly.

'I need to sit down, love,' she said.

Colin led the way. 'Comfy chair for your grandma,' he barked at Ryan who jumped to it.

Colin pulled up another chair for himself and sat down next to his mother. 'You all right, Mum?' he asked, taking her hand. Susie was doing the decent and manoeuvring the twins towards the bar with promises of coke and crisps.

Gill looked at him. The truth was she was fine. Her heart was still beating thirteen to the dozen and had been ever since they'd told her that he, Colin, had woken up. They'd had to tell her three times. But she was fine.

'It's a miracle,' Gill had said eventually.

'It's very rare but it's not unknown,' the nurse had said, the sullen one. 'Not even a record. People have woken up after 19, 20 years in a coma.'

Gill looked at her so-handsome, amazingly-alive son – not even a record holder. 'I'm fine,' she said.

He patted her hand and her heart nearly broke free from its mooring.

'Mum,' said Colin. 'Did Chris Caton come to see me? Or did I dream it?'

'He was definitely there once,' said Gill. 'But it was when they took you out for your prostate op. I don't think he actually saw you then. But perhaps he was there another time.'

'What was he doing in Biscuit Town?'

'He was interested in Gary, that redhead skinhead, I think.'

Colin laughed. She'd forgotten how much she loved to hear him laugh. The thought of never hearing it again...

'He came all the way down from London for a bicycle thief?'

'I don't know,' said Gill. 'He came round one night. We had fish and chips.'

Colin laughed again. 'Chris, you mean. Not Gary Shad.'

Something distracted Gill. She couldn't quite say what it was. A slight reduction in the volume of chitter-chatter. A slight fall in room temperature. Had they dimmed the lights? Perhaps all of these. The crowd parted. Given that most of the mourners were her mother's age, this happened quite slowly. She had an uninterrupted view of the double doors, with their fine Edwardian handles, which led from the hotel lobby into the lounge bar where the mourners were assembled. One minute he wasn't there and the next minute he was. Gill had no idea why she'd looked over in that direction but, for the first time, her heart was not pounding. She breathed, two, three conscious breaths. She felt fine. She felt fine.

'Colin, who's that old man who's just come in?'

She felt Colin's hand grip just a little tighter around hers. 'Bloody hell, Mum,' he said softly. 'I've been out of the game for a while but I still don't need bloody glasses. It's Dad. It's Cliff.'

Gill would normally have rebuked her son for two 'bloody's in a single sentence – just out of a coma or not – but, on this occasion, his words were, if anything, inadequate descriptors for her surprise.

'Pinch me and tell me I'm not dreaming,' she said.

'You're not dreaming, Mum.'

'Bloody hell,' she said.

Colin watched as his mother rose from her chair and moved across the parquet towards his father. Was it not a dream of all children of divorce that their parents should get back together? And here he was watching it. He sipped his pint. Don't get ahead of yourself, Colin. She'll probably clock the bastard. But she didn't. They spoke for a few moments and then they both exited through the double doors, his father gallantly holding the door open and chaperoning his mother through with a flourish of the arm.

His father was slightly stooped, and certainly greyer and thinner now, but he was quite clearly his old man. Colin had last seen him in a pub in Covent Garden back in... well, it was ages ago, before the smoking ban in pubs because the old man had been smoking. He hadn't told his mum about the meeting which Colin, up in London for a training course, had initiated. It must have been getting on for a quarter of century since she'd last seen him.

He gave them five minutes, downed his pint and then he got up and followed them out to the lobby. After all, what were they going to do? Get a room?

He found them sitting beneath the TV in a pair of elegant Bergère-style armchairs.

'Get you a pint, Dad?' he said, making the customary arm-raising gesture across the lobby to his father.

His dad didn't look remotely surprised. 'I think you'd better get your mother something stronger, son,' he said. He hadn't changed. You couldn't help smiling.

When Colin returned to the lobby from the bar, his parents were, like the half-a-dozen other people in the lobby, staff and guests, taking a moment to attend to the TV screen on which the new Prime Minister was, as far Colin knew, anyway, making his first appearance since being elected. It wasn't the usual old platitudinous, patriotic bollocks either. He was actually talking about taxation. He seemed to be saying that corporation tax was to be abolished and replaced with a tax on things that couldn't be moved, hidden or magicked away with creative accountancy. That boiled down to sales and assets, apparently. 'We will remove the smokescreen. What is illegal and what is immoral will be one and the same, and this will enable companies to act not only in their own interest but in the interest of the rest of society. It will finally mean that, after centuries of supposedly trying, economic growth really will benefit everybody.'

Even Andrew Marr – or was it David Dimbleby, he could never remember – seemed gobsmacked by that one.

'Pinch me and tell me I'm not dreaming,' said Colin, handing his father a pint and his mother another sherry.

'Don't believe a bloody word of it, son,' said Cliff. 'They make it all up as they bloody go along.'

'Cliff!' snapped Gill automatically. 'This is...' She could have said 'a funeral' or 'a respectable establishment' but she settled for 'a nice surprise'.

'Well, I was always fond of your mother.'

Gill laughed at this blatant lie like she hadn't laughed for years. For her, it was a nice surprise – just not the nicest.

A quarter of a mile away, Denise Gann really was dreaming. She'd finally fallen asleep on the sofa where Jess would find her in two hours time, snoring away, in the deepest of deep sleeps, dreaming of a brave new world.

# 6.5.

Ron stopped at the top of Moonshine Point, close to the edge but not too close. It was a gorgeous day, no sign of mist, bright blue sky and a singing green sea. Not a grey note anywhere. He was even awake as Martha might have put it. He put his earbuds in and turned on her 'Body Scan practice (shorter)'.

He became aware of his breath and focused on it. The Body Scan was a very specific Mindfulness technique. In her soft, soporific voice, Martha went through the body parts one by one, beginning with the toes and working her way up. You, the participant, were encouraged to zone in on the sensations in those parts of the body. Today Ron was determined to engage. Today it would be different. Indeed, it felt different already. As he began, Ron had a revelation, something like a grey mist being lifted from before his own eyes. Ron was aware of how his two feet did not quite make contact with the ground in exactly the same way, the pressure of the chalky soil beneath the left foot was slightly different from that beneath the right. Not a lot, but noticeable. It was the bullet he'd taken that had left him with a slight limp. But Ron had never really acknowledged that limp, had he? He had continued to bound along like an eager PC out on his very first beat, straining every sinew in his body to 'walk properly'. Of course, when he first returned to duty after the shooting, there was a certain logic in this. You needed to prove that you were still up to the job, not some sort of hopping invalid. But it made no sense now. It was just denial, wasn't it? Wasn't that what they called it, the psychiatrists? Perhaps that's why he could never 'get' Mindfulness. He was in denial about what he was feeling in his body, so no wonder he couldn't scan its component parts. He wiggled his toes. Compared to his right foot, only about three-quarters of his left actually touched the ground. He was, as far as that foot was concerned, literally walking on the edge.

Martha was moving up the body. And Ron, having acknowledged that variation between his two lower limbs felt the difference rise through his being too. The left knee had long been a bit sore from bowling but, now he'd given up that tedious game and his bowls had gone, he was aware less of any overt soreness and more of how it was at a slight angle, the knee cap, compared to the other, and bent outwards a little. It wasn't painful, it was just noticeable.

The giggling schoolboy deep inside Ron had always been the first to react to Martha's encouragement to be aware of the 'sensations in the groin region'. On one occasion, while Eileen was still alive, the sensation in his groin region had been embarrassingly stark. It had been at one of the actual Mindfulness sessions and Martha had been doing the practice 'live', so to speak. She hadn't been wearing, doing or saying anything particularly memorable and the whole tone of the class, which was middle class and middle-aged, was anything but sexual. And Ron had had his eyes closed anyway. But he'd still got an erection, just like that giggling schoolboy. It was mortifying in those tracksuit bottoms and had reminded him of Eileen (and Le Sex) in a way that made him feel guilty and tearful, alive and alone and a vast gamut of emotions he couldn't pin down – an avalanche of Mindfulness. Today, he let it go. It was a good thing that it could still happen at his age, surely? Today he was more aware of the numbness in his hip and at the top of the thigh, the point of entry of the bullet.

The sensation in Ron's abdomen was very pleasant, a satisfying sense of fullness after his fish and chips (and not that bubble of bloating you sometimes got if the batter mix was too old. No danger of that at Gregory's.) He could still taste the fish on his lips, but that would be to get ahead of Martha, the mind marching ahead much as Ron was inclined to. He put his hand on his stomach and felt the organ doing its digestive best. There was the gentle rumbling of a soft machine.

'We leave the abdomen and go down the arms to the fingers.'

His hands weren't shaking as they had once been. They were steady. He was aware of the grease at the tips of several fingers, Gregory's chips again, and, on one, the tiniest fleck of crispy bit. He licked it off. Was licking allowed in Mindfulness? Martha had never mentioned it.

His shoulder ached though, that was for sure. That felt like it had taken a bullet (it hadn't). All thanks to that wretched bowling bag and its heavyweight contents. He must have strained it lifting the bag above his head. Actually, it really was, now that he was focusing on it, quite painful.

'The mind will wander – that's what minds do,' said Martha and Ron was hopeful that his would wander away from the pain in his shoulder. He wondered what Eileen would have made of the Mindfulness. Oh, she'd known he'd been doing it, but they'd never really discussed it. It was just one of those things that got him out of the house like the bowling. He'd told her what it was and she'd said she'd had a few pupils who could have done with a bit of it, but that was as far as it had gone. Eileen would have been sceptical. Well, it wasn't science, was it? Eileen liked facts. Did it work? Where was the data? If it worked, how did it work? What was the mechanism, the sequence of events, the A that led to B that led to C. Yes, she was very black and white, Eileen. Well, they both were. Or, at least, both had been. He was wondering now whether being certain, being sure, had very much to recommend it, really. He shuffled a few paces closer to the edge of the cliff. You could see where bits were falling off, the chalk was white instead of grey.

He looked up. It really was a lovely day. Nobody could argue with summer. It was here in all its warm, multi-coloured cleansing glory. The grey that could hang over Biscuit Town even in the spring and sometimes long into the afternoon was nowhere to be seen, burned away by the fire of the sun. He became aware of Martha's soothing voice again. His mind had wandered about as far as it could go really, hadn't it?

Martha was wrapping up. 'You are fine. Fine just as you are,' she said. 'In this moment.'

# WHO'S WHO

Who's who in Biscuit Town and beyond. (Number in brackets indicates chapter in which character first appears.)

**Blair HENRY**
Financial journalist (2.12)
**Bradley COOMBES-WALKER**
DCI Edgar Corrigan's deputy (5.2)

**Camila BROWNE**
Dog-walker in park opposite Gill's mother's house (2.3)
**Chancellor of the Exchequer** (4.8)
**Cherrianne DIXON**
Brighton-based sweet-toothed colleague of Dan at corporatesponger.co.uk (2.12)
**Chris CATON**
Detective Sergeant in the Met, currently on restricted duties in Biscuit Town (2.1)
**Colin GRAHAM**
Firefighter and son of Gill Graham (1.6)
**Conrad**
Works at corporatesponger.co.uk (3.2)

**Dan MANN**
Scooter-rider, keen fisherman and founder of corporatesponger.co.uk (2.12)
**Darren**
UKIP-supporting former school friend of Gary (1.2)
**Deborah GANN**
Sister of Denise Gann and aunt of Jessica Gann (1.4)
**Denise GANN**
Jessica's mother (6.1)
**Des WESTMORELAND**
Civil Service colleague of Dominic (3.14)

**Edgar CORRIGAN**
Detective Chief Inspector, Chris's boss and Dominic's contact in the police (2.1)

**Dominic MASON**
Cabinet Office civil servant and Edgar Corrigan's contact in government (3.3)

**Eileen NEWTON (Mrs Newton)**
Former school teacher, wife of Ron, cancer patient (1.4)

**Elizabeth ROBB**
Monaco-residing wife of Peter (3.5)

**ELLIS**
Special Advisor (Spad) to the Prime Minister (3.14)

**Francine CATON (Madame Caton)**
Chris's French mother, lives on the South Downs (2.13)

**Gabby GARNIER-SENDER**
French former model and wife of Stufff boss Jack Sender, accompanying Chris Caton (2.2)

**Gary SHAD**
Friendly-neighbourhood criminal, lives in same run-down apartment block as Jess (1.2)

**Gavin HENLEY (Gav)**
Financial consultant, resident of swanky Estuary Sands, father of Pip Henley and husband of Malvina (1.2)

**Gill GRAHAM**
Mother to Colin (and wife of absent Cliff), retired and caring for her mother (1.8)

**Greta HENLEY**
Gavin's first wife, Pip's mother (4.7)

**Heather MASON**
Nurse, wife of Dominic (3.6)

**(Mrs) HENNESSEY**
Neighbour of Gill (2.3)
**Hovis**
UKIP-supporting former school friend of Gary (1.2)

**Jack SENDER**
Owner of online warehouse Stufff (2.1)
**Jake GRAHAM**
Colin's son, Gill's grandson, twin of Ryan (2.3)
**Jen WHITE**
Lee's wife (4.13)
**Jessica GANN (Jess)**
Three-jobs Jess is a barmaid at The Smugglers', an au-pair to Gavin Henley and a dog walker (1.4)
**Josh FINKELSTEIN**
Sidekick of Tommy Lockhart (1.1)

**Kaylee WHITE**
Lee and Jen's daughter (4.13)
**Kirsty CARLISLE**
Pupil of Pip, injured by crumbling cliff (1.1)

**(PC) Lawrence PENNEY**
Biscuit Town copper (5.14)
**Lee WHITE**
Geordie son of a miner working in Stufff warehouse (1.5)
**Lucas FORSBERG**
Swedish boss of MöblA furniture superstores (3.8)

**Malvina HENLEY**
Gavin's wife, Pip's stepmother, believed to be Russian (3.10)
**(Sergeant) MARINELLI**
Biscuit Town copper (5.14)
**Martha**
Ron and Gill's Mindfulness teacher (1.4)

**Melissa BRINK**
Student, housemate of Pip (1.1)

**Peter ROBB**
Owner of the high street clothing chain that bears his name (3.3)
**Pip HENLEY**
Student teacher and daughter of Gavin Henley (1.1)
**Prime Minister**
Add your own description (1.8)

**Rachel THOMAS BROWN**
Zak's wife (4.9)
**ROBBINS**
Peter Robb's bodyguard (4.10)
**Roger WILKINS**
Friend of Dominic, now at the Treasury (3.7)
**Ron NEWTON**
Retired Police Sergeant and husband of Eileen (1.2)
**'Ruby Tuesday'**
Cancer-beating sidekick of Deborah Gann (1.4)
**Ryan GRAHAM**
Colin's son, Gill's grandson, twin of Jake (2.3)

**Susie GRAHAM**
Wife of firefighter Colin, mother to Jake and Ryan, daughter-in-law to Gill (1.6)

**Tanisha**
Student, housemate of Pip (1.1)
**Tommy LOCKHART**
Student, housemate of Pip (1.1)
**Tori**
Malvina and Gavin's toddler daughter, Pip's half-sister (3.10)

**Vic HOOPER**
Landlord of The Smugglers', 'arguably the worst pub on the South Coast' (1.2)

**'Walt'**
Dominic and Heather's next-door neighbour (3.6)

**Warren RUFF**
Boss of internet giant Comm-N (3.8)

**Wilson**
Barrista at Brewed Awakening (5.4)

**Zak THOMAS BROWN**
CEO of Boomer's Coffee (2.9)

# Acknowledgements

Thanks very much to retired Watch Manager Gary Dyer for reading the chapter involving firefighting and for his advice. Thanks also to Police Family Liaison Officer Linda Hugo for answering my questions on policing matters. Although my police characters are generally unencumbered by any notions of standard practice and procedure, I also found 'The Crime Writer's Guide to Police Practice and Procedure' by Michael O'Byrne useful.

Much credit to Allen Watkin, Liz West and Susanne Nilsson for the cover photos 'White Cliff', 'Mishap' and 'Walking the dog' which were kindly made available through the Creative Commons. (There are links on the Tartaruga Books website.)

Enormous, drinks-on-me-next-time-we-meet-sized thanks to my early readers for their insightful and constructive comments, you know who you are.

Last but not least, bigger thanks than I can express to the best proofreader in the world, Bela, for unyielding support, close reading of the earlier drafts of the manuscript and even closer scrutiny of the plot – always in my heart.

Thanks are always due to songwriters but, specifically here, to the creators of the following which appear in the story, random though some of the connections might be. (Links can again be found on the website)

Communication Breakdown – Led Zeppelin
Rosalita – Bruce Springsteen
How Does It Feel? – Slade
Wishing On A Star – Rose Royce
The Night – Frankie Valli and the Four Seasons
Is Vic There? – Department S
Here Comes The Sun – George Harrison
Something Changed – Pulp
Valerie – Amy Winehouse

Theme to The Big Bang Theory – Barenaked Ladies
Turn, Turn, Turn – The Byrds
I Can't Stand The Rain – Ann Peebles
Ruby Tuesday – The Rolling Stones
Theme from Jaws – John Williams

Made on a Mac, using Scrivener and In Design.

Jim Pollard, Feb 2017
jimpollard.co.uk
notonlywords.co.uk/tartaruga

# Want Some More?

Look out for other Biscuit Town titles and other formats.

More information at notonlywords.co.uk/tartaruga

Printed in Great Britain
by Amazon